My Pet Serial Killer

My Pet Serial Killer

MICHAEL J SEIDLINGER

FANGORIA

FANGORIA.COM
@FANGORIA
DALLAS, TX

PRAISE FOR MY PET SERIAL KILLER

"*Fifty Shades of Grey* with cataracts of blood."

—Kirkus Reviews

"A rowdy menagerie of the unexpected, this book will delight and disturb even the bravest of readers; all preconceptions of what to trust and what to fear are masterfully upended."

—Alissa Nutting, author of *Made for Love*

"It's rare to be able to say so, but, in this case, it's hard to say otherwise: Seidlinger's book is unlike anything I've read before. Strange and alarming, unique and capacious, this novel will surprise you."

—R.O. Kwon, author of *The Incendiaries*

"Michael J. Seidlinger's *My Pet Serial Killer* is wickedly subversive and, at times, just plain wicked. Seidlinger's use of the grotesque is masterful and his novel deserves to be on the shelf next to Poppy Z. Brite's *Exquisite Corpse* and Cormac McCarthy's *Child of God*, and, baby, once it gets its claws into you, this dark masterpiece will keep you reading long into the night."

—Nick White, author of *Sweet and Low*

"In Michael J Seidlinger's *My Pet Serial Killer*, the pleasure of the gaze and violence of the gaze and repulsion of the gaze and necessity of the gaze perform acrobatics, leaving the reader breathlessly disturbed. In this world, the cameras are always rolling. Violence is both real and performed, with viewers and actors who overlap and ripple, layer after layer. We are transfixed, we are afraid. We follow Claire and her pet, though we, too, might be her pet in this dark world. What are our expectations? What are we desperate to see? Seidlinger deftly offers space for us to answer those questions for ourselves, and it's uncomfortable. Perfectly so. *My Pet Serial Killer* functions as a cultural critique that is both disturbing and enjoyable, both real and surreal, and ultimately hard to put down."

—Tessa Fontaine, author of ***The Electric Woman: A Memoir in Death-Defying Acts***

My Pet Serial Killer

ISBN 9781946487025 *(paperback)*
ISBN 9781946487032 *(e-book)*

Library of Congress Control Number: 2017930079

Published by Fangoria
www.fangoria.com
Dallas, Texas

COVER BY **ASHLEY DETMERING**

DESIGN & LAYOUT ASHLEY DETMERING
TYPESETTER KIRBY GANN
COPYEDITORS MOLLY WOLCHANSKY
DISTRIBUTOR CONSORTIUM BOOK SALES & DISTRIBUTION
ASSOCIATE PUBLISHER JESSICA SAFAVIMEHR
PRODUCER & PUBLISHER DALLAS SONNIER
AUTHOR MICHAEL J SEIDLINGER

First Edition September 2018

Printed in the United States of America

Table of Contents

YOU'RE MINE.

BE MINE.

Claire, student, master.

0.

She'd like to meet you. She really would.
What's your type?

Being found as a number of clever pickup lines.

1.

Start with the first and the last.

What is and will always be.

I went to class. I listened to the lecture. I participated in the discussion, telling them my side of the narrow story. I spoke of what might be something I'd like to study. It's getting to be that time… it's assumed I've learned enough, and now peers and professors demanded that I teach them something in return. A thesis posited and presented; learn from me, learn about something.

I went to class.

Have I learned anything?

2.

There's always a party.

Since there's always a need to forget, there'll be a party so that people can escape themselves while seemingly finding one another.

It's why I'll be there. I have yet to find and be found.

I hope there's someone.

It's something I have to continually remind myself.

Keep searching. Keep talking to people.

Never know when you'll find someone new.

When there's a serial killer living next door, the end is predictable. The end isn't what's exciting. At the end, the killer will kill every single one of us. The end is boring and bloody.

Where's the fun in that?

Life and death are boring, but you got to keep going.

That's why I'm standing around, watching everyone as they arrive. It's the "Who's Who" party and things have yet to pick up, so what else can I do?

I'm watching people magnetically assemble into perfect conversation circles with the strict purpose being for—what else—gossip and gloating.

And I see people sitting on the couch, leaning against walls and other fixtures, writing rapidly on white cards, and they're hiding what they write from everyone else—no one can see—because it's not their turn yet.

And I'm looking at my card. My card is blank.

It's early, and the frat house hasn't even begun to spill-over, but people are already playing the field. Some guy's standing next to me with his back turned, and he's writing too, and when he notices me looking at what he's writing, he doesn't cover up with his other hand like everyone else does. This is where this guy would sense that maybe, just maybe, I'm interested too.

But I'm not.

I'm looking him up and down. There's really no fight in him.

He wouldn't, couldn't, shouldn't. . . so often it's the excuses that give them away and leave me disinterested. So often they're already tamed. Where's the fight in them? Like, when I'm not interested, shouldn't they try harder? Aren't we all looking for the same thing?

And then I'm looking back down at my card, pen in hand, and I don't have anything to write down. I'm not going to write anything down—not my name (Claire Wilkinson), my age (26), my real hair color (brown), my current hair color (blonde), my eye color (blue), my major (forensics), my turn-ons and turn-offs (you wish), my birthplace/hometown (yeah, right); and there's no use in trying because I probably won't end up going anyway.

Whatever I do is like whatever I drink: For appearance more so than approach.

I know what's going to happen.

I'm a great observer.

Key to any of these college parties is the fact that there's really nothing more than an everlasting momentum slowly increasing until it meets its peak and then it's all about letting it slide until just before dawn.

If you want hard facts and a clear pickup game, you go to clubs and bars downtown. People get caught up in each other's mistakes and murmurs going to these parties. It's always a momentum that leaves most feeling welcome, but lost all at the same time. You're only at these parties if you're still new to the game we all play.

Different night, different crowd, same intentions, same results. It becomes the same kind of game after a couple; these parties are practice and nothing more.

There's a gimmick to get everyone started on the drinks and the smokes and the pills and the specialties and the thought that it's okay to speak up and speak out because that's what everyone believes this party, and every party, is for. But even if it wasn't, after a drink or two, no one's going to care what is said and who's saying it.

People fall into each other.

This is how they get lost.

This is how anyone is found.

Easy enough to get.

Since I already explained the first couple hours of any university party, skip forward to where we are now. They start talking and I'm thinking I should say something because, well, I'm standing close enough–my fault, I'm not usually this close–to make it look like I'm supposed to be in on their little chat. I'm in the circle, but I'm not talking, not yet, so I feel like I have to.

I've got to say something.

And what do I say?

"I've heard Professor Derrick's paper is going to be thirty pages."

It's the perfect thing to say if you don't want anyone to say anything back.

They nod, and that's that.

And their gaze pans across the party and now I'm supposed to feel out of place. I've become uninteresting and unappealing. I'm free to leave them for another corner, another random spot at the party. Wherever I'm planning on going it'll be precisely the same—the ten second attention spans, the desperate need to get drunk soon. Now, now, ten minutes ago. People trying to be found, wanting to effortlessly join in on whatever it is that's going on.

What are they talking about?

Take it from me, they aren't talking about anything.

People that don't really know each other, pretending they've known each other all along. Going around passing drinks, passing stories, passing around the tray of temptation because, inevitably, we're all here wanting to be found.

Person, find me.

How about this person. . .will you find me?

But it's not that easy.

Try this one for instance–

Says he's a Foreign Language major and goes on and on about the subtle differences of a language, any language, but he gets the big things mixed up. He says Spanglish. He says Chinese when he means Japanese. He's talking and talking and talking and I'm pretending to listen. I've already written him off as just another somebody.

He might make someone happy. . . maybe not. . .but that person won't be me.

So, what does it feel like to be left out? I couldn't tell you. I don't feel I'm being left out. I don't feel like I belong; you can't really be left out if you never were brought in to begin with.

I'm only here to observe. That's what I do, and I feel like I'm on the verge of something.

I'm always looking and looking, but I feel like I might figure it all out soon. I might find what I want to find. Until then, it's more of the same, where the same is kind of like the words and sentences running together, and the images too, but the worst part is when the sound is ever-so-slightly off and whatever it is I'm doing, I end up doing either too early or too late.

People are talking and I'll never know who's talking, much less becoming the one that talks and carries the entire circle. Circles always hold on for dear life.

What I'm accustomed to: smiling, nodding and—

Everything that's done to hide the fact that I'm searching.

That's what I'm accustomed to, and it's probably not what you were expecting.

People are no longer writing on their cards. They're all now laughing and turning to other people and laughing, forming even more premeditative party circles like this one. The music's so loud that it's impossible for anyone to feel like dancing. The music's so loud that it's hard to hear the rhythm. Everything's a bass-beat and an earthquake.

People are quaking to get started.

And the circles around me keep switching topics—from majors to comparing class schedules to rating this week's celebrities—and I'm considering where the circles will go next. It can only be something from a very short list. I bet I could get it right if I wanted to.

Now people are lining up for the big drink-starter.

It's the same sort of start-up and end, but the biggest difference is that everyone's going to finally put themselves out there.

The gimmick of a party is everything.

With these parties it isn't about saying something catchy; it's about saying something so easy to remember it can't really mean anything. Everyone is trying to figure out how to do it.

How to introduce themselves.

What isn't yet obvious to them is how impossible it is to do just that.

They'll inevitably settle for something that'll never really amount to anything. It'll be something to say, and something to stand by for the rest of the party, but watch how quickly it fades away.

"You're studying pre-law?"

The following day, the only thing that can be said is, "Oh, I must have forgotten."

This party's about to pop, about to really fall into place;

everyone's ready so they're eagerly lined up. People are practicing the process of the "Who's Who" by thinking about how to say their names; they are trying to think of something interesting about themselves.

There I am, observing them all from near the keg.

People, they're all getting nervous, feeling faint when the first person starts reading from his card, and it's something right out of pop culture, references, lyrics, and all.

And everyone's frantically writing on their cards again. I'm watching them sip the cheap, watered-down beer; the first person to go just ruined it for everyone else.

The gimmick has changed, just like that, from "Who are you?" to "Which celebrity/idol would you rather be?" This isn't as interesting a gimmick as it might seem, but maybe it's more suitable for the people, this party. Everyone seems to give off the same glow of desperation.

Probably why I'm not paying much attention, and it's probably why I'm not going to find what I'm looking for. Not tonight.

Instead of self-deprecating humor and introductions, we get a couple dozen people all pretending to be the same pop idol. My attention's coming and going; I'm watching one celebrity impersonation-as-introduction after another, and then they're given a congratulatory drink and they're chugging it, spilling it all over themselves. But it's a party, and everybody takes the sight with that desperately booming laughter, and then I'm watching the previous hug, the one going next, and it all starts over again. Over and over and over and over.

Getting tired of this yet?

Imagine how I feel, but I'm constantly reminding myself that I'm here for a reason. And whoever it is I'm talking to (probably talking to myself) should still understand that this is me, this is only me, and it's about what I need to become.

And now I'm watching a couple that might not actually be a couple arguing. I assume they'd never met, but then the girl is shouting at the guy. It's the kind of shout that isn't directed to strangers. I'm hearing the familiar twinge of unrequited proclamations. I'm seeing an anger that isn't just anger; it's also an inadvertent attack based on the girl's knowledge that the guy might not be as into her as she is to him. The guy doesn't seem to take it well, but can't do anything about it. Since the introductions, people have caught up on the drinking. Many are drunk, and this guy, he's nowhere near sober. So when he hits her, it makes sense, even for her. She takes the smack in stride and delivers one of her own. The circle nearest to them cheers the couple on. It goes back and forth like this, one slap after the other, until they are bleeding, but just barely. My attention wavers when I realize it was going to end up forgotten too.

Just another one of those typical flare-ups, done partly for the attention.

Always about attention.

And then what happens? Well, the same thing that happens every night.

The room gets smaller, so I'm stepping aside as much as I can, as often as I can. I'm moving out of the action, watching it all blend together.

People choke on body heat, but they're way too into it now to stop.

They've got to see this through.

At some point I leave, go home, and pass out. Whatever I drink is never enough to defeat me, but I always feel the effects of it, a shallow numbness climbing on top of me, trying to fuck me over when I wake up the next morning for yet another day of graduate research and class.

All that goes on between the time I get home and the time I pass out resets and starts over again. It's the kind of stuff that is never worth thinking about later. All I know is when I'm awake again, whatever happened is gone. Forgotten. For the many that are involved, this is what they'd call a success. They have forgotten and been forgotten.

If I haven't found what I was searching for, it's going to be the same thing tomorrow night. Different but same effect.

I get by.

And I'll keep reminding myself I'm a great observer and that I know exactly what I'm looking for. I'll downplay the fact that I'm still searching.

It's been such a long time, it seems like.

But I'm bound to find what I'm looking for.

If it happened before, it'll happen again.

Until then, I will get by. Since every day and every night is the same, I'm pretty sure I know what to expect. No surprises, and I'm still searching.

3.

I went to class.

Eavesdropped talk about someone unlucky last night, but what everyone's hearing is just what managed to reach the mainstream media.

More about plan-of-study and stock market prices on the decline.

Everyone's half asleep and/or half interested.

Everyone's recovering from last night.

Everything will lead up to tonight.

*4.

No use resisting. Before it can start, you've got to sit through the "Coming Attractions." The lights in the auditorium dim, and the screen flickers as the first few frames of the paid-for promotion struggles to commence. The audience anchors itself with snack foods and beverage, settling in for the night's most anticipated feature.

Do you ever feel like you're simply too content with life? Do you ever sit in some majestic club, with the love of your life, with all questions answered, with a million-dollar car valet-parked outside, an estate valued at five million dollars awaiting your return, completely satisfied with your situation and yourself, but you're asking, Why am I so happy?

Do you ever wonder what it's like to feel like shit; feel like you don't belong? How does it feel to open up your wallet and find out you don't have enough cash to pay for the food you just ate, or to have the register ring up "credit card declined?"

Do you ever wonder what it feels like to be that someone who goes store-to-store asking for work? Do you view the homeless as free advertisement?

What must it feel like to be turned down, rejected, when that something you reached for turned out to not be interested? What must it feel like to live under an overpass, dumpster diving for dysentery? What must it feel like to work a dead-end job with crummy pay?

Do you ever want to have nightmares while awake? The feeling you're falling?

Do you ever think about trying life from someone else's shoes?

Do you make a backup for your backup plan just in case it doesn't work out? Does this plan "Z" have anything to do with suicide?

Do you often find yourself detaching from daily tasks, mulling over the machinations of the criminal? Do you ever wonder what it might be like to be someone else? Someone institutionalized?

Do you ever compare your life to the life of the institutionalized? Prison or asylum? Do you often feel the urge to do something, really do something, change something, alter something, destroy something. . . but never the confidence or courage to follow through?

Well if you answered "yes" to any of those questions, there is a state-of-mind perfect for someone like you!

Welcome to "Nothing Ever Happens," a state-of-mind that allows you to find, above all, every occasion, everything that happens in their cities and your city, in their countries and yours, which leads to absolutely nothing. It is assured that your involvement in such activities can only end in regret, remorse, spoiled moods, and scarring that'll haunt you for a lifetime.

In "Nothing Ever Happens," you'll undeniably learn to hate yourself, because hating yourself is the closest thing to an escape you'll ever find.

In "Nothing Ever Happens," you'll be the same person in ten years that you are now.

In "Nothing Ever Happens," you live the very same life you've built up for yourself, but now everything you've earned and everything you've owned will slowly spoil. You'll see that valuable estate plummet; you'll see that fiancée and financially capable job flounder. You'll find yourself in deep deliberation, and wonder as if it isn't your life that's falling apart, but someone else's. You'll stand in line. You'll buy the first ticket to the tragedy that's entirely yours.

In "Nothing Ever Happens," you live a life full of certainties until you come across a mystery, and whatever you do to make sense of this mystery only feeds that mystery.

You swear that the mystery involves a man and a woman.

You abide by the mystery in which a life is built from the ground up by the cash-advances on one's dreams and soul.

You view life as a part of the mystery as it unfolds.

The mystery is rarely what's wanted and is rarely what's found.

The mystery has no true form.

It maps and molds to the mood of man and woman.

The mystery is everything you don't understand.

Buying into the mystery, you're buying into self-murder.

You're trying to make something of nonsense.

There's a mystery to every movement in life. When your life is idle, it's more than likely the mystery ends up becoming your best friend. In "Nothing Ever Happens," the mystery visits your recently repossessed estate, syringe in tow. The mystery is there to make everything better. Don't be startled. The mystery is here to visit. Here to help you.

In "Nothing Ever Happens," mystery is really the only reason to live. The fact that there's something out there, something unsolved, something above and beyond the norm is enough to keep living through the civil stalemate of your estate.

How about picturing yourself later in life, when everything's spent? You're poor, but the mystery is there to keep you company until you're numb and ready for the knife.

Only then does it make any sense.

The mystery came to visit you. The mystery is the only reason you're sitting here, waiting and watching in wonder—in attendance to a show that seems to lack a main character.

Take some solace from the fact that you became part of the mystery. The same mystery that's everywhere and involves a national infatuation with death, disease, and tragedy.

"Nothing Ever Happens."

With such a state-of-mind, it's a good enough reason to let deviance be our director.

The show's about to start!

5. . . 4. . . 3. . .

2. . .

1. . .

And now, our Feature Presentation.

**scenes set in italics are considered optional.*

There can only be three walls if you plan on having a window.

1.

I went to class.

Crowded campus today doesn't help lessen how lonely I feel.

Not used to just being me. Lots about how it gets easier with time. Not with my kind of time. Slow time forces me to study every scar.

I'm scarred, but beautiful.

How many people really know each other?

See them together, what do they want? What do they really want?

Searched during class today.

I walked to and from class the same way.

Alone.

2.

Open wide on an over-emphasized trendy club on any given night. A mile-long wrap-around bar surrounds a dance floor full of attractive single women. Intermingling between these feminine rave dancers are the confident and brave single men with enough charisma and courage to approach the ungodly specimens of amazing beauty. The majority of the men stay near the bar, buying up as much alcohol as they can to keep themselves buzzed and busy while waiting to build up the bravery for the dance floor and the meeting of a girl.

But it can't be all that bad because most of the woman have a man by their side.

Those at the bar, they aren't men; they are boys too embarrassed to approach the opposite sex, too demeaned by what it must mean to stand at the bar to pull things together and walk the dance floor, making first contact.

The trendy club sets the scene with strobe lights, vintage appeal, and modern electronic music. It's a familiar scene of girls teasing guys.

This is a club that caters to the classical modes of courtship, but everyone here is here for the same intentions, and I have to stress how certain I am of this, even if they aren't.

This is the runway, the primetime. I get to stand there, swaying back and forth, scanning every man, waiting, as always, for somebody that's just my type.

Whenever I hit the clubs, I feel optimistic.

It isn't like the parties. A lot can happen in one night.

You and I, we're here undercover from looking irresistible. Looking irresistible is the easy part. I'm watching the night unfold. I can see it now:

A number of things happening, from the sighting of a dating savant–one hell of a gentleman–right on down to a group of university students thinking they've got what it takes, really got what it takes, to be someone that can give me, or anyone else, everything they want. Kind of boastful, don't you think?

But me, I'm not accepting anything less.

I'm getting better at sighting the patterns, the pleasures, everything in this pickup game we play. They have all sorts of names for it, but we're all really just looking to be picked up. Wanting so badly, so very badly, to be found.

Those at the bar, they aren't men; they are boys too embarrassed to approach the opposite sex, too demeaned by what it must mean to stand at the bar to pull things together and walk the dance floor, making first contact.

The trendy club sets the scene with strobe lights, vintage appeal, and modern electronic music. It's a familiar scene of girls teasing guys. I'm near enough to be where I need to be if I find myself looking to be picked up and wanted by any one of these guys.

For now, I'm watching something interesting happening between two young guys, seemingly friends and mutually absorbed in the inevitable failure of the night. Though they haven't yet tried, both have clearly dismissed the chances of meeting a girl tonight. They waste their time with meaningless banter, the fetishizing of discussion and debate. I'm not observing because I find them in any away attractive. Rather, I'm watching them being watched by a man that I've never seen before. He's eyeing them like they've stolen something from him, and it's there, in that glare, that I see a glimpse of something promising.

Might he be. . .

But I'm swaying to the music. I'm not supposed to be aware of what happens next.

Both of the young guys hold drinks in their hands like life-preservers. Sip, gulp, refill. They are dressed in current fashion, which does nothing for me but make it easier to lose them in the sea of clubbers looking, acting, smelling, and smiling similarly.

I have a very specific type.

"Duh," and they go back to their drinks.

"Hey man, I'm just trying to make a point here," and take a sip.

"So we have a murder victim, then what else happens?" Sip.

"The murder victim makes it impossible to move on. People never look at you the same way. That's prison for you. It's why Jeff's life is ruined." Sip.

"Duh." Getting that buzz going. It's the only thing "going" for these guys tonight.

"You're not getting it."

Oh this guy is really letting himself go. Clearly not at all worried about what'll happen later. Moderation? Fuck that.

"What am I not getting?" Another drink bartender.

"We have a killer. Our friend is a killer." Take a shot.

You could say I'm getting really interested in their conversation now, and I am, but not because of what they're actually talking about.

No, I'm interested in the man walking over to them. Their conversation is drunk talk, and drunk talk is the equivalent to starting a metaphysical thriller an hour in. You won't understand anything, but maybe it's because there's really no substance, just a smattering of ideas and a desperate attempt at trying to make everything connect together as one.

"Of course we have a killer; when don't we have a killer on the loose?" Finishes drink. Asks for whiskey on the rocks having realized he's out of cash and this drink will be his last.

"Jeff is a killer… I'm having trouble accepting it."

"There are a legion of active killers that we have absolutely no control over, and no clue whatsoever as to their origins, methods, and kill-patterns. Fuck if Jeff is a killer because he isn't alone. It just so happens he was caught. It doesn't change anything about human nature. It doesn't change anything about this or that."

I observe the two young guys, buzzed and with their drink budget blown for the night, they nurse their last drinks like lifelines-in-hand.

"I don't get your point. . . so we all know killers and those killers are commonplace?" Sip.

"Yes, that's exactly what I'm saying. Choose any kind of sample, small or large, it's still going to be a "one in three" scenario. If there is no killer in a group, it's only a matter of time. The killer has to gain confidence while losing faith in humanity." Looks out at the dance floor.

"Did you pick that up in one of your sociology classes?" Orders his last drink.

"Maybe, but it's damn fucking true. You're an asshole if you don't believe it." Watches two girls walking side by side, holding hands, passing by the bar and towards the restrooms.

"I think the real killer is a window into our lives." Sips drink.

"The killer inside someone is waiting for the moment of self-depreciation. That would-be killer will need friends and family, work and hobbies, more than ever. If the killer lacks in any of those departments, well, better call in advance, letting the authorities know another killer is being born. Jeff turned to friends and family after graduating and having nowhere to go, no job found, and what happened?" Let's the drink sit, ice melting, diluting the whiskey.

"Society kicked his ass." Sips drink.

"Society is a filthy bitch, anyway." Catches himself

grooving with the club music and stops, looking around, pretending no one noticed.

The other guy gazes out at the dance floor watching the impossible features of immaculate creatures, those confident and culturally relevant socialites dominating this club. For a moment, our eyes meet, but only I'm sober and observant enough to understand what's happening between the both of us. He could have tried to walk over to me but he lacked the hunter, the instinct, the confidence to do it. What would I have said to him if he tried?

I would have said, "How about a drink?"

And that would be the end of it because he's broke. But this is all a waste of deliberation and time because he wouldn't, couldn't, never will. But the man that watches the two young guys. . .he's near the dance floor; he appraises what he sees. It's clear he could have any one of the women, and he probably will, but right now, something about the two young guys interests him. I'm watching the start of something that'll end with both guys, days later, strung out and walking out of a jail cell, on bail.

"Check out that redhead in the white top." The guy with the whiskey nudges the other in the arm with his elbow. Spills some of his whiskey in the process.

"Huh? Oh. Very nice." Sip.

"Yeah." Sip.

"I'm into redheads."

"Same here." Sips his whiskey.

"And brunettes." Almost mistakenly finishes his drink, stops, sets it down on the bar disappointingly.

"And blondes." Sips his whiskey, frowns at the fading flavor of the whiskey after being watered down by the melting ice. Abandons the drink and steals the drink of someone next to him. Doesn't seem at all worried about what might be in the drink. Just needs a drink. Can't be here without a drink.

"Except blondes."

"What do you have against blondes?" Flicks a little piece of napkin at the other guy.

"They're boring. Everyone's a blonde these days. I like a little character."

"So a blonde lacks character?"

"Yes, a blonde lacks character. Blame it on the media." Finishes drink.

"You blame everything on the media." Discovers the wrapper of a cigar in the drink. Takes it out and continues drinking anyway.

"The media has its eyes in everything. Problem is their eyes are cataracts. They only see what they want to see."

Rolls up the damp wrapper. "So, you gonna talk to the redhead?"

"Are you?"

Shakes head. "You can have her."

"Why? You're the one that noticed her first."

"I'll find someone else. Lots of really hot chicks left."

"What, are you afraid?"

"Far from it."

"Then go talk to her."

"You're the one that's afraid." Finishes the drink and slams his fist against the counter.

"Hey man, don't say that. Don't make me show you how it's done. You know how it works. If I end up with the redhead, you're alone on trying to find a ride home tonight."

"I'll take my chances."

I'm rolling my eyes. That is such a turn-off.

But then I'm watching the man walk over to the two guys.

I'm noticing for the first time the slicked-back hair, the

professional demeanor, expensive suit, not a single shred of self-consciousness. The man turns at the last minute and targets the redhead the two guys were talking about.

"Looks like you're too late anyway." One says to the other.

Both guys watch the man lean in and whisper something in the redhead's ear. The redhead reveals a genuine flirtatious smile, while the man says nothing more. He looks at her a moment before taking her by the arm. The redhead grips onto his arm and the man walks with redhead down one of the hallways leading to the lounge in the back.

"Fuck."

"That guy's a pro at this."

Seconds later the man returns from the lounge alone.

"Look he's back."

"Where's the girl?"

"Don't know."

The man effortlessly weaves in and around the dance floor to a blonde with red streaks and a pink top. He reaches out and grabs her hand. Holding her hand, the man whispers something in her ear. It looks like the girl's laughing. The man takes her by the hand just like the redhead and he walks out of sight.

"The guy's a savant, man."

"Damn man, he's back again."

"He's going for that hot blonde hanging near the DJ."

"Okay this is ridiculous. What's he doing?"

"Fuck if I know."

"We have to talk to him."

"He's already leaving with the girl."

"Stockpiling girls, he'll be back."

The man returns and the two young guys nod.

"See?"

"Well then let's talk to him before he leaves."

"Right."

The two guys have no trouble walking up to the man. I don't hear what they hear because I'm moving into position. I want to meet this man. He's all I'm watching, and he's all I'm going to be thinking about until I find out whether or not he's my type.

I'm pushing through the dance floor when the man spots me.

We exchange a look. It's right then that I know:

He is my type.

The man passes a little piece of paper to one of the young guys. The man coolly leaves the two guys fawning over the piece of paper. I'm his next target.

He walks over to me. The two guys are watching, dazed and utterly confused.

I say something, he says something. We speak like we're sharing the same life story.

We are walking by, towards the hallway, towards the lounge.

The man passes nods towards the two young guys as we pass.

To them, I'm just another attractive female being picked up by a professional.

There's a lot going on that few will ever notice. So quickly the scene changes. If you don't know the threats and the patterns, the looks and the temptations, you'll never get past the fact that it's just a night club. It's never just a night club, just like it's never just a party.

Peel back the surface layer and you'll find a dozen more. The pickup game is played on as many levels as there are pickup lines.

Now the two young guys are the ones watching, huddled together, unaware of the fact that I am the one that picked up the man and not the other way around.

What was said between the two of us remains a closely guarded secret. Like the two young guys, you'll never know what we shared.

When we're gone, the two young guys read what's on the scrap of paper:

"You just witnessed the death of women. You are accessories to their murder."

3.

I went to class.

Had trouble paying attention. Didn't really participate. When there are only ten in the class, professor always notices who speaks versus who doesn't speak.

Frankly I really don't care.

There's a serial killer back at my apartment, sleeping.

I have that to go home to.

Which is why I couldn't have cared. A, B, C, or D. . .

Couldn't give a fuck. I've saved it all for him.

Just give me the grade and let me go.

4.

I'd like to keep last night a secret so that it can be remain selfishly mine, but that was before I felt whole again. I have to gush, if only a little. So here I am, talking to myself, maybe hoping someone else on the bus to campus is listening, but everyone here has their headphones on, ears pressed to cellphones, text messages and video-screens demanding their full attention.

So I'm kind of thinking I should talk a little bit about what this leads to, but I can't talk about later if it hasn't happened yet, even if I know what will happen.

I can't, I won't. I'll start with what already happened.

I'll start with last night.

He was someone with potential. Someone that was my type, but just because I brought him home didn't mean it would build up to anything.

But, thankfully, it did.

I brought him home. I brought him inside, showing him around. Little did either of us realize at the time that this was the tour of what would be his new home. It's just like any other apartment–kitchen, two bedrooms, and a common area—except for what I had done to the common area. All the other rooms looked like they belonged, but not the common area.

Across what should have opened up into the balcony was a grey wall. Across all three walls I had studio-quality soundproofing installed. Where the common area should have linked up with the hallway, where we'd use to come and go from the apartment as we pleased, stood a window without a frame.

You had to crawl through the window to get into what was an insulated cage.

The floors are carpeted everywhere within. I had

someone come in and shave down the carpet bare, installing smooth linoleum where it mattered most.

Since having it all done, it has seen some use.

Before we went to bed, he gave it a look, tapping the soundproofed walls, listening for any faults, but I knew there weren't. It was perfect.

The moment, me observing him, was perfect.

He hadn't trusted me or understood what I had to offer. And in a way I hadn't yet really mustered up the right lines, much less anything but a few empty words.

This night was only about mending.

I'd been alone for such a long time. . . I was only looking to be consumed for one night.

Poking his head through the window, he asked me, "Were you looking for me?"

I had picked him up so I didn't have to say anything. Not a single word if I didn't want to. It was he that was required to do the talking. Whatever I did, it was optional. My choice.

"Were you anticipating my presence?"

He could tell the cage would be perfect for his work.

"It's built with the best quality materials."

He nodded.

"Got to be prepared."

A hand over his slicked back hair loosened a strand and it fell over his left eye. Before he could brush it back, I grabbed him and showed him my bedroom.

I showed him me, and all that I could be. He showed me what he was, and where he had been. In each of us was a brand new, unfamiliar city full of delights and desires never before experienced. Bed was our bus stop. We wanted to explore each other's cities.

And it was then that I felt it:

He was the one I'd been searching for.

We slept near each other, arms crossed, elbows touching. Somewhere between sleep and awake, I could feel myself trembling. I was feeling his arms reaching around me, bringing me close. Connected, together, I didn't have to observe. I could feel every twitch and touch as it entered and exited my body, his body, my voice, his voice.

He dared not cut my skin like he had all women in his life, and I treated this knowledge not with surprise, but expectation. It was I that picked him up, and it was I that would drop him down. I'd be the one directing what can and will happen versus what won't and never will occur.

Early morning I watched him sleep in the minutes before I had to leave for what would inevitably be yet another one of those days, as repetitious and predictable as pulling the trigger of a gun. I would go only to return hours later, feeling as though I've wasted my time. But now I had something to make up for the hours I'd lose.

I wasn't worried whether or not he'd be there when I got back from class. I was someone he'd never met before. He'd met his match.

Would he satisfy me like I'd satisfy him?

I wondered if he knew what he was getting himself into.

Who he was would soon turn into who I pictured him to be.

Who I am would be his saving grace.

What I feel is what most people feel when they say they are in love. Am I in love? To that I say, who can truly be in love with anyone but themselves?

After last night, it was obvious there was going to be a lot more to experience and explore together as one, as individuals, as visitors of each other's bodies.

There can be no shame in the secrets we keep to ourselves.

But this secret, I'm forcing myself to let it out into the

wilds of indifference.

I can't help it, just like I can't help the frenzy of wanton avarice soon to follow.

5.

No matter what the film's about, everyone ends up traveling. It's a mystery that anyone knows what the hell's going on this early in the narrative, but you have to keep with it. You've got to be patient and observant until the mystery unfolds.

Keep on driving until it all makes sense.

Some drive until the road ends. Some turn around and try learning a different road. Some never find a place with their name on it. They commit to theories that speak of a life that only ends up coiled around mystery.

It's always a matter of having grown too comfortable, too confused, for the people and places shared. Everyone becomes a part of a mystery that can't be solved.

Fade in on the mystery driving down the interstate picking up theories.

Theories like to hitchhike using red gloves. Look for them. Thumbs up!

Without too much time, the scene evolves to include a subject. She stands in the rain, hair and clothing glued to her frame. Soaked, but still hopeful, she holds that thumb out for all to see.

Why are you hitchhiking in this weather?

Nowhere else to go. Have to keep going. Why? I have to find something to live for.

There's room in this car for one more.

Of course she's thankful. They all are.

Watch as the clothes come off. Mind if I dry up?

Of course not. Showing some skin is good for the critics; it's good for any horror flick.

Can't have horror without some honest and wholesome nudity.

She's down to her wet underwear and she's wearing white today. Might as well not even wear the underwear.

There are some clothes in her bag.

Fresh shirt and mesh shorts.

Cover up. That's better. Bearing all for just long enough for the voyeur's glimpse.

Watch as the mystery continues to elude her inquiries.

The passenger's a naïve blabbermouth.

Where she's going. What's the point? Why not take a bus? Aren't you scared? Felt like touring the country. Never have. I don't know what's out there. Oh, there's a lot out there.

So much of the country is a mystery.

The mystery is about to take a sharp turn.

She's getting comfortable. She reclines back, making it so much easier to see past the front seats.

Don't you recognize me?

She doesn't seem to, and asks, what do you mean when you say you're a mystery?

It's all about the mystery, right?

Traveling down this road you hope for some discovery.

It starts with one lie–sometimes it's you that lies to yourself–and it keeps going until the dead end of this night. It's a double feature.

Got to make this last.

It's going to be a long drive.

Better get used to the mystery.

Better start crying.

Had enough exposition. It's about time she starts noticing she's in danger.

Oh. You just missed the exit. . . is there another way?

She squirms in her seat, worried about what this means.

What are you talking about?

There's only the one planned stop, and it's our final destination.

Seems she's the only one confused, the only one that hasn't read the script.

You should keep up to date with the news. It might have saved your life.

It's around now that she'll start crying.

She starts pleading, let me go.

The bargaining doesn't usually come until after anger. She's switching the steps.

She tries the door. It's locked from the driver's side.

It's going to be a long drive. Get comfortable.

Since when has everything been about murder?

Since it became marketable and entertaining for an audience, any audience.

Go ahead. There's some popcorn in the back seat.

Might as well sit back and enjoy the ride.

Give in. She's going to give up soon enough.

It's time for anger and screams. Her screams startle the audience. Hurts the ears, adds urgency to the scene unfolding.

Go ahead and scream.

No one uses this interstate. This, an interstate without a number; an interstate abandoned by time. The only use of such an interstate is the mystery that drives up and down its entire expanse, leaving only to refuel.

Screams turn to anguished blood curdling cries.

The mystery slouches in its seat, one arm on the steering wheel, getting comfortable.

This is getting good.

Your ego is the only reason you are here.

1.

So, you know, given the way the world is, it's not that difficult to find what you're looking for. Keep searching and you'll eventually find it, whatever it might be. Even if it's just a picture online, you'll find it. If there's any demand, it will be captured. If this were two days, two weeks, two months ago, I wouldn't be as optimistic.

But that's only because of what you might already know.

Yes, I am talking about him.

Victor Hent. The slicked back hair, the expensive suit, the deadly gaze, the general demeanor and confidence.

Our beloved gentleman killer.

I wake up and fall asleep to the same series of pictures.

What am I picturing? Is it possible for me to capture what you demand to see?

I'm picturing everything you'll never get to see with your own two eyes.

I'm picturing what he'll leave behind after all is said and done.

I'm picturing him driving across the country, picking up women with relative ease; all he needs to do is speak to them and they'll be wanted.

I'm picturing a woman walking across campus, a dreary bag of secrets weighing down her handbag. It's what keeps her going, and these images don't weigh that much. She can take them along too.

I'm picturing a man and a woman comparing the angle and shape of their curves.

I'm picturing the Gentleman Killer in bold, white capital letters on the six-o-clock news.

I'm picturing a dinner party where the topic of conversation is whether or not the Gentleman Killer will seduce their wives.

I'm picturing a rainy day like any other day, a woman dripping wet.

I'm picturing the night I returned to my apartment, soaked, and there he was, turning one body into two. I'm picturing it split down the middle because it sounds so much better that way.

I'm picturing what I said and what I didn't say.

I'm picturing his face when he realized I was serious, my offer, serious and true.

I'm picturing our kiss.

I'm picturing everything you can't picture, and it makes it so much better knowing that it's mine and mine alone.

But see how I'm not really telling you the whole story, and I'm not going to, because leaving a bit of it to mystery keeps everyone guessing. It turns a person's mind into a powerful weapon. Guess all you want, but you're not going to figure it all out. And then you're thinking maybe it's impossible to figure out. Eventually you might give up, but the mystery never gives up on anyone. It'll return as a passing thought, something that triggers during a cup of coffee, while riding the subway to work, or maybe when you're people watching, the mystery will return. It's a sitcom rerun that was never viewed in its entirety.

Bits and pieces get pieced away, left on the cutting room floor.

I'm picturing a dirty floor, scraps of skin and bone where there should only be books, magazines, and dirty laundry.

I'm picturing your face right as you realize what he's going to do to you.

I'm picturing all the things I imagine people see right before their breath is no longer their breath. I'm picturing a world in recession, the world at present.

I'm picturing my pet, by all accounts a gentleman

and cultivated cultural icon, attaining the higher twenties.

I met him like he meets all his ladies—under the intention of swooning and swaying them towards being free and willing, letting themselves be taken. To bed, not to death.

Or so they hoped.

But you see, I was different. I am different.

I knew what he had planned. What I offered him no one else has ever offered. I offered him more than my body.

More than my love. I offered him my home.

My kindness, my secret, my safety.

He would be mine and I would keep him to his craft.

I'm going to help him increase that number.

2.

I went to class.

Talked about current events and culture of fear.

Good topics. Good mood today.

More so because of what's happening tonight.

After class I attended a meeting with my thesis council.

Topic was what I want to study. I think I know what I plan on studying.

Everyone agrees I'm smart and a great observer. I know people.

Not actual people, but just "people," figuratively speaking.

I'm great at profiling. Told them what I think I'm going to study.

They are all in agreement.

"Serial murder is quite popular." Their words not mine.

Seems like I agree with that statement.

3.

Wanting so very much to know what he's doing back at home.

I'm not there, but he is. There's something arousing about having this knowledge. His business is there. Home. Where she is. His latest. She probably still believes he's the one. The one perfect for her, and that they're about to share something intimate and personal.

Oh Victor. She'll always know his name.

What he says and does are perfectly timed. It's always the right thing. For her at least. Always for the one he has in mind at the time.

There's something fragile about the scene he projects. He expends so much energy trying to make it happen, not showing how much of a fighter he is deep down, beyond the expensive clothing, the practiced gestures, and the beautiful, flirtatious things he says.

She's saying, "I can't believe this. You're too good to be true."

They aren't like me. They're the women of the world too oblivious to see past his projected image. He's not your type. He is my type. And that's why you can't imagine what it is he's doing to you. I'm telling you, I love every minute of it.

It's like sex but he's really killing her.

He's telling the woman, "I love you."

But what does that even mean?

He's telling the woman, "You have beautiful eyes," right as everything goes right for him and wrong for her. So quickly the scene can unfold without notice.

The smell of his expensive cologne counters the smell of her shitting herself. Thankfully he's already making use of the cage. He localizes the mess to one corner where the slaughter can be flushed out with a simple turn of a nearby faucet. In this rainy city, a victim's remains wash out the following day, long before the morning turns over to afternoon. And the neighbors below me are too afraid of what it all is. They wouldn't care either way.

He's excusing every sound as his own—"Pardon me," and when her necklace breaks and drops to the floor, he's saying, "Let me get that for you."

He places it in the open palm of one of her hands. She'll try but fail to close her hand. The sound of dripping isn't just urine. Hear the blood dripping down into the drainpipe.

He addresses every victim as "Miss" or "Ma'am," and I'm certain he continues to do and say the same things until there's nothing left but the body. There won't be a mess when I get back. There'll only be him, the perfect gentleman. When he's with me, he turns into pleasure, natural pleasure. And we're talking about her, and her, and the other her, whoever his last one was, like we might be able to surpass one with the one that'll inevitably come next.

I'm always thankful to see what he's done to them when I return from class.

He cleans up the body after every bloodletting. "I'll take care of that," and "There you go, all better!" His kind regards make them all look like perfect, porcelain dolls. And the way he leaves them, they're seldom any more than a fixture of his mounting legacy.

Like a true gentleman, when I return home dinner is ready.

And I'm hungry for everything.

And he's willing to give.

Saying, "Pardon," and "Allow me."

When I arrive, he's pulling off the gentleman disguise and he's turning into someone I can no longer live without. That expensive suit is his disguise and that's fine for her. But me, I'm craving the scene under his clothing, the scene he saves for me.

4.

Just in case she's still conscious enough to see my face, I turn the knob three times. That's the warning we've discussed. Unlike him, I'm not so open about letting her know anything about me, be it my face or my name.

Maybe she's not going to last much longer, but I'm not comfortable with it, and so I give the warning, wanting to get the hell inside because it's raining again—when is it not?—and I want to take off these wet clothes and warm up next to his body.

I unlock the door and slip through, the door never open any wider than a crack.

He's already done with her, with the meal, and I catch him slipping out of his underwear.

I say, "Hi," in as cute a voice as I can manage.

He's not quite smiling, not quite nodding, "Hello."

This is the killer inside. I get to see what goes on, behavior and otherwise.

Whenever I'm around, I take over, and he's nothing but a man waiting to satisfy my every beckon and call. I tell him what to do.

"Sit down," and he sits down.

I drop my purse next to the front door and, in five steps, I have all my clothes off. I stop at the thermostat and turn up the heat.

"Where is she?" I ask.

His head drops, staring blankly at the placemat in front of him.

I'm walking over to the cage and I'm poking my head through the windowless frame.

Not a mark remains, and I'm wearing an unsatisfied smirk as I sit down at the table. He's standing back up to portion out the meal.

He made me curry, exactly what I wanted tonight.

I didn't have to tell him that. He knows what I'll want and when I'll want it. It's all part of our agreement.

He's sitting back down and I'm telling him, "Explain to me your day," because that's also part of our agreement.

He isn't protesting—why would he?—and he's telling me about her, where he found her, how he kissed her. Told her the story about a bad breakup and how he toyed with calling her all day before finally doing so. All throughout the explanation, we take in mouthfuls of curry. It seems to lighten his mood a little, the more he talks about how he tended to her. A truly perfect gentleman, he's telling me about how he made sure the blood didn't settle on the floor for too long. If it had, the blood would stain. I'd have to get the linoleum replaced. It has happened before, and I told him to keep the cage really clean. I stressed how important it was to stick to protocol in order to keep the neighbors from smelling her, whoever she is and whenever she comes and finally goes, and he agreed. For the time being, he's been great about it.

What isn't so great, and what I'm finding myself more than a little annoyed, is how bad he is with explanations.

"I need details," I'm saying.

He's replying, "But I already told you. . ."

I'm all about forgiveness if its justified, but this is a big part of our agreement.

I support you financially. I give you a place to hide. I make sure you are never under suspicion of being what you really are, a cold-blooded psychotic killer (so hot), and in return you clue me into your process. You become mine.

You do what I say, when I say it.

You keep everything to the letter, clean and proficient, and I'll always be your best friend, your best lover, your perfect and reasonable master.

Master and pet.

This isn't something impossible to maintain. I've done it before and I'm willing to do it again, better than ever before. But he has to give me those details.

"I need every single aspect of it explained." He's looking a little doubtful and it's enough to turn me off. Turn me away. Make me not want to walk around naked.

But he's trying again, better this time, but it's still not good enough.

Dinner is over.

He's standing up, using the opportunity to gather all the details, but then I'm standing up too, walking into the kitchen, right at his side.

I'm grabbing and saying, "Don't drop the plate. It will shatter all over you."

It wasn't supposed to be a threat, but it turns into one, and he's going over every single word, every single thing I told him—the if/else statement—and he's maybe already buckling under the weight of my own demands. But it's my roof, my place, my support structure, and I've already made my investment, so I give him a chance.

I'm finding myself wanting him more because of all that he's done prior to meeting me. He's not inexperienced. He is a professional.

I'm still remembering the loneliness and the searching, ceaseless searching, and I don't have it in me to go right back to it again, so I'm telling him:

"I'll figure something out."

I give him a stroke or two, and it's enough to calm him. He's turning to me and touching me. The half-inch or less of space between us is warm and getting warmer. He's placing the plate in the sink and we're entering my bedroom and we're getting hot, real hot.

His gentleman persona lends itself well to improvisation, and he's quickly adapting to my every demand; everything I'm wanting he's giving, and I'm enjoying the time we have together. It makes me totally forget about class, about all my responsibilities, and I'm indulging, we're indulging, in the possibilities still to be posed.

When we're finished, we're touching ourselves where we're raw. I'm touching my lip and there's blood, but only a little. He's using his saliva to wipe away what I did to his arm.

I'm pointing to the ceiling of my room, "Maybe a few there and there," and he's agreeing, and I'm adding, "Your room too. If you see me, I see you."

And he can't do anything but agree.

So I'm also thinking it's necessary in the common area, right in the cage, so that he won't have to tell me anything. I'll see it for myself.

Every single second recorded on camera.

And we're getting ready, getting warmer and warmer, after growing limp and cold, and we're going for round two, saving ourselves for rounds three and four, because this is how our nights have unraveled before, and how they'll continue to unravel for as long as I see fit.

I'm wanting him to say it, and say it again. One more time.

He's hesitating, so I begin to pull him away, but then he's buckling, "I'm yours! I'm yours!" And then I'm telling him, it's all easy if you're willing to do everything I say. As long as he lends every inch of himself, as well as every aspect of his work to me, everything will be taken care of. He'll never be found and I'll do all the finding for him.

No one will ever be the same.

Our beloved gentleman killer will cross all boundaries while the authorities look everywhere only to find nothing but what's beautiful and bothersome by design.

I'm whispering to him, "They'll remember you."

Textbooks written about him and the impossibility of his escape.

The mystery will consume everyone and I'm the only one that'll have known every inch and angle. I'll have seen everything as it turned into common knowledge.

I'll have been there, telling him what to clear and what to keep.

And I'll be saying to him every line that no one else will hear.

Every line of that mystery.

Every line of you and me.

5.

The wide-open road aches for the next scene.

Getting closer to our destination. Sobbing but no longer screaming, she rests her head between her knees. Spot the syringe full of clear liquid.

By the time she notices, it's already too late.

Soon after the injection comes the silence.

She falls back in the seat, eyes cloudy. Close up on her face.

A single stream of saliva drips down the side of her mouth.

Every pore on her face can be seen. Otherwise lifeless eyes are blinking—letting the audience know she's still alive.

No clear shot on the driver keeps the audience curious and guessing.

The mystery feels it's necessary for the wide shot.

The mystery presses down on the gas pedal. Watch as the car peels out, kicking up waves of filthy water as it speeds down the interstate and out of view.

Plenty of horsepower. Plenty of muscle. To-die-for.

The more observant audience members will have noticed the missing license plate. Add it to the mystery. How about a nice shot of a rain-drenched interstate?

Not a single light source down this particular highway. Spotting no headlights.

It rains in thick sheets making it hard to see into the distance. The mystery is meant for a destination somewhere down the interstate.

It isn't time for new reveals.

Don't choke on your popcorn.

The best part is yet to come.

There's a serial killer living next door.

1.

This is what I want, and I won't feel like myself until everything is exactly right.

Two cameras to a room. Both rooms, because I need him to have his own room whenever I don't want him close to me.

I'm not saying that I ever would, but I want to know that I have the ability to choose. One camera on the bed, front and center, and the other scanning, searching for movement.

I need eyes on everything he does with doors closed and windows shut.

The same goes for my room, too. I have one right on me at all times. Watch me sleep; watch me as I toss and turn. Watch me when you feel alone.

Watch me when I want you to watch me.

Watch me when I don't want you to. Watch me. . .

The second camera is aimed low on a seat I use for one thing and one thing only. As a reminder, I should say that I don't need to speak if I don't want to, but you must note that my room is just like his, except for what I won't let him have. He should be thankful that I let him have what he has because he could continue on his own, never amounting to anything more than a short-lived stint followed by death row and an anticlimactic execution.

He wants more than that.

Like a gentleman, he wants it all, and that's why I'm going to get everything I can out of him. And you have to assume that I chose him for a reason.

The tech guy looked at me weird when I told him I wanted four cameras installed in the cage. He refused to go into the cage alone; I had to be in there too. Somehow he figured that if I was in there too, nothing bad would happen. How little people know about shivers and sin...

The four cameras scan left and right, but never cross each other's sight. Each corner is covered by a camera.

In addition to the cameras, I had the tech guy install all the necessary hardware and software so that my pet and I could constantly record every inch of the apartment, every single day. Never will there be a moment when nobody's watching. Everything between us is open, intimate, and shared. But only I have admin status. Only I can analyze, edit, erase, and access his computer. Though he might have a window into the online world, I would be able to watch and communicate with him anytime I feel like it.

He wouldn't dare cross me.

We're in this together.

Oh, sweet gentleman.

The tech guy was paid handsomely not to question or care. The oddity of his objective, never, not even once, derived a need to understand how these cameras would be used. In fact, I'm sure he wouldn't want to know, even if I was willing to tell him. He wouldn't want to know that I paid him using the money procured from the pockets of a few missing, forgotten women, their names infamous only because they no longer exist. We were the last people to know of them, just before a gentleman let the red drip like a leak in the ceiling to wash the area around our feet a dark red, sticky the longer we let it stay.

The tech guy wouldn't want me to tell him about that one time there was someone strapped into the chair he sat in. I forget how long... long enough to piss herself and leave a stain that, if seen with the right set of eyes, looked like the heart shape of a former obsession. He wouldn't want me to tell him about all the forgotten that disappear not because they want to, not because they partied too hard, but because someone else was looking to find someone, and that someone happened to be them. The forgotten are the ones people fixate upon more than those near and dear.

The tech guy wouldn't want me to tell him about how easy it is to disappear, to become the product of someone else's delicate masterpiece. He wouldn't want me to tell him about how easy it is to banish someone into the world of victim and unmarked graves.

He wouldn't want me to tell him. No, he wouldn't want that.

He just wanted to get paid and leave. As soon as possible.

Fine, go ahead and leave.

Minuteman.

2.

When you're a professional student, forever stuck between the successful completion of a class and the beginnings of another, switching roles between teacher and the one being taught, you have to waste your life away on the objects of language and theory.

You're often forced to give a shit about the people that study with you.

It's why tonight I'm telling him beforehand to stay in his room.

He's never stayed in his room before.

"Watch us from above," I'm saying to him when someone knocks on the front door. The first to arrive. He's leaving me for his bedroom while I'm making sure the cage is closed off so that it'll look like a third bedroom. I was smart enough to come up with it early enough, but not without first having a delivery boy and the superintendent both notice something wrong with the apartment. I'm learning like everyone else. Since those two separate mishaps, I've had a drop down panel designed to make it look like a wall with a door that, if tried, goes to nowhere.

When I open the door, they're there, three of the five, energetic and anxious.

My peers, here for caffeine and a caustic cram session.

Tomorrow half the class will pass while the other half will fail out of the graduate program. I'm the only one that can't be concerned about where I'll be placed. But they all insisted on having a last-minute collaborative cram session.

The topic is modern crime.

The exam is an essay-based test.

Application of one's mastery of modern theory. There's no getting out of this with a simple relay of textbook facts.

I'm telling them we'll study in my bedroom. "There's

more room there."

"Yeah, your apartment is way too cramped."

I am agreeing, "It is when you share the apartment with two other roommates."

"I thought this was a two bedroom."

I'm shrugging, "It was until money was tight enough to need a new roommate." I can be so good, so very good, at lies.

It helps to get caught up in the lies yourself. Everything I say and do might as well be real because I'm indifferent to what they really mean.

What I say is gospel, how about that?

I'm facilitating the cram session.

The subject of modern crime ends up on the big three:

Fraud/robbery, serial/spree murder, and sex trafficking.

"Correlations between separate crimes and motive."

I'm getting this all on camera, every single thing, and I'm aware of him watching us and I'm watching them as they start grappling with the prompt while the last to arrive finds us and is saying how he claims all motives originate from a desperation, a dire lacking.

One of them is saying desire is a big part of it.

Someone else is trying to explain how desire can be considered a form of lacking.

I'm getting this all on camera, so I let them all have a say.

I'm imagining him watching them, watching me, maybe turned on enough to pull down his pants and get a good stroke going.

I'm finding myself really into what's going on, and I'm having trouble focusing on my own views of the prompt, so I'm letting them get it all out, finish what they have to say, and then I'm moving on, moving in closer on concepts having to do with social isolation and more about motives.

The prompts given to us by our professor will be potential exam questions and we're all stressing each and every single one so that we not only understand what can and can't be argued, but also what we'll hopefully retain for approximately a day, long enough to release it all onto paper for one time and one time only.

He's watching. . .

And now they're talking about media icons and murder.

I'm saying something, elaborating upon a point previously brought up by one of the others. It has everything to do with the mystery and the image a mystery projects. Many of them are agreeing that serial and spree murders are prone to garnering media attention due to the hasty and often hopeless end-result of the crime scenes found.

Without extensive forensic science, the public is left to wonder.

If you leave the public to wonder, they'll wither in the face of their own overactive and irrational imaginations and minds.

I'm finding myself wanting to look up at one of the cameras, but I don't.

He's watching and he's hearing them now, talking about serial killers that were a) never caught or b) still active.

I'm hearing about the Zodiac. I'm hearing about Jack the Ripper. I'm hearing them yawn and grow bored, sipping their energy drinks, and I'm riffing off one of their comments about how tired and old the big-names are:

"Big name escapes are ancient history."

Many of them are agreeing, "Is anachronistic."

"Get with the times," I'm saying.

And then it's so magical because it happens while he's watching from a room away.

One of them is gulping the energy drink and then saying, mid-burp, "You hear about the Gentleman Killer?"

And they are all remembering now, how he's "big news"

and "brand new."

Something about fresh interest, and I'm nodding with the rest of them, and they are all fighting over who gets to use Gentleman Killer in their exam and who doesn't. They're talking about how they can't all answer the prompt using the same example.

But then I'm saying, "Why not?"

And he's watching.

And they are realizing that its valid. He's valid.

"The Gentleman Killer has killed twenty-four women."

"26," I'm correcting them.

They are going to believe me because I'm the one in the class, every class, that doesn't try very hard, and yet has some kind of natural link or facility for retaining all this morbid information and theory. I'm a natural observer and I'm best when I'm noting how people act and react, and I know more about the Gentleman Killer than any of them could.

I know that he's watching.

I know that he's mine.

And I know that tomorrow, my response to the prompt will land me a spot on the passing side and, even more than that, I'll be highlighted as a bright and shining scholarly star.

My professor will want to talk to me. Everyone will want to befriend me.

I'm going to be valuable for what I know and what I hide.

I'll take the mystery to my grave.

He's watching them as they gush and gloat about their own theories about him, my beloved gentleman killer. They're bringing up the theories that discuss the inherent fear and simultaneous interest these killers and murderers project. "There's a serial killer next door," and they're using this example to explain how the proximity and believability of the danger increases as interest and closeness increases.

At its utmost height, they're potential victims, and yet they can't resist the adventure and enticement that comes with trying to keep up and uncover the true identity and shape of the danger, the killer. And then they're starting to scrutinize each other and any theory and idea that's brought up, and I'm letting them go all-out, spreading lies, spreading thoughts about him that are simply not true.

He isn't an old man. A pervert. A woman. A terrorist.

And no, he isn't a media-created lie.

He exists, and he's watching in the next room.

After they've gone, as oblivious leaving as they were coming in, he and I will have quite the laugh. We'll laugh while we get naked, and then afterwards, we'll plan ahead to tomorrow night, deciding what will be read about hours later online and in the morning paper.

And I'll get a perfect score, accolades, while he'll inch closer to 30.

30 women. And this, I'm finding myself saying quite often, "It's only the beginning. By the time we're really close that number will be doubled."

His eyes would light up and I'd be pushing him into his room, telling him to get online, get on camera, and that I'm wanting him fully, in frame, ready and recording.

There's no better way to know every little thing about another by seeing them naked and alone, with only the dark lights and threat of humiliation forming around them from the bleak corners of their room.

Him in his room, and me in mine—this is us, and we're getting to know each other.

3.

What is this, what is that? Look into the camera. I can lust over nothing else.

Speak to me with every press of the key.

—He agrees.

Let me see you. Manipulate you, manipulate me. We cannot get any closer than the screens and the demands broadcast between camera and keyboard. I want your body next to me when I'm looking to fuck and not be found.

Find me online. Find me on camera. Type to me.

—He does.

Say everything that can't leave your lips.

Bare text. Don't let the bare text fool you. Bare text is like airbrushed nude pics where you're not getting the full-effect. Let's see those freckles. Let's see those stretch marks. It's far better to see in video than the bare text of any blog.

I'm what you call a purist. I want every ounce, every fold, every tuck.

Every fuck.

The need to feel something teases me with the thought that I can satisfy my urges.

But I can never have enough.

—And neither can he.

Move to minimize three windows while I enlarge one. I hesitate right after.

I feel my lips quiver. I see my hands shaking.

I look up at the camera, imagining that you're as excited as me.

—He's watching me.

I look down at myself. I am seated where he can see right through me.

I've shaved today just for this. Call it show time. Call it seeing the real side of a person. Call it the daily grind. Call it loving yourself. Call it whatever you want to call it as long as you come when I say.

The real me, and not the one I let strangers see.

I'm probably classifiable an egomaniac, a battle-torn being.

I'm bitter and I'm bored.

I'm a city with a thousand faces, but I need to come before I can find the one I need, the one that fits me. Look at me. Don't look at my fingers thrusting in and out.

Look at me.

—He looks.

They look at me and see only what's on the surface.

You look at me and what do you see?

I know what's coming and it's me, and it's them, and it never gets old.

The window bares all.

The camera captures parts of me—every moan, every misery, every desire. Yet it won't ever capture all of me. I'm the deluge. I'm a girl with serious demands. I'm resourceful. I've built a business around the thought of glimpsing perfection, all feeling, all touch, all taste, all sensation, all at once.

Perfection is something you cannot pay for.

Perfection is something worth dying for.

Some windows are two-way. He watches me and I watch him.

He has no reason to hide from me. He must let me see him.

Let me see what I want to see.

Do what I say.

—He does what I say.

Dominate me. . .

Dominate me!

—He dominates me.

I want to look him in the eye right before we both climax.

And when we do, I'm the one ready again. He seems to slow down, tiring out, and look who's on top, riding you limp, wanting more?

—He wants to please me.

How many people really want to be found?

1.

I'm here because he's insatiable, which really means I'm searching not for someone, but for something, her, and she's potentially anyone and everyone. The chances are good that anyone might fit into what she needs to be. Just like there might be a serial killer living next door, it means the chances are great, the greatest they've ever been, that anyone is everyone and everyone is simply a matter of who I'm choosing, labeling: "That's her."

I'm here looking to pick her up. Her—number twenty-eight.

We are continually being lost and found in the game we all play.

So when it's all so exciting and hopelessly final, the serial killer next door may be knocking, showing its true self as your father, your best friend, your sister or brother. You're ready to think about purpose and meaning. When you start letting those ideas roam free, it sounds something like trying to compare and contrast what "I am" compared to everyone else.

When a weapon is made murder weapon, and the location is made crime scene, the last thing that's important is whether or not the victim was a good human being or not.

The media's going to make the victim look as innocent as possible. No matter what the victim might have done, there'll be a disconnection between reality and fiction. It doesn't really mean that much to answer why. No matter how hard I try, I'm not going to be saying what you want to hear.

I don't really know what you want and I don't know the answer.

So, you see why I'd prefer not to talk. I keep things to myself most of the time.

But I end up getting texts from him and he's telling me about how number twenty-seven couldn't last that long and so maybe the one I find, the one that'll be her, number twenty-eight, should be a little feistier, more aggressive, more willing to break free from us in the cold rainy night so that we could both chase her down like a good girl. After that we'd both see how long it'll take to bleed her dry.

I've been to so many parties, and I've pretended to be all sorts of social people, but it's never me and it's never the "me" I want it to be. Yet here I am, once again, searching for him.

I'm never going to get used to all the waiting; waiting for the right people, the right crowd. I always feel off, almost anxious, pretending to look busy, staring into my phone. Rereading old texts make me feel even more like I've wasted my time. And I might start believing that I'm wasting my time, and I'm almost ready to start telling him that I'm not going to find her, but this is the first time, the very first time I'm helping him. I am going to find her, Miss Number 28. The twenty-seven that came before won't compare to her.

Miss Number 28. I guarantee it.

She'll change his life.

I'm waiting in someone else's car, someone—one of the grad students who routinely wish it was I they could seduce—and he's doing all the talking while I'm listening, most definitely waiting to get this over with.

I'm still not used to hearing the music and the party spillover in the parking lots. It's always a surprise; I'll always feel like the party's trying to reach out and strangle me. But it's alright because she's here tonight. I know it.

"You look beautiful, Claire! You really need to stop worrying. Take a deep breath. You'll be the prettiest one at the party." That's what my fellow grad student is saying. I'm apparently giving off vibes of anxiety and unease when, in fact, I'm simply uninterested with sights and sounds; I'm into the kind of atmosphere that'll drop all attendees on their rightful heads, turning them into dumb drunks, free for the taking.

But this guy is thinking I'm with him and not my gentleman, my beloved and true gentleman, who wouldn't have any qualms about removing this guy's tongue just so that I'd never have to hear him ramble, which is what he always seems to do. I'm really wishing it'll happen because he's still going on and on.

The damn party hasn't swelled enough yet to bother showing up. Everyone with self-respect is as late to the party as possible. Let the loners have first dibs, get drunker than us—quicker, faster—so that they might not find themselves in the same situation the following morning.

Take deep breaths. Take deep breaths. I'm checking and rechecking myself.

I'm calm. He's the one that's anxious, and he's anxious because he's trying to find me, trying to get close to me, and by close what else can it mean without making very little sense? I'm probably doing pretty well to keep things from crossing that invisible line separating, going too far, and not going far enough because he isn't trying very hard. And maybe I'm not making much sense but, here's to hoping, that when the entire scene is sculpted, you'll see through it all to the seriousness of his desires and mine.

"No one's here yet. I doubt they've even set up the blacklights yet."

So I'm forced to hear the same thing repeated over and over again because he's anxious and more than likely unable to calm himself.

But I'm thinking about having my beloved gentleman under me, right now, at all times, mine, mine, mine, mine,

mine, mine, mine, mine, mine. . .

Look at this guy, not a single shred of confidence or danger in him, yet he's trying to meet me halfway. He's trying to find me. He's incapable of laying a finger on anything, much less me, but that isn't stopping him from trying to find me, trying to get lucky, matching massacres with my well-maintained body and mind.

I'm rambling.

I'm getting bored.

It's good to have someone there that knows the signs. That's what I am to him and he is to me. The structure is solid, more solid than I'm used to, and we're poised to see the gentleman continue to find her over and over again. Gain ground until he knows the various tastes and tempers traceable when you take them out the right way. Her?

I see her before she even joins the party.

That's her, I'm thinking. Miss lucky number twenty-eight. Hey miss?

I'm watching her, observing the way she walks, and this guy is saying to me, "I've seen her before. Do you know her?"

And I'm responding, "I know everyone worth knowing."

This guy, he's still going, still rambling incoherently about who she might be but I'm already exiting the car, walking towards the source of the party. Maybe it's a little too early, but I know what I want. I've found her and she's going to be perfect all dressed up and docile.

The number twenty-eight looks perfect on you, miss.

This guy is going to follow me. I know he is. I'm not forcing him. In fact, I'm not saying anything to this guy, but he's not about to let me go that easily. He wants to at least think he's trying to figure me out, but all I'm thinking is, "Sir you have no idea."

Can you tell that you're going to end up lost in the

party crowd?

He's saying how great it'll be, and he's talking like he's a connoisseur of socialite events—parties, junkets, benders, and other brags—but he's a grad student in forensics, which means he spends his days and nights reading and applying theory, profiling, and trying to build the necessary skillset to be someone that's a professional at being forgotten. It's the nature of any forensic scientist to be influential but unmemorable. That way they're never in danger and never anything more than a stimulus, an ingredient in the complex social stew of whatever-the-fuck and maybe-I-care.

It's a fragile balance, if you dare.

"See? Now there's the kind of sass and dry wit I know you have, Claire."

But what I'm saying is the truth, and this guy hasn't a clue who I really am.

"It is the truth. It's you."

And I'm wanting to say that you have no right to use my name.

I don't, because I'm finding myself already at the door and I'm being judged by appearance and whether or not I am wearing a white shirt. I am. And I'm being let in even though I haven't a clue of who these people are—just people, random without a single interesting prospect between the lot of them—but my Miss Number 28 isn't too far away and I'm going to find her. I'm going to find her. We'll be best of friends tonight and in the quiet and gentle morning drizzle outside, I'll wake up to her anguished moans as he finds her too.

2.

It's hard to tell what's what in blacklight. I've since lost the guy I arrived with, but that's alright because she's with me and we're talking like we've known each other throughout undergrad. She seems to have her own little backstory, motivations and all, but I'm not that person that'll need to know, much less care. I'm acting drunk while she's getting drunk and I'm saying, "Dressed to impress!" when she looks at me with her hazy, batty eyes, and then the witty tilt of her head and the slinging back of yet another gulp of whatever she's drinking.

If parties are this predictable, imagine how predictable people must be.

I'm being super nice to her and she's talking in the third person, which you'd think would make it easier to remember her name. Her name's irrelevant; I'm finding her suitable and that's all that really matters.

And I'm saying something like, "You know, these parties are basically the only way people these days can face off and compare each other's worth!" I shout over the music, but she's hearing something else entirely. She's responding with something like, "I can't get enough," which makes me think that she probably misheard what I said as, "You know, these parties are basically the only way people these days fuck off and compare each other's size."

On second thought, I'm thinking no.

I'm wondering if anyone here's aware of how close a killer can be to them, but with the way they are acting, there's nothing in them to suggest they could save themselves, much less anyone else. It's just another party, but for most of the students in attendance, it's seemingly enough of a reason for them to drink until it all comes back up.

Anything to break the monotony of class, cram session,

repeat.

Peoples' teeth glow a decadent ghastly grin and while I'm expecting everyone to peer into the grins as good natured, I'm finding myself staring through to the grimness within. Their clothes are luminescent enough to give you a headache.

I'm looking down at my clothes and they're barely glowing. I feel like I'm going to be pulled into the negative black space because there's so much white.

Under blacklight everybody looks the same. I'm the only one that looks different.

The gimmick of the night turns everybody wearing white into a ghost and they're all smiling, their eyes missing, and I'm beginning to see the change in people.

They're well on their way to being lost.

I'm pulling a name from the early twenties, one that I only heard about from him, and I'm asking Miss Number 28, "Have you seen Jessie?"

And she's asking me to speak up because she can't hear me.

I ask her again, "Jessie— have you seen her?"

She's shrugging, saying she doesn't know.

"Maybe?"

She's drunker than I expected. I watch her fall to the floor; people should be laughing but we're not in high school anymore and no one notices and no one really cares.

By now the party is getting good.

Miss Number 28 is about done and I'm preparing my excuse to leave the party early.

It's getting bright in the center of the room, a mashing of white shirts moving, blending, and changing shape.

I'm in the negative space where a great observer is able to watch, search, and find.

I'm relaxing and taking my time. I've already found her;

she isn't leaving my side.

We're sitting near a cluster of chairs. She's got her head on my shoulder and she's saying, over and over again, "What shitty beer."

"I've good stuff at my place."

And she's asking me, "What kind of stuff?"

"The good stuff."

Mystery works wonders.

I'm watching everyone in their white shirts trying to make up for the lack of fight and inner spirit, and I'm pretending to judge them, but I don't care about any of these people.

They have no faces.

The faceless start drawing on themselves. I'm leaning forward like I'm home watching a movie. I'm the interested viewer trying to figure out what's being written. I can't make out what they're writing. They keep moving. They keep drawing.

And I keep trying.

Now Miss Number 28 is giving up and getting used to the idea of a quieter place to drink, and I'm implying that I have more than just booze. And then I'm pretending I knew what kind of party this was all along when really I didn't, not until they all start writing the same thing on their shirts:

"I'm going to die."

And I'm nodding and I'm sort of happy they figured it out because, of course, they're going to die. Everyone's got a killer inside but only a few are capable of murder.

It's all based on the fight and whether or not they can let it surface.

Miss Number 28 is saying, "I'm sobering up."

And I'm saying, "Wanna go?"

"Yeah."

And just as well. If a normal university party is red hot, a death party is as blue as the blacklight used to reveal their invisible statements.

I'm going to die.

I'm going to die.

I'm going to die.

I'm texting him details as well as what he should do, how he should get ready, and how long it'll take for her to agree to a threesome.

When we're all naked and she's floating between consciousness and coma, I'll just sit there, watching him take her like a true gentleman. For a fuck or two they'll be just like new lovers, exploring the taste and touch of each other's private spaces, but then he'll kiss her where he kisses them all, every number before her, and she'll giggle.

She always giggles.

And I'll giggle too, but only because I know what'll happen next. I'll comment here or there, but mostly I'll just observe.

I'm into letting things fall into place before I factor myself into the evolution of each step. He's as excitable as he's ever been and Miss Number 28, I can tell, he completely approves.

I'm commenting, "Do whatever it is you feel like doing. I want to see her inside-out."

I want to see what's inside her. But it's never what you expect. You expect to see something else, something more interesting, more complex, and multi-faceted, when you see through the practiced social demeanor, but in the end we'll get to see her organs, her insides, and the source of her sexual stench, but little else.

He's a believer and I'm a great observer and we both know we need to keep looking. If not twenty-eight then twenty-nine. . .

There's always another.

Before Miss number 28 can wake up, she's passed on and he's showing me what he's got and I'm impressed. He's talented, got a real fire inside.

I'm thinking he's the best yet and that he'll be here to stay.

I'm so impressed I'm believing it, and every time he looks up at me, I'm staring back, knowing that he's starting to get used to me, his support structure.

I see more fire and more fight the deeper I look. He's a city partially explored. I want to dig up the catacombs. I want to meet number seventy and number eighty.

I'm going to be there to meet the one that preaches his story and I'll be the genius that successfully profiles him.

"You need to talk to me. You need to hear my voice," is what I'm saying when he grips the cartilage near her nose, looking up at me. I'm sure he can't help it, asking for my approval.

I'm saying to him that he's doing well; I'm saying that I'm impressed, but I don't say too much. I leave him curious about what it takes to satisfy me.

The more I think about it, the more I realize there's no way to satisfy me.

Too much of me is a battlefield, a city in demise. I've never been fully repaired. He looks at me like I look at anyone else, but I'm seeing something beyond his gaze. I'm noticing it now more than ever.

Tonight is the night I reappear with someone he would never have found without my help.

Twenty-eight is purer than all twenty-seven combined.

I see what he sees right as he finishes with them.

I see fear.

I'm ecstatic, pure delight.

If it's true, he'll do well to satisfy me, his most important master, for the killing period to come. If he wants my continued support, he'll do his damnedest to satisfy me and let me change him. Let me in. Fully.

Lend me your everything, my pet.

Lend me it all. Let yourself be mine like I know you already have.

Tonight you've taken your twenty-eighth while I've found myself a new fixation.

The pet to fully please me.

3.

It's a mystery no one ever fights back.

It's a scene that jumps from one scene to another. Jump shot, sighting her with the man of mystery. Quick, rapid flashes of her holding hands with the man. The mystery peeling out of the apartment complex. Audience gets first glimpse of what the man might look like.

Jump shot of the stretcher. Outline of the victim's face.

Return to this shot twice while audience sees extended shots of the mystery unfolding somewhere nearby. See her in the front passenger seat. See the mystery treating her perfectly. Hear the sound of nervous heartbeats as she leaves the lounge with the man. Heartbeats starting to slow down as she falls asleep in the passenger seat.

Where is he taking her? Where is the mystery going?

Heartbeats rise up until everything else is inaudible. The audience hears one last heartbeat skipping and then the sound of a door locking.

The mystery is right outside an apartment complex—location unknown—during some early hour of the night. The parking lot is overrun by emergency vehicles and police squad cars. Bystanders trickle out from the bottom floors. People collect in the streets, hoping for a better view. A body is rolled out on a stretcher, covered by a sheet. The audience is left guessing.

Gain no confidence from such a spectacle.

Who just died? What is the audience looking at?

Zoom in on the stretcher. Hear comments from the officers standing around making sure no bystanders interfere with the crime scene.

—Young one.

—Questioned a sample. No one noticed anything.

—Where'd they find the body?

—One of the bedrooms.

—There's always a dozen or more people crammed into the place.

—Place is a real dive. Have you taken a look at the bathroom?

—It's where we found the victim's stomach.

In her last conscious gasps, she felt that warmth.

The body left behind is warm before growing cold.

Who sleeps in your bed besides shame and sadness?

1.

For the first time but certainly not the last—
I skipped class.
My absence would have been noticeable.
Would have counted against me.
But the real world is on my side.
Measuring up every insertion and assertion in terms of what I see.
Soft conditioning.
The support of a pet and perilous cause.
I skipped class.
Knowing I would learn more by not going.
Learn more by doing.
Learn more by being.

2.

I'm discovering he's not much of a talker. Everything's practiced until he's out of memorized and rehearsed material. He's awkward at his most pure, and he's incapable of matching my gaze when I'm still there, looking for more. He's without another quirky and/or confident line to dispense, so there's this awkward atmosphere billowing into the apartment, tempting to ruin what I've established. So I'm telling him to go into his room, not mine, to start on the footage of number twenty-eight hoping to figure out how number twenty-nine was such a problem. He has to learn somehow.

Done it so many times before, but when it came to her, we had to ditch her because he picked up the wrong kind of victim. She was a half-hearted pain in the ass. I thought he had better sense, higher standards, but there he is, on-camera, taking in another drunk, lonely freshman college chick.

He's returning from his room with the laptop I supplied. He sits next to me at the kitchen table. I'm saying, "I'll show you where you're wrong."

He replies, "How do you know all this?"

But I'm not saying anything and he's answering for me, "You've done this before."

I'm starting up the video software.

He's staring at my screen. With no direction, he focuses in on the one thing that so effortlessly demands a person's attention, the computer screen.

I'm telling him, "Follow the leader."

And so he's opening his video software too, going through every step to match mine.

We watch what became of her.

I'm saying, "First of all, did you not see how she was

walking and talking?"

He's not going to say anything.

"Look at her. With a face and body like that, you have little to work with."

I'm letting the recorded footage play until I stop on the last moment, right when she began to leave her body for death.

"Okay, look at how long it took for the dosage to kick in. Eleven seconds. Not a big deal for us, but it's a red-flag for anyone that knows about quality."

He's listening, making sure to pause on the same time-stamp as me, failing to do so, starting, rewinding, and stopping and trying once, twice, a third time, until I raise my voice tell him to stop.

"She's built up a resistance and that's enough to notice how little she's worth."

He's staring at his laptop screen, wide eyed, noticeably intimidated.

The way he looks right now, he's not the slicked back hair, confident and completely smooth gentleman I picked up maybe a week or two ago. He's my pet, and I've pulled every single protective layer from his exterior leaving only the paleness, the shame, the hidden core, the frontline of fight.

I'm saying, "Do you understand?"

He's hesitating.

I'm forcing a reply.

He's replying, "Yes, yes, I understand."

I fast forward to the first lacerations. I'm telling him he could be a little slower, a lot more precise, with each incision, because you have to treat the body with surgical precision in order to really enjoy it.

I'm criticizing his methods as something akin to a binge-eater or batch-a-fuck sleaze, taking in mounds of food, fucking large groups of nobodies, in order to escape what is hidden inside. I'm noticing how he's not liking the position he's in, so I'm reminding him:

"You remember the rules. You can't afford to be confident."

Let it sink in.

He watches the video of himself cutting her deep—so deep the blood doesn't spew. It escapes and forms a pool up to his forearms. He's pushing through instead of controlling the blood. I'm shaking my head, and he's noticing, but this time I didn't mean for him to see.

I'm telling him to fast forward. "We've seen enough," and then we're watching the end where he discovers he's cut her too deep, ruining the organs underneath.

This is where I'm telling him if he wants to really transcend simple serial killer, he's going to have to increase his skill enough to baffle the people in forensics.

"Like any other person, you have to affect them to the core, so deep they won't be the same person ever again. The reason you're such a catch is because you can't be caught. You're doing all the catching. You have to change every little bit about them. If you don't, you're just another cry for publicity. Killing isn't enough anymore. . ."

We take a moment to fully absorb what I've said. Even I'm taking a moment to really comprehend it and comprehend it fully. I'm agreeing with myself and he's agreeing too.

And he's talking about choosing better next time and I'm shaking my head, "No—you work on the bodies, changing the person inside and out. I'll work on finding her. You no longer have to worry about ever leaving this apartment. The cage is yours; the room is yours. I'll bring you everything you want and need."

He doesn't seem to react to this.

Is this a good thing or a bad thing?

We're listening to the steady patter of rain on the balcony outside.

It feels like late night but it's noon on a Wednesday.

Uncertain until he gives in. He's nodding and I can't help myself, telling him to take his laptop, sign into our 1-on-1 password protected chat room and get started.

I'm telling him, "I'll be right with you."

Talking craft turns me on and I want to see more of him. He's going to have to see more of me. He does what he's told, door closing gently. He's in his room and I'm walking into mine, stopping at the mirror for a moment, checking myself out.

What I see is beautiful. What everyone else sees is what I want them to see.

I am their type when I want to be.

When I don't, I'm just another nobody in the crowd, being forgotten.

I'm touching myself, "He wants me, he wants me, he wants me, he wants me," but I'm catching myself not thinking about him.

I can't take it any longer. I retreat to my bedroom, winking to the camera, to him, as I get into position on my precious little seat.

When I imagine him watching me I'm nowhere else but deep inside.

Deep inside me.

Deep inside, revealing the real me. The one so willing to fight I coach those with enough potential to bring out the red in all of us.

I'm a radiant light waiting to wash out the withdrawn.

3.

Call me a fiend.

—He calls me a fiend.

Call me a force of confusion.

—He calls me what I want him to call me.

Call me a caring friend.

—He calls me a friend.

Call me whatever you want, but will you come for me?

—He comes into his hand while I watch.

Look me in the eye. Type out the words that come to mind. Don't think. Just type.

—He won't look away.

I lick my lips when our eyes meet. Don't worry about the lag; we'll meet when we moan together. Let me hear you moan.

I'm already touching myself.

Why do you think we're all prone to deviance? Deviance reminds us of our mortality.

I'm close. Are you?

We grow closer with every breath. Every stroke. Every thrust. Every second I get wetter, you get more and more tense.

Release. Release me.

—He wants to be free.

I stop and watch your body tense up from head to toe. And in the seconds after you're spoiled, I grin a fiendish smile and get myself to climax too, right on command.

I know my urges.

I know my body inside and out.

Call it experience. Call it stability.

I don't regret a thing. When you know yourself so well, you don't worry about whether what you're doing is right or wrong. What's right feels right. Whatever makes you feel alive, live it and be like me. The first thing a person does after coming is close their window.

Don't you flee me in fear. Not until I tell you to. Come and go, you're mine.

—He pledges to be my pet.

If you'd look at me, you'd find yourself.

Hello my name is. . .

—He'll never know my real name.

Calling. Oh, I am calling. I'm calling your name the way you wish I would.

I'm telling you I'm fine. I'm saying nothing but bittersweet phrases out of a romance novel I've never read. I'm whispering your name when you're resisting because I know well that any resistance is really an act of instinct and survival.

That's just the kind of person I am.

I'm your little girl, if you'd like.

I'm your mother, if you'd like.

I'm your dream, if you'd like.

I'm your nightmare.

—He withers when I want him to.

I'm anything you'd like me to be as long as I remain master.

As master, I can never be your victim.

You want to talk. Really talk? Fine, let's talk.

I'll do as you say but on one condition—

I'll meet you halfway and I won't be wearing a thing.

The last thing that's going to bring me down are cotton fibers and other forms of elasticity. They are tethers; they are daggers digging into my shoulder blades. The body was never meant to wear those trendy clothes.

And when people see me walking naked down the street—how is it a crime if everyone's enjoying the sight? I turn the heads of every man and more than a few women.

—He wants me.

We're comparing curves. Everyone's aligning to their standards and wondering where I've been all their lives. I'd have them too, but only if you'd be a gentleman to them afterwards.

We meet halfway. I'm listening to you, yes, don't deny that I'm not. I am myself. I can't be anybody but "me."

—He dominates me.

This is me. We can go anywhere you like.

If I go missing it's because I chose to go missing. This isn't a kidnapping if I'm the one agreeing to go somewhere more secluded. I'll go to your apartment.

It's okay to look at me there. I don't mind.

This is all about satisfaction and I'll soon be getting mine.

You tell me it's insanity, but I'm telling you I'm perfectly fine.

Somehow I already know your name, but you claim you don't know mine. Or rather, you're telling me that you don't know who I am anymore, like we've known each other for quite some time. It's quite the night for a little fun, don't you think?

I need the satisfaction and you need whatever it is you need, so how is it any worse than what I'd do on webcam on any given night?

But you're the resistant type, and you're telling me I've gone too far.

—He says only what I want him to say.

What I'd say is we haven't gone far enough.

If this is the case, who's owning who?

I won't be the one to deny that I didn't expect the feeling to be mutual. Is it possible to go missing in the night when you didn't mean to? More so, is it possible to be the kidnapper of someone you hadn't yet taken?

Just like sex it comes in so many different varieties.

If there's any reason to keep going it's to see what else is out there, being created as we speak, while you tell me to calm down—but I'm calm it's you who isn't calm—and to put something on. I'm ready to leave.

Your that kind of client that wants to rationalize your own version of dignity with me, and I'm the person who says there's no argument. I'm leaving.

I've got the rest of the night to make up for the disappointment.
—He climaxes too early.
—He is ashamed.
—He knows I'm disappointed.
The disappointment, it's you.

Shh, don't say anything you'll regret in the morning.

1.

He wanted me to call him Victor.
I only call him my pet.
He wanted to know my name.
I'd never tell.
He'd only know me as master.
Master observes.
Master finds real fighters.
Master makes him a better serial murderer.
Remember to thank me, my pet. . .
Without me, you would have already been caught.
The pickup game is a deadly switch of sex and violence.

2.

I know firsthand the anatomy of a scene.

She'll look you right in your eyes. She'll grip onto you so tightly it'll make you blush. There's nothing like such a girl to make you feel alive, just as there's nothing like a girl to mess with your head. Stay focused. She'll remind you of your first time. She'll make you feel like you're inadequate. You'll begin to think you're not ready, but that's just part of the game.

You have to remember: You are taking her home.

She isn't yours to have.

Her brown hair slips out of its ponytail and brushes his arm while they walk to the lounge in the back.

She's asking, "Where are we going?"

Don't ignore her. It's better to talk to the girl. There's nothing worse than getting her only to lose her halfway across the club because you were acting suspicious.

You reply, "There's a lounge in the back."

"Do they have a bar there too?"

Nodding, "Yup."

She tightens her grip. Stomach tightens with her every touch. This is intentional.

You get used to it. If you're a natural, by the third time there's nothing to it.

Don't think of the mystery, just think of the moment.

The brunette reaches out and grabs your hand. The brunette holds on for dear life.

What goes on in her head?

Not sure it's possible to explain. You're someone she just met. You're interesting, mysterious, and she'll stay with you because you are just that: an enigma.

You're someone that's come into her life. You're maybe someone new, never tried before, but after a long stretch with a certain type, she's ready to try something else. She's desperate. Who isn't?

Not too long ago, you were another observer spending every dreary rainy night alone on the dance floor, watching, scanning, searching. You worry about the chances you'll end up in the same situation again. It's enough to try to make it worth it with him, and all sighs and gasps lead to a positive result.

It's why you're out tonight, needing new streets and boulevards to explore.

Another bit of advice is to never lead them on long enough for them to begin questioning who you are and whether or not you're worth it.

It's likely they'll decide that you're not.

Too many people end up going home with someone less just because they want to feel something, anything. The girl doesn't think you're less. She thinks you're a catch. She's excited. She wants to know more about you than you're willing to show.

This is about getting the girl as soon as possible. It's that simple, okay?

Don't think about it. Do it.

What's going on in your head?

The lounge is empty. You do what's worked time and time before. You lead the brunette to one of the back corner booths and you sit with her.

The brunette sits next to you, rather than across, and begins asking about your life, your loves, your losses—the little things. She plays with your shirt; she nibbles on your cheek.

It's all a game.

You remain somewhat silent.

The brunette begins to notice. "Perk up, why don't ya? It was you that came to me."

Everyone is lonely. Everyone is desperate to have someone at their side.

You act the part, getting her right where you need her.

"It's complicated."

"What's complicated?"

"What I'm going to do to you. . ."

The brunette laughs, "Oh yeah? What are you going to do to me?" She runs a hand up your shirt and begins fondling your left breast. You're not wearing a bra.

If it gets too personal, too intimate, drag out each question until it's time. Until it's perfect. When will it be time? You'll know.

"You're so tense. It's good that we have the lounge to ourselves."

You respond, "The lounge is never full."

She rests her head on your lap. In a playful, half-interested voice, she asks, "Why's that?"

"Because people don't go here to lounge."

"Well yeah," and she is beginning to pick up the clue, knowing what you want.

You say something like, "People are drugged here and dragged home."

Startled, you let her push away and fumble to her feet.

No use going anywhere, girl. You drugged her so seamlessly it is without notice or description. It happened between actions and touching. A bit later, after the girl is in the cage and stripped clean, you run through a mental checklist—who might know her, and who might want to find her—you can't have anyone searching around later.

You checked her purse, right?

"Right."

You made note of who might have noticed you and her together, right?

"Right."

You recovered her car and all extraneous belongings and identification, right?

"Right."

Then what else is wrong?

"I want to know that she's quality."

If she seemed to react the way the others did, she can't be inferior, can she?

"Just confirm that she's capable."

Capable of what?

"Capable of replacing me. Us."

What you don't know is just cause for potential danger.

Picture this—you're tending to her and somehow she still stirs and manages a sharp metal object right into your hand.

There should be some excitement accompanying that thought.

"Yeah."

Look at him. Look. Look at your pet.

He's ecstatic.

And this is how I can tell the fighters from the truly forgotten.

This is how I turn number twenty-nine into number thirty-five in two nights trailing a series of clubs where everyone's playing; everyone's dying to be picked up.

Me—I'm just another player looking to expand her horizons.

Am I? Am I really?

3.

I went to class.

My turn to make up for my absences.

A letter grade lost because I wasn't there to explain.

It's my turn to teach and my turn to show them how.

A killer makes the victim feel like there's still something left in life; a new "take" on it.

A killer is often searching for something that is unrecognizable.

A killer is adept at seeking the surfacing of its subconscious.

I taught ten clueless forensics grad students and one associate professor about how the Gentleman Killer made the rounds:

He plays flirtatious bachelor.

He targets semi-aggressive, equally-eligible females.

The one he targets is the one he's supposed to want.

He waits for the female to open up, if only just a little.

All he needs is for her to take one look.

Gentleman Killer tells the women, "Any man would have you."

Gentleman Killer tells the women they are irresistible.

He is an artist.

He is a scientist.

He's popular news.

Gentleman Killer might sit next to you in class. He asks for your notes.

He stands in line for lunch with the rest of the students.

He sells you your textbooks.

The campus is blanketed in disclaimer flyers, his own doing.

These words are his. The flyer you hold—you'll wish you never read it.

Treat this flyer by its would-be intention: A warning.

Keep your eyes open and your hearts cold.

He wants you by his side and, if he chooses you, you won't be able to say no.

Like any true gentleman, he will always be "your type."

You know it's true. You know him better than you know yourself, just as he can see you better than you can see yourself in natural light.

You're squinting to have a look while he sees you plainly, and is at-present deciding whether or not you're a worthy enough target, a worthy enough victim.

Life's flashing before your eyes and it makes you forget everything else.

They are tamed, apprehensive about my profile of the killer-at-large.

None in agreement, but they don't know how to prove me wrong.

I am satiated. The professor pulled me aside, explaining to me his thoughts.

I told him what's so bothersome is how he can be anyone and everyone. No one is normal; under the surface of our practiced social disguises exists a glimmer of fight.

Humbled. Hasty with his reply. He told me about the possibilities of research.

This topic, my thesis, a fellowship with funding to help find him—Gentleman Killer.

I have better things to do. Professor said, "Think about it," and handed me my grade.

I went to class and recovered effortlessly the letter grade I had lost.

4.

I try and try and try, but he still won't tell me what they taste like after. He's eager to let me know what he did to her to make her, every side of her, unique, but when it comes down to the way they taste on second suck, second lick, second insertion, he's stopping short, falling silent, moving on to the next one and then the one after that.

What does she taste like after her breath falls and her heart stops?

He's eager to tell me about Melanie, who tastes like cinnamon. He penetrated her with as many insertables as possible before he saw tearing and blood.

He's eager to tell me about Stephanie, who he didn't seem to enjoy as much.

His second wasn't as good as his first? But barring any disappointment, he still managed to try out his recent online auction purchase—a pear of anguish. That did wonders, I'm sure.

He's not waiting for my reply. I'm finding his sudden splurge of enthusiasm quite compelling. He's going on about his third, Jessica, who really loved the phrase, "My dear," and how she tasted like apple. She squealed like a pig when he used the expanding prods.

Jessica screamed like no one else screamed before.

When Mildred came around, he shocked her again in hopes of hearing the same squeal. Not to be, but it only fueled him more.

He's smacking his lips when he talks about Christy, how she tasted of vanilla. He used razor wire pipe on every inch of her that cut like butter. Alexandra tasted like chocolate, and to celebrate the discovery, he treated her to stucco and plastic shards.

He laughs when he talks about Lexis, Jenny, Christina,

and Shannon, who all tasted like sour apple. He made a joke about how this must be why so many men fail to please a woman down there. They pucker up like a kiss when they should be loose, letting their tongues please every fold. He got used to the pear of anguish and used it on all four.

He's shrugging, "But then the pear became my 'thing' and I had to stop using it."

He's talking up this Maggie because she was the first to taste like cherries. He treated her to an old fashioned cut of the knife, you know, just to change things up.

Athena was a name to remember attached to someone who tasted and acted like everyone else. He shoved the barrel of a .45 inside her and pulled the trigger.

I'm shaking my head.

He's pouting, saying, "Why?"

I'm not upset about what he did, but rather where he did it. "A gun shot in a loft apartment downtown? Good thing you're lucky because anyone else would have had neighbors and local cops knocking on their doors five minutes later."

He's acting all confident and saying that he left her there a minute later, not bothering to examine her insides, but I'm still shaking my head. He doesn't know what else to say, so he's moving on to Althea who he expanded with a 2x4 after finding out she tasted like nothing.

Lauren wouldn't stop talking about computers, so after tasting her—he's stopping for a moment to explain her taste, "It's like. . . I think it's. . . butterscotch"—he took apart an old computer and inserted pieces of a motherboard in that butterscotch tasting snatch, watching as she didn't seem to notice at first, the small pieces before the bigger ones.

He's blushing, "She kept pleading with me, 'Please,

please no, please,' and for the first time, I got hard." Lauren's squirming and victimizing pleas left a mark.

He's stopping to say how I look like her.

"Like who?"

And of course he's saying, her, Nicole, a redhead who tasted like honey.

He's smacking his lips again.

I'm saying, "I am no Nicole."

He's nodding and talking about how he froze tacks and water into eight-inch-long popsicles and used that to get her going.

"And she got going," he says while making the sound of an airborne siren.

Victoria, Gabriella, and Christine tasted the same. Butterscotch.

He used wax and fire and various vegetables.

I'm saying that it's actually quite common for it to taste something like that if it's clean, and I'm also saying that it's also common for it to taste sour, too.

"It all depends."

And then he's not saying anything.

"Go ahead. Keep going."

Crystal liked the sound of his voice when he was angry, so he got real angry and only managed a lick before he got at her with the pear of anguish. He's saying she probably preferred to have it end this way. "Her way about things was dismal and defeatist."

Green-eyed Nadia, somewhat of a drug addict, made for the usual torture and dismantling, but not before he tried her and recoiled in disgust. Sour flavor after a series of butterscotch really doesn't work. He couldn't stand her all of a sudden, so he drugged her, inserted needles, and various dosages. He made it look like one hell of an overdose.

He's saying, "At least it wasn't predictable."

I'm saying, "You leave every single one in bed, seemingly post-fuck. You are predictable."

I'm letting it hurt. It stings him deeply. Oh, it does.

With nothing else to do, he continues talking about quite a few more but they all sound the same—flavor, pear of anguish, followed by the same modus operandi.

It isn't until Kayla, the flavor of vanilla, and the jaws of life that got me interested again.

Hazel with her—big surprise—hazel eyes had that cherry flavor, and he used saw blades he found in the alley on the way to her apartment.

Dawn was a musician of some sort, or at least she wanted to be. She tasted wrong, just wrong, not like any of the others, and how he reacted by inserting one end of the guitar as far inside as possible until she couldn't take anymore.

Hannah was his second gunshot. He got the gun barrel really deep inside of her and he's talking about how she liked it, "Didn't even ask if it was loaded or not," and how she was honey flavor too. The trigger pulled; he made sure to be out of there in no time.

Ingrid was tattooed in all the wrong places but had the flavor of strawberry, her clitoral hood pierced. He tasted her for what felt like an hour, smothering his face with her flavor. He did a little piercing here, piercing there, and she enjoyed it until he took the piercing gun right inside of her and pierced what wasn't meant to be pierced.

He's talking about how he played with her more than the others, how she was the one that really helped him develop his creativity.

Then what am I?

Now he's talking about Marlowe, his most recent, and how he played out her fantasy, cuffing, beating, forced blowing and insertion, "The kinky sex stuff," and then he waited until the last minute to taste her and heated water, pouring it over her body.

He's never satisfied. Always left with more fight in him.

I'm saying, "You've used the appropriate chemicals with all of them right?"

He nods.

Can't afford to leave behind a trace. She's recovered like a mannequin smelling like it's disinfected a dozen times.

He's sweating and I'm starving.

Breathless, he's staring at me and getting ideas. He wants what I want, and I'm ready to throw him back into his room, back on camera, but not before I tell him, guaranteeing three more, a trifecta, by the dead end of night.

"My dear, you are insatiable."

He buckles as he's blown.

I'm telling him, "Get in there."

He does as he's told.

I'm walking into my room and I feel damp down there. It couldn't be.

That's simply not possible. But it's true.

I'm filthy. Everything I do and say is filthy.

Yet the acceptance does nothing. I'm wiping it away and having a taste, pretending to be him, and what do I taste like?

It's a mystery.

5.

He's trying to remember who he was before he met me. Time is always fading and I begin to relate explicably with time. I feel like I'm fading. I am here, barren. The webbing portal of perversion and perfection, crossing paths, always a promise. One last time, one last lusting. Tonight. Like the rain outside, it is ceaseless.

The searching. . . the savoring. . . the seduction. . . the seething. . .the need. . .

My needs. He's here to satisfy my needs.

Don't talk to me about needs. I'm not in the mood.

It's under the pretenses of disappointment and the anxiety of it being, quite possibly, a wasted night that I discover a new thrill. I am going to hurt you.

You are going to try to hurt me.

Watch as I take this, and I put it where you didn't expect me to put it. Watch me as I tell you who is master and who is pet.

I'll tell you every sick little thing you'd like to hear. I'll make you tag every single frame to watch again later. I'm willing to beat you senseless.

Is it good for you?

He covers his mouth in shame.

It's great for me.

Every form of gratification is just a variation of the same climax.

End result and the desire for more.

You don't know what you've lost until I'm finding it easier to resist rather than give.

You can't have me until you're on all fours, begging for supplication. No penetrations that aren't my own. My taste changes based on my discoveries. I am ruler of a certain city and the populace is in shock. Tonight there was surprise.

Laying prone. Lotioned up and casual.

I'm waiting. He covers his mouth.

I'll be watching as you taste them too.

I won't let you move forward until you tell me what they taste like afterwards.

This body is young, firm, and glorious. These frames reveal the perfect paleness of my luscious skin.

You'll get what you deserve.

He covers his mouth. He isn't supposed to upset me.

Bloodletting is a certain fancy, often as alluring as any other bodily fluids in that it's a reminder of so much that's hidden inside. I've bled before.

I bleed and I am dripping wet elsewhere.

Tell me that I'm wrong. You're only fueling me even more. I implore what's wrong and detrimental to show me what it feels like to be too far gone to be affected.

You will bleed.

He drops his hand. His lower lip quivers.

You have bled before.

You will bleed again.

I wipe the blood across my body and I can see the room chatter, the fires blaring, the flame of their fantasies being fulfilled. The fact that it's mine makes this natural.

I write a name, just any name, or maybe it's a specific name. Her name. If we're ever going to tell the truth, we're going to have to confess. I wrote my confession out long ago.

What's your fantasy?

He covers his mouth again.

Lust is lust no matter the color and shade, the force of each thrust. It's beyond any mere sexual act, and it's my reasoning that every sexual act is violent and every violent act is sexual. In that cluttered, cloudy pool that's the result of your release is where satisfaction turns into continual gratification.

But you begin to adore the waiting period. It strikes your fancy.

I let blood dribble from both of my forearms while I beckon you to do a little bloodletting too. I see it in some of his eyes.

Commit to me, I ask.

He says he's mine.

What you don't realize is how you've already committed.

You can't keep doing the things you do without my support.

The age-old show me yours and I'll show you mine. This was a pact. Throughout time, we show each other ours in hopes of making a connection that transcends touch and talk.

I clean this up but my sheets will continue to glow. Dots of erratic notice read like a book written in pain. The confusion I have—how will I ever top this satisfaction?

What else can I discover?

I crave. I crave blood from this breast.

And this leg.

And this finger.

The taste is familiar. The taste is undeniably mine.

My pale skin has brown streaks where I have left it smeared. Such a sight gets to arousal in no time and I'm only talking about the average. Where I am, I'm more than satisfied, but I keep going, laying here on my bed, white sheets speckled in reddish-brown dry spots.

I ask you what they taste like and nothing you say makes any sense. No one tastes like anything after they're gone. It's only what you imagine them to taste like while they're alive that takes on any kind of sense. The way they are now, they're dead.

They aren't worth the taste.

Just like they aren't worth the time.

He covers his eyes like he covers his mouth. He says and does what I want him to say and do. But he holds back.

I want him to uncover his mouth. I want him to have a taste.

He agrees but doesn't pull his hand away from his mouth.

You tell me lies.

I remind you of what you are to me.

I remind you of what I am to you.

Now do as I say.

He is withdrawn.

Call me when you need someone to talk to.

1.

I went to class.

I went to the seminar.

I attended the conference.

All the while aware of what I was missing.

I talked about violence and future crime with fellow students and scholars.

The future of this. The future of that.

I would have been taking part in sex and violence if I stayed behind.

Days like these, I remind myself everything I do is in the name of research.

Fine research.

In the name of research all can and will be done.

Behind every subject is a slipstream of secrets and mysteries.

I went to class, went to the seminar, attended the conference, knowing beforehand that the majority here haven't a clue about the breadth of any and all secrets existing around the concealing shroud of this, that, any mystery.

The mystery of ourselves.

And who we are there—beyond sculpting and repair.

Can't teach that. Can't even discuss that. Got to go out there and learn it like you do learning to tie your shoelaces, learning to drive, learning to survive the coldness of societies disinterest in your general well-being. Can't even get extra credit for a single secret shared.

These mysteries are our first and last, our beginning and end.

No surprise that these mysteries are the ones undoing us, forcing us to unravel without being able to regain control.

We can't ever remember our births and we will be incapable of seeing our death after it's done. Oh my, my god, my beloved gentleman, if only you sat next to me as they spoke of serial murder and the lifestyle of a sexually active individual.

The mystery is there to keep us interested.

The mystery, a lot like our lives, is only there to be enjoyed.

The mystery is incapable of being completely solved.

2.

It's just the answering machine. It isn't her. It's only her voice speaking in code that he hasn't yet figured out completely. Time and place, and the dreariness of whoever's involved.

These last few days he's been less of a fighter and more like the dead. I'm finding loose ends unaccounted for. For instance, what did he do with the body parts, and where did he go while I was in class? He's not supposed to be leaving the apartment at all. I do all the leaving and finding, but lately he's been slipping out to a nearby park where he'll sit there, watching the trees, sunlight coating his face. I know because I've followed him, seen him where he shouldn't be. I call to leave messages. Lately my messages have kept him indoors.

My days have become a campus-throwdown where every moment of my waking day is dodging the rainfall as I move from building to building conducting residency instruction and working to write my thesis paper. Even then it isn't over because I'll have to turn my thesis into a real research project. It's exhausting and, seemingly, it never ends.

I picture my pet frightened and drained, staring fearfully at the answering machine.

Not picking up. Not really listening.

What is it that I'm saying?

I'm telling him where we'll meet up tonight, which club (they all seem to be the same), and what time we'll meet. But he's not picking up.

I'm talking, rambling really, waiting for him to pick up, but he's not.

The machine cuts me off and I call back.

Fourth time it's done that. I'm getting angry now, "Pick up, pick up, hey! Pick. Up."

Eventually he does, but not soon enough, not fast enough to undo all that has been done. I'm starting to question what's happening. What's wrong with him?

I'm not working him too hard. The Gentleman Killer is barely considered obscene at this point. He's a novelty item. He's not my kind of big-news item. There's so much left to be done.

If he wants to be a killer to remember, he needs to do more.

And over the past few days, ever since thirty-six, I've been feeling a sudden lapse in effort and care on his end of things. I'm the only one putting in the fight.

I don't give a fuck what he does as long as he does what I say.

So why is he having trouble explaining himself?

Hmm?

I'm asking him, "Who's the master? Hmm? Who's the master?"

"You."

"I didn't hear you!"

"You are the master."

"And what are you?!"

"Pet. . ."

"What are you?"

"A pet."

"My pet!"

"Your pet. . ."

"So do what I say—okay? It's not difficult! I'm doing this for you. You will thank me one day when you're up there with the Ripper and the Zodiac. When the term 'gentleman' can't be used without having people recalling your work, your legacy."

He's not saying anything.

This is irritating.

What is wrong with my pet? This can't be happening. Not again.

Nothing happens for a minute or two. We listen to each other's breaths.

I'm getting turned on, but now's not the time.

I'm sitting in a campus diner, no surprise when I look at everyone around me I see the dead—no fighters. None are capable of doing what needs to be done to get what they want, and I mean what they truly want.

What anyone wants.

He's muttering something.

I'm replying, "Yes, what?"

"Where?"

I'm telling him the name of the club.

"What time?"

I can barely hear him. I'm tired. I choose to ignore this.

He's now used to me gathering the girls. He's probably rusty.

I'm telling him this is something else.

And at first he's not understanding so I have to make him understand.

He's nervous, says that he understands, but I know he doesn't; his words are empty, without aim or definition. I tell him to hang up before he makes a real fool of himself.

After every five or so, it's worth finding a few suspects. Now's that time.

We're looking for two patsies tonight.

Two eligible bachelors, gentlemen of "some regard."

Two lucky men will think they've found me, only to discover that they've been lost. I'll do my best to have it be the detectives that find them, cuff them, and tell them how their life, from this point on, might in fact be ruined. Once you're mistaken for being a serial murderer, no one ever looks at you the same way again. So many lives are ruined on a daily basis.

I'm only doing my part to make that number borderline unbelievable.

3.

My dear pet,

As I sit here, between classes, I am in a daze, a desperate wonder. Why do you look the way you do? How can I save you? How can I know that you're okay? It's been a few days since you've been with her. Neither you nor I have found her, Miss Number 37. Is this why? Are you feeling deprived? My dear pet, I can't have you acting all sick and tired. A gentleman does not pass on pity. A gentleman passes on pain. My dear pet, what will I do with you if you can't be my pet tonight?

Love,
Claire

The body is still warm.

1.

I find a piece of paper in my pocket. It's nearly illegible. Seems I've written a really bad poem in pencil. It's addressed to my pet. I toss it as I go for my phone, making sure he's here, inside the club, which is how I want this to play out.

I told him, "Just like before. Remember when we first met."

It's going to be just like that.

He will have to turn on the charm. I only hope he isn't too rusty.

When he messages me back, I'm reading his words, "You've done this before, haven't you?" and I'm finding his message more than a little disconcerting. Of course I've done this before. How could he not know that I've done it to him?

This is the pickup game.

It's all part of being picked up, being found, being wanted, being with another. We are all alone, individuals of our self-righteous thrones, until we are searching for something to savor.

I text back, "In position?"

He's quick to respond, "Yes."

I walk inside the club. All clubs are the same. Same dynamic. Bar is the focal point, the touchstone and the dance floor is where peoples' lives are made and ruined.

Liquor and specialty drugs fluctuate between attendees in hopes of facilitating the forgetting. It's the same at every club; it's the same at every party. The only difference is in theme, and this club's theme is all about getting lost in a previous generation, even if you weren't a part of that generation. By the looks of it, the majority here would fail to qualify.

I'm watching them, whispering to myself, "I could pick any of you up and I'd be your perfect match. Just your type."

I'm a social chameleon. Always been.

I change hairstyles and speech based on the demands of the social setting.

The big problem for me is how fickle the pickup game really is. I can pick any of them up, sure, but none of them are what I'm looking for. I need someone that'll need me, want me, covet me, consume me, captivate me, just as much as I do all those things and more to them.

I'm selective in that way.

But really, how can you not be?

I wander over to the edge of the bar, getting a drink because you have to in order to

fit in. Right now I need to fit in. I need to wait it out, find the right guys, find him, wait for him to finish his part. I'm taking my first sip of my martini as I spot him, and I'm instantly relieved because he's looking, acting in precisely the same manner as when I first spotted him that night dozens of girls ago. I'm watching him eye women, gaining their attention only to ditch them on the way to one of the private booths in the back of the club.

It's always worth a laugh to see how the competition—other males looking to pick someone up—react to those that seemingly rise above the rest. Few understand what's going on when you go to these clubs, these parties, and mingle, flirt, fuck around.

They're clueless.

They know so little. To get with the pickup game, it's all about grasping the basics. The rules, and there are definitely rules. Get it straight. Get caught up with reality. The pickup may be like a game but this is as much a measurement of your worth as it is a measurement of one's primal urges. Display the inner fight because, think about it: That girl, that guy, doesn't need you. They'll get what they want. If they are being picked up, it's because they are not the aggressors, the players; they aren't capable of putting up a fight. They know they don't have any fight in them so they wait it out, hoping to be found by other fighters, the ones capable of getting anything they want be it one hour or the rest of your life.

There are standards. There are expectations.

You'll see a pattern if you're wanting to be seen at all.

A pickup isn't over until they ask you where you want to go. Only then are you in control. When you're in control, you have been given access to both body and mind.

Don't be foolish and think it's an access to their heart.

That's not what any of this is about.

Never was. It's about possession and being a part of the possession.

Knowing all this, I'm watching with enthusiasm as he puts it into practice like a professional. After seeing him for his true self, I've forgotten how he looks from afar, where he only shows a little glimmer, a small shred, of himself.

It's commendable, watching him pick up women only to leave them wanting. The other players believing they have whatever it takes to make it work.

Yet they cannot fathom how my pet can and will do whatever it takes to possess them.

He's known thirty-six of them. Sure enough, he had my help, but he channeled the fight in order to make it possible at all.

The game of pickup operates on the basics, yet it's open to interpretation.

I finish my first drink, watching as two overdressed guys desperately wave my pet over. First off, he's going to tell them about the club dynamic, just to gain their confidence. He'll be a little more confident than needed because in such a scenario, it'll get the other guys hanging on his every word.

He'll say something like, "Take a look at everything that's offered. Choose a popular and crowded club. It needs to be a popular club because I'm not going to be there to collect on used goods and other slut-bags. The girl needs to be fresh, new, attractive, but not a perfect ten. Look for realistic charm and beauty, not synthetic silicon brides. Prospects need to be casual looking to have fun tonight because tomorrow they'll be going to class and studying for their midterms."

The two guys are laughing, doing some kind handshake with each other, and he's just waiting patiently as they finish.

"Make sure you know your competition. Don't get caught in arguments. You blow your cool and that's it. No good, no go."

They agree. He tries to leave but they both call after, proof that he's got them right where we want them. Now it's my turn to pick him up.

Time save my pet.

I'm quickly taking my position, a perfect distance between him and the guys sitting at the table and me. This is a good searching distance.

They don't seem to want him to leave, so, of course, they follow his every step.

He pretends to spot me; he reacts naturally.

He's saying stuff like, "Need pointers? Watch me."

Pointers include:

"Survey the floor. Mark potentials as targets. Figure out their situation. Don't try to move in other players' territories if you don't need to."

He's in my face now, preaching the lines that he usually pulls on the other girls.

I'm forcing to play along as he elbows them, pretending that I'm the example, just another girl that's ditsy and/or drunk, receptive to his amazing charm.

He's shouting over the music. I can hear them but I'm pretending not to, pretending to dance. I'm pretending to be oblivious.

"No pickup lines. A pickup taunt is more like it. Focus on the art of touch and poise and you'll never have to say anything other than a little prototypical hello."

He's turning to me, showcasing what he just said. I'm playing along, more than a little angry, wondering if this is some kind of revenge. Afterwards he leans over to them and says, "Playing with their senses gets them going. The perfect combination of cologne, cigar smoke, taste in clothing, behavior and voice gets the girl interested. Picture yourself as a ghost dropping in, changing her life. You are changing their lives."

I'm playing out revenge scenarios in my head when he starts encouraging them to do the same to other women. The two guys disappear into the crowd, so easily influenced.

He's looking over to me, straight faced, as if he's trying to hide something from me.

I grab his arm and we turn to leave the club. On the way out, a woman barely able to stand up straight grabs him and pulls him close, but I can still hear her ask, "Have we met?"

And I'm a great observer, so I remember her as one of the women from a previous night, one of the decoy girls, someone he picked up only to leave midway so as to get in the clear with the one he really wanted. And what he should have said was, "No," but instead he said, "We have." It's something a killer should never say, and so I'm forced to take over. Just a little glare, letting the drunk chick get a glimpse of the fight I hide inside.

She pushes him toward me and stumbles away.

I'm escorting him to my car and I'm telling him to wait there, saying something like, "We'll talk about what you did later," in a tone that's a mixture between angry and tired.

He watches me from the passenger side window. I walk back into the club. I'm not about to let her get away with that. She's not too far from where we left her. I have found her.

Maybe she isn't the best candidate but I see potential. More so than that, I want revenge.

I find her near one of the bar-backs, trying to order another drink.

Hello Miss Number 37.

2.

Right about now those two guys are being linked to dozens of dead women.

I'm with him—with the only one I'd want to be—in the cage where thirty-seven is being examined. He's more like himself now, and that sends a shrill little spark up my spine.

It feels a lot like what we used to do before.

"Look what you've done."

I'm getting comfortable as master.

What has he done?

He's giving up, giving in completely to me, my pet.

Number thirty-seven is a naked body, unconscious, on the cold steel of his operating table. Since our agreement, he's transformed this cage into his own. Not to say much has changed. In fact, it's practically the same except for the smells, the sensation I'm getting when I have a look. Tonight we're both here, in his comfort zone, and I'm getting to watch him piece together what will become his thirty-seventh sensory experience.

"The skin is a sheath. The sooner you get it off, the sooner we can do something about it."

He's petting her stomach, the mons venus, and I'm annoyed because he shouldn't be wasting time on such things. Have a taste and get on with it.

I'm watching and finding myself getting more and more involved.

He doesn't want instruction but, as master, I'm feeling like I need to show him how it's supposed to be done.

He's too lenient on method.

No wonder we find ourselves needing to find patsies, covering our tracks every few girls. I'm willing to show him how it's done, but he's shoving his face between her legs, pretending he can't (and won't) hear me.

I'm saying, "You can't just covet that body. Take the surgical knife and carve."

He's coming up for air and saying, "She tastes like strawberries!"

I'm shaking my head, wanting to move things forward.

"You've gotten your taste. Now what are we going to do now?"

He's sighing a loud sigh and I'm hearing it, raspy and apprehensive.

I'm asking him, "Hey, what's wrong with you?"

He's not telling me.

Enough is enough. I can't have him acting up like this.

"What does a pet do, hmm?"

He's ignoring me as he grabs the knife resting next to a series of utensils and starts carving, violently cutting through sinew and bone. She's waking up.

I'm shouting, "You didn't drug her?!"

Apparently he didn't. This girl, this Andrea, Miss Number 37, had blacked out on all the booze. He was supposed to send a dosage up her bloodstream on the car ride home.

Clearly he did not.

"You. . . how can you be so. . ." I'm seeing the next segment from the future, grabbing him and shaking him. My pleas, my repeated queries about what's going wrong. His resistance, pulling away from my grip. Slapping him, kicking him in the stomach. Coughing, his dry heaves, an intended vomit.

His breathy shout, his confession, how my support has drained the thrill out of the game, out of his craft, and my disappointment, a complete and total disappointment, as thirty-seven is bleeding into her hands and falling off the operating table.

"Killer must kill," I'm saying, much to his dismay.

Thirty-seven bites him, teeth digging hard. I back away saying, "If you want to do it alone, fine."

I sit in the corner of the cage, watching him struggle.

She's bleeding all over his expensive suit. He's going to have to figure out how to get bloodstains out of a tan suit.

Good luck. If it were me, I'd know which combination of cleaners and stain-removers to use for the most effective result. But he thinks it's all boring, what we're doing, so I'm backing away. Fine. Fine. . .

I'm taking it harder than expected.

Fine.

He's really struggling now and I'm laughing, "Oh, she's more than I expected."

I really know how to pick them. He disappoints me, really saddens me. I thought we had something special. Now I'm not so sure. I've been in other relationships before, but the person I pick up has never been this willing to comply and be mine.

I guess it was too good to be true.

He's calling to me for help.

I'm watching, not as much as a single twitch. I'm not going anywhere.

"Master. . .help!"

I should enjoy his pleas, but you know I'm not.

I'm saying, "You're the killer, do what you do best."

He isn't able to wrestle free from thirty-seven's locked legs around his chest, pushing the air out of his lungs. His face is a stain of dark red and thirty-seven, I'm watching her breasts hang, her hair knotted with blood, her eyes a dark black when I had thought they were green.

It's a pathetic sight, my pet unable to function on his own.

He needs me.

He's realizing how much he needs me.

I feel like nothing will ever be the same again.

I stand up and leave the cage.

He's shouting, "Master! Master!"

I'm going to take care of this but only because it's too late to undo what has already been done. His shouts are way too loud. The cage might be soundproofed but you can't ever trap 100% of the sound. Somewhere, through a tiny crack, people are hearing his cries and thinking it's some really kinky sex.

In the kitchen I put the kettle on and sit, listening patiently.

I'm still in the future, seeing 37's burned body, a killer begging to its master, asking for a second chance, and worst of all, my inability to go back to the way things were.

I'm saying to myself, "They're all the same. You can't tame them."

And I'm starting to believe it.

I'm also believing that he's ruined and I'm the one that ruined him. If I let him go free, we'd hear of the Gentleman Killer caught by day's end.

The kettle's piercing squeal breaks my thread of thought.

I'm picking it up and walking back into the cage.

I'm kicking thirty-seven in the kidney and she's buckling, letting go of him. He's crawling toward me, gripping my legs, hiding behind me. I'm disgusted, but the heat of the handle sends notices of increasing pain from the tips of my fingers, nerves sending out that warning, so I'm pouring the scalding water all over her bare side, chest, and back.

I enjoy a scream only killers get to enjoy firsthand.

Her skin bubbles and peels and I'm mocking her as I tell her, "Don't move. It'll hurt less if you don't move."

Yeah, but she can't help it so the skin peels off with ease as she twitches and rolls to one side of the cage and stays there.

I kick him free, "There, now you've got a new challenge." I leave him in the cage to tend to a partially dead version of what should have been a glorious celebration.

He won't taste her now unless he likes the flavor of burnt flesh.

3.

The only thing you're capable of killing is your legacy.

I hate to say it but. . .*you're not so much a mystery as you are a mistake.*

The killer calls
every morning.

1.

I went to class.

I let my pet have the apartment.

I spent most of my days on campus, working and studying, formulating this thesis of mine. If I wasn't on campus, I was getting food or staying at a nearby motel.

Room 201.

My pet wanted freedom so I let him, knowing how much it would hurt.

He called me every day.

I ignored his calls.

Knew why he was calling.

2.

I picked up once. This is what was said.

And it didn't matter who said what.

I think it's obvious who said what.

"There was a body here but now it's gone."

"How do you figure?"

"What do you mean 'how do I figure?'"

"There was a dead girl's body in the cage but it's gone now."

"Oh."

"Look, okay—how long have we been doing this?"

"A long time."

"Four months. For me, it's been four months. And it's been a little over a month since you became a supporter of my craft."

"Okay. What's your point?"

"My point is, the both of us, we might not be as safe as we thought."

"Duh. Someone's probably tapped the phones and cameras."

"What?"

"Yes."

"Huh? But, if the bodies are disappearing, what's happening to them? Where are they going? Other guys aren't meeting women so that they can't sleep with them."

"Don't forget that someone must be breaking into the apartment and stealing the bodies."

"You have to help me."

"What's your number?"

"I don't want to know."

"Last time I checked it was forty-one, but only thirty-six, maybe thirty-seven of them are really yours. The rest are uncalled for. Poof, disappearing act."

"I'm not using the cameras and computers. I never open the front door."

"The door opened all by itself. There was a body here."

"Now it's gone. . ."

"The body was of a girl you picked up twenty minutes ago."

Every time he leaves the apartment, I sneak back in and take the bodies. Through a hole in the wall, I hang out with our next door neighbor, a guy who's high most of the day and selling most of the night. Convenient for me, I get to use his apartment to spy on my pet.

I am punishing my pet.

This is what I tell myself. This is what I'm doing.

He must learn how to appreciate his master. Honestly, I am already noticing a change.

It's working.

3.

And another time I reacted to a voicemail with a one-sided conversation where I asked him questions while ignoring his answers. He wanted advice.

I gave him open-ended queries of the killer inside:

Does a killer decide or choose?

He rambles.

What about a killer derives confidence?

He asks for forgiveness.

Is it true that a killer is considered popular culture?

He tries to get angry and blames me.

How many kills does it take a killer to get comfortable with his craft?

He apologizes.

Does a killer keep killing, or does a killer stop once the passion is gone?

He wants me home.

Might a killer simply be someone trying to find themselves?

He tries to seduce me.

Is a killer capable of finding value in another person?

He breaks down.

Or is the killer just taking life?

He sobs.

I hang up.

4.

I went to class.
I went to class.
I am in class.
I am studying.
I am onto something. . .

5.

Jump back to the dark, desolate interstate. A scene from a killer's past, when the mystery was as alone as the vehicle appearing in the distance, singled out by the darkness of the night.

The mystery holds onto her like she's a mannequin, signing the registry and receiving the key with zero suspicion and zero effort. The receptionist never looks up from the book he's reading. 201—remember the number.

It's a wonder the man doesn't drug her ahead of time. Got to be careful with these things. The mystery lays out a series of syringes, all new, still capped with the protective plastic seal.

Too much, and there goes the most important part.

Too little, and it's nothing more than a stupid, ignorant fight like in any horror film.

Time for your medication. . .

She'll try to escape. She wakes up in a cold sweat. Panic.

It's still wet enough outside; in the aged gravel of the parking lot footsteps can be seen. Focus in on those footsteps. Pull back to see a new set being printed next to hers. The man walks with hers, a familiar image out of Catholic fable. During those hard times, the mystery carries the burden, solitary footsteps in the sand.

Familiar imagery flickers; call it nostalgia. Jump cut to her running down the dead interstate. The interstate leads back to the motel. It only leads back to the mystery.

The man waits patiently. When she sees the mystery, she stumbles, trips, falls, and tears up her knees.

Oh come on, I thought we'd had enough of these kinds of chase scenes.

Do we really need to be derivative?

The mystery turns to the audience.

Frame skip—static interlaced while focusing right on the mystery, then cuts to the motel.

Man has her in arm, bleeding.

You're a feisty one.

She's naked on the bed, and there's a close-up shot of the syringe, the end being pulled, the needle pricking the vial, the medication squirting in one long stream. Focus on her neck. The needle punctures skin.

The audience wants what it wants. Will it get it? Will they be satisfied?

The man sits on the side of the bed.

Waiting.

You know, it's not all bad. I don't intend on being a fantasy.

You get to be the first. There's something to that.

Hear me, you'll be remembered.

You're my first.

The mystery cuffs her to the bed.

Various shots of her naked body, lifeless eyes releasing tears, the man drinking wine. Putting on latex gloves. Lighting a sheet of paper on fire to test the fire alarms in the motel room. Alarm doesn't go off. Man puts a plastic bag over it anyway.

These are shots of the mystery unfolding.

Man leaning in and sticking two fingers inside of her. Looking for a reaction, gets no reaction from her so he tries again. This time three fingers. No reaction.

Four fingers. Again, no reaction.

Man looks around the room, looking for the remote.

Insertion proves to be difficult but the man is able to fit the end of the remote into her and, yet again, no reaction.

I bet this would hurt if you could feel it.

How about I tell you what I'm doing?

I've tried my fingers. I've tried this remote. I'm going to try. . .hmm, what am I going to try? Crazy how the human body can be so fragile, yet so versatile. How about. . .

Focus on the man. Focus on the mystery. Zoom in close on his face.

Notice the excitement.

Cut to much later. The body looks the same but something's off. Something about it isn't right and there's no mystery. She's dead.

The man sits on the edge of the bed.

Man takes a few puffs from a cigar. Knocks over the glass of wine. Splatters it down the side of the bed. The sheets being white makes it clear, almost like blood. Man mutters profanities. Stands up and walks to a bin seemingly empty until the angle changes and inside there are numerous latex gloves, garments, used syringes, and a plastic sheet speckled in red.

The mystery might not make sense, but it has been planned.

Everything up to the wine. That was an accident.

Jump to the man standing over the body. Glances out the window.

It's going to be light soon.

Montage of the man cleaning and deciding to leave the body dressed in lingerie. Leave the body cuffed, cleaning the body of any and all fingerprints and DNA with a series of chemicals. The body begins to look more like porcelain than a dead corpse.

The man sings, catering to the mystery.

The end of the montage leaves the body and audience behind. Man leaves just before dawn. Shot of the bin placed near the dumpster, ash and melted nothingness within.

The audience is left in bed with the mystery.

Everlasting over the entire scene is the feeling that it had just begun.

What part of human nature is a mystery?

1.

I left class early to have a look.

I knock on neighbor's door. Nobody answers, so I try turning the knob. No surprise it's open. Doubtful whether or not he ever locks the door.

Doesn't really matter. There's nothing in here worth stealing.

I wander over and look through the hole in the wall.

I watch the killer watch TV.

He didn't used to watch TV.

He's changing. He's changed.

He's watching the news story about himself, and when it's done he rewinds it and watches the news story again, and again, and again.

The killer is worried.

At some point I must have fallen asleep. I wake up when I hear him slam the front door. I hear the sound of the door locking.

I know where he's going.

I leave one apartment for the next.

I go inside my apartment and see two women drugged and near death in the cage, unaccounted for. What are their names?

I notice all the small details.

He's letting both craft and domicile go to waste.

I take both women, one by one, down to my car.

No one seems to notice what I'm doing.

To them I'm a woman with a piece of luggage.

With both bodies safely stowed in my car, I return to the apartment to gather a few things and to leave behind a little something. Something small, insignificant, noticeable.

I wander each room wondering what it might be.

After a few minutes of contemplation, I fill the kettle

with water and place it on the stove.

I remember the cameras, recording everything.

I return to my room, sign into the video software noticing that he signed in recently. I'm amused rather than angry, and I proceed to remove the entire visit from all angles.

I climb out onto the balcony and down the fire escape.

It isn't until I'm free of the two bodies, in the pensive quiet of the motel room, that I realize my heart beats quicker, my body warm and aroused when I think of what I just did.

I plan on doing more.

I aspire to control from behind the scenes, recording a killer's sanity unraveling.

I'm laughing, touching myself, as I turn to the new laptop I borrowed from the forensics department for the purposes of my research. I turn on the webcam.

I watch myself on webcam.

I unclothe myself.

I turn to the various internet sex chats.

I say hello.

They have no idea who they're talking to.

And I find it compelling.

2.

Whole eras begin and end at night. A narrow shot down an alley at the moment of sunset. The thing about mysteries, you've got to keep up with all the details or you'll end up lost in the big picture. It's good that you're patient, waiting for the man to reappear.

Glimpse the bare feet walking, stepping in putrid puddles of rainwater, drunken vomit, and dog shit. Pan up showing ankles, legs, a bare heart-shaped behind, bare back with long, blonde, no, maybe brown hair draped over skin the color of porcelain.

See this woman? Want to see the other side of her, the full-frontal?

The thing about mysteries—they're written to give prying minds a means of flexing mental muscle, but, inevitably, the quality of any mystery is in its management of ambiguity.

The more given, the less mysterious she becomes.

Woman casually walks the length of this decrepit alley without a care at all.

Untouchable.

Surely the woman is out of place. Strange. And the question is, why is there a woman?

How is she not being attacked?

The mystery yawns wide, falling into a loose embrace with the audience.

Woman stops at door labeled, Employees Only.

In the pale blue light cast by a single bulb hanging right above the door, the woman is finally seen, full-frontal, her face blurred out.

Panning in circles, the audience tries to get a good look at her.

Despite what's left unseen, it's unanimous. She is beautiful.

The woman knocks on the door and waits.

She's got nothing to hide.

Close-up as the woman licks her lips. The audience is silent.

Various quick shots of the woman in showcase, every naked angle of her body but her face. The face is pristine. The face is left unseen.

The door opens. There's no one on the other side.

The woman walks in, leaving the audience behind. Zooming out, the audience is bound to the retreating shot, backtracking down the alley, being pulled away from the woman they had just met. A retreating shot makes it feel like the glimpse given was an accident. It wasn't intended. Someone slipped in a series of shots from a scene.

Where did the woman come from?

The mystery doesn't want to be solved.

Getting too close, it's time to back off before the mystery notices that the rest of the scene is erased. The existence of the woman cannot be reversed. The woman—the only other that knows the reason behind the mystery. The solution is in the hands of a naked woman that'll let you see her entire body before she'll let you see her face.

3.

The killer returns to the sound of a blood-thinning screeching.

The killer doesn't notice that she's watching.

The killer is running to the source, leaving her behind, the one he picked up tonight. The killer finds the kettle nearing full capacity. Steam escapes from the spout and threatens to overflow and spill onto the stove.

The killer burns his hand but manages take the kettle off the stove.

She's laughing, and by "she" we don't mean her standing by his side, drug dosage beginning to kick in.

She's laughing, "You're a wreck without me."

The killer wanders into the bathroom.

The killer returns with a tray full of toys and a bandaged hand.

She's watching blissfully as he reenters the cage.

The killer exhales deeply and holds back a few tears.

Only she knows why.

"Where's your master when you need her most?"

The killer wants his master.

The killer isn't much of a killer without her.

This is how she perceives the scene.

This is what she believes is occurring as she watches from next door, bird's eye view via the cameras, and an ear pressed to the hole in the wall.

She can hear him crying.

4.

Fade in on an auditorium in the heart of modern American academia. Counting sixty seats; spread out stadium seating. With a lonely professor at the podium, he speaks too closely to the microphone muffling his speech. The mystery is in the back. Watching.

The mystery is the offhand inquiry, asking—

How does anyone learn anything in this kind of environment?

And the audience already knows the answer, having experienced this personally.

"I know that I'm wanted," murmurs the lonely professor, lips pressed to the microphone.

"Want to go watch a movie?" Lonely professor is reading, desperately reading, from today's prepared lecture.

Students take notes. Pretend the students take notes.

Pretend the students want to be here.

Pretend the students know what they're majoring in.

Pretend the students are being taught how to be apathetic, vicious and heartless victims.

Victims of the system they will one day dismantle from the bottom-up.

The mystery throws in a scene of absent humility to throw the audience off the scent of the man's trail. The man waits elsewhere, noticing he hasn't been followed for a few hours now.

Something's wrong. The mystery was once exclusively the man's, and the man won't want to share even a second of the feature presentation with the woman.

Too bad. It's a done deal.

The man needed the support of a woman to make this work.

"Want to go to a show?" Poor lonely professor. The audience is already bored with you.

"Want to go to the beach?"

"What do you want to do? I'm up for anything!"

The woman is here as a contingency, having stumbled upon the man's activities.

"I just don't want to be alone," the lonely professor looks for approval. Students remain busied with their laptops. Not even one looks up at the professor.

The professor is alone at the podium.

The mystery derails while this woman remains front-and-center. Every shot of the woman distracts. How can the woman not be a diversion?

The audience is beginning to see how they're directly involved.

Hitting new highs means hitting moral lows.

"People do bad things when they're left alone."

Clock strikes twelve. It's about that time. The class is officially over. Jump shots, picture-in-picture of students rushing to close their laptops, packing up their things, center shot remaining fixed on the lonely professor who keeps talking, "Loneliness is a killer of confidence. Who wants to be around someone who lacks confidence?"

The professor's pleas fall on deaf ears.

Glance at the back of the auditorium. The woman is gone.

If there's a mystery, it's impossible to be alone as long as the mystery is alive. The mystery provides everyone involved a meaning to keep moving, keep making connections with others. There's always at least one with the answer and at least one other trying to solve it.

When there's no mystery, well, there's only a professor, alone swimming in his misery.

The professor is on the verge of tears, an emotionally anchoring scene, but the audience is too busy looking for evidence of where the woman went.

The woman reserves the audience's full attention.

Glimpses here.

Glimpses there.

The audience is getting desperate waiting for the scene to finish.

The scene doesn't end. It stays on the professor, as if by sheer willpower, the professor takes the stand and refuses to let this finish without winning over the audience.

It's a part of the mystery that gets the audience down, discouraged. . .wondering if this is going anywhere or if they're missing something.

What is this scene about?

There's a question in need of being answered. Help the audience help you.

He cannot hear the audience. He cannot hear anyone.

As the shot stays and slowly, achingly, like the drooping of an eyelid, the professor is the audience's direct focus. The lonely professor reminisces past events in his life that he refers to as a "past life." The professor talks about a wife, a divorce.

Audience begins to suspect the point of the scene is the professor. The professor is lingering, speaking of something—he knows something about the mystery. The professor is speaking about victimization, about brutality, about the end.

The screen quickly fades, as if there was a technical malfunction.

Audience is left in the dark, staring at a black screen, the professor's muffled voice barely audible over the censor beeps. Suddenly, the woman is seen again, transparent; the same scene in the dark alley from before.

But this time, a new shot has slipped in between the last glimpse of a pulled back view of the naked woman in alley and the first close-up of the woman in pale blue light facing the Employees Only back door. In this new shot, the woman looks right at the audience.

Gasp. Confusion. Dread.

Everyone has seen this face before.

The mystery wears a mask of horror.

5.

I no longer went to class. Class went along with me.

I was offered a scholarship and a paid-for stint of independent study.

All they need is a meeting once a week where I update the department chair on any and all new developments. *Sure thing.* That's what I said.

I'd surely show them something.

But what I would show them would be like the disguise we offer to others during first introductions. The meat of my research wouldn't be found until you cut through to the bone.

I rigged remote access to my laptop and his.

I made it possible to watch and document and erase from my motel room.

My pet, my petty subject, hadn't a clue I was close by.

I wouldn't let him.

Everything I gave him he failed to appreciate.

Everything he gets, from this point on, he'll have to earn.

Be my pet. My perfect, perfect pet.

Does this sound like someone you might know?

1.

There is no precision in what you do.

I watch from a twin monitor setup lent to me by the department.

Room 201 is approximately two miles down the road from where he sits staring into the cage.

The cage is filthy, containing a decomposing body, because I'm not there to clean it up.

No. Not this time. And that's the least of his problems.

I can switch to recorded video, but I know what I'll find.

Him, sitting and staring through her, whoever she is (does it even matter?), and for a killer he isn't killing her right. He isn't killing her at all. She won't stop screaming.

I mute the live feed. I'm wishing these cameras could zoom in, but they are stationary, stagnant, just like him.

He's sitting, depleted.

She's in pain.

He hasn't so much as tasted her.

I know her as Laura, but only because I've decided to call her that.

I wish I could speak to him.

I watch the degradation of a killer without his master.

The fight dribbles out the side of his mouth, saliva pooling into his sleeve, getting damper, until I'm noticing him standing and I'm saying, "Finally."

He's walking inside the cage.

I don't switch to the camera in the cage.

I unmute the video feed.

I listen.

Her screams.

Laura's precious, escaping cries.

And then silence.

I imagine the pool of blood collecting.

I imagine the killer inside failing to come out.

Where's the fight?

I don't switch cameras.

There's nothing worth seeing.

The killer should do everything right. The killer should leave in the night, the remains of his most recent in a black overnight bag. With his return, he has neither bag nor remains. The killer is based in efficiency and routine. The killer mustn't rely on anyone but himself. All of these things are necessities. This is everything a Gentleman Killer lacks.

I'm whispering, "You lack everything."

I'm writing something down, "What happens to a killer without any fight left?"

I'm also adding, "What did I see in you? And where did it go?"

A thought, "Might it be my fault?"

This can't be the precursor to a breakup.

This can't be the beginnings of the end.

This isn't that.

And I'm not enjoying the distance apart.

Not at all.

2.

Might be wondering how there can be a battle without any bloodshed, but it's fairly obvious most of this is happening within a certain frame-of-mind. My frame-of-mind sees people as fighters based on the verve or value hidden within. Once you see behind their frontline defenses, those dreaded sociable exteriors worn and worn well, you see who they really are, whether they're alive or dead. You don't have to be six feet under to be dead. The majority of the dead keep to a routine. They stay active. They're losers out of battle, out of touch. The battle is a game of mental wits, clashing conceptual angles to see which couple has enough fortitude to consume the other. This is how I really see people.

With or without any real fight, you're only alive if you're willing to explore.

I take the motel.

He takes the apartment.

My apartment.

Part of me thinks about who got the better end of this. He gets his bed. He gets her. I'm watching a roach skitter across the room, disappearing into the darkened and lifeless bathroom.

I'm next door when I want more of him. When I want to watch, I have the video feed, but I still don't have my pet to talk to. I have to take a peek through the hole, the hole that the neighbor once claimed to have been a glory hole installed in hopes of the previous tenants of my apartment to fellate him after a month of what he perceived to be intense flirting.

This shared wall is all that separates us, me and my pet.

But I can't let my pet see me.

He is being punished.

I want him back and I can't have him if I let him get what he wants. If I reenter his life.

I must train him to kill on his own.

My beloved little pet, "Gentleman Killer," what have you done to yourself?

No, it is not yet time.

I watch him continue to pick them up, yet fail to finish them off.

A series of five girls teeter towards utter demise while he avoids the cage altogether.

The smell must be unbearable.

He busies himself with food preparation, watching people come and go from their apartments via the peephole.

I have taken to leaving via the fire escape or showing up after he leaves for yet another dominance-display at a nearby club or party.

I was the one that taught him the difference between club and party.

"The club is where you go to compete and look at those with fighting potential. The party is where you go for scraps, easy padding, but just be careful of dead weight. There's typically nothing but duds at parties. People without even the capability of killing a stray cat much less a person. Get it good, club. Get it quick, party."

I taught him everything.

My instruction.

Back when he had a mere twenty kills, I showed him the way.

I'm wondering if he remembers or if what he's really doing is trying to find me.

He misses me, for sure. I wonder what about me he's missing.

Me, or my support?

I sniff the air passing through the hole in the wall.

I whisper to nobody in particular, "You've ruined my apartment."

I tell myself during times of weakness, "This has everything to do with intervention."

3.

Conversation from the cutting room floor.

Everyone's out for the scent.

They sell victims. They sell friends. They're selling victims drugged up and ready to be fed to your pet serial killer.

They provide a service. These stores help pet owners keep their serial killers healthy.

Ticket to a serial killer's health is to keep them creative.

My serial killer welcomes me home with a ten-minute hunt in the shadows.

My serial killer likes to play American Dream.

I can have whatever I want.

A serial killer is something best kept a secret.

I have a secret that no one will ever know.

You're a mystery.

I am the mystery.

What can I do for you tonight?

What they sell are products that'll feed the mystery.

The woman is here to buy a week's worth of victims.

My serial killer likes women more than men.

I'm a woman.

You're a mystery.

I'd be a good friend.

You'd be a good killer.

That's everyone's role.

It's possible to switch and share roles.

Who are you talking to?

What are you looking for?

You're losing sight of reality.

The woman is here to buy a replacement pet.

The man is searching for a new master.

It's hard to find friends.

But it's easy to find killers.

A handful of voices, none of them hers.

She found you first...
never forget it.

1.

I haven't even begun; that's what tonight is for.

I'm home. My place.

A little foreplay—wearing latex gloves, I walk through the apartment.

I begin working on his computer.

I wear a mask. The mask smells of somewhere else.

It smells of him.

He altered his laptop to be password protected.

I know the password.

I know all his passwords.

I've made my decision.

Even with the past we've shared, I am free to do as I please.

And what I find pleasing is keeping him paranoid, on his feet, alert every step of the way.

I need to do something about those bodies.

Some of them are dead.

I want to say he's met the fifty mark, but when all I see is a tossed out body with little to identify with, I get the feeling that he's ruining it.

I've kept up with the news. **Missing Persons** reports have become linked to Gentleman Killer. He is as interesting as he was prior to my enforced banishment.

The key to power—by that I mean any kind of power—is in how the media handles the mystery. So far he's been lucky. He's been lucky every step of the way.

But not tonight. Not anymore.

I will teach him a lesson and use his reaction as data.

I play with myself while playing with his computer.

I find his phone on the kitchen counter.

I add a few phone numbers.

Every phone number is someone I've never met.

Each phone number comes from one of my classes, people I've never cared for, people with which affability comes easy.

I toy around with security software.

I alter the past so that it looks like I have yet to return to the apartment.

I make it look like his computer hasn't been accessed.

I momentarily consider taking the bodies.

Just to make sure, I leave for next door around the time he typically returns with his newfound lays, but he doesn't come back, so I get right back to work.

When was the last time I've been aroused?

I can't be sure.

I play with myself but I won't be getting off.

I can't.

I'm naked to keep my outfit from smelling and being stained.

I walk from room to room, a finger where it feels good.

Occasionally I wipe my wet finger across random surfaces—coffee table, couch, carpet, keyboard—noting what I had touched. The cameras are recording. The cameras are recording. . .

I tend to the bodies.

What a waste. He could have at least tasted her.

The bodies go where they need to go to disappear.

But nothing's ever completely erased.

I make note of how many—eight—and I don't bother cleaning up the body fluids crusted and coated throughout the entire cage.

I take out some perfume and spray the surfaces my finger touched.

I return to my room when I've left the smells and cleaned out the bodies.

Check the footage.

I decide to keep and alter the footage rather than it being erased.

I hide my face in every shot.

I make sure that whatever he does see is undoubtedly me.

Check her form.

Check her breast size.

Check her nice long legs.

She looks a lot like your type, huh?

Don't like blondes? That's okay, because she's a brunette too.

What he'll see is a lot of what he's already seen in private display.

We used to talk to each other, record every touch, the camera catching our true forms, letting us fuck each other with our own hands.

What am I?

I am his type.

She is his type.

She is your type.

I edit the footage and leave it as-is, knowing well that he'll be back to check.

The scraps are forever erased.

I leave no trace.

I sign into an anonymous email account, a name made up and an email most unfamiliar, and I title it, "SORRY TO HAVE MISSED YOU."

In the body of the email I write:

"They all look the same once you've let them retire."

I am adding to the mystery.

"Where do they go, if they've got no fight left in them? I see vermin but they look a lot like the girl on the 6-o-clock news. Don't worry. They might not spread your secret around. . ."

I sign it with XOXO and then, post script, I add:
"Say hello. Wave to me."
I want him to remember who found who first.
I picked you up, not the other way around.
Remember? Hearts and kisses!

2.

THIS:

What happens?

THAT:

What happened?

Where it's believed to be that "Nothing Ever Happens," there's a lot going on wherever people aren't paying attention.

But who's believing who?

Cryptic mysteries are seldom easy to explain.

Well, try this:

3.

A scene from the past. Not just any kid's room—the woman's childhood bedroom. Panning shot around the room shows the same walls covered in watercolors and other artistic treasures. The bed is covered with teddy bear sheets and on the windowsill the same telescope she used every night to glimpse a world that was never hers to understand.

There's a child guarding this room. The only person th child lets in is the woman. The woman belongs here. The reason why isn't a mystery.

The real mystery is why the child hasn't aged.

The room seems to shrink and shake to the sounds of footsteps outside.

The audience watches the room buckle and bend.

Mom and Dad are angry. You missed curfew.

Mom and Dad will punish you.

Easy for you, you're the favorite.

It's not my fault. It's important to be confident.

Mom and Dad want a sensible daughter.

Mom and dad want me, not you.

Hear that? It's Dad. He's here to do it again.

He won't, not again. Not after all this time.

He'll keep doing it until you learn.

Why don't you help me stop him instead of hiding under the bed?

Nothing I do matters. I've got the bravery, the looks, and the brains to do anything, but I lack one thing, one important element.

And what's that?

I can only live through you.

The child's words are the woman's and the woman's are the child's.

Of course, the audience knows this.

The room coils around the woman as if meant to protect her from what bangs on the door. The audience standing in unison, hairs on their neck standing as they stand, the tension built up so obscurely it has left the audience a wreck, a loss for words while searching for an understanding. Bang—someone's at the door.

Who is it?

Don't bother. We already know.

Don't let him pull me out of the room.

I won't.

I need to stay in the room.

As long as you're in this room, you'll be safe.

The room has always protected you.

I can protect you too.

Bang—the door's not going to hold.

The woman takes a step back. The room reconfigures to hide everything but her face.

Zoom in on the woman's face. The audience can see everything.

Mug shot—see the source of the woman's fear, anxiety, and inadequacy.

Jump shot to the door splintering into pieces. Perfectly centered in the door frame, the light coming from the hallway darkening his shape: A man.

That isn't Dad.

I know who it is.

What's he doing here?

He's here to take back his secret. . .but I'm not going to let him do that.

Though the man tries, he can't step one foot into the room.

"You aren't welcome here!"

The woman is spoken for.

The man doesn't say a word. He isn't here for her; he's here for the mystery.

It's his and he's taking it back.

He's not going to leave.

He'll have to leave sometime.

No, you don't get it. He isn't leaving.

I'm not giving it back.

Give it back.

No.

Give the mystery back to the man. It's his, not yours, Claire.

I won't give it back.

Have I ever been wrong?

You're stubborn. Always was a stubborn bitch. You'll start a war.

Then let's start the war.

You're willing to go to war with your pet?

He's been a bad pet. He's turning on his master.

The man patiently waits at the door while the woman walks forward. Close up shot of her face, then his; the first time the audience sees his face.

They were meant to reveal more of themselves. Bit by bit, until each seeks the destruction of the other. This is the only way the mystery will be solved.

With a war.

You'll regret it, Claire.

No I won't.

Then what the fuck do you want, Claire?

I want control. It's all I've ever wanted. Complete control over an entire person.

You don't get it. This is for me.

Claire. . .

I'm breaking down the walls.

Stop talking like you're me.

1.

I was there watching as it all fell into place.

I recorded each item as data.

I had enough data to corroborate what I had hypothesized.

There was only one thing I hadn't expected.

2.

The killer returns home in the morning.
The killer has someone with him.
Drugged, she's failing.
She tries to kiss him.
The killer kisses her back.
When he pulls back, his mouth is bloody.
The killer spits it out into the kitchen sink.
Watches as she falls.
The killer drags her into the cage.
It is then that he first notices another change.
The others are missing.
What are you doing, fine sir?
The killer stops abruptly.
The killer seems angered.
Data recorded.

3.

The killer notices the email.

The killer watches the footage.

The killer breaks down.

Sobbing and silence.

Flat packing sounds, the sound of the killer tending to her body.

Sliding and then disposal.

Miss Whatever Number wasn't enjoyable at all.

Screams.

The killer screams.

Anger.

The killer is shouting.

The killer is begging.

The killer is shouting her name in anger.

The killer is shouting her name in apology.

Data recorded.

4.

The killer receives phone calls from women late at night.

Different voice every time.

The killer loops the video footage.

The killer can't get rid of the smell of perfume even though the smell of the freshly dead body overlaps, overpowering the entire apartment.

The killer picks up the phone.

A familiar tone, the way she talks.

His face is expressionless.

What is he thinking?

My pet serial killer, my pretty, pretty pet.

The killer remains seated at his laptop.

The killer picks up the phone and listens to her talk.

The killer watches the footage.

The killer does this all day.

Like the sound of the rain outside, the killer is steady and constant.

Unmoving.

The killer answers the phone without looking at the number.

Listens to the masked voice reciting the same thing.

"This is your fault. This is your fault."

Over and over again until master hangs up.

The killer watches the footage.

What's most important is what the killer is thinking about, but that can't be recorded.

The killer sits still. The killer might be playing dead.

Data recorded.

5.

Sometime late into the night, the killer begins moving again.

The killer takes out his cellphone.

The killer sits there a moment, considering his options.

The killer begins inputting numbers.

The killer dials, hangs up before saying a word.

The killer hits play on the video footage.

Leans in close, analyzing what he sees.

The killer narrows his eyes.

Crosses his arms, uncrosses them. Sighs.

The killer stands up.

The killer starts taking off his clothes.

First the shirt, then the pants.

Lastly his underwear.

He is erect, stroking.

The killer looks up directly at one of the cameras.

The killer, instead of sitting back down, he walks off camera.

The killer doesn't appear on any of the other cameras.

One by one the cameras go black.

Spray paint across the lens, the hissing of an aerosol can. Nothing is seen, only heard.

The killer moves around the apartment.

Only sound remains.

The killer is typing something on the keyboard.

The killer is talking to someone on the phone.

The killer hangs up.

He curses to himself.

Tries again.

Sounds like a different number.

The killer is talking to someone.

The killer is talking to someone.

He is talking to someone.

Voice muffled, difficult to determine who it is.

It's enough to disturb the master keeping track of his every move.

Data recorded.

6.

So this is where things start to lean more in his favor rather than mine. I hadn't expected him to resist, or at least I hadn't expected him to resist so quickly.

I've barely pushed him, yet he's passing me over.

Doing something I would never, ever allow.

I'm. . .I don't know what I'm feeling.

Shouldn't I be angry?

I should, right?

I should be angry.

But I'm not. I'm feeling like I should go to the apartment, like right now, but I'm also wondering if he sprayed the cameras as a means of getting me back.

Do I ignore or pursue?

Nothing about this is easy.

I shouldn't go.

If I do he'll have the upper hand.

We have to remember our roles and what each side brings to this relationship. I am master while he is pet. It's fair. Right down the middle. He does what he does and gets what he needs. I give what he needs and get what I want in return. I used to think this was acceptable enough but then. . .

I should go.

No.

Yes.

I should go because if I don't there's no telling if he's going to stay. I don't want to track him down. I know as much about him as he knows about me. So in a way. he can't just leave. The look on his face. . .

He knows something.

I'm going.

I'm going to pack up my things and ditch this motel room.

Yes.
That's exactly what I'm going to do.
It's what I need to do.
He is my pet.
He is my pet.
I am master.
I am master.
Yes.
I'm leaving.
I'm on my way now.
Right now.
Yes.

7.

There'll be a movie about a killer that meets another killer who is destined to be a future killer—while the concept of another killer is forever a possibility, capable of being found, and that's where killer and killer assume another source. The killer inside is a fight that runs in circles. How does the audience know which one is the main killer? The audience has to figure it out. That's the mystery. That's why the movie will be a mystery. This movie will sell well, as with any other graphic crime-thriller. This movie is called. . .

After the movie there is nothing.

Before the movie there is nothing.

The movie is about a killer, and the one killer that transcends the hour-and-a-half long story to continue as a killer like so many others.

Man, woman, and mystery.

This is cause for celebration. What's one scene have anything to do with another?

Flicker. Cue the booming, rhythmic bass of rave music. Flicker. It's a club, Saturday night. Flicker. DJ bobbing his head. Flicker. A certain shot is desperately trying to be seen.

The audience is receptive to a number of flickering, establishing shots of the club's clientele—bar, people drinking, people dancing, people mingling, people making out. Flicker. An empty lounge. Flicker. A three second close-up shot of a pool of blood, dark enough to look like spilt oil. Flicker. People trading numbers. Flicker.

A familiar man talking to a woman. Flicker. Then another woman. Flicker. Yet another woman. The scene starts fittingly with this man. He's quite the player. He's in a good mood.

It must have been a good day.

The audience watches him whisper something in a woman's ear. She smiles. She nods when he asks her something inaudible, blanketed by the rave music.

The audience hears nothing but rave music.

No laughter. No sound effects. Nothing but the rave track throughout the entire scene.

The audience watches the man with a series of women—jump shots, making it appear like girls are being interchangeably swapped in and out like templates with a seamless charge. The man finds a woman on the dance floor, talks to her, seduces her, walks with her to the edge of the dance floor, up the stairs, and out of sight.

When the man returns, he returns alone.

Flicker. Close-up on the young man's face, a look of fear.

Flicker. A naked woman on the dance floor.

Flicker. The woman standing, splitting the dance floor like the parting of a sea.

Flicker. Accelerating, rapid second-long still image shots of the man trying to get closer to the woman. The woman is fully nude, wandering around the club. The man runs away and hides within a group of people. The woman looks at the audience and smiles.

The music stops. Complete silence.

The audience doesn't notice.

The people at the club don't notice.

No one misses a step.

Why don't you dance?

Anything behind a locked door is there for a reason.

1.

For the first and last time, I found myself in the position of being a patsy.

I went back to the apartment.

He wasn't there.

I saw her, face down with the skin of her back missing, but he wasn't there.

"He left her."

One of the most important rules—if there were rules—would be to never leave her.

Never leave me.

But most importantly, "Don't ditch the bodies!"

I made sure to bathe the bodies I collected. Dispose of them promptly. Yes, the night club with the seemingly forgotten basements and nearby storage units. Leaving the body there for a little less than a day, bathed in powerful chemical, there'll be nothing left.

Set them side by side, each in their own plastic carton, and they'll be primed.

But he's leaving her here, thinking they'll disappear.

At least this is what I first thought until I checked around, inspecting everything in the apartment for clues—I am a woman of forensics—and what did I find, oh, what did I find. . .

I went back to the apartment and found that he hoped to flee, making me the prime suspect. A woman responsible for the Gentleman Killer series of murders?

Now that makes for a great news story.

It makes me laugh.

Not the story, but rather the fact he thinks he can turn on me.

Me.

Master.

2.

But of course he wouldn't get that far without having to go back and he wasn't really trying to run away. He enjoyed the freedom of fleeing only to grasp that endless series of mistakes, every single one of them stringing together so beautifully, no one would have to fill in any of the plot-holes. It wouldn't be a mystery. But what's the fun in that?

Before his return, I cleaned up the apartment. Why not?

I'm not done with him yet.

The neighbor next door, I had to tend to him before everything could be set into place.

But that's where it started.

The breaking-up.

The betrayal.

Let it be recorded: He broke our agreement.

It was he that started it all.

I wanted to give him everything. I thought I saw the inner fight inside.

But I guess not.

What do I see?

I see someone masquerading as popular device.

3.

I'm knocking on the door and there's no answer. I'm about to break in when the neighbor opens the door. He's staring blankly at me, head rocking back and forth ever so slightly, and I'm pushing him aside, walking into his apartment.

He's barely there. He's laughing, calling me a witch because, with my hair wet, it curls at the ends and takes on a frazzled look. I mean, I guess that's why he's calling me that.

According to him, "You've been living in the woods or some shit!"

He offers and why not. I breathe in and cough.

He's grinning widely, "Good shit huh? I know where to get the good shit!"

I'm telling him he needs to go.

Amid laughter, he can only manage to repeat the word "go."

"Yes, go, and here, take all this, stay away for a week. I only need a week. If you accept this, you are officially homeless for a week, get it? I'll change the locks if I have to."

The sight of the money straightens his face and sobers him instantly, "Whoh hey now."

I'm not slowing down to explain it to him. I'm not explaining any of it to him.

He's laying out the bills, counting the money like a first-grader still new to handling money. I'm repeating the same sentences until they stick:

"This is my apartment for a week."

Repeat it enough times and he'll get it.

"Shit, I'm gonna kick it at the beach."

"Yeah, you do that. Just don't come back here for a week."

"Shit you can have this place. I don't need it."

"Only a week."

"Yeah. . ."

"One week."

I'm pushing him towards the front door; otherwise, he may never leave.

At the door, I'm asking, "How old are you?"

He's not going to answer. We share an awkward moment before I start pushing him out the door and looking at him a moment longer, realizing he won't be able to answer, I slam the door shut. Neighbor tries the front door but it's locked.

Did he forget already? He did.

I'm saying, "Anything behind a locked door is there for a reason."

But after jiggling the doorknob for a bit I hear him say, "Oh right, my bad."

4.

I'm still ahead of schedule. I take my time with this apartment.

I'm aware that I'm not completely sober but that's more than acceptable because what needs to be done might as well already be done.

It's exactly how I want it.

What I want:

This apartment leaning as close to mine as possible.

And it is.

To hear every single thing that happens, as it happens.

And I will.

The cameras, newly repaired, backed up by a series of holes drilled across the walls, covered with a descending panel to prevent light (or smoke) to pour in from the wrong side.

And let it be.

Him, instantly confused and regretting every moment of his so-called life until he's ready to give up and take his own life.

And believe in him.

Him, wondering why he did the things he did, betray the one he betrayed, waver and become withdrawn when it's clear he still had some fight left in him.

And wonder too the worry this brings.

A killer is only capable of one kind of murder.

Is this true?

A killer is capable of knowing himself fully but after seeing yourself in true shape it might be true that you can't ever retain form again.

You are knowledgeable of your every angle yet you cannot stand by one.

You cannot stand tall. You cannot settle for one.

Just as I can't settle for you.

When you can't leave me behind, returning defeated to

the apartment, I will be waiting.

I will be watching, like before. This time, I'm next door.

I have seen, in the mirror, a million different faces looking back at me.

But what I am, what you might already have figured out, is what you are now trying to escape: If I am that who supports a serial killer, what does that make me? Surely I'm not just a student. I'm a scholar. I'm a practitioner of a particular hands-on kind of exploratory search.

I know what I want, just like I know what I'm studying.

Just like I know what I am.

And I know what I'm going to do with you.

No pet of mine has ever tried turning on me.

I've been attacked. I've been strangled. I've been in the position of having to give chase to one that simply ran and ran and ran but they all end with the same image:

A **mystery** wrapped around a serial killer image where the killer seemingly ended its own life. My last time, he found the intestinal tract of a human being fascinating, how it can run on for miles and how it can all be there, in that compact midsection of the human body. He wondered how long he was. As my last gift to him, I showed him. He stretched for miles like he said, wrapping around him like a python, strangling him until dead. See?

I am not new to this, my pet.

I have a big heart but you mustn't cross me.

And why, then, must they always cut what they cannot straighten out? My, my, I only want to give those capable of taking the ability to take, but they always ruin it. Always. Never fail. It ends with entrails being uncoiled from a dead body by people like me.

The forensics team, they have a look, get a kick out of what they see.

Me, I'm the only one that knows the secret.

It's stupid to think I do this for sinister reasons.

My reasons are my own. I must say—it's amazing how people always assume that I'm troubled. I know what I'm doing just like I know what I want.

Perhaps it's the game we play that's perilous and full of pain.

Has no one thought about that possibility?

Either way, I'm still going to have to tend to him.

When he arrives, I'll be waiting.

5.

The real mystery is that we're able to get along at all. Is it possible to get to know someone without feeling the urge to murder them after seeing who they really are?

The audience demanded it and now they're going to get it.

Skipping over rising action, it's about time for climax and catharsis.

What is the audience looking at?

A park setting? No. The club setting? No. That dank alley? No.

Open wide on an apartment; no, make it two apartments.

Side by side, the shot is pulled back to fit both floor plans. And worse, to make the shot work, the roofs must come off; the element of reality must be disrupted all in the name of cinematic effect.

The mystery will be solved. Finally.

The mystery is hidden away, somewhere in one of these apartments.

But there's more to the man. There's more to the woman.

We see one apartment in the present, one in the past.

In the past, man and woman are together in bed; man and woman enjoying what they see, on screen with each other, chatting, and becoming one.

In the present, the apartment is draped in technology, every single item has its own protective plastic casing. The bed is rigged with bars on both sides so that between nightly tossing and turning, nocturnal fluctuations won't end with an injured arm or leg.

There is nobody in the apartment.

Yet in the past someone is watching.

The audience gets a feel for both apartments.

The audience leans back and soaks it all in. Something dreadful is about to happen.

Action impending—you can see how it might all end. It's pretty obvious, yet it's still worth watching in hopes of seeing how the wall will be broken, figuratively speaking.

What is this? What is that?

It's time to ask the audience. The audience builds a scene. Their scene. What they want to see, the sickening and somehow senseless things they might want to see.

What are we seeing?

Man and woman press their naked bodies against the shared wall.

They listen for movement but hear nothing coming from either side of the wall.

Voice-over:

Someone was recently victimized there. Please, a moment of silence.

Man and woman knock on the wall.

The wall between them is symbolic, defiantly important.

The wall will not yet fall. The wall will remain standing, pushing both man and woman away from each other. Man and woman whisper through the wall, calling for the same person.

The name sounds familiar.

Of course it does.

They call out for their own names. Man and woman, they whisper their names.

Victor. Claire.

They want to speak, but they haven't been formally introduced.

There's something missing between the both of them.

Man and woman, they are similar and yet opposite.

They listen to the sound of rainfall outside.

They want to be together. They hate being alone.

All they need to do is start over.

All they need to do is introduce themselves.

Hello, my name is. . .

A man.

Hello, my name is. . .

A woman.

The audience has voted and it seems they want pet and master, master and pet, man and woman, woman and man, to have that happy ending. And yet, they can't stomach seeing the past erased. The audience isn't satisfied with this scene.

The audience watches as the wall shakes and buckles in anger.

They can't seem to agree.

But that's still not enough. An agreement? The concept might be silly.

This is indeed silly. It's odd. How much of this is really happening and how much of it is the product of human imagination?

Can there be any other possible ending to a story involving pet and master?

Second chances. Strip that scene and start over.

This isn't commentary. This isn't anything.

It's an intermission.

The shifting of sore bodies in small theater seats.

The pensiveness of wanting something else without seeing everything change.

New but familiar. Familiar but foreign.

The mystery—it keeps them there.

We're all being watched.

Students write "I'm going to die" on their shirts.

1.

I go to the weekly meeting.

On the way to and from the department building, I see students gathered at the center of campus, in protest.

The students wear white shirts, writing "I'm going to die" one shirt after the other.

When they're done, they take their shirts off and put another one on.

Their bodies are their message.

What they wear and what they write is what they believe.

I don't bother to watch long enough to figure out the cause.

What they're protesting.

I have my own protest.

I preach my thesis and my data to the department chair.

He is confused but captivated. This has happened all before.

After a bit of discussion, I am given approval. One week extension.

Another week is all I need.

On the way back I ask one of the protesting students, "What is this all about?"

The student said, "We're protesting the value of our lives."

With death creeping up, students fight like they're actually still alive.

No one tells them that they're already dead.

Me? I'm not wasting my time.

2.

He's walking into the apartment like he's always done.

The first thing I say causes some surprise, "What is the value of your life?"

Every kill wipes away the previous kill, so he can't say that the killing affords him some value. It isn't the killing that holds value; it's the killer and what it stands for.

The killer as an object.

The killer as a voice.

But he's using his kill count, "I've got sixty-one under me and I'm still unharmed," and I'm shaking my head and denying it.

I'm telling him why it doesn't count.

He's pretending to be confused. That's bullshit. He knows exactly what I'm saying. He knows exactly what's going on. Just like he knows exactly what he's done. So pathetic, my pet, so very pathetic, and as a result I'm changing my mind.

I'm not going to tell him.

Instead, I'm going to move right on to begging. I'm going to make him beg for mercy.

He'll beg for everything to be the same again.

Oh yes, he will.

He's pacing up and down the hall while I sit casually at the kitchen table. He's not realizing how bad off he really is. I've decided to let it all fall apart on its own.

He complains how I disappeared, saying that I left him vulnerable, *at a loss,* and that he could have easily been caught, "The entire thing we talked about, Gentleman's legacy completely ruined and wasted."

He doesn't mention why I left. Maybe he doesn't know why I left. He doesn't know or care because to him it's not a contract, an agreement; it's something he's already won.

Me.

And he thinks he's won me rather than the other way around:

I won him.

There's no winning, though, and I have to say that he's not mine and I'm not his. Not this way. Not the way we've left ourselves. This is not what I've searched for and this is not what I've worked so hard to support.

He's accusing me of what's happened:

All the bodies unaccounted for.

All the kills lacking any real crime-spree, any motive, any meaning; he's blaming me for his shameless pickups.

He's even blaming me for the collapse of this once well-kept and pleasant apartment.

After he exhausts himself, he sits down, but his legs still twitch.

I don't need to do anything.

He's letting it all implode on himself.

Now he's trying to confide in me.

A glance in my direction. I give him nothing.

Even after all this, he still doesn't want to.

Doesn't want to confess.

Doesn't want to apologize.

I count the seconds.

He waits thirty-eight seconds before he breaks down, that familiar sobbing, and he's saying he didn't mean to do it. His excuse is desperation, about how he wasn't sure I was alive and/or on his side. He's rambling on and on about how he never doubted our agreement and never meant to break it. He thought it was already broken, the missing pieces being the impossibilities made possible (disappearing bodies, hidden voices, and something he calls the smell of seduction seeping through the apartment walls all day and night), and this was all his way of getting back at what didn't work and what didn't seem to fit.

He wants to be pardoned.

He wants me to forgive him.

I accept his apology; or rather, I say that I do.

He's telling me about all the things he will do to make it up for me:

—Clean the apartment until it looks new.

—Tell me about every single girl he's picked up.

—Let me choose who's next.

—He'll erase the document on his computer. He'll burn everything and erase everything until it's no more.

He can't come up with anything exact, but he says, falling to his knees, begging, "I'll do anything, I'll do anything!"

And that might be enough.

But the truth is, it'll never be enough. He's not my type.

I've seen his true self, the fight, and it's little more than a single stab, a little bloodletting. I'm looking for someone better; I'm looking for someone that'll show me how different and easy it is to be what I want them to be.

He begs and begs until he offers me enough to design a breakup, a perfect separation.

I tell him, "The first thing you can do is tell me about that night."

"What night?"

"The night we first met."

He's looking at me, as if trying to figure out whether my request is sincere or not.

But it is, and he's looking up at me and then back down at the ground.

He's nervous.

And he should be.

This isn't working.

We aren't meant to be together.

What's on your mind at this very moment?

1.

The day it stopped raining, I woke up early, way too early.

My pet, still in the cage I put him in, stared at me, wide-eyed and pathetic.

I pointed at him, shook my head.

No speaking.

We both knew. This was strange weather.

Not something that's happened before.

The city had subterranean ducts and tunnels, an intricate patchwork of city planning to make sure the flooding never rose above ankle-deep.

What would happen to all that water in a rain-free day?

The chirping of birds. Where did they come from?

The sunlight is something unexpected.

I enjoyed the feeling.

That feeling of something new and unexpected.

I told my pet, "This is what I want."

I let the mystery not make sense for as long as I could.

But in reality, it was only a Monday.

The rain started again while I was in the shower.

2.

He's not resisting, not at all. He's letting me take control of him.

My pet on loan, my pet with ulterior motives.

I tell him to fuck the mannequin I brought back from the clothing store while the one he picked up the night before, bound head to toe, suspended from the ceiling of the cage, watched.

And he did what I said.

To him the cameras were still rolling, but in reality I held onto a control device that turned them on and off at will. I recorded the best scenes—the scenes I had designed to pass before I put them into motion.

I'm a great observer. I know what it takes to see the scene through to its conclusion.

He says he's at sixty-one, but I'm telling him, "You're still at thirty-eight."

He grits his teeth.

I stare down at his flaccid penis, still dripping of semen, and he's following my gaze, eyes darting over to her, and he closes them, gasps, feels completely embarrassed.

"No one found them bound to their beds. Therefore, it's cold murder. No creativity. You wasted for the sake of wasting."

He agrees because he has to agree.

He's my pet.

"Stand up."

He's standing up.

"Walk over to her."

He's walking over to her.

"Spread her legs."

He's spreading her legs.

The condition down there, after more than a day bound,

is far from acceptable, but I force him to have a taste. He's resisting, but only a little.

It's enough of a reason for me to raise my voice, "Taste."

I do this while reclined in a chair I've placed in the way of the front door, if only to casually remind him that he'll never be able to leave.

"Really munch on it. Come on."

Her moan is not one of pleasure.

He's pulling back, gagging. He throws up a yellow stream.

"What does it taste like?"

He's trying to speak but more vomit spills from his mouth.

"Calm down and wipe your mouth. Now, tell me?"

And he tells me what it tastes like.

He says it tastes like spoiled and sour flesh.

"Thank you." I'm adding, "You could have told me before, you know. It didn't have to come to this. You could have told me but, no, you had to tease me. You had to disappoint me."

He's sickened, retching, but manages to say he's sorry.

I'm saying, "Oh, we're not even close yet."

He's got so much more to do.

So much more to get on camera.

And he still thinks I might let him go.

3.

But I'm not going to let him go.

It's obvious, right?

He's still in the apartment. I told him to stay in the cage. "Stay with her."

He's in time-out; he believes he's being punished and demeaned for his negligence.

My pet must learn.

My pet must learn if it wants to become a legacy.

Gentleman Killer has been off the media radar lately, hasn't he?

It has, and it's not my fault.

He must learn. He must learn that there's nothing he can do to make this any better.

It was the intention of making me patsy that finally did it.

I'm next door and watching as his legs begin to buckle, the needle-prick of impending numbness setting in. He can't sit down, leave the cage, or do anything until I return.

I placed the mannequin in his line-of-sight so that he has nothing else to look at but the very object that crystallized his shame.

Its vacant smile.

Its vigilance standing tall as he begins to lean on one leg and then the other; I'm seeing it on his face. The mannequin is really getting to him.

What's he going to do? I'm hitting record as he shouts into the mannequin's face and he's now going against my command, kicking at the mannequin's stomach.

He's shouting incoherent lines. This is perfect footage.

Really, it's great stuff.

He has an erection. He's pouncing on the mannequin and fucking it for a second time.

When he's done, he runs into the kitchen looking for something, but he doesn't find it so he goes into my room, my room (a big no-no) and comes back with a sledgehammer.

He bashes the mannequin into pieces and screams in its cracked face.

He's going back to her, bound and motionless.

By the way he reacts, it's a good guess that she's no longer proper.

The body is still warm.

He touches her neck, touches her there. He's hard again. He's fucking her, but I'm looking away in disgust. I'm not looking away because I'm disgusted with what he's doing.

No, I'm not.

Rather, I'm shocked that he'd be so impulsive, such an amateur with a dead body.

It's a rookie mistake. After he's finished, I enjoy the look of sheer terror when he realizes what he has just done.

I'm still recording. I won't bother to shut it off now.

He cuts her into pieces and then smaller pieces. It might just work except for the fact that he's slowing down, cautious yet uncertain of what he's going to do.

He hasn't a clue. I've been taking care of disposal all this time.

The killer has forgotten how to kill.

He's beginning to sob again and he's talking to himself, breathy shouts between pain-induced laughter:

"What have you done?"

Laughter. Why is he laughing?

"What have you done?"

I'm whispering my response, "What have you done?"

I consider returning to the apartment but I look outside.

"It's raining. . ." When is it not?

I look at the time.

There's a little bit of time before I have to be off. I could leave or edit.

I decide to work on editing the footage.

From the hole in the wall, I hear him talking to himself.

What happens when a killer is burnt-out?

This is what I'm trying to study.

4.

This no longer directly involves you. The longer you are here, the more you are in danger.

Screams and shout—the man in tears turns the doorknob but the door remains shut.

There are voices drowning out every other sound.

The audience hears the voices running together as intended. The contradictory nature of each line makes it seem like there's really only one voice.

It sounds like the woman's voice.

Get it? Get it? Of course the audience gets it.

It's the characters that don't. Not yet.

This leaves only the woman and her needs.

Her needs battled out via internal dialogue:

They can't see you.

I know they can't see me.

Doesn't that frighten you?

No, I think nothing of it.

Well you should. There's a reason it always rains.

I don't know.

The rain washes away the confusion.

It leaves only the mystery without its various solutions.

I know that by your bedside, you used to think you were safe.

I know that this all revolves around you.

What revolves—around who?

Around you.

People gravitate to you.

I don't gravitate towards them; they gravitate towards me.

What are you, the serial killer's muse?

Maybe I am.

I know what you are: You are a black hole.

I am Claire Wilkinson.

I know what I want and I know what I am. I have no need of explaining it. People turn to me because they're turned on by the mystery that surrounds—

Don't interrupt me.

Look at the walls, they're weeping.

Look at the ceilings, they're gone. I can see them watching us.

This has been nothing more than a big production.

Is this your idea of a sick joke?

There's a man and there's a woman.

Isn't every story about a man and a woman?

Most of the time.

You think you know someone, but no one ever really knew you.

You're a trick, a gimmick, something to wear until the flair wears out.

No need to break down the door, it wilts on its own.

Yeah, you get bored. The killer never satisfies you and so you look for someone else.

And what's wrong with that? Aren't we all looking for someone to get along with?

Most of us play for keeps.

I don't see your point. That's exactly what I'm doing. I'm looking for my type, the kind of guy in touch with his instincts and his emotions.

But I'm left somewhere between wanting to be forgotten and wanting to be found.

Well with Victor, he didn't have a chance.

He didn't know what he was getting into when he first agreed.

Have any of your exes?

I'd like to say my breakups are always mutual.

On a scale of 1 to 10 stars, 10 being the best, how would you rate me?

1.

When I walk through the front door, he resists.

Master is home. He should be catering to my every need—*take off my shoes, rub my feet, draw a bath, massage my back*—but he's not and maybe it's because he can't stand the sight of me. If that's the case, then everything's right on schedule.

I'm instructing him before I even see him, back still turned, taking off my raincoat. I take off all my clothes. "The pet treats the master with a nice warm meal and bath when returning home from a day in the rain."

Naked, his resistance crumbles.

He's torn between dinner and the bath. What to do, what to do?

I'm supposed to tell him what to do. Instead I sit him down at the kitchen table.

I bring him his laptop.

I open mine.

We face each other via webcam.

There's nothing more intimate than this.

It's here that I tell him the truth.

Everything he isn't. Everything he lacks as a killer.

I can see his face coiling, redder and redder, eyes bloodshot, the pain so unbearable, rooted in mental harm.

He needs to hear this.

He needs to break to pieces.

Sometimes words aren't enough. I'm telling him to stand up.

I'm telling him to put on some clothes.

He doesn't have any clean clothes so I'm lending him a dress. Even better. He closes his eyes as I force the dress over his head and tell him to remain in place.

I ask him, "What exactly are you trying to do?"

He doesn't say anything.

I ask him again, "What have you done with yourself?"

He lacks the confidence to speak about himself honestly and with poise.

"Did you ever wonder where the bodies might be going?

"Why did you agree to be with me if you had absolutely no feelings for me?"

"You obviously lack the ability to commit. Why didn't you tell me beforehand that you're better off dead? That you're already dead?"

"Hmm?"

I tell him not to look at me. He doesn't deserve to see me.

I sit back down at the table while he remains standing.

"Gentleman Killer—now that's something from *last month!*"

He's trying to speak but it's simply a mixture of stutters.

I'm rolling my eyes and telling him he smells.

It's not his usual smell.

He smells different. I don't like the smell.

I stand up and shove his nose under my armpit while saying, "This is how a woman smells." I shove his face between my legs, "This is what a woman tastes like. We're not candy. We're far better than fifty-one flavors."

I take him in both hands and I try to get him hard but he can't and I point and laugh.

He's not taking this well and, of course, it's meant to leave him as less.

Much less.

I push him to the kitchen floor, forcing him to lick the linoleum.

"You are my pet, remember that."

I see it in the way he can't move.

I see it in how the vein in his neck throbs. I see it in his flaccid state.

He loathes me.

And with that, the lesson is complete. We're finished.

I tell him to clean everything up while I go into my bedroom and sleep.

I warn him, "Fall asleep and you'll wish you were dead."

I enter my room and lock the door. I crawl through an area of space joining my apartment and the neighbor's; it's where I'll be, watching, as he breaks down for the final time.

I'll be watching and recording.

It's time to watch and learn something new.

2.

When he starts talking about me, I hit record.

He doesn't know my name, so he can only call me master. As master, I sound like a dictator unkind to his solitary citizen, a poor killer no longer capable of serializing his suffering.

It's perfect, really. He's pacing back and forth, while shouting to himself, frantic nonsense, a series of threats. These threats are directed at me.

"She's a killer of killers!"

But that's not true.

I haven't killed anyone.

My pets do all the killing. They use while I preserve the fight within.

It's better that way. I'm always wanting more and more and more and the fight within seems to gain strength. I'm not against the thought of killing though. People that have it in them to let out the fight turns me on, turns me sideways, horizontal, ready for everything.

He's calling me all kinds of things.

I don't mind.

Some of it is true.

A lot of it is misplaced, the lingering trace of fight escaping. It's the leftovers.

This and that.

This and that.

It's hot in there.

Must be. Look at him sweat.

I'm thinking this is going to end perfectly. I've never done this before—the perfect ending thing. Maybe not perfect for others but it's perfect for me.

I stop recording.

He's trying to find me.

My name. He's in my room. He's getting close. I quiet down, just to make sure he doesn't hear me on the other side of the wall.

He won't.

He doesn't.

He's on one of the laptops.

The laptop I left there purposefully because I bugged it.

Rigged to record.

I open up the remote-access software and record from within his feed.

His cursor drags all over the place. He's looking for something.

I let him find my name.

He's saying it, "Jessie McAndrews."

You and I both know it's not my name. It's simply one of the names attached to one of the phone numbers I used once and it's the name and number he's calling next.

I have the number set to call a program on my laptop.

I quickly mute my laptop before any sound can escape it.

He's on the other side of the wall. Really close, sitting on a chair of sex, the one I had used so many times before. He must smell my smell.

It must be overpowering.

Let it ring.

Let it go to voicemail.

I let him record a message that, as planned, works in both tone and message.

Oh, the desperation.

It's a message that'll be used as evidence like the rest of what I've edited and recorded.

He moves on to porn websites, indulging in the free samples, the pictures both tame and fetishized, but he can't seem to get hard enough. He keeps trying and I'm watching and waiting; he has to be on my laptop for more than my name and porn.

After he realizes porn won't arouse him fully, he moves on. I record his email address and password—*good to know*—and he's continuing, or at least trying to continue, what he already started.

Amusing to think he can get away with this.

His email address with his name attached.

Where's the benefit? Think about it for a second –

Let's say Victor Hent is an innocent man, shy, not as much as a single spark of fight inside. He's come across (somehow) information/evidence pertaining to the Gentleman Killer case. Why would he put himself in danger by going to the media?

Why would the media believe him?

He lacks the kind of material and evidence required to hook them in.

But he's not thinking straight—this much is obvious—and I'm going to let him finish writing that email.

Let it be known that he'll never receive any response.

Not even an auto-response.

He begins surfing around the various local club websites and university forums for information on tonight's events. Nothing to see here:

Just a killer without a spine returning to the only thing he knows how to do—

Play the pickup game.

No matter how demeaned and demoralized, he's still able to be that eligible player, effortlessly picking women up with overt tactics and unrelenting charm. So much for that.

Under the surface he's a killer with nothing left, not even a personal reason, for doing the things that he still thinks he's doing.

But I have him and everything that I need. What's missing is how I'll phrase it and what I'll do with myself later.

No time to think about that.

There's work to be done.

Everything went as planned.

Now I'm going for the perfect finish.

3.

He's going to think it's a gesture of forgiveness, and that maybe, just maybe, we'll be alright—he'll still have me and I'll have him—but these four women, effectively four, that I picked up under the pretenses of having access to recreational drugs and the willingness to explore bisexuality, they are already fading well when I return with them to the apartment.

The first thing they see is too much for them to bear.

They see him, nude, partly-erect, a shell of a killer with nothing else to do but attempt to masturbate. One or two laugh while the others gasp.

One walks closer, intrigued by the concept of an orgy.

I remain at the door.

I take off all my clothes.

The four women act drunk when in fact they're drowsy from the drugs.

I toy with them in the minutes before falling to the floor.

Seeing me naked, they want to get naked too. He's still gripping himself in disbelief, but more than willing to make do with being "made up," everything fitting back into place.

We trade smiles.

That's my way of saying, *We're okay, you and I. Master and pet.*

And he's getting hard, standing right up.

He treats the four women as a marathon meal.

One's naked and the other three are close when they seem to succumb to the drugs.

We both take turns dragging the bodies into the cage.

I strip all but one naked, leaving him one as a gesture of respect.

I grab him, pulling him, and I can feel it twitch in my

hand. I bring him close, an inch from our lips touching, and I say, "Do what you do best."

He's excited. He enters the cage.

I walk into my room, shouting back, "We've got to catch up!"

I hit record before missing anything of value.

He's tasting their bodies, one after the other.

He calls out to me. I hit stop, crawl back, and meet him in the cage.

"She tastes like cinnamon!"

He's stroking himself.

I'm replying, "I didn't think this was about sex."

He's smiling and for a moment he's the spitting image of that beloved gentleman I once met. He says, "Everything's about sex and everything's about violence."

He offers her to me.

I know what I taste like but I've never really thought about anyone else's.

I shrug, "Why not?"

I lean in for a taste.

I feel pressure on the back of my head. He's holding me there, "Eat it. Eat it!"

I bite down and taste copper more than cinnamon.

Her blood, I suck it in and keep it in my mouth. Breaking free, I spit in his eyes.

I'm scolding him, "What the hell was that?"

"That's how it's done."

The killer's way of showing me how it's done.

Some fight left in him, but I know better.

I'm nodding and he's tasting the second and third, "Cherry!" and "Chocolate," but I'm crawling back into the other room muttering to myself, "All women taste more or less the same."

Hitting record, he's beginning with the cutting but

then stops and calls over to me. I stop recording and, tired of crawling back and forth, I shout, "What?!"

He's trying to flatter me, "You really know how to pick 'em!"

"Yeah!"

And then I'm immediately adding, "Master knows best!"

On camera he doesn't seem to notice or suspect why I'm in my room rather than in the cage with him and the four of them. He doesn't because he's too busy indulging.

His actions are those of a new killer, one with no real understanding or reason from which he needs to taste, and cut, and prod, and tear, and feel.

He just does.

And in the process he expels the craving without considering the purpose.

I'm shocked to find that I care about his feelings.

I want him to enjoy them. I enjoy watching him enjoy their mutilation and chemical bath. Truly it's like he's never done this before. . .

This is why I'm finding it so arousing.

I start up my webcam but there's no one to broadcast to. I broadcast to myself.

I let the cameras record and capture his method.

When he's done, I'll get into my car with the dead bodies and I'll find beds for them. Just like I used to do. This is a night of nostalgia.

This is a night where my arousal is almost what it used to be.

He is satiated.

And so am I.

If everything ended with this night, this might be a happy ending.

Happy.

Where's the mystery in that?

4.

It all started with a little bloodletting.

Blood, saliva, and other bodily fluids are just that, fluids. It's because of what I know. What I know is that the liquid, that fluid, isn't yours. It isn't theirs. It's mine. It came from me. We leave smells, trails, and splatter wherever we go but here I am, telling a story with every moan. A moan, like a scream, tells so much more than simple words.

The blood that is mine binds to every surface. The floor at my feet I let collect small drying pools. I bring my foot up, dripping in it, and you ask me to suck my toe.

Does it feel right? Does it feel good?

Are you ready to commit to me?

Are you ready now?

I do things for you that no one else would. And you know what, it's because you're mine and I know more about your urges than you do.

Mark this as method.

Look at me from any angle.

Play with you.

I play with you.

It's what you and I do.

It's what we all do.

Some play harder than others.

The knife? It could always be sharper.

It doesn't matter that this is all imagined, speared by the digital data transfer.

What is your mystery?

I know you.

Like you claim you know me.

Do you like to party?

Do you play pet or master?

And who am I?

I hope you'll remember me and what I did for you.
I feel like we've done this before.
With a fleeting kiss, I bid you goodbye.

Their mystery is a cliffhanger ending.

1.

If there's an attraction, burn it to disc.

If there's a correlation, be sure to bring that disc with you.

I definitely did.

The day was a highlight because the rain didn't come down as hard as it usually did, as if giving me a three-hour window to make it on campus and inside the department building before it started up again.

One of the professors joking about the nonexistence of reality, "Whoever's controlling the rain must hate his job."

Another professor replies, "What makes you think it's a guy?"

Five of them and me. Six of us in total.

Today is the day.

I'm ready to defend my thesis.

I walk up to the front of the room and to the computer equipped with all the necessary lecture tools like projector and dimmer switches. I take out the disc and load up a video edited to play continuously, cast against the wall behind me, as I discuss my thesis, my hypothesis, and my results. There's only one starring character in this show and it's not me.

It's him.

And ten minutes into the fifteen-minute presentation all five are leaning forward, captivated, smiling widely.

At one point a professor exchanges an enthusiastic nod with the department head.

It does nothing to slow me down from delivering my presentation as I had intended.

I gain my applause and a round of acclaim.

But I feel nothing.

Not until I'm certain everything will fit together.

They've set up a little reception in the conference room

across from the class room.

The head of the department keeps me within arm's reach the entire time as if I'm his pet and he's making sure I don't run away.

When has he had an opportunity like this during his reign in the department?

I'm a lowly student but they see something that I've already seen. This isn't just research. For me, my presentation is not yet complete. They have an array of finger foods ranging from cheese and crackers all the way up to store-bought sushi.

When I reach for a piece of sushi, an assistant professor asks, "Why are you wearing latex gloves?"

I'm lying—as good at lying as I am at observing, "I was going to use it as an example, but I totally forgot to incorporate it into my presentation. I guess I was nervous."

Chuckle. Acceptable reply.

Everyone stands around and mingles while someone turns on the projector, letting a situational crime scene drama be the backdrop of the reception.

A joke or two regarding the show spreads throughout the faculty.

Two doctorate candidates make a game out of pointing out the seemingly endless possibilities made possible in the crime scene drama.

I'm enjoying a piece or two of sushi but I'll admit to being a little more concerned than normal. I try not to appear any different than normal as one professor after the next offers their congratulations about my successful thesis defense.

The show is interrupted by the laser sound effect and the title **Breaking News.**

A hush falls on the entire reception as the words **Gentleman Killer Arrested** scrolls across the screen for the first time.

The news report immediately settles in on how he was apprehended.

Video footage of his capture at one of the more popular night clubs in the city as two undercover women agents put into use the profile submitted to them by a young graduate student. It shouldn't be difficult to wonder who provided the information. It quickly dawns on everyone in attendance, and the next thing I know the department chair is shaking my hand after implying that I'd be a shoe-in as a doctorate candidate at the department.

I merely smiled and, as expected, everyone else filled in the gaps.

Like any mystery, their minds wrapped around what was missing.

They commented on my presentation and how I successfully created accurate footage of the killer tending to his victims. Set side by side the details provided by the local news, my information and profile is a perfect match.

They treat me like a genius.

It's only now that I can relax.

I half-listen to their compliments as I observe the news story, his face appearing on screen. I'm imagining how it happened. How it must have felt for him, everything seemingly coming together again, on the rise, only to have it implode on him, crushing him completely.

"Who did you get to act as killer? So amazing, so prescient, so candid!"

"I can't believe he let you film him erect like that!"

What was most obvious was how cutthroat it all was. Not two hours ago, a young man now sitting alone in front of the food, pretending to be really hungry, had been the department's pride and joy. In two hours he had the limelight stolen by none other than me.

His face cast against the projector screen, I don't feel anything for him either. I feel neither joy nor disgust. It is what it is. But what I'm beginning to realize now is what I have to do next. I can wait it out awhile, but I'll again feel the way I always feel. I'll begin to feel my independence, my single presence, and I'll feel that loneliness. When that happens, I have trouble living with only myself. I feel like coming apart, the fight spilling out and I, myself, becoming what I'd rather have with me instead.

I'll end up where I end up.

I'll have to start searching.

2.

The mystery is a man.

The mystery is a woman.

The mystery is you.

The mystery is me.

Do we tell stories or do we tell lies?

As long as there's the element of mystery, we're telling no story at all. We're revealing shades of reality, shades of ourselves.

After long, it becomes evident that the mystery consumes us all.

3.

"What are you doing here?"

"What do you mean? I visit all my ex-s."

"You had me arrested. . ."

"No, no. That's not true. You were faltering. It was only a matter of time before you fucked up your legacy."

"But. . ."

"Hey now, I'm just here to make sure there are no hard feelings—only physical harm!"

That look, I'll admit it's priceless. Worth the long drive to the state prison and the annoyance of having to see someone I'd otherwise never again desire to see.

"Oh come on. . .don't worry about it. What's prison but another cage? Hmm? You'll get used to it. You adapt well. Prison is good for the fight within. It keeps you sharp. Maybe you can start something in here!"

"Not with how everyone views me."

I'm shaking my head, "The rain will wash away whatever remains of their short attention spans. By month's end, they'll have forgotten. They'll be like. . .Gentleman who?"

But he's not buying it and he's obviously not supposed to. This is mostly for me. I'm beaming, really acting like I'm having the time of my life.

This is actually an important part —the follow-up—to make sure I show him what he lost. My support, my beauty, my poise. . .

And I don't stay for any longer than a minute. I'm standing up, "Well I should be off. I have a class I need to teach in an hour and a half!"

I don't say goodbye. I say nothing more. He's not saying or doing anything.

He's just watching me leave, leave for the last time. Down there he's shrinking into himself. He's barely a man, much less a killer.

My plan, by design, is fully complete.

4.

She stood at the bar not drinking, just watching, searching, keeping an eye on the situation of the club. She observes the manager of the club:

He reports earnings on an hourly basis.

He makes sure no clubbers get trampled.

He watches the alcohol intake because he doesn't trust his bartenders.

He keeps track of who's lost and who's found.

He knows his business is temporary. It'll transform when the current trend is over into a theme that caters to the next trend. And then the next trend after that—and so on.

He understands the only constant is the game.

The pickup game.

She observes, takes her time. If not tonight, there's tomorrow. The day after that. As long as it takes, but she's found him before. She's certain there are plenty more.

This is supposed to happen. Him? What about him? No. . .

There's no fight in him.

She moves through the crowd keeping distance like she's capable of her own invisible bubble of space. Though she's dancing, she isn't dancing with anybody. She isn't dancing in rhythm with the song.

She seems out of place.

People don't seem to notice her.

No one notices a naked woman on the dance floor.

There is no waiting for a song to end. The perpetual rave is treated with perpetual dance.

The setting of the pickup game might do well to be considered a ritual, one where the ultimate purposes is to possess someone else.

There is a man.

She notices him before he notices her.

He'll get as close to her as he can but he'll never reach her, not unless she thinks he's her type. She walks casually to the back lounge and through the door. Seconds later, a woman, fully clothed, passes through, closing the door so that no one can see what's back there. A bit of bright light pours out just before the door can be closed.

She returns and stands where she can be seen.

He spots her.

It's just another rainy night in a club that takes on a series of purposes depending on the person and who's picking up who.

This is the club where people are discovered and ruined in one night.

This is the club where you know you're being watched.

This is the club where danger is written right into the tagline.

This is the club where she gets to look exactly like she wants to look and she hopes to find him, someone just her type.

The man, she finds him interesting, the way he walks, his glow. . .

He has potential.

She waits until he tries to walk over before she interjects and makes first contact.

Hello, my name is. . .

Hello, my name is. . .

I've been called quite the intellectual, he says.

I'm often told I'm a mystery, she says in return.

She's thinking about it. It's obvious she knows what she wants, and who knows, maybe he really is it. It's early. Plenty of time.

It's not too late into the night to be found. He's hoping.

She can tell that he wants her.

But does she want him?

Is he her type?

She accepts a drink and accepts a seat at his table where they stare at each other, a silent exchange of eye contact and facial gesture. He looks away to the dance floor. She observes him as he watches them dance. He's holding back. There's something he wants to say, something he wants to do, but doesn't. He chooses not to because it's what he's always done. It's what he felt was right. She winks at him. There's a killer on every corner, even if they don't know inside if they have what it takes. She'll show them how.

On one condition, and one condition only. . .

The audience, the viewer.

0.

What did you think? I don't really know; it hasn't sunk in yet. I liked it. I hated it.

You hated it?

It was too indulgent. It didn't know if it wanted to be a thriller or a mystery.

I'd like to think a thriller is a mystery. I would have liked it if the mystery was solved. It was solved. Was it?

Was it really?

Yes!

Then what happened?

It was all in Claire's head!

No it wasn't!

Yeah, I don't believe it's all just a lie. Claire is real. The killer is real.

The real Mystery is who the next killer is and what that means for the rest of society. The fact that her type is something capable of being found in a crowd.

Was it really based on a true story?

Probably.

Which killer was it?

Umm. . .

So the Mystery is that Claire was insane and that she was an accomplice?

I guess.

What did you think about the voyeur element, how she started watching him from afar? I personally loved it. I thought it was cool how they made us sit back like we're watching some sock-puppet play.

Yeah, some of the cinematography techniques were interesting. Like the "false" technical difficulties in the middle.

Yeah but what about Claire?

What about Claire?

Is she supposed to be us, "normal sexually active socialite?"

That's kind of up for debate.

True.

Yeah. The entire thing was filmed to be two things at once.

Sometimes three.

Sometimes three. Yeah.

I like how they brought us into the film.

Well, as much as they could.

Right.

You know, the more I think about it, Claire might an undercover cop.

What the fuck?

That makes no sense at all!

Hey. . .shut up! I'm trying!

What we have to mention is Claire is a succubus. . .but for, like, killer instinct. Or something.

No, no—you're onto something there. It's like she knew ahead of time that the killer wouldn't meet her requirements.

Whatever they were.

Right, it's not really explained what her demands were expected to be satisfied.

That's how it works.

The whole film is about the fetish and the allure of the fetish.

Fetish?

What fetish?

Sex, violence, destruction—apathy—all that shit.

I don't think so.

Does anyone else agree with me?!

I agree that the film was about the possibility for the "impossible" to actually occur near us and through us, the so-called normal people. I also think that people can choose to be good people but sometimes they simply don't have control over the result of what they're doing. They could be helping someone, but that someone might actually be a killer and they simply didn't know it. Maybe we're all insane. . .

The film is trying to show how subjective everything is.

The whole "I see one thing. . .you see another."

You mean subjectivity.

Right.

What I don't get is the point of the sponsor.

Huh?

"Nothing Ever Happens."

Yeah, what was that?

Makes me want to look it up and find out.

I know.

Then the sponsor succeeded.

I want to know more.

What else is there to know?

Plenty.

I want to learn about the Gentleman Killer.

I want to try and find Claire downtown at the clubs.

Or at the parties.

Yeah, or at some party somewhere. . .

And maybe that was the point too.

Of the film?

Of course the film.

It wants to support the crimes of others.

Stop thinking so superficially. The film is entertainment. What's sick is that we considered this "entertainment." When it's BASED ON A TRUE STORY *it makes it even more interesting because we get to glimpse a fragment of the world that isn't next door.*

But the killer is everyone that has the capacity to kill.

Yup.

Huh? You didn't catch the fourth wall breaking cleverness?

Yeah I did but what are you trying to say?

The mystery is trivializing the "fiction" by making it "now" and "real" because we are watching. We are involved. We are able to note things and commentate. We're also characters of her mind.

That's cool.

I get it.

It falls back on subjectivity again.

Subjectivity is cool.

It's so loose and yet so tight.

Still, I'm not sure I liked the film.

What was it called anyway?

Umm. . .

They don't have any posters up.

That's strange.

Yeah it is.

No one remembers the film?

Really?

If we really wanted to, we could argue that it wasn't a film. . .

None of it was real. . .

Okay, now you guys are starting to freak me out. Can we just go get food now?

I want to get drunk, real drunk.

I want to talk more about the killer.

We will. When we're alone.

Let's get something to eat.

Something to drink.

Right.

Cheers!

All in all, I think it was a good film!

(whispers) Me too but everyone's a critic. Someone will like it and someone else will loathe it. That's the way it always is. Creating at all means putting yourself out there.

Everything's a date.

We're all trying to "pick up" and seduce people into befriending us.

Just like what Claire does.

And so it revolves.

Man, you could argue about pretty much anything. . .especially if it's meant to be argued.

Food.

Petty pleasures. . .

Is anyone else hungry. . .?!

We're leaving!!!

Okay, okay.

Good film.

Whatever it was called.

YOU'RE MINE.

Every body is found.

1.

I'm different. I'd be the first to confess to this.

But how different am I really, compared to you?

We all have the same needs. We all need a place to call home. We all need friends, financial sustainability, and hobbies. We all need to feel ambitious even if we can't be sure what to feel ambitious about, and there's no doubt that we will all grow older. We might feel wiser, when the complete opposite tends to be true. We grow comfortable, reticent, against the introduction of new pleasures and new bodies to our lives. We all need so much but we never find it all.

We need love like we need to stop lingering on why we haven't found love.

That's where we are different. That's not me. No way.

I've found what I've been looking for.

And if he'd ask, I have a dozen reasons why:

Reason 1—I love you.

Reason 2—I love you.

Reason 3—I love you.

Reason 4—I love you.

Reason 5—I love you.

Reason 5—I love you.

Reason 6—I love you.

Reason 7—I love you.

Reason 8—I love you.

Reason 9—I love you.

Reason 10—I love you.

Reason 11—I love you.

Reason 12—The biggest reason of all:

You love me more.

2.

There's always a need to keep ahead of the curve.

If it isn't one credential it's something else. They want me to prove to them that I can be a professor. They want me to prove to them that I can offer more to academia than the adjunct. I have taught classes. I have been a student for decades. But they want more. If it's not one thesis, it's another study. There's always one thing left thing to do.

That's why I'm here. I'm not teaching today—no—but they have me here early; the first round of classes haven't started yet and we're already in a stuffy meeting room in the Sociology/Criminology department. They cram us all in—the four tenured professors alongside every single adjunct and PHD candidate that are here for reasons that have to do with what I've already said. All here because we have reason to contest, reason to be something more than what we currently are.

I'm kind of slacking, and they should know that. I've graduated, yet I've found myself in another attention-seeking situation.

After graduate studies there are doctorate studies; after doctorate studies there's a reason to be something more. I'm here because they don't yet understand that I've already found that "something more."

When you've seen the limits of what a person can do, there's nothing better than turning the camera on what they couldn't manage to achieve.

Focus in on the lack of performance, the failure.

That's what I can't help but focus on. Lately I see people for what they are; I see people for all of their fallen actions, everything they've done that never stuck. Sitting in this room, I don't see a single person alive. They're all as drowsy inside as they are out.

Me, I'm red hot. I'm always searching.

I'm always looking, seeing the fight and finding nothing but more failure.

Failure walks faster than most would think; failure is a whole lot like fear: It gets people places but it doesn't give them the chance to see what's around them.

It gets you into meetings like these where you think it might end as something better. I know how this'll end.

Focus in on what's really going on here.

The meeting is between the department's trusted, meaning four of them, sitting with their coffees with their cellphones set down in front of them, and they are here to dispense with opportunities.

I have the opportunity but that's not why I'm here.

I'm here because of him. He's sitting in the far corner. He's sitting there stealing split-second glances in my direction. He knows me.

I know him. He was my teacher's assistant for a semester. Deviant Behavior 3051. He is here because he's about to fail out of grad school. I'm here as support.

You didn't think I was here because they got the better of me, did you? I spoke with one of the tenured professors the other day. I'm all about the opportunity she pitched to me. Independent study. And I get to choose who's on my team. And I get to choose what I'm studying. I am a young professor on the verge of becoming an assistant professor.

They like what I've done.

They like what I'm doing.

They don't really know what I'm doing but they like that they don't know what I'm doing. I have something to show them, something to show you, but that'll have to wait. Wait until the show starts, and the mystery unfolds.

I'm all about mystery, really. Way I'm sitting here, I'm a mystery to those that sit on the edge of their seats, worried about this meeting.

I'm sitting the way anyone might want to sit, but most importantly, I'm sitting as myself. I can only be who I am; the difference between me and anyone else has everything to do with taste. I've chosen Criminology while many of them have chosen LGBT studies; one of them is into Poverty and Homelessness. The point being that we all have our interests and those interests help identify our true tastes.

We've only got one thing in common, all of us including the tenured folk, we have been taught and we will have to be teachers too.

Quite a few have trouble grasping the concept; they spend their entire career barely able to overcome the anxiety of teaching and lecturing, much else actually making a connection with their students.

But not me.

I'm on that site, where students rate their professors, and I'm considered hot.

I've got a 4.5 rating. I lose half a point because I make them work. They might think Miss Wilkinson is nice, but they know. They know that they're only seeing what I want them to see. Something about how I teach, I always leave them wanting more.

The mystery is that any of them manage to pass my classes. I really make them work for it. I've taught enough to see that it isn't the grade that matters; it's how much they can get away with before losing touch with their own interests. I'm seeing that in tenured professors—they aren't interested in anything, not anymore. It's probably why they have so many meetings. Perhaps they believe in order.

I'm noticing that the room is like all other rooms in the department: Windowless.

You wouldn't know if it's storming outside or a beautiful day.

They get the meeting going and it's quickly a matter of "agenda."

Grant funding, PHD defenses, undergrad graduation, and special circumstances.

I factor in the last category. He factors into the third.

They don't bother with the third until the very end. Most of the time they talk openly about grant funding and how important it is for the department. The strength of the department. So they bore everyone else because they are all here for almost no reason at all. They ended up here because they ended up here. I've talked about this already.

Seems they fail to grasp the fact that this will only end in another scheduled meeting.

So I'm wrapping my mind around what I already know and what I need to still figure out. They need grant funding. I've been told that I need a few more credentials, which means nothing; it means the same as I need to prove to them that I can generate funding.

I'm in need of supporting the support structure that supports me.

Sure, it's like any other social circle; the needs outweigh the ideal. In the end, the circle needs strength and strength in academia is funding. Funding is given only when those involved are good enough to spark the interest that ironically would generate funding on its own. Money. That's what it is. They need money and the people that have money want to make sure their money is spent on what will generate interest in others.

Whenever I yawn, they look. They don't mention it, but they look.

He's been looking the entire time.

When I leave the room, he follows.

Every time I have something in mind, I leave it to the mystery. It isn't my problem if they are left in the dark.

They'll figure it out. No crime is without its consequence.

Every body is found.

The meeting ends before it really ever begins; very little determined and the extent of it is mostly empty promises and more filler for the discussion, the one that persists. Not sure what the discussion is, but that's what keeps everyone attending every meeting.

But I have that understanding.

He waits around the corner while I talk to one of the tenured professors. She is accommodating; I know what I am to them. I am an anomaly. I am someone that is unpredictable. I am also one of their best students. There hasn't been a mark on my record and there won't ever be anything but the letter "A" on any transcript.

So when I tell her, she is intrigued.

So when I tell her more, she gives me the go-ahead. No meeting needed.

So when I tell her I need two assistants, a budget, and a few weeks, she pauses, tells me to wait in her office, and quickly looks for the head of the department.

The guy that's always smoking outside.

The guy that always ties pornography into deviance.

Because she tells me to wait in her office, I tell him to wait in the hall where no one can see. I wait and he waits. This part is understood completely.

We haven't said anything to each other and I can already see it. He isn't like the others. There is fight in him. He can understand without needing things spelled out. Sitting in the office, waiting, I can't stop thinking about what he might look like on camera. What would he do if filmed? What might he think in the moments after his first victim?

She returns, sits down at her desk and exhales.

I already know everything she tells me.

She leans forward, hands crossed, "It's like out of the

movies. . ."

I already know what she'll say next.

"How much do you need?"

The mystery wraps itself around the problem and the fact that it might generate interest is enough to let it slide.

We exchange information. We talk about what it might be called. She writes it in as an independent study, but we both know that it's nothing at all like that.

What did I propose?

I told her I wanted to study incarcerated serial killers.

I told her I wanted to drive across the East coast, visiting well-documented serial killers, filming interviews, generating data in hopes of corroborating a theory I have been developing since undergrad. I told her that I would need two assistants. I told her that it could take a month. I told her it might be controversial and that some of the interrogations might border on dangerous.

I tell her, "I'm willing to subject myself to the dangers."

She likes that I said that.

I add, "We study alarming material. We should be willing to inspect fearlessly in order to better understand the culture of fear and fascination surrounding violent crime and deviance at large."

It's exactly what someone like her wants to hear.

It's ambition. It sounds earnest and it fits in perfectly with the department's never-ending funding problem.

What I don't tell her is the true nature of the mystery:

I know every single one of them. Many of them still think about me.

They had fight, but they met failure after long. Some of them wanted to never stop fighting, but their fear got the best of them. I supported them and helped build them into what they could have been. Most of them were killers with no concept before I met them.

Before I kissed them. Before I showed them how to kill.

But I come up with the idea of visiting them a second time only because I want to show them, want so very much to show them all, how well I've been doing.

I've done well for myself.

I've found someone and he is willing. Not even a single flicker of doubt.

I'm doing well. Want so very much to get to know him more.

There's a budget, there's a need for time. There's an interest, and I already know that there's love. I can see it in the way he abides.

He wants to be educated.

He wants to be around me.

After I showed him the possibilities, he was the first to say it.

I was the first to point the camera lens. I was the first to capture what he might be capable of. I can see the fight, bubbling to the surface, turning his cheeks red, his eyes wide, his chest clenched. He wants to dominate me, but only after I've dominated him.

He creates fantasies where he's the victim and I curate the fight as master. And he lets me; he doesn't resist. And he wants it now, not later. And he wants me. And he can see it in people too. And he wants what's best for us. And that means we will travel well, on the department's dime.

And we will film every part of it.

3.

Would-be threat or would-be love?

Before any of it can begin again, before the vehicles take to the interstate and drive the entirety of the coast, north to south, the audience needs to know what this is about. Though the mystery will keep them watching every week, the mystery needs an objective. The mystery needs your support.

The mystery mustn't be esoteric; it isn't an image being played out on its own, without commentary. The audience needs a lens of their own.

Watcher watches all. Cameras set to all angles of the stage.

The audience needs a voice of their own. The voice of the audience is the voice of the show.

Everything you do is in reaction to the audience's response.

There's a need to generate interest.

Send the footage to the editor. Send the edited footage to the focus groups.

The show's got to be just right to keep them from switching channels or worse, turning to an entirely different form of media. Panning shots across the possibilities of this show, and a running list of needs and wants, the audience's interest growing. Our interests, our needs to be entertained, must be satisfied.

Audience participation. Audience involvement.

A successful story is the same as a successful show.

Dynamically involved and diverse: Season after season the camera captures more of a world, a story that stretches as far beyond what is managed to be caught on camera.

Much more than a mere APPLAUSE prompt.

The audience involvement is everything and it creates all kinds of questions. The audience gets to choose! Yours to sculpt. Help master and pet. Become an active participant of the audience.

The mystery needs an audience. There's a need to ask, and there's a need to tell.

Watch them watch you. Ask them questions and they ask you. Fill in the blanks. Watch as the mystery continues to unfold:

Are they a perfect couple?

Who do they kill next?

Is it true that every body is found? No crime left incomplete?

What do you want to see?

Do you think the mystery will keep you interested for more than a few episodes, a few seasons?

How much of this is scripted versus unscripted? Reality or fiction?

How long will her assistants last before realizing the implication of each interrogation?

How long before her assistants understand that they have become accessories?

Do you think their cover stories are good enough to thwart the authorities?

What kind of vehicle will she drive? What about him?

What will she wear? What will he wear?

What is your definition of true love?

Are you male or female?

How old are you?

Have you ever met a killer?

Do you seek reality or does reality seek you? Have you ever auditioned to be a part of a story? Does your story have a happy ending or a sad ending? Ever forget the days of the week? Are you alarmed by violence proliferating through popular culture?

Does sex as a subject alarm you?

Might you be the first to reconsider censorship?

Do you find yourself seeking out fetishes, different forms of entertainment that are contrary to the norm? What is your definition of "norm?" How about "niche?"

How about "sex?" How about "violence?"

Where do you think sex crosses the line? What about violence?

Have you ever found yourself unsettled by graphic depictions of sex? Violence?

What is your definition of the perfect mate? Is she/he anything like her? Like him?

Do you find yourself uncomfortable if pieces of the story aren't fully explained?

If given the opportunity, would you be interested in involving yourself in the feature?

Might you like to be an extra?

Would you like to meet her? Or him?

These are the kinds of questions generated from a truly interested audience.

It's their show and you, as audience members, are watching. You get to watch as their lives unfold. You get to peer into the most intimate of areas. If you like, everything will be exposed; if you like, more will be explored. For the mystery to work, the audience must be attentive.

We want you to be involved. We need you to be every bit a part of the story as our starring cast. As the show begins, know that your vote really does count.

No one is passive. No one is a viewer.

They want to explore; you want to solve. We need your help, and just like you, we want to be entertained. Your continued interest keeps the cameras rolling.

Their interest in each other is equal to your interest in the mystery.

For the mystery to maintain our interest, we must become participants.

Every road leads somewhere.

Every exit leads elsewhere.

It's often a reason enough to take the first exit that comes along. Can't always worry about what can go wrong. Never know where it'll take you.

So let's drive.

Danger drives 95mph.

1.

I drove through the night.

We drive in separate cars. We wear disguises.

We leave behind unmarked videotapes that tell of not the basics, but what we've been doing. We don't want to miss a moment. He needs to keep going, keep following me. Following us.

He's in training and I'm his trainer. Master and pet, we are loves firmly met.

The assistants look like me and I look like them. But I'm the only one that can really be Claire. Anyone else couldn't tell, so what if I changed my hair color? I'm a redhead for the sake of keeping this clandestine. The one that's blonde is naturally blonde and the brunette, I had her dye her hair from what was a dirty blonde to nearly jet-black. Because it's part of the study.

We drive the coast, the study in full effect.

No searching, we've found each destination, marked on a map.

I know where we're going, and he lets me figure out where that is. I imagine, and he does exactly as I've imagined. My pet, master misses you.

The camera keeps us from ever being lonely.

2.

Close shot on what looks like a mirror but is soon understood to be the chrome rear bumper of a red convertible speeding down the left lane of an unknown interstate, midday, roof pulled back. The mirror image could be the fact that you see three of the same: same jean shorts, same black tank top, same pair of sunglasses. Mirrored, x3. Same motions, same giggles, same mannerisms.

We've practiced this. They're both graduate students assigned to my study.

Any passing vehicle will take notice at the fact that we are dressed for ulterior motives; they look a whole lot like me at first glance. This is appropriate. I've wanted it to be like this because, well, you wouldn't be able to tell the difference. But he could.

He would spot me in a second.

The rest, they'll see seduction wear thin as we do exactly what's needed to keep them looking without really looking. See us speeding down the interstate, we're instantly typecast as attractive. I do this because I don't want anyone thinking anything but the lesser of possibilities.

We're young and we want to party. We're searching for a party. How's that for the typical sociological stereotype? Attractive female college students seeking an escape from their studies during the small break we've been afforded?

Sounds like a horror flick in the making.

A reality television show.

It's not a coincidence. And the cameras are always rolling. I collect data via the constantly filmed interstate. If it's not the road, it's my assistants. If it's not my assistants, it's the possibilities of where we'll go next.

I'm the one that does the driving, not them. Not unless I tell them to, and then they'll do the driving. Only because I said so. Well understood. They seem to understand what's about to happen.

We're visiting incarcerated serial killers.

We're trying to gather data on a culture of fear.

I'm trying my best to make my pet everything he can be. He's on the verge, ready.

I'm seeing him in my rearview mirror, old brown coupe carrying his own cover story. His story is for him to play out, and so is mine. We have each other; we don't need to dabble in victim and fantasies. Fantasies are perfect cover stories. No one thinks a fantasy is real.

Fantasies are imagined; they are a form of highway hypnosis.

He drives slower—according to plan.

I'm driving faster. I'll get there first.

Exit 94 is a few miles ahead. The red convertible takes to the momentum like I've become taken with his ability to be exactly what I want him to be. He is my fantasy reborn true.

My assistants giggle.

"That's not good enough," I tell them.

It sounds fake.

They apologize.

"Try again," I'm saying.

Second attempt isn't any better than the first.

"Listen," I'm already lecturing this early on.

Between giggles, I look at him in his coupe. Look in the rearview mirror, imagining.

Imagining everything that is going to happen versus everything that might give me some surprise. The possibilities turn me on. I giggle for real.

This is exactly how it's meant to be.

They try, and it's better.

"Good, but keep working on it," I'm saying while

changing lanes.

Cut off this one car going slower, get in front of another; the assistants grip onto their seats. Watch how they tense up. I'm telling them to relax.

"You both are participating in something important."

What they deem important has nothing to do with me. They assume what maybe you assume, that the importance is in the study, when the real importance is in how him and I will get to know each other. With each expression I get more and more excited.

Soon we will have nothing but footage between the both of us examining every single inch, every single action. And I will watch the footage over and over again.

Data recorded of our love.

I'm starting to get excited so I force them to do something for the camera.

They are caught off-guard by it. I dangle the concept of prestige, a famous and controversial sociological study (which means instant career success for everyone involved), and it shuts them up.

"Act more like me," I'm telling them.

So they do it.

And for the sake of the camera lens, I turn it away so that you only hear them.

Fantasy. Taste. Lick. Moan.

Meanwhile I watch him in the rearview mirror.

I'm changing lanes and he's changing lanes. He is hunter and victim, love and killer, all rolled into one. Hearing them and seeing him gets me more excited.

I'm driving faster.

One car keeps up. A man, thirties, caught a glimpse of my assistants.

He caught a glimpse of me. Smile. And the camera captures him too. He looks, he doesn't know what to expect so I fill in the blanks, just enough to show something. Just enough to get him even more interested before moving on.

The interstate is paved in fantasies.

I'm doing my part. As payment, we all get off on the touch and the feel of each fantasy.

They finish and I tell them, "You'll get used to each other's taste."

This is recorded too.

One of them asks and I tell them, "Yes."

It'll all be added as data.

Blushing now, the brunette.

"We've all got personalities," I'm saying, "so we need to show them off."

Listen up, assistants. Listen well: "You didn't think this was going to be anything you expected, did you?"

The answer is: Of course not.

I'm pressing down harder on the gas. They will learn; once they get a real glimpse, the fantasy will become real. And then they'll become every bit a part of this as anyone else watching.

They use their real names.

I'm shouting to them, "Your name is Claire!"

I thought I told them this already, but apparently assistants cannot be bothered by the importance of uncut footage. Everything, everything, is caught on film.

I'm forced to say it again. I change lanes and say it a second time.

Claire.

Say it.

"Claire."

Your name is Claire.

"My name is Claire."

Blonde hesitates. Say it!

"My name is Claire."

I'm eyeing him again. I'm telling them, "You're supposed to act this way. I'm the only one that knows where this is going."

It's about now that I start telling them how we'll be doing this. Process is 99% of it. Keeping to the process is the other 1%. How it'll work, listen to me. Keep the camera on the road, on the subject—this is data. I tell them about who's first.

Then I'm going on and on about ethics and other things that a social scientist is supposed to know. I'm their teacher, in effect, and as such they must be everything I am, but less.

Just enough to maintain the cover story.

Just enough to maintain my needs.

"Understand?"

Their answer is your answer. It's the answer I want. People want what isn't there; people imagine exactly what is implied, but made more their own if you let them. And I will let them. I do this by being as much on camera as the other two. The redhead needs to play victim too.

The redhead on camera is everything I'd expect you to see. And more.

I'm exiting via Exit 94. A service area for the tired, a place for me to touch him. I'm turning and he's turning. I'm turned on and he's all about doing what I need him to do to make this exactly what I want. And he's perfect because he knows without having to be told. He parks away from my convertible. He wanders around with his camera, talking to it, playing naïve. He pretends he's clueless as I wait for him in a bathroom stall. And with cameras turned to the assistants, to the rest of the Thomas Edison Service Area, we are two bodies crammed into a stall made for one.

Footage pans across the prototypical:

Think of it as stock footage. This is where the title

would get its due, placed prominently on the pulled back shot of the interstate.

In the stall, we are. And you can only add it to the mystery. We'll leave wearing scars that we won't hide under any bandage. On camera, you can see them. If you look where I want you to look, you'll see them. Get close enough you can taste it. I'm leaving with a tape; he's leaving with one too.

In any mirror he is everything I've expected him to be. Soon, there'll be nothing left of the mystery to hide. An important fact, so hot:

He's never killed before.

I'm touching myself, and I can't help it.

Fantasy has gotten the best of me as I pull the convertible into drive.

3.

No matter what his gimmick will be, a first kill is the sincerest of all possible expressions.

His first kill, he'll dedicate it to me.

Between you and me, I'll go right out and say it. It's my confession, and you, the audience, get to hear it. You wouldn't tell him, would you?

I'm having trouble imagining that he'll meet my expectations.

Can't wrap my mind around how he'll deal with the sodomy, with the knife and the orifices.

My ex is one of the most intense; he really tried to please me. He only got going the moment he met me. And then he took the name—The Demon—to heart. He idolized libertinism. He sought enough to meet his own expectations, which were compounded with my own.

He wanted me to accept him.

But he couldn't be pet. Wouldn't ever let me be the master I wanted to be.

I can't wrap my mind around how he'll be able to so effortlessly take The Demon's life.

His first might be my worst.

The Demon tried to take my life. It was when I finally decided if they couldn't then I wouldn't hold back. I would stop trying. I'd let the data go; I'd let it swim the channels, ending up with the authorities.

The Demon was one of my first, and so too will it be for him.

But can I tell you, will you keep it a secret?

You will, right?

My expectation has made it so that I'm seeing the kill for what I want it to be; I'm setting myself up to be disappointed. How might he be able to kill a man that has killed nearly 120? A man who idolized the libertine lifestyle—a man that turned his sadism into the gimmick I created for him?

I see it the only way I can see it—in frame with missing details.

I don't know how he'll wield the knife. I don't know how he'll use what's available to him.

I don't know how much of a sadist he'll be, but the way I see it, the way I want to see it caught on film, is the perfect form, the sodomy, the coprophagia; everything that the Demon used on his victims matched to the way he forces Demon to rest. I see it.

Here's how he'd do it:

Waiting in the showers, waiting for the guard to bring The Demon to him, paid off and paid well, he has, at his disposal—close up shots on a knife, a second knife bladed (used for gouging), gloves, bleach, a plate, and a few bottles of miscellaneous liquids—everything he might need to make this possible.

Guard forces a shackled Demon into the showers.

Guard turns on the showers, not enough to cover future terror but at least something to dissuade. In my mind, the rest of the cellblock hears everything. They hear everything and they're happy. Something that should have happened already. In my version, The Demon doesn't interact well with the rest of the inmates. Given what he's done to his victims, the only thing they'd want of him is to kill himself.

Once the showers are on, it's action.

See, this is where I'm having trouble explaining it.

It's perfectly on point: he forces the Demon to take off his wet clothes. Forces the Demon to kneel down.

Forces the Demon to open his mouth. Forces the demon to eat the knife.

Forces the knife deep into his throat, holds it a second, and then pulls out.

Blood in pools at Demon's knees. I. . .

And then I. . .can see it, everything releases. The smell, it's horrible.

He's not stopping though. In my version he acts like this is his last kill rather than his first.

He picks up the excrement and forces Demon to eat it. Demon chokes and bleeds more.

The knife wouldn't be cleaned; no time. He'd have to go at it with the gouging knife, just enough to keep him alive. And then, and then. . .

Does any of this make any sense?

I can barely put it into words. But my biggest worry is that when I see the tape, he will have merely gone through with the kill. It takes a practiced killer to withstand the complete humiliation of a victim.

It takes a killer that is willing to be a victim, to understand how it feels, to be humiliated, in order to be the better killer. I will show him; I know I will. He's mine and he knows it.

But I want the best from him, and my confession is that I have begun to doubt it.

You all are more like me than you're probably willing to admit. You probably can't believe it.

Can't believe he'd even begin to do away with it like this, but then we're sort of seeing it with similar disdain.

No, we aren't that different are we?

Well, keep my confession.

My pet has a whole lot to learn.

I hope his debut is worth stomaching.

We can't hide what the camera sees.

4.

Cut to my first words. Not hello, but instead, "Long time, no see."

Oh how informalities make it sound so much worse. Makes you feel good while it makes the situation awkward. For him, it's worse. The Demon hasn't aged well.

I recall his meekness being more believable. I'm remembering brown eyes bold enough to break a victim's spirits. His eyes might as well be grey. In the fluorescent light of the room, I'm breaking what the Demon understood as my code.

I only visit them once.

No doubt he's suspected me of more. I can't be lonely forever; he didn't think that I'd end up with nothing, did he?

There are better killers than you.

He'd deny it, but no one's watching to see an old fling caught up on who's doing better than who. I've already made it obvious: I'm doing just fine and according to the guard I spoke to and slipped a couple hundred for safekeeping, Demon's duc for the end in a month or less.

"About damn time," I said with a wink.

Doesn't take much to get them on your side when the victim's a killer that got caught. Nothing remarkable about a killer that couldn't keep the gimmick straight.

"How are you?" I'm holding back laughter.

Insert a shot of the Demon when they kicked down my apartment door. Dusting for fingerprints only resulted in more evidence stacked against him.

"Why are you here?"

"Well that's not very imaginative, huh? We used to talk in code."

I'm still talking in code but he doesn't have the codex.

Silence isn't awkward for anyone but him. By the way

he moves his hands, I see how he's grown used to the handcuffs. He watches me. I look into the camera, the camera he hadn't noticed, until I made it clear that he was being filmed. He has no choice; like the others he will be filmed because in order for this to work, you need to see what I see.

The data must be analyzed.

The data must be recorded.

Skip over expected resistance; cut to where I'm getting right down to it, mostly because I don't need to talk to them for any more than I need to get the questions out:

Number one, **"How many fan letters have you received?"**

He's fumbling so I get one of the assistants to walk in and hold up cue cards.

He'll read them. They'll all read them.

He's seeing double and now he's stuttering, "Hu-hun-hundreds."

"I need a number. Feel free to estimate." I have blonde Claire hold the cue card up higher.

He says exactly what it says, "Lots of them are scholars mostly. They're factoring me into their research on sadism and the libertines. Lots of long essays studying the result of my victims."

He almost messes it up, looking down at his dirty palms, but finishes more or less how I'd like it to be, "Something like a thousand letters and calls, stuff like that."

Good enough.

On to number two.

"Have you been able to accept what you've done?"

He's saying yes but I'm getting the brunette Claire to make him take it back. She's under the table, pulling at his ankle cuffs, cutting into his skin.

My assistants, they've been told that this will be different. Despite suspicion, they agreed based on the promise of the study. They view it all as potential success.

If it means treating someone inhuman like scum, so be it. If it means becoming someone unrestrained for the camera, so be it. So be it.

Now answer.

He's going to answer.

And when he does, I have her tighten the cuffs so that he can concentrate on nothing more than the pain. He's going to say what I want him to say. He's going to concentrate on me.

He says, "No," and via the cue card, he delivers the line, "I think about what I could still be doing, if I could have finished what I started."

That's perfect for the audience.

Perfect for the camera. Perfect for me.

Number three, **"What are you afraid of?"**

The recycled answer, the one I want from every single one of my exes, is what he says to the camera; it's what he says and it'll be the line you get from every single one of them.

It's what's bleeped out, all part of the mystery. He says a name. A name like any other; it's what I want to hear, what I need to hear, before it happens. Before my pet goes through with it.

And then I have the two assistants leave. I have the camera close up on his face; I make it so that he's paying attention to me, the pain gone, the pressure freed.

I have one last question and I'm wanting him to look into my eyes as he answers truthfully, honestly; I'm giving him no cues.

Number four, **"Why haven't you tried to kill yourself yet?"**

This is where "the Demon," in all his cultural infamy, dies:

He says it, and I couldn't have written it better myself.

"I've tried. I've tried but I can't go through with it."

Those are tears, what I'm seeing running down his face. What else can you say, watching what was once feared now shudder and cry? That's what you call disappointment, a taboo crossed and filmed. Those are real. They signal the end of this interview.

It's the end of my part but it's only the beginning of the experience. The real experience, he's up. And I can hardly wait to see what he might do.

The Demon will die as his victims died: defiled and completely alone.

Data recorded.

A fantasy is worth pursuing.

1.

I held the tape in my hand, told the assistants to get in the trunk, and hit play.

After the first minute, I couldn't help myself.

2.

I watched. I'm watching. I'm being watched.

Every frame tells more of the story. In every frame, there he was, or rather, there is where he'd be. And you'd see too, what I see.

I'm seeing him, not even a gimmick or a name to call his own, but I see him acting like he's been at this for a dozen kills. A dozen kills to his name. I might consider that he remains nameless. Nameless—because we haven't discussed names.

I've yet to tell him what he could be.

This is his first and his first is mine.

He's mine and he's showing me everything.

Nothing held back. He turns on the showers, just like I expected. He waits in the shadows, exactly as a killer should. You want this. You want this bad. But you wait, wait for the guard's cue. Wait for the Demon's due. Matter-of-factly, you are a man waiting to do something you've never done before. My pet, my perfect little pet, you are young but the way you stand, the way you are in no way nervous, the way you remain in the shadows, not a single error in both filming and fighting back nerves, you are everything I had hoped for.

He's filming the Demon led to the showers.

Demon doesn't understand.

Or Demon knows well what's about to happen.

No one else here, Demon notices.

He's adjusting the angle, zooming in close on Demon's face.

I see it in his eyes. . .That's worry. Oh, I can hardly contain myself.

And then the guard is cuffing Demon in place. Guard doesn't look back. Guard was paid well. The camera moves;

my pet is moving. He's doing exactly what he's supposed to.

New killers usually lose touch with the fight; they stutter and stumble. Looking into the eyes of their victim, they lose their nerve. They become careless. They usually want something but not the laceration or gunshot. They'd rather lie to themselves than go through with it.

But not him. He's made this film just for me.

And I'm sharing it with you.

Watch, are you really watching? Our mutual mystery is unfolding.

There's the knife, the liquids, the gloves.

There's the fear, the fear so much better when it's the fear of a killer.

Demon gets down to his knees. I can't quite hear my pet's voice over the sound of the shower, but I can hear Demon's guttural shrieks as he uses the knife to dislodge Demon's left eye.

Held in his other hand, I see that he's carrying a book. The book is damp and beginning to unfurl. But my pet reads, and he reads in such a way that I can hear only his words, the lines ringing out the words of a true libertine. He reads with poise as if it is where he's getting his inspiration.

And then I see it: He's doing what Demon's never done before.

My pet mimics Demon's method. Every step of the way, he inserts the blade and cuts. He forces Demon eat what Demon's made all hundred or so of his own eat before being completely disemboweled. Demon anticipates what comes next as my pet removes an ear.

Demon never did that. Then he's moving the camera under the shower, no regard for whether or not the camera will survive, in order to get the following shot:

The gouging knife hooks the side of Demon's mouth.

Blood pouring from the fresh wound looks dark red right before it joins the downpour of water.

He's capturing that very moment. He's filmed this for me.

Every frame was his to choose, his expression, his sole means of showing how much I mean to him. He's reading and being the true representation of the book's myriad of possibilities.

The camera continues filming, and I imagine he's used a waterproofing shell, something a young killer wouldn't think of until it was too late.

He asks Demon, close up shot, "Are you a cockmonger?"

He's tearing out pages from the book and placing them on top of Demon's head. The pages clump together, sagging and sticking to the shape of Demon's head like fresh biopsied skin.

He runs through a number of qualifications.

"If you aren't a cockmonger, are you one of the servants?"

Page torn.

"How about one of the boys?"

The camera pans down to see that he's stored the knife in Demon's side for safe keeping. It remains lodged in what I imagine is a punctured kidney.

"How inventive," I'm catching myself say aloud.

"One of the girls?"

Demon doesn't have the means of saying anything other than sounds.

Another page torn.

My pet took the tongue out between shots. The blood from Demon's mouth pools and dribbles down the sides of his mouth handsomely. I'd imagine it a nice addition to what Demon never did. He's aiming the camera lens on something else, something I hadn't been shown yet.

He has removed Demon's genitals and reinserted them up Demon's anus.

I gasp—amazed at his creativity.

My pet is performing to the full extent that Demon never could.

"You fancy yourself one of the Lords of Sodom?"

He rests the camera on Demon's shoulder. Watch as he wanders over to the chemicals. Three jugs, and I can imagine the sound of the screams long before they finally pour through the tiny camera speaker. He picks back up the camera.

The tape skips over the next few frames but I can still hear.

"Then let me wash the shit from your skin. Let me make sure you look the part."

He pours a pink chemical.

I'm imagining the smell, licking my lips.

My pet kicks Demon in the chest. Given that he's in a kneeling position, the impact causes him to fall onto his back.

"Would the Marquis share the pleasure with you?"

He's rolling Demon onto his stomach, severed penis removed and sliced to pieces. He's throwing them into a plastic container where they will be dissolved.

"The pleasure is all mine."

Knife is dislodged from Demon's side. He's barebacked with the knife.

He's careful not to show his face on camera.

That's not what my pet would do; it wouldn't fit what Demon would do. And I'm finding myself completely satisfied and even a bit compelled by his accuracy. His reenactment becomes true revision. My pet fixes the errors of another. Demon is written off with his inaccuracies. He is dissolved like his genitals are dissolved in the container.

He's reading more from the book, but the book has come to pieces, and there's little left but a sliver and the damp glue mush of a spine. He's placing the leftovers of the book like a ball-gag in Demon's mouth.

"You should study your influences before joining their side."

The white of my knuckles show the strength of my grip.

Demon has one thing left to do:

Die.

My pet helps, using a clear liquid poured into the open cavity of Demon's groin.

With it over, he's ripe with the adrenaline release but he doesn't let the quality of the footage falter. I'm witness to a long ornate panning shot across the entirety of my pet's first kill.

The showers are shut off.

The imagined chemical stench overlaps the smell of stomach acids and partially digested food, excrement and other bodily fluids.

Nothing seems to faze him.

Soon he's dripping in something other than tap water.

He cleans up and keeps each frame perfect:

As if I had been there as this happened.

With him. Him—who can only be mine.

The tape skips and then stops.

Duration over. This isn't data; this is the mark of my pet.

He is no longer the virginal menace. He has tried and exceeded my expectations.

I cannot help myself. I drive a few miles with the assistants in the trunk.

The sun is clear and shining, not a glimmer of rain in sight.

3.

Maybe you didn't watch the entire tape, or maybe you did.

So you're a viewer now. You are privy to information that you couldn't have known about until watching more than one episode.

You are involved. Aware of the ongoing mystery.

More so you are enthralled, curious, interested.

You are also slightly ashamed by the level of graphic content. Somewhere you started to reconsider your first impression. You might not fully understand what is about to occur, but you've got an inkling that it has already happened. What you are seeing isn't always live.

It may be that the woman on camera has been filmed in a different capacity.

It may be that the woman on camera is shown in a certain light that might not be straight-on.

She might be partially abstracted, and him, who has quickly become the reason anyone is watching, feels more like an extension of the woman's initiative, her needs, rather than someone you, the audience member, can fully relate to. But then there's that concern:

Why are you relating to this at all?

It is obscene; it is full of gore and violence.

Sexual undertones quickly expand into the literal.

And this has only just begun, that much is clear.

Why do you watch?

And why does the woman seem to be holding back, made half of what she really is?

You are full of questions, and for that reason alone the mystery becomes increasingly complex.

You must see more.

You want full-frontal.

The show will at least give you that. It will peel back the skin and show you how foreign the human body can seem. A nightmare is unfolding as a man and a woman begin their affair.

The road is their cradle; the camera is their affection.

With each tape there will be a kill. With each kill there will be more to who he is.

Gimmicks are first impressions.

The reality of your interest is in your cooperation.

Your attendance.

You are given a look, and, upon invested in the mystery, the show becomes a part of your life.

She becomes a part of your life. He becomes key to every single potential concept of crime and deviant behavior. The longer you watch, the more you will come to see her as part of your life.

You then shudder to think what it must be on the flipside.

She sees you as part of her life.

She could be anywhere, and anyone. She just might be coming for you.

He is quick to follow her every command. . .

4.

So, you know, given the way the world works, I still manage to be surprised.

I'm surprised by his behavior and how he exhibits no hesitance, no resistance either.

Against my own rules, I call him. And this is what we say to each other.

"I love you," as I'm letting the assistants out of the trunk.

"I love you," as he's pulling out of a parking space, heading back to the interstate, headed for his second.

"I love you," as I'm back behind the wheel, the assistants barely able to hold back tears.

"I love you," as it's clear to him that I'm proud of my pet. Master is proud.

"I love you," as he makes it clear that he did it for me. He'll always do it for me.

And again, speeding down the interstate, "I love you," because I'm beginning to see the possibilities. Master just might know what you are now capable of.

"I love you," as the assistants begin complaining.

"I love you," as he's coming down from the adrenaline rush. My pet quick to demand more. And my, oh my, do I want to see him.

"I love you," as he's back on the interstate, the name clear, the plan never more clear than now, sight and sound vivid, bold, and impossible to enjoy.

My pet can't enjoy anything I haven't allowed him to enjoy.

He wants more, craves more.

And I crave him.

"I love you" are the words that summarize our actions.

We need nothing else.

This will be his training.

He will be fully mine and, in turn, he will have his legacy.

The road twists and turns but he'll be around every corner.

I'll be underneath it all, the one controlling the puppet, the one curating the shape and size of the mystery. "I love you," as he and I are back into position.

I keep him on the line.

I demand that he does the same.

He won't refuse me.

My pet.

5.

What am I picturing?

Is it possible for me to fully capture what I know he'll be?

I'm picturing a name that won't yet be a name, not until the media begins noting his work. He will be notable before noteworthy, a slight mention before he becomes a movement, something everyone can't stop thinking or talking about.

I'm picturing the fact that he kills the already killed, the ones that are less human as they are the very reason prisons still exist, will be the reason why our plans will go off without much of a hitch.

I'm picturing his method, and how it takes into question their method.

I'm picturing how each kill is exactly how my ex killed.

I'm picturing my perfect little pet having no problem with that.

I'm picturing yet again a lack of policing, a fumble, the authorities three days behind at their best.

I'm picturing the way he'll appear to the general public.

I'm picturing something pleasing. They will cheer for him more than most.

I'm picturing a sort of image—one they'll use mostly because so many have killed using gimmick, have tried to become as much a menace as they were practitioners of the fight we all hide within.

I'm picturing they'll cut him slack.

I'm picturing a social media presence wherein thousands upon thousands praise his work and quickly spread buzz like wildfire.

I'm picturing real fires, burning down prisons and whole towns, roads and all.

I'm picturing my perfect pet, and he is perfect. He is

all I see.

I'm picturing the end of this interstate, down south, where no one can see.

I'm picturing something different. I'm picturing a nice twist.

I'm picturing the entire mystery becoming an ongoing hot topic.

I'm picturing how easy, how pleasing to the touch, this will be.

I'm picturing full arousal when his work is viewed as a whole.

I'm picturing debate, discussion, and extensive studies on his method when it's all said and done. I'm picturing a subgenre, a new category, an entire estate based on the intellectual property of his namesake. I'm picturing the past as a sort of roadmap, the one that I'm currently navigating.

And most of all, I'm picturing what I'll have him do to me; what I'll do to him when a mystery meets its natural conclusion.

Most of all, I'm picturing its would-be solution.

Master and pet—there will be no doubt between the both of us.

But you, you'll have to ask.

And because you'll ask, I'm picturing the kind of ending you'll want, and it's an ending that's a bit too predictable, and too obvious. You really don't think it'll be that simple, right?

I'm picturing you, with blood on your tongue.

I'm picturing an entire audience watching.

An entire audience waiting and reacting.

An entire audience spreading the word.

My pet, my perfect pet, your potential nearly gets the best of me.

I can hardly hold back, and by the time I reach the next

mile-marker, I will have determined that there's no reason for holding back.

I'm picturing how I'll taste you when you're once again in my presence.

I'm picturing exactly what you'll be, my pet, everything they were, but better.

And I'll teach you. On one condition, and one condition only.

6.

We have reason to meet in person. You don't ask why. You don't ask why.

Him and I, we meet because I want to meet.

We aren't made to meet at every juncture; it will slow us down, but a heartbeat is bound to quicken its pace when something happens, and I mean something really happens.

I've made the rules, and a concession is in order.

My petty assistants have been startled; they have begun to understand the true nature of this study. I'm a social scientist willing to record the data true to its source.

I take the next exit, driving down a side road full of quiet two-story homes.

In minutes his coupe is behind me.

In the minute after he parks the car, I am behind him.

"I love you," I'm saying.

He's saying the same thing.

They are watching, but he knows which one is me.

They are shocked but still watching. Think of the perfect shot and film it as you'd like. It's what they capture, blonde then brunette passing the camera back and forth as I get him to do as I say. This happens, they might say.

We're only saying what is destined to make any sense.

"I love you."

A pet loves his master.

A master must in turn learn to love her pet.

I can still smell the chemicals on him.

My assistants begin to sob, and I'm taking the camera, putting them on the spot.

"Get out of the car."

They get out of the car with only the slightest bit of hesitation.

The sky above darkens, a thunderstorm will soon

reach us.

Lights dim, and the way this looks on camera, the way you see it, it might as well be night.

A tinge of noir based on the way I capture them on camera, I force them to their knees.

"Don't make a sound."

We aren't wasting time on exposition.

The show must go on.

My assistants quickly understand that they cannot hold back either. They are my assistants and for that reason they have become subordinates.

Involved. Accessories.

I watch as they look over at him.

"What was that just now?"

I provoke them for an answer.

When one cries, I slap both across the face.

"I didn't hear you!"

I'm the person with the camera. I'm the master walking the line I've drawn. My pet remains on all fours, waiting and enjoying what he sees.

If I wanted to, he would take them for me.

They would resist and in resisting they would be perfect victims.

But not right now, I tell myself.

That time may come, but not at this point, so early, so fresh on our trail.

My assistants are armchair social scientists. I ask them what they did just now.

You'll never hear their voices unless I feel a need for them to be recorded on camera. You don't have to hear them to know that they are inadequate.

They are fearful. They also looked at him not with fear, but with something else.

And I will keep track of what that "something else"

might be.

"You are involved," I'm saying.

More about the study.

It was their fault that they failed to understand what this was about.

"Didn't think you signed up for this?"

And sure they're quick to shake their heads. I turn to my pet, and he is commanded to stand back up. He's done so well I want to kiss him.

But I don't. Not yet.

The camera wouldn't capture it correctly.

They're watching, so I bite him.

I tell him to bite back.

Drawing blood, I spit at them. Blood splatters across their faces.

"This has always been the same study. It seems you both never fully understood the cost of doing what you love."

Brunette pees herself. I tell her to take off the clothes.

I force her to remain naked even though there are spares in the trunk.

Both up off their knees, I have him walk up to them. I have my pet show them the footage, both of what he did to Demon and what I filmed of them just now.

I take the camera from him, and he goes back to his car.

He waits, but knows what the waiting will do:

It will leave a time discrepancy in our records.

But this was needed. Their loyalty will now be set in stone.

When I show them the final bit of footage, of both tasting each other, they are wondrously everything I expected them to be. I'm saying that they are my assistants.

Both shut up and become obedient carbon copies of me.

To any viewer, they look just like me with different affectations.

Hair color, tan lines...take your pick. What's your type?

I am everybody's type.

To all of you, they will be just what I need when my hands are full.

Camera captures the brunette completely: spread cheeks, on all fours, wet. When that's over, I'm saying, "Now does it all make sense?"

They both nod, slowly.

He mouths, "I love you," from the driver's seat.

As I drive off, I'm mouthing the very same words looking back at him via the rearview mirror. Only him and I know the full extent of their meaning.

Data recorded.

7.

My pet is taking requests.
Would you care to die by his hands?
He'll love you right until the end.
Your deepest, darkest fantasies will come true.
And you too will be mine.

Why watch what you don't understand?

1.

I drove through the storm to get back to the limelight of this study.

Wanting so very much to see him back there, but instead I see the storm clouds, the rains set to downpour. No amount of rain will wash away what's been done and what will become the basic facts of my disgust. The facts, they're both of these sentences:

They slowed it down. They didn't assist.

I blame the assistants for his death.

My pet has no one to kill.

The assistants shiver but they don't see me, equally wet from the storm, shivering. I'm red hot on the trail.

We've no one for him to kill. His would-be second, the man that had been called the "Butcher of Brooklyn" was executed.

I had them drenched. But the rain wouldn't wash away how I felt.

How I feel. So maybe, wanting them to better understand. . .

Then I see it and that's all it takes.

It is done.

Two cars behind, in the lane to my right, a blue van. The blue van, the one we had been following since finding out that the Butcher was no more.

He thought she could replace me, huh? Thought marrying into something would wash away his past? If watching rainfall teaches you anything about consequence, let it be the fact that nothing completely washes away. Everything that disappears washes up somewhere else.

The Butcher of Brooklyn, he's all washed up.

He got married to this woman. He got married to her just so that he would have someone visit him in jail. And it looks like she married out of the Butcher's life, opting to start on another.

It's all in the blue van: Two kids, a dog, and will you look at that. . .

The man driving, that couldn't be the Butcher, could it?

Butcher's veins were pumped full of a lethal dosage.

He's a corpse in a grave six feet under. We're too late but this, the blue van, will have to do. Oh well, look at that: She seems to understand that they're being followed.

I want to say hello.

I'm having trouble juggling all the possibilities. So much can go wrong when traveling down the interstate. So much—and I'm looking to have us be one of those wrong turns.

Side-by-side the blue van, I have them wave. I have the blonde drive so that I can do what needs to be done. I'm flashing my bare chest and so that means they have to show theirs too.

What do they see, what do they see?

The camera sees them.

My pet drives past us, pulls in front of the blue van and speeds down the interstate.

Preparing for elsewhere, I imagine. But this, this is ours.

My pet, I'll show you later. I'll show you everything.

We're playing a game; can't you see? Cat and mouse, and who might be the mouse here?

Look at me: Would you consider me anything like a kitty cat?

Meow.

The guy driving doesn't seem to think so. He speeds up, passing cars, switching lanes, doing his best to create distance.

Every time we get close, we touch each other. Metal on metal leaves dents. It leaves scars.

Our convertible is fine. I'm liking the dented look, the

look of heavy petting. In adoration of the well explored body.

I stand up on the front passenger seat.

Order the assistants to leave their tops off.

You'll see it. You'll see it!

I have the guy see. More importantly, I have her see.

I know she sees us.

"Why don't you look?!"

Camera pans to the back seat. Dog barking, fogging up the window.

I wave to the dog, shouting the words, "I have a pet too!"

The kids are crying.

I look at the young boy. I blow him a kiss.

I touch my left nipple. I shout, "We're all wet!"

Blue van speeds up again.

I shout, "Hey I know you!"

Guilty by association, we are wet bodies past the storm, looking to get past this, looking to pass on the fact that he was ours to kill and because the Butcher is dead, they'll have to do.

Next of kin. Executer of estate.

She shows up on every record. I'm all about fairness. Look at my fair skin. I can be as tender as porcelain, as honest as long as you play fair.

If you're not, I'm snapping my fingers. Blonde is driving faster. Brunette is handing me oranges. If not. . .

"We're going to have to play a different game!"

I whisper those words, the words exclusively understood by no one but my perfect pet, as I hurl that first orange at the blue van. It lands on the windshield.

Continuous shot as I tend to the oranges. Each hurled orange is an expression of adoration.

Each hurled orange is one more scar to heal, a dent to mark the blue a different color.

She sees me now. And I'm telling her, it's because of

him. Yes, him. Her husband, the one that's dead. The one that's alive and cowering behind the wheel hears me. He hasn't heard of the information, hasn't figured his wife for one attracted to a serial killer.

But then, no one is until they are. By then they are in bed with a killer, and they just might be like me, wanting so much to change them. Make him better.

She knew the moment she saw me. Butcher must have told her all about me.

Up until now, there was nothing to prove to her that I exist. But see these? I cup them, I feel them, the van on the side of the road, I push her face into them.

Smother her. And then, "Yes, for the camera."

Butcher liked to cook the bodies. We'd do a little roadside cooking.

I have them hold the camera just so that he can see. You'll want to see this.

I'm sure you're interested. I have one of the assistants look in the back of the van. Sure enough he has a portable grill.

I ask the young girl, "How was the picnic?"

Of course she isn't valuable enough to be given a line in the script.

Sure—I enjoy this. I enjoy it more because you're watching.

I enjoy it because he's well ahead of me, he's moving on.

He's got an appetite like me.

We're all hungry,

You can cut a whole lot from the human body before it becomes fatal. I force her to try some of her meat.

"Tender huh?"

The assistants look the part but I warn the brunette, "You better not!" when she breathes deeply, wave of nausea hitting her hard.

"Eat it."

We all have a taste.

Marinated in her own blood, it tastes a little flat, but the meat, it is tender.

Perhaps the man behind the wheel is a bit of a wife beater. . .I look at her arms, the side of her face, there are bruises, signs of a lesser man's weakness.

This troubles me. I see those with no fight in them as the weakest, most disgusting of the bunch. The man behind the wheel won't look me in the eye.

I shout at him. I have the assistants pull him out but he holds onto the wheel for dear life.

"Fine," I say, realizing that he's not worth the effort.

He's not really alive. "Maybe you won't feel this," I say right as I slam the door on his arm once, twice, three times, before locking him in that van.

"Kids, circle around."

None of this is for the cars passing by. No one will stop. They will drive faster. Danger ahead. You should know of the dangers one can experience while driving.

Fade to black as the lights go out. It is sunny, a kind of natural stage light on our red convertible. Tops off, we continue driving. The assistants have no mind to resist now. I took care of it. I had the assistants do something they'll never forget. Think about it: It's not difficult to take a person's life when they do nothing to save it.

"Wait on the side of the road kids," I'm telling them.

Their father hasn't moved from the driver's seat. Not even a single flicker of fight in him. Oh, what a surprise. I hand the young boy the rest of his mother.

"In case you get hungry."

The boy doesn't look me in the eye. He looks at my chest. Looks at their chests too. He's bound by the urge. I see it and tell him, "You've got a lot of potential."

I glance up at the kid's dad, watching me. I tell the boy,

"Don't grow up dead like your dad."

I let him feel my breast. He starts crying. The girl looks at the bag. Blood leaks from the bottom, drips down to the asphalt.

No rain will wash away the memory of our game.

The kids will take it with them. Define the rest of their days.

We know each other, don't we?

You're watching this, and I'd like to think that we liked the way she tasted.

2.

We'd really like to know what you think. A few episodes in, we're getting to that point of the show where your suggestions become an integral part.

This is as much your show as it is his or her, so please, if you can spare a few minutes, vote!

Your opinion really does count!

Each questionnaire is answered anonymously, so by all means, be honest. Use the extra room to write in a more personal response. We're building something together, folks, and it's important to us that we see in her exactly what you'd like to see; we want what's best for him. Many have already voiced their opinion on what a natural born killer like him should act like, and evolve into, and so it's really moments like these that become imperative for the functionality of his training.

She does need your help, and the camera, you see, is always watching.

You're never anywhere else but right up front.

1. Should the mystery involve more of the assistants or less of the assistants?

a) More b) Less c) Other: ______________________________

____

____

2. The woman has been seen topless. Would you prefer more or less nudity?

a) More b) Less c) Other: ______________________________

____

____

3. The man has yet to have a serial killer name. If you could name him, what would you name him?

____

____

4. The network wants to know: is a half hour twice a week more attractive than one hour once a week?

a) 2 Half-hour episodes b) One-hour episode c) Other: ___

____

____

5. The woman has quickly become quite the antagonist, and yet audience and critics equally, have had trouble placing where she fits. What do you think she is, to you? What does Claire mean to you?

a) Protagonist b) Antagonist c) Other: ____________

____

____

____

6. The man hasn't said a word. His trust is in the woman's hands. The master/pet dynamic hinges on trust. Would you like to hear from him at any point?

a) Yes b) No c) Other: __________________

____

____

____

7. Would you like to know how many exes the woman's had?

a) Yes b) No c) Other: __________________

____

____

____

8. What part of the mystery are you currently enjoying the most?

____

____

9. What part of the mystery are you currently enjoying the least?

____

____

10. For you loyal viewers that watch every single episode, what is it about the show that keeps you coming back, week after week?

____

____

Thank you for your time. The mystery has only just begun to unfold; we can't wait to show you more.

She'll show you everything, if you let her.

3.

She tasted pretty good. I'll admit it—but it was an appetizer compared to the main course.

I'm hungry, aren't you? I'm driving, the yellow lines of the highway quickly setting me into a daydream. I look back at the assistants; they cover their breasts with their arms, ashamed of their nudity. I look at myself. I see no reason to be ashamed.

This is a body. A body is supposed to be used.

I'm in a daze thinking about how he didn't get to taste her.

I'm imagining a scenario where my pet takes it upon himself to treat me to a very special dinner where everyone is there, watching, as we try a number of different delicacies.

At some point we both laugh and say, "We aren't cannibals."

But I'm also imagining a scenario where we are. It becomes probable the moment it becomes worth watching. And you can imagine to the full extent, a horizon of possibilities.

I don't have time to check the footage before sending it to him but, you see, that's what makes this all the more interesting. We aren't seeing what I want to see; you're seeing everything. He's showing me only what happened; when everything happened. I'm left breathless and horny.

The drive is torture when I'm hungry.

I call him just to see if he'll be all that he can be. And yet again, I'm impressed.

He isn't supposed to use his phone. I'm picturing what he's done: Probably lost the phone. It's probably under the driver's seat or something.

I think about what he's filming—did he really decide

to go ahead with the next?

If he's there first, I've told him to wait; an obedient pet will only keep to the rules long enough until an opportunity arises to do something that'll win favor.

He wants to please me.

I need to be pleased.

The assistants are in each other's arms, asleep.

Looking at them, the way they look, I think; so young but too old for new liberties. They won't understand what I'm doing; they'll likely figure me for the worst person they've ever met. And what we're doing, I'm under the impression that they don't feel they'll make it past this.

This isn't an occasion.

This is the one occasion—the one to end all.

I have big plans for my pet and me. They will be able to join us. . .but only if they be as obedient as possible. They must be just like me.

But not like me. If that's confusing, it's because you aren't them and your life isn't in danger. I could easily let my pet have his way with them. I'd use both of our cameras.

Get two angles of the same kill.

I'd watch both tapes twice, just to whet my appetite.

The hunger is unbearable. Where's a restaurant when you need it?

The hushed nature of this drive causes me to doze just enough to forget that I need to take this next exit. The assistants wake up when I make a sharp turn off the interstate.

Car horns are perfect alarm clocks.

"Yeah, wake up," I need you to retrieve the tape.

I force the brunette to dig through a dumpster topless even though it seems to be the worst I've made her do based on how much she resists.

I dangle the treat in front of her:

"Do you want to be part of this landmark study or not?"

It wasn't a question and she doesn't answer.

The blonde seems satisfied that she didn't have to be the one to dig through the dumpster. I see her smile and for a brief moment I like what I see.

But then I also know what that means so I tell her to get out of the car. I tell her to start walking. I force her to walk back to the interstate. Her nudity brandishes her shame.

These assistants are so entitled.

They are part of **my** study.

Like you, watching, they are privy to what is being shown to them; if the cameras were to go dead, there wouldn't be anything you could do. If I killed the assistants now, they wouldn't be able to do anything about it. Not that they'd be able to do something later.

But the point is—I'm master of this.

I'm director. I'm the star.

I'm confident, but don't think I'm an egomaniac. I'm not. I just believe in what I believe in.

And I'm really fucking hungry.

When I'm hungry, I get irritable.

The smell of garbage turns me on more; I get hungrier. I like that he's chosen to hide his tape in the garbage. What must he show me that required a whole tape?

The brunette hands me the tape but it's still in the plastic bag.

I push it away, "Take it out, come on!"

I hand the brunette a shirt, "Here."

I drive back towards the interstate, pick up the blonde, who didn't even make it a mile, and quickly readjust my expectations for the next visit.

Giles, I wonder what's become of you. Have your tattoos faded?

But long before that, I need to get off. I need to eat.

A few exits down, I see a sign. It's one of those franchise

restaurants. This one looks like a log cabin on the outside; has a store full of candy and trinkets that you have to go through to get to the cafeteria-style seating arrangement. Southern cooking is what they sell.

Sure—I tell them to go get a table.

Before anything else can happen, I need to watch the tape.

I see him, and only him.

He has with him a gun.

I don't know where he got the gun.

"That's interesting," I say to myself.

He says the words, "I love you," as he holds the gun to his head.

"I love you," again as he pulls the trigger. The gun, not loaded, makes a loud clicking sound.

"I love you," as he sets down the gun, looks around the inside of the coupe, holds up a new tape, picks up the phone and speaks to his family.

I didn't tell him to talk to his family.

He says the words, same words we've shared, to the person on the other line.

Who is it? Who is it?

Dad, Mom, sister? Or someone else?

My face feels hot. I clench my jaw. What is this? Are you taunting me?

My pet takes the phone and lets it fall from his hands. It disappears from the shot. He turns to me, holds the gun, looks into the camera, nods twice, and places his hands together.

Then I understand.

He wants my approval. Will this be how he wants to get off?

Right here? Holding the gun?

Surely he does. He's already erect when he pulls down

his pants.

He presses his penis against the gun. I remove my panties.

I imagine the barrel of the gun as my fingers.

I look out the passenger window, seeing a couple looking in my direction as they walk towards their car. I moan louder.

He aims the lens down at his groin.

He lets it splatter all over the lens when he's done.

My pet. . .I moan.

I feel everything right before I feel, once again, nothing.

He is not here and will not be here until he's exactly what I want him to be.

My pet.

I will never be fully satisfied until then.

We can explore every inch of our bodies; we film it all so that we can save the memory, so that we can express to you what it means to say "I love you." We say those words right before we shove a gun in our mouths; we say those words before we continue building his legacy.

We say those words before and after we climax.

But it's only the beginning. It isn't satisfying.

It can't be the complete expression. Not yet.

Until then, this is all we can really have.

Masturbation.

To love anyone you must first love yourself.

1.

My pet was here. He ate and spoke to me from behind a camera lens.

We may have crossed paths but it's not on camera, not on film, so you don't know that.

You only know what we show, and if we're showing you everything, what does it mean when it isn't in any frame? It might be that it never happened.

Maybe it can happen later.

Have a piece of this pancake, or how about some hash browns?

I hear their mashed potatoes are lovely.

My assistants both seem to enjoy the food. Everything is eaten, but how much of the food did they really taste?

I ask.

I'm not getting a definitive answer.

This cannot do—people made that food. They cooked it so that you'd enjoy it.

"Wrong," I'm telling them.

I order another round of the same. They'll get this right.

A list of commands, instructions if you will.

I'm showing them how to properly eat with a fork and knife, spoon when needed. Just enough syrup to increase the flavor of the pancakes; just enough salt and pepper on their hash browns; just enough to increase the meal.

Unsatisfied, I'm sighing, head tilted down. Nothing to see here, eyes closed.

Even when they do it right, they're still doing it wrong.

Sip of coffee. Look what they've done now.

Now they're not eating. I've nearly had enough of this.

I'm slamming the fork down onto the table.

"Get up." They'll have to make up for this. Wonder what the cook's interested in sampling. . .everyone's got a craving. Everyone's has their own taste.

What's his?

I know mine. My pet, did you finish your plate or did you seek out a proper dessert? Did you clean your palate? The best way to fully enjoy every flavor is to wash it with its exact opposite.

Blonde goes first.

"Do it," I tell her.

We'll stay right here, won't we? I look at the brunette.

Wait our turn.

I'm handing the camera to the blonde. If she's smart she'll go ahead and do it; if she's stupid. . .well then the odds are definitely against her.

"Go." Way I say it—can't be any more firm than that. She may think her rack is firmer but—ha—yeah right.

Brunette and I sit back down.

I'm staring at her. She's having trouble staring back.

You see, this part isn't on film so you'll have to bear with me. Nothing will be bared: All you'll know is what I tell you.

I can already tell what's going on.

"You can't replace me," I warn her.

She won't be able to really be Claire. But the blonde's going to try.

Wonder what she's saying? My pet gets first dibs. He'll watch it and if it's worth anything, I'll see it on the blonde's face. If it's as good it can be, we'll hear it from the kitchen.

The full view—that's left for a different show. Too busy watching the main event to be busy with any offshoots, huh?

Then I hear it, and I'm more than pleased.

Seems blonde turned the camera into a weapon.

"What part of the camera did you use?"

Don't tell me it's the damn lens. But it was. Good to know I've budgeted for this. Creativity means casualties, lots of casualties. Put the camera to bed and you're bound to take its life.

Manager had it coming hmm?

Blonde gains a few brownie points.

"Are we still hungry?"

Blonde shakes her head.

We should probably pay the bill. Waitress looks concerned.

I'm shaking my head, pouty face, "Thought we weren't going to leave you a tip?"

How's a few $20 bills, hmm? You think that's one hell of a tip?

My, my—no one is surprised anymore, huh? Waitress might even be glad that blonde did away with her boss. Had it coming.

Brunette's going to have to show me something.

I can't have my assistants playing victim. In the convertible, I let the blonde drive.

Arm around the brunette in the backseat.

I'm look down her shirt, "That pushup bra isn't cutting it."

But then she wants to be me, or at least is pretending to be me.

For the cover story to work, they need to believe that they're me. They must love themselves before they can begin to love anyone else. A victim feels sorry for itself. A victim wants to be saved; someone that needs saving has little self-worth. If they had any self-worth, they'd learn to save themselves. "Where's the fight? Hmm?"

Brunette looks away. I'm telling the blonde, "I'm going to need the both of you. . ."

I have his tape in my hand, new camera in the other.

Catch the blonde looking back at me.

So ask, "What happens when one is valued greater than

the other?"

Look who's on camera?

"They're all watching. They want to be entertained. What do you do?"

Brunette looks away.

Panning shot of the sunset.

2.

Wave to the studio audience!

—Hey all!

It's been an intense few episodes huh?

—You can say that [laughter]

We're capturing some really great stuff. I'm just amazed at what you've already been subjected to. . .were you expecting anything at all like this?

—No! Definitely not. . .and I'm still kind of shocked. I don't know what's going to happen but it really does feel like this is it, you know? There's nothing after this if it keeps getting worse. "No way out" kind of thing. I'm afraid, but I am also stunned to find that, you know, I'm quickly getting used to this.

What's it like working for the woman?

—Oh, I don't know. I mean, I've always been intrigued by deviant behavior, always been addicted to, you know, all sorts of crime dramas, serial killer books, stuff like that. It was what made me choose Criminology as my major. She's intense, really intense. . .but everyone in the department knows that. I knew that when I signed up for this. I mean, well. . .[long pause] she's become infamous among all the criminologists. Every paper she's published has given her instant attention. I guess I had no choice. . .

How did you hear about the study?

—I didn't actually. That's something to talk about. Yeah, see I was approached by her. I got this text message from a friend of a friend that basically said "this woman was looking for you. . ." and it's really weird to explain it now, but at the time, I already knew who it was. And what it was for. Yeah, doesn't really make a whole lot of sense. . .

It makes some kind of sense. Given the nature of the program, we have to ask: What are your limits? Where do you draw the line?

—I don't know. Guess that's kind of why I'm in this to begin

with. If I had limits, I wouldn't have signed up for this. You could feel the heaviness of it, how it wasn't going to be anything even remotely understandable, you know? Going on the road with her and someone else, undercover, draped with cameras, hunting down serial killers, interrogating them. . .it's all so insane. . .

And then the murders started.

—Murder followed us from the very beginning. He's out there, you know?

What do you mean "out there?"

—Nothing really. He's another car driving around. He's her new fling.

Do you find him attractive?

—Not really. I mean maybe a little. I don't know.

Do you find it weird that we're asking?

—No.

And?

—What else? You're all watching so I imagine that you're trying to make sense of the mystery.

About that—the mystery—what exactly is it? In your own definition?

—It's you guys. The camera. The show. The study at large. That's what I'd say. I mean, right? It's entertainment; it's the attention span. I feel like I might be getting this wrong. . .

No-no, it's a good answer.

—Really?

Yes.

—Can I ask why?

Why not? It's your answer. How can it not be good?

—Aww thanks [blushes]

[To audience] Would you like anything else to ask the lovely assistant?

Someone has a question.

—Sure.

Why do you look so much like her?

—Isn't. . .that the point?

The point? Could you elaborate?

—Oh right, I'm so sorry. Not sure if I'm supposed to tell you this but, yeah, it's not a coincidence that I'm acting and looking like her. My peer is the same way. We're supposed to look like this, act like this, that kind of thing. And we can't even use our real names. We have to use hers.

Is this part of the study?

—Sure? Why not.

The audience would like to know more.

—I'm not sure I'm supposed to be telling you this.

Ruining the mystery?

—Maybe, I guess.

One last question from the audience.

—Okay.

Do you think she'll get what she wants? I.e. do you think it'll turn out the way she wants?

—Yeah, I think so. It's a scary thought but looks that way. I wouldn't doubt it. Not ever.

Not at all?

—Nope. No doubt about it. And even if there was some doubt, I refuse to be the person to say it.

Thank you for your time.

—Thanks.

[Audience applause]

3.

After paying the guard with funds from the brunette's checking account, I've had enough with this. Driving. The momentum's way ahead of us, no worry about that. I have another thing in mind. This can't stay lopsided. She's got to learn a thing or two.

I deny the blonde's offer to take over driving duties.

We are stopping here. Side of the road. Watch other cars pass us by.

Watch the hitchhiker, see what I see.

I'm looking at the brunette.

If this were the blonde, she'd understand what's about to happen.

Let me elaborate, hmm?

I'm telling her that she's nothing like what I expected and that she's too meek, too much like her true self. I'm telling her that he needs to be more like me. I'm telling her that she needs to perk up, shoulders up, voice confident and true. I'm telling her that she needs to be more like the blonde. She needs to say my name. Say my name!

"Claire. . ."

Again.

"Claire."

Again!

"Claire!"

Not good enough—she's going to have to pick someone up if she's got any chance of picking the pieces of herself crapped out on the floor of the convertible.

Brunette's a wreck and I'm starting to feel ashamed.

To the blonde, "Camera," and to the brunette, "Get out."

"Off." She starts taking her top off.

"All of it."

She's embarrassed, arms not at her sides, instead covering the areas that the meek would be too nervous to let the camera see. What's the use, hmm? Here's what I see:

Me.

I see everything I am, minus the fight, the confidence, the good taste.

She doesn't tie the rope tight enough so it begins to chafe against her hips as we put the convertible in neutral. See what I mean?

I'm having to show her what it means to be tight enough. She's not even wet.

Rope around her waist, I let the blonde have a little fun. Neutral at 10-15MPH causes the brunette to stumble forward, forced to keep up given the situation.

Ever wonder what a nude woman tied to the bumper of a moving vehicle looks like?

Taillights drape her body in red.

When we pass the hitchhiker, I motion for him to keep up.

He walks with her. A lesser man would have gone right for it but, lucky for the brunette, he's at least talking to her. No touching, only the narrowest of glances at her body.

She shouldn't be ashamed. He's the one that's worthless. He can't help himself. There's a difference between shame and sexuality, there's a difference between taste and torture.

Seems few get this. I'm trying to teach my assistants a thing or two.

If we're going to keep at this, I need carbon copies of myself.

I'm repeating myself. . .

But that's what teaching is:

Repetition.

My assistants, you must leave everything at the door.

But after a half-mile, we're making progress. The camera captures seduction.

Brunette fends for what she might imagine as safety by saying the right kind of thing, just enough to turn potential assailant into a whipped and salivating animal.

The hitchhiker's yours, I'm telling her.

The blonde speeds up.

Now we're really running.

"What do you want to say to the camera?!" I'm shouting to them.

"This is your scene!" I tell her. And in that moment, she's a survivor.

In that moment, I'd liken it to her emulating me. I ask for nothing more from these two. They have to look like me if we're going to ride the rest of the interstate.

We're looking good. I exhale, satisfied to see that the rope is now on the hitchhiker's waist. Brunette got him to do everything: Untie her, tie himself up.

Power of suggestion. One word can rival a thousand.

And now he's left alone running after us.

Brunette gets a kiss on the cheek from me. I catch her grinning.

That's more like it. I picked them both for a reason; they weren't just the most charming, they both had some fight in them. They want what they want, just like me.

Hitchhiker can really run.

"Give him another 5MPH," I'm telling the blonde.

Cast in the red light, the hitchhiker looks like he's running after us, running away from the past. I just know my pet is going to love this. There's a whole lot to get off on when you get creative enough. My, my—he's really running. "We got a marathon runner," I'm telling them.

I ask the brunette what she wants us to do.

"It's yours," I'm saying when she gives me that look, a look that says, 'Really I get to choose?' And of course she gets to choose.

What are her choices, hmm? What do you think?

She chooses the latter, the one that the audience wants but would never say. For this, I get the blonde to give me the wheel.

"Go ahead, get it all on camera. Enjoy yourself."

Careful with this, you see—you can't just slam on the gas. You can't just speed up. Small increments spare him the fear that'll leave him twisted, stumbling over his two feet. Small increments mean we'll get more of a scene. More out of this.

3-5MPH increments. Perfect.

He's starting to shout something.

Really can't understand what it is but let's go with something practical:

"HELP!"

Yeah that works.

Better yet, "Please, stop!"

Begs for his life. Makes sense.

"Are you getting this?" I'm asking. That's a nod. She is.

He puts in enough, probably just because he's got nothing but adrenaline flowing; when something like this happens, it's doubtful that you're thinking, I'm going to die. Really you're functioning purely on gut reaction, basic survival instincts. The hitchhiker's got just enough to last longer than I expected him to, but, really now, what did you think was going to happen?

We stop the car to get a closer look at what's left.

I do it more for him. I'm sure it would make for a good lesson.

A good first-look at the possibilities. Proof that in anything there can be beauty.

What does he look like? Well, I'm kind of a liar when I'm this excited—I like to exaggerate and fill in the gaps with my own version—but I'll say this:

I never knew a face could be this flat.

4.

Wave to the studio audience!

[She waves]

Talk about a hell of a time, huh?

—Yeah.

We're really seeing some unexpected turns. It's rendering us all pleasantly intrigued and just a little bit confused. But right at the top, we have to ask: Are you okay?

—I'm okay.

You don't sound okay.

—No, I am. I'm a little frazzled, that's all. It's all happened so quickly. Kind of expected a slow start but then this happened.

Yeah, but that's perhaps why we're all so intrigued.

[She nods]

So that answers our first question, so we'll be able to move—

—What was the first question?

Oh, it went along the lines of "were you expecting anything like this?"

—Yeah, I wasn't, but now I don't expect anything.

Nothing?

—The past is the past and with it, I begin to see that I wasn't prepared for this.

Are you prepared now?

—No. But that won't stop it from continuing.

Why not fight it?

—That won't do anything.

No—it probably won't. Moving on.

—Okay.

What's it like working for the woman?

—It's hell.

Wow, how succinct.

—It's the truth. It's hell because everything is going to get worse and I can't stop it. It's hell because I don't want to stop it. I'm letting it go. I let myself go.

You really think you let yourself go?

—Not in a physical way. More in a moral way. I thought I understood boundaries but then I do something like this and I would be lying to the audience if I didn't say that I'm enjoying it.

We're getting a call-in.

Oh—would you be okay answering?

—Okay.

I will preface this by saying that it's her.

—Okay what does she need?

She's asking you why.

—Why?

Yes.

—Why what?

We're. . .not sure. She wants clarification. She's saying she wants proof.

—She's asking. . .

She's asking about something you previously. . .

—[Interrupts] I know what she's asking! Why—why did I like what I did? Of course I can't avoid it. I can't avoid her. Why, why, why, why. . .

Why?

—Because.

That's not good enough, apparently.

—Because I hated that he looked at me that way; I've never done anything like this before. Because I can't help myself. Because I find myself more interested in why she's attracted to this stuff, not just to criminology and deviant behavior, but more so to what has no name.

Obscenity?

—Love.

I don't think we follow. . .

—You're not supposed to. Part of the mystery.

[Audience silence]

—You'll have to keep watching. You're going to anyway. You all are just like me and we're in too deep.

5.

I'm touching the tape like it's part of him. I'm smelling it because there's nothing to taste. I'm stroking it in the seconds before I insert it and begin. He's been so busy, busy enough to have been left behind a good 30 minutes. Somewhere my pet wanted to please me.

He started and finished without any need of my presence.

The result is this tape. And you're watching even though you have to blink. You're watching even though you worry it might be worse.

I'm watching because he's mine and no one else can have him.

I let the assistants watch in celebration of their recent efforts. I let them watch but I'm telling them that I don't want them near me. I want them out of sight; I don't want to hear them. And because of that they sit in the back of the convertible, duct taped mouths.

We can begin. Aren't you excited:

Establishing shot of a handful of nails. Camera pulls back, establishing the first surprise: He did it in the jail cell. He didn't opt for something a bit more secluded. There would be a lot of noise. Cut to Giles the Great looking exactly the same. I would still be attracted to him if it weren't for his humiliating downfall. What killer cries, begs for his mommy, as they drag him away?

Giles the Great (more like Giles the Lesser) is roped up on a piece of plywood.

My pet enters the shot. He's wearing a featureless black mask. Giles never did that.

This is new. I don't know how to feel about it. Surprised, sure, but I'm more surprised because of my reaction. I'm not wholly pleased. I've given him some liberty, some license to express himself, but if he keeps doing this without my explicit instructions. . .well, I'm going to let it slide.

It's no big deal. We're still getting to know each other. I'm quite sure it was just because he wanted to please me. Anything I say, he'll do.

I told him to act like a victim. That's his best cover story.

I told him to embrace naivety. That's his best cover story.

I told him to pretend that he's on his own. That's his best cover story.

He follows these things and for that, I'm pleased. I am.

Inmates are watching too. The guards let them; everyone wants someone like Giles dead. Enough of a cash transfer and it doesn't matter what is done; inmate will clean up the mess. The guards get to split the dough. Money, as they say, talks.

Giles in his "greatest moments" liked to peel back skin.

Skin peeled back looks a whole lot like the texture of undercooked chicken.

He liked to douse them with paint. He wanted to be a painter. For a time he was everything, as is the case when you decide to express yourself by taking lives.

Paint on fresh wounds creates a runny mess. The paint and blood don't mix well.

My pet seems annoyed by it and rushes here. That's an error—Giles took his time.

Throughout this, I am wondering, distantly, who's filming him.

I don't find out until the very end.

Split screen shot of footage I kept of Giles and that of what I'm now watching. My pet is, stroke-for-stroke, on target. But there's something else missing.

When the paint doesn't dry fast enough, he gets creative. Once again, the shot establishing shot of nails, but this time we get more than the three seconds from the start of the tape. We get his hand dipped in paint, the nails dripping in various colors.

A hammer doesn't work that well when he tries, the nails only going halfway in before hitting bone. Screams of all sorts drown out the audio—inmates cheering, Giles sobbing.

My pet trades in the hammer for a nail gun. Each dipped and dripping nail goes in one after the other. Again, and again, and again:

Nailed. The nails are different colors but always end up looking the same.

When the first nail punctures Giles's stomach, everything inside it comes out as vomit.

Another sort of response from the inmates, but my pet is vigilant.

He isn't annoyed, disgusted: No expression.

I look at my assistants. They watch intently. Too intently.

But disregard—I don't want to miss this. Various insertions in the shoulders, arms, thighs, and groin culminate with one last one, the one that'll go through Giles's forehead.

Again, Giles is begging.

Before I can muster up a true sense of anger, my pet does something about it; he nails Giles's mouth shut. It only takes three nails shot through from the top lip down.

One of them tears when Giles makes a pained face.

My pet attempts to fix it but instead the nail cracks one of Giles's front teeth.

Some of the inmates stop watching. They look away. Sounds, unsettling sounds.

My pet holds back a moment, appreciating his work.

Looks at the camera. Whoever's filming it ruins our moment when he says, "This is fucked," enthusiastically. This upsets him and he should know that it upsets me just as much, if not more.

But later—we will deal with this later.

He finishes the job. The nail through the forehead is almost enough but there's still heartbeat. For that it takes a number of nails. Giles might still be alive; he's a pest like that.

But my pet doesn't seem interested. What's done is done.

And I'm fairly satisfied. Thought just now, I should be fulfilled.

But I'm not. By the look of it, he isn't either.

He looks into the camera, and here we have a moment.

And I understand. He wants to see me. More of me. He wants to catch up to me, all of me. And most of all, he wants to learn more. He needs more practice.

And yet, there's something else I haven't placed. It might just be me. . .

I could be adding more to this than there really is.

The tape ends with the sound of an inmate cheering. There we are, revealed: Looking into the camera, revealing the identity of who had, once upon a time, been a part of the mystery. That inmate—Eugene Carson, 25 years for embezzlement—will not survive this study.

The mystery will envelop him. One day he'll just disappear.

Only a select few will know where he ended up. Everyone should know that he won't be the first. When everyone's talking about murder, it's clear people want to be involved.

The more they watch, the more they are willing to talk about it.

Data recorded.

Trade in a walk in the park
for a walk in the dark.

1.

By night, we walked the side of the interstate.

Walked barefoot, bare skin. Woke up the dozing drivers with a game of chicken, three lanes of traffic turning and evading at the sight of what they could only assume was us.

In the dark of night, we looked like ghost flashes across a damp windshield.

Rouse the driver into a new car crash and maybe he'll thank me. I saved his life. He had been waiting for an accident to happen. Now he can cross it off. We do this less for you, the audience, and more for him, my pet. He went above and beyond what I had intended.

Those sounds are theirs to keep. Each blare of the horn only makes me run faster.

Again I rush through traffic.

Again I'm thinking this is fun.

These are the moments I'd imagine would be only possible after finding meaning for those words. My pet, I'm thinking about you. I'm saying the words to myself as I cup my breasts, mid-sprint, the feeling of them sway and jiggle sometimes discomforting.

I'm saying the words, and nobody but you can hear them over the sounds of screeching tires, car horns trying to tell me I'm beautiful.

"I love you," in case you hadn't known.

"You love me more," because I know it's true.

We know it's true. The assistants know it's true. When they run through traffic, they slow down as the vehicle nears; when they run through traffic, they believe they're in danger. They might be hit. This is where I am the most different.

When I run, I'm heading towards something. Anything that might be in the way is merely that—in the way—and it will move. It will move on its own; if not, I will make them.

Either end of the interstate, we are still the same. See those rocks? Don't you want to see how far they can travel before cracking in half, or cracking something? We're as close to the state line as we need to be. On this night, I'm letting them vent their frustrations.

Give it a toss.

It feels good to be letting go of something.

The night is wearing thin, running long, and us Claires need to feel something more than what we've been feeling. I'm more interested in seeing you as you pass.

We're waiting for cars to slow down.

We're waiting for cars to speed up.

Closer angle on my ass as I lean down to pick up another rock. And you know the camera can do nothing but look. Really look. I don't mind. I'm not ashamed.

In one long continuous shot, the following happens:

Rocks hitting windshields and windows. Cars swerving into each other, a near accident. Blonde trapped between two cars, jumping into a free lane, cutting the side of her leg. No worries, though; she doesn't feel it and in no time it'll be gone. Not even a scratch. Brunette has a fairly good arm, landing more than a few to the tires, which proves to be far worse than shattered glass.

In concert with each other, I leave them for a sign that you'll see.

You're almost here.

I need it to be written. On pieces of cardboard I write the words over and over again. When you'll see them you'll know. It'll be so obvious; it would be embarrassing to have seen it at all. I'm pretending it's not, but it is. . .and really if you're my pet, you'll be too far into the fantasy to separate the two. If I called you, you'd act like you were someone else. We have to if we're going to be invisible to the authorities. I've seen three pass by since we've disrobed, and not even one has noticed. Shot-for-shot, I'm not slowing down. Into the camera, I'm letting you have a good look. The audience will think it's for them but we know what's true.

After placing the signs, I'm waiting for you to pass by. I'm looking around. See what I see: Blonde picking up sticks and trying to light them on fire. Brunette squatting to urinate. And in front of us, the vehicle that'll take us from here. We've walked this far. They've probably found the convertible by now. It starts to rain—feels good on my skin.

Cool before getting warm, I'm tilting my neck back and opening my mouth. Tasteless, but oh, so satisfying, like most things. And when you do finally pass, I'm not there to see your car. But I know it was then because this is how we agreed for it to happen.

Between blinks, it's like you were never here.

And when I'm behind the wheel of the SUV, the same could be said for us.

2.

I'm here because he's perfect, which really means I'm training him to be more. With every tape, I'm giving him exactly what he needs to hear. These are lessons, but they aren't lectures; these are "I love yous," but they aren't formal expressions. We save that for murder. I've taught so many, all it takes is the brush of a strand of hair over the ear, a little blush of the cheek, a giggle, and/or maybe a blink of an eye. The chances are good that neither assistant will make it in the end. The chances are even greater that we won't find some of my exes, but I'm willing to look, and that's why I have the back of the SUV full of weapons of all sorts. I'll never be sure when I'll need them, but when I do, my pet, you'll be well equipped. As well-equipped as I'm sure you are well-endowed.

Size isn't everything—it's all about what I see beyond the murderous sparkle of your eyes.

People are born for this. . .and if not, well they're just another tired driver on this interstate at 1AM on a weekday. That's to say, they're lost, and got nothing in them worth being more than anyone else. They'll maybe drive some more to figure it out, whereas we're driving to finish having already figured out who we are.

My beloved pet has driven so many miles.

Seeing the sign:

Maryland Welcomes You

Does nothing but increase the itch to keep going. So true, isn't it?

My heart beats faster thinking of the possibilities.

Tell time via the mile markers and the amount of tape we have left to record. What will the next ten minutes bring? The next twenty?

I'm getting excited enough to drive faster. By now

we're sharing the same patch of road; by now I'm swerving in and out of lanes, frightening the truckers, RVs, and other vehicles. Black SUV swerving across three lanes of traffic. This isn't exhaustion; it is enticing.

So when it's all so exciting and hopeful, the pet at my side drives with me. He swerves with me. He speeds up. I slow down. We take to lanes, playing that kind of game.

And when I start chasing him, he is quick to flee.

Like a good pet, he is the one being chased. He keeps the coupe at 95MPH. The SUV can go much faster than his used Japanese coupe, but when we're expressing ourselves, 95MPH will have to do. He gets behind a pickup truck but manages to ride the grassy side of the road until the pickup truck switches lanes.

The SUV gets right up on the pickup truck's rear. I'm going to make the pickup truck move. This vehicle does not change lanes for anyone.

In this game we're playing, it's about master and pet. It's not about them. They are merely in the way. Now leave. Give the truck the high beams and it happens.

And I'm right up on my pet, close enough to see the back of his head slightly hidden by the headrest. I'm noticing that he's taped up the camera to the dashboard.

"He's filming 24/7 now. . . " I'm saying to myself.

I'm hearing from the back, the blonde, "So clever."

I'm telling the both of them—they should have been asleep—that they have no part in this. This is between him and me.

If they don't close their eyes, duct tape their mouths and ears; I'm going to have to do something else. Quick with the duct tape. So they've learned something.

I'm whispering, "I love you," as I nudge his bumper.

He's swerving, but oh, you know he's enjoying it.

He's enjoying it so much that he's nudging me back.

We each take turns. Love taps.

And I'm loving every tap. In this game we're playing, we're sleepless and together. We're continually being lost and found. And together we're laughing as we both switch to the left lane, a semi-truck inches from being the one that takes us down.

I'm enjoying the thought—my pet melded with the back of the trailer, master and the love of his life melded between twisted metal and other dark fluids into one big wreck.

That would be where we'd be fully found. If it had to end that way, no one would be able to tell us apart. Our bodies wouldn't be found between the explosions, fires, chassis damage, and body contortions. It would be the perfect vehicular expression, if I'd imagine it correctly in any way.

What's the camera seeing?

Are you getting any of this?

Held back, resting by the strap, the footage isn't at all like his; his would be far more precise; from my end the shakiness of the footage matches my heartbeat.

But there's more to be had, so hold on.

Your nausea may be another form of attraction for someone else.

I'm riding towards the exit until he changes his mind and swerves last-minute back into the right lane. The SUV doesn't take the collision perfectly and for what feels like one breathless forever, the vehicle spins before I'm able to regain control.

He's watching it happen long before it's happened.

I'm watching the next frame and the frames after that where we are on the median, where he's blacking out as the car goes in the wrong direction.

We go against traffic for a half mile.

The few vehicles heading our way are nowhere near as

in love as we are.

This is perfect, so perfect I have only those three words to say.

But at the last second I decide not to say them. He knows, and so I'm looking away from the road to the camera. This is where the observer gets to provide commentary.

Hear other people's voices.

The cars might crash but it'll be for the sake of how my pet and I feel.

For one blacked out moment, we're going in reverse before we're, once again, heading in the right direction. And then we're back to position one, him being chased and me, the chaser.

I'm asking the assistants how they feel.

Nothing, hear nothing, while I press down on the gas, speeding past 95MPH, to catch up to him. Slamming on the breaks when a sedan of some sort slowly switches lanes, obstructing my path.

Speak with the sound other horn, telling the driver that she doesn't belong.

I'm asking the assistants how they feel.

Me, I've felt so much it's difficult to feel much of anything exact, but it's all rushing through my veins, my nerves tense, my skin damp with sweat, my eyeliner running just enough to create a streak down my cheeks. In the darkness of this late night, this is a chase between two similar minds.

And everyone's clearly along for the ride.

It becomes a scene that jumps from one to the next with no clear order.

He's winning. He's winning and I'm satisfied.

He's winning and maybe I'm letting him win. For him to win means I've gotten the payoff I wanted. One last grand altercation begins when two passing cars choose to get involved, attempting to switch into my lane. When I attempt to switch lanes, one car speeds up. When I try to slow down and try to outmaneuver them, they slow down too.

There's nothing else to be done and so, as I ask the assistants how they feel, I ram into the side one car and then the next, the SUV taking most of the damage, nothing wrong with a little dent.

I'm observing how, at this speed, it feels so much like we're standing still.

Momentum this great, I can only quantify it in breaths held. I go from holding my breath for a second to holding my breath for thirty seconds as I'm pushing through those that simply do not understand. Exhaling, I'm asking the assistants how they feel.

If they're saying anything, I can't hear them over the thudding of my heartbeat.

I'm shouting to the assistants a bunch of things—can't quite be sure what—I'm so excited. At this very moment, I'm not sure what I feel. At this exact moment, I'm pretty sure a person can't expect anything greater than what I'm feeling.

And then he ducks behind another van, switches lanes into the far left before I can even get close enough. I'm mouthing goodbyes because I can't talk I'm so out of breath.

Then he's nowhere to be seen, two, three, four cars ahead.

I'm waving goodbye, slowing the SUV down, I'm asking you what you think. Who won and who lost? And really, would you be stupid enough to think that I did anything other than let my pet win? This isn't merely for pleasure; I'm training my pet. And he's doing oh, so well.

To the next juncture and lesson, my pet. I can only be satisfied when he's doing exactly what I tell him. I'm looking in the backseat.

"Gross. You're going to have to bleach the hell out of the upholstery."

Bodily fluids rarely carry the kind of aroma you'd be fine with keeping around; most of it has to do with the acridness that carries the unconscious fact that it came from something living. It's why bodily fluids are so curious; when ingested you are taking in something that belongs to another.

When it is shed, it's someone marking it as theirs.

Whether they intend to or not, spilled fluid is a mark left with the scent of another.

It begins to rain softly, but I wait until exhaustion hits to switch on the windshield wipers.

The assistants are silent in the back. I'm reaching for the camera—don't you want to see me one last time before the episode's over? I'm hearing nothing the gentle press of a few piano keys, tracing the gentile music to its source. It's coming from the SUV's speakers.

Part of the transition. Music to accompany this episode's ending credits.

This is the calm before the next storm. It fades to black with breathless ease.

Data recorded.

3.

What is this, what is that? Look at the camera.

Doesn't she look familiar? It's because today, we'll be interviewing the star of the show, the center of the mystery, Claire Wilkinson! [Audience chatter] No, no—not the Clair,e but rather, we will speak to a number of individuals that claim to be Claire's spitting image. They believe to carry the same characteristics, and, what's more, they believe that they have done some of what Claire has done.

[More audience chatter] That's right!

We'll get a first-hand glimpse at Claire's greatest fans.

We'll get to ask the questions we've been wanting to ask.

We'll peer into the boundless psyche of a mystery all its own.

All this and more after the commercial break!

[Commercial break] During the commercial break, glimpse a trailer for a surrealistic thriller, a commercial for another network television show, and a featured spot for the upcoming high definition season one release of the mystery, complete with the now infamous shot of Claire as its cover art.

[Back to show] [Audience applause]

And we're back with four of the most unusual and captivating guests we've interviewed.

Say hello to our assortment of Claires!

[Audience greeting]

Who'd like to go first?

—I will.

Now there's a courageous one.

—What are you getting at? We're not courageous?

No, no—I'm not saying that.

—You were implying it.

—Yeah he was.

If there were any unintended implications, I apologize but, well, let's just get right down to the interview.

—I'd like to interview you.

—Me too.

—I think it would be appropriate if all four of us ask this man some questions.

—My first one would be, why that suit and not any other suit? You chose the worst possible suit to wear and I'm beginning to think that maybe you've always worn the same shitty suits.

I. . .umm. . .wear what wardrobe provides.

—Seems a lot is wrong with the way the camera is being run.

—Someone's got to clean the lens.

—Why are you talking like that?

I. . .I'm talking like I always talk.

—I'm thinking you're talking like that because you have confidence issues. You don't seem to be high up on the confidence chart.

—Yup.

—Not a single ounce of fight in the guy.

—Couldn't even hold a knife right to save his life.

I. . .

—Who's got a knife with them?

—Yeah, let's see if he can.

—What's he doing?

—Show's off the air.

—Couldn't take the heat?

—We're just being ourselves.

—Can't be anything but who we are.

—I'm sure of myself. Are you?

[Off air] View the static image that reads, "The show must go on, but 'SORRY'—we're currently experiencing technical difficulties. 'STANDBY.'"]

—How long is a viewer expected to really "standby?"

—I'd switch channels.

—I'd go watch something else.

—I know we would, but they wouldn't.

—They want to watch me.

—You mean me.

—No I'm talking about me.

—You're both confused. The camera's on me.

[Producer's voice] Please, ladies, we can't go back on air until there is some sense of order.

—Seems fine to me.

Please understand that you cannot verbally attack the host of this show.

—I'm not doing anything to the guy.

—He's disgusting.

—Kind of guy I wouldn't dare even look at much less talk to at a party.

—Parties are full of them.

—We're in agreement there.

The show will not go on until I have unanimous agreement between the lot of you:

No heckling, no verbally attacking the host of this show!

[Camera flickers back on]

—I don't think so.

[Producer's voice] Who may I ask is speaking?

—You know who.

[Producer into headset] Get her on camera. Who needs these fakes if we've got the real deal!

[Host chimes in] Everyone, please give a round of applause for our surprise gues—

—Save it. I don't approve of what's going on here.

I. . .apologize. [Host looks more than a little anxious from the pressure, practiced cool gone]

—No, I think I'll be paying more attention at what goes on behind the camera.

[Producer chimes in] Excuse me?

—[To the host]You've been written out of the narrative. Before you can say anything, save it.

This is no longer the place for it.

I'm going to have you disappear. There's got to be a mystery or else no one would be watching. From this point on, audience, speak up. If you expect to understand reality, you've got to embrace the mystery. No more letting transcripts and audience-cues give you the blues.

You're involved. Speak up. Your involvement helps make me beautiful.

4.

The camera captures everything but the feel of night air against skin, the smell of burning rubber, the bloodcurdling screams of my nubile assistants here. The not-quite Claires.

Come as you are. We're merely getting to know each other. I'm sure you, yes you, watching would like to think you know a thing or two about me. If I gave you my body, what would you stimulate first? Do you think I like my nipples bitten, my asshole licked? What's your fetish? The camera sees all. And if it doesn't, it'll be the most patient one of all. Eventually you'll start to treat me as your own; I'll play a part in your own fantasy. I'll feel real to the touch in the context of your wet dream. I'll make you young again. Boys and girls, we'll need no bedsheets.

We keep the lights on.

For all to see. No reason to be ashamed.

And as night becomes day, I want you to understand something.

You've been watching the entire time.

Lives aren't shared,
they're stolen.

1.

I drove down a narrow dirt road by daylight.

Couldn't see due to the glare, but the real world was on my side.

He wasn't there, you see. He wasn't there.

Second time it's happened. Death row doesn't last forever.

So we had to make up for it.

My pet needs someone else to kill. And I can't let all my exes die by other hands.

Down this road and a right turn, we'll see a house. We'll see a barn.

We'll see a man. The Candy Man's brother. Not much of anything, frankly.

But he'll have to do.

The executioner can take Candy Man's life.

Only I can take a legacy.

2.

I'm quickly finding out that just because you're related to a killer, it doesn't mean you have it in you to do the same. He's a stutterer. When he sees us, he can't get a word out.

I already know his name.

I already know what we're doing here.

I already know how it'll all play out.

A few basic facts: His name is Jeff. He's the older of the two. The Candy Man, as he was called, his younger brother, I started him after his second kill. He always had a sweet tooth and I sweetened him up so that he couldn't have a lick without taking a life too.

Weren't really lives to him though.

I'm thinking Candy Man thought of this as a sugar-coated dream.

He came from a lackluster lineage. Lineage with generations of schizophrenia.

I'm thinking I stayed with Candy Man because he was just so fucking funny.

He knew how to make me laugh. Oh, the things he'd do to them. I'd laugh for hours.

One time I laughed for days.

I'm thinking I should be ashamed of my time with Candy Man, but I wasn't. I'd still watch the footage I've kept of him. Back then he was unquenchable.

He'd lick just to lick. Didn't matter how dirty of a situation it was, he'd lick.

I fell for humor. I'm not proud of it.

Another fact to add: Jeff will be the last of the family to go.

I won't even do much of anything. It's the assistants that'll be combing the haystacks for the mother hiding, fighting off the father with a pitchfork.

We have the weapons in the SUV.

Might as well use them. It's why we walk the way we walk. It's why the assistants don't talk when Jeff shows up, intrigued to see us. Don't be fooled: He acts like he knows us but really he's never seen us before. He doesn't look very much like his brother. That's a shame.

But not like it would have made a difference. It'll still end the way it's supposed to end. I would have liked to have Jeff be a bit more representative of his sibling. That way the mystery could have been upheld. Oh well. Hear me now:

It's going to happen and that's all there is to it.

So get on with it. I'm walking faster.

"Keep up," I'm shouting to the assistants.

"You've got a lot to do," I'm also saying that they shouldn't be wearing so many clothes. I'm down to my underwear. My pale skin's going to tan a little bit. Would you like to see darker skin?

Leave it to the mystery to be blunt when you least expect it.

So we're beginning to realize how hot it can get this far away from the interstate.

So I'm already getting tired of Jeff.

Things are said.

I'm not saying them.

I'm walking. Doing nothing more than that.

It's worth feeling a little sorry for Jeff.

Jeff's oblivious, and more than a little naïve. Do you feel sorry for the guy?

No? I'm thinking we need a little more camera time before things heat up. Enough of bright light on bare skin, look at the victim. Dossier on victimization and what it means to watch as a victim completes his part.

"Hello Jeff, smile for the camera."

"What you filming?"

Pointing to the assistants, "I'm filming for a study."

"You don't look like a scientist," Jeff's saying with a laugh.

Right out of some kind of cheesy horror flick, we have Jeff, dim witted and close-minded. He carries the same concepts of normalcy as the most conservative bunch you'll find. Flip through a book of tropes and archetypes and he'd be in there:

Typical small town/small minded slasher victim.

Kind of makes you feel the opposite of sorry. He's not putting much thought into any of this. He sees attractive females; he's thinking with his dick, nothing else.

I'm asking, "What's your definition of a scientist?"

The assistants are lost in thought, thinking two steps ahead. They know what they'll have to do, so get the ChapStick out. Those chapped lips won't do.

I'm not interested in his response, and by the looks of it, neither is the audience.

Skip over the meaningless talk, get right to the last few lines. In the case of getting as much as you give, Jeffy boy isn't giving much.

Gets interesting when this line is delivered:

"Where's your dad?"

And then, "In the barn."

"And your mom?"

"She's bakin' for breakfast. I dunno what I'm supposta do till breakfast."

And then, "How about helping your mom with the cooking?"

"Dunno how to do that."

"Do you know how to do anything?"

"I'm good at feeding the animals."

And then, "What kind of animals do you and your family have?"

"All kinds."

Skip this part because it's not worth mentioning. No hurting the animals unless the animals hurt you first. I've never found any worth in harming them. They know their boundaries better than, say, Jeffy boy here. They'll leave you to your own business. They understand life and death. More so, an animal tends to their lives like it's leaning towards the dark end. The big "D." And no, I'm not talking about dick. I'm sure someone watching would think of it. Maybe it has more to do with you thinking it when you hear "big D" than what's being said here. A lot can be understood from connotation and what you choose to imagine given the cues.

I'm full of cues.

I'm more about giving cues than giving due.

What are you thinking right now?

3.

I'm tired of the heat. More so, I'm tired of how typical this is. Deserted road leads to run down farm leads to a family that's stuck out of time. Family that might be pulled from some B-movie. They stick out and do nothing for the mystery. You don't want to see the assistants the way they are now. So shameful. You call that a blowjob? You call that a blow to the head?

You call that humiliation?

Seems they're the ones that are more humiliated. I'm beginning to think that they're fucking with me. They've learned so much and then this happens. One minute they're obedient and interested in what we're doing, next minute they're acting like I kidnapped them. Against their will.

They want to be Claires don't they?!

See how they nod with certainty when I ask them?

They're fucking with me. Now it's up to them to tend to the bodies.

They're going to have to try blowing Jeff a second time. They couldn't even make archetypal dim-witted boy cum. How's that for pathetic?

The audience expects better.

The audience wants to see something definitive.

How is a dick that won't get hard definitive?

I'm ashamed of this. This is a scene that should be left on the cutting room floor. But see the floors covered with bodies and those that should be tending to their removal are too busy clamming up in front of the camera.

Jeff seems to be completely indifferent to it.

Forgets all about his dying family in the barn.

Offers us food.

I push them out of the way. Pan around the kitchen to

see how stereotypical of a kitchen it is. I'll give you a cue:

Floral pattern wallpaper.

It's time for this to go somewhere.

Cut to Jeff in the kitchen. Blank-faced. The opposite of someone aroused.

Cut to us with the father. I'm talking to him like I'm the one bargaining. Really though, it's the blonde that finally drives the knife into the father's neck.

Brunette sits back, holding the camera. Thinks she can get away with not doing much of anything because she's operating the camera. But I'm aware. Oh, I'm aware.

Cut to Jeff right as his face contorts in pain.

Cut back to the barn, mother in tears over the dead father's body.

I'm taking the camera from the brunette. No more hiding. She's right in the center of this.

"Don't you want to end her sorrow?" I'm saying, pointing at the mother.

She's in tears. She's been dead a long time. As far as I'm seeing it, the desperation and loneliness got to her decades ago; it's only now that anyone bothered to kill her.

Camera zooms in on the mother's face. Tired eyes and tears, hollow gasps, and the subtle inkling that this isn't genuine. She's crying because that's what people do when someone close to them dies. Does she really feel anything?

I'm sure if that were a question on some test it would be a no-brainer, a freebie.

Not that I'd ever put something like that on one of my tests. They'd probably get it wrong, then I'd have to grade on a curve so that it looks like people actually learn something.

Cut back to the brunette.

"Yes you are," I'm saying.

She's going to, or she's going to be the one with the

gun in her mouth.

Cut back to Jeff, wincing in pain. A little bit of blood.

Apparently he bit his lip. No—no one's hurt him yet. Kind of expected it to be something else, didn't you? I'm all about making it more interesting. More interesting means more fun. My pet likes to be fully engrossed in the scene. You like seeing how it works, shot for shot, don't you?

Cut back to the brunette, gun in hand.

I'm saying, "If you don't do it now I'm going to take that gun and if I take that gun you know exactly where it's going."

So what else is she going to do?

She pulls the trigger. It makes a loud enough sound to mess with the audio levels of the camera, a crackling muted sound, before it fades.

I'm standing there, looking.

Brunette is standing there, frozen in place, gun still aimed at the now useless sight.

Blonde is looking away, mostly out of boredom. I catch her holding something but we're cutting to the next shot before I can have a look.

Cut back to the kitchen. Jeff eating.

Someone under the table.

Make that two.

"It's not a popsicle."

Jeff is amused.

4.

So audience, what shall we call him, hmm?

Speak up! I can't hear you!

That's better. Our man here is privy to a number of things he hasn't yet done. But with the help of my assistants, he will get off. He will feel what it feels like to blow his load.

Our man here, you want to be a man don't you?

[Jeff response]

He says he doesn't know. What's that supposed to mean?

The audience wants to know!

Okay—here's what we're going to do, Jeffy boy.

First—don't move.

Good. The audience is watching and they know what they want. Don't fuck up.

Second—You're going to meet a man. He's going to seem pretty normal. He will need help.

You will help him.

Understand? Good.

Hey audience, which would you prefer:

a) My pet sees what's inside the barn

b) My pet doesn't see what's inside the barn

[Audience poll]

Looks like it's done.

Three—you aren't going to show him the barn.

Hear me?

Good.

Four—you are going to act like everything's okay. Everything is okay.

If you don't, we're just around the corner.

You don't agree? I'll make them bite. They've got you inside their mouths; all it takes is one bite and. . .

[Audience gasps]

Hey audience, what do you think?

a) I stick around and film my pet interacting with Jeffy boy

b) We leave and tend to my pet's broken coupe

c) We go get some candy somewhere. Or some yogurt. Maybe both

Looks like we have a tie between (b) and (c).

Well, this is interesting. I'm sure there's no reason why we can't do both.

Five—We're watching you, so I expect you to extend the same level of hospitality to him as you did to me. Just because he doesn't have tits and a vagina doesn't mean you can't be civil to the guy.

Six—You're going to help him. I can't stress that enough. For the mystery to work, you need to be yourself. Our presence here mustn't change a single thing.

Got me?

Good.

Do all this and I won't chop it off.

It's engorged right now. If I were to say, use these hedgers here...

[Audience gasp]

It'll be less manhood and more a spout.

Ever been completely embarrassed in public?

Didn't think so.

You'll want to be a good boy.

Or else you'll be like your brother.

Didn't know?

[Audience laughter]

Your brother and I were close.

Didn't work out but we've got a past.

You could say he's nothing but the past now.

[Audience applause]

[To the blonde] Cover his ears.

They covered? Okay, before the next scene, I want to share how I've designed it.

See, The Candy Man got his gimmick from how he dealt with his victim's bodies, not the other way around. He didn't sell candy and he didn't have an ice cream truck. I found most of his victims. I'd leave them tied up and gagged and he'd walk in when he's interested. He'd treat them like friends, playing videogames with them, that kind of thing. But eventually, when he worked himself up, the anticipation killing him, he'd have his meal.

He wasn't a cannibal. That's not really it. He just liked the warmth.

He liked to use their fingers to scoop up fudge and chocolate pudding.

He liked how it tasted when you mixed honey and little bit of blood.

Towards the end, he started eating out of parts of the victim's body. He drank urine.

He started exploring without any adherence to the rules I've assigned.

You see, my pet's going to do just that: He will take Jeff and effortlessly do away with his life.

Simple shot to the head. The kill itself won't be interesting.

He'll drench Jeff in syrup and eat breakfast using his body as the plate.

Some of the body will be eaten. But my pet does this because it's what the Candy Man did.

I'm seeing what he's capable of, and perhaps what he'll fully embody.

But not yet. We will be patient. For the mystery to work, I can't just give him a name and show him how he'll treat each of his victims. He has to learn, and a lot of learning is done by doing.

I'll show him right from wrong later.

Jeffy boy here—you can let go of his ears now—will play an important role!

Let's give him a hand!

[Audience applause]

Close up shot on Jeff grinning before dissolving into the next shot.

5.

We're somewhere near the gas station when I watch the tape.

Inhale and exhale, I'd like to push away all assumptions. I'll watch it while waiting for him to catch up. He's going to have to walk the entire dirt road and a good few miles on the interstate before he gets here. For it to work, timing is everything.

So I waited to watch the tape.

I wanted to have something to look forward to.

But when I start the tape, it doesn't begin the way I wanted it to. It doesn't start with the two of them at the table. It starts with a dirt road.

It doesn't have the two of them talking.

My pet killed Jeff and dragged him in the dirt.

I say the words like they're in reaction to something that I'll never hear again.

"I love you. . ." I look around and see that the assistants are watching too.

The blonde seems amused.

I slap her across the face and tell her to get in the back with the brunette.

Duct tape. They forced me to do it.

My pet ruined the kill. Fumbled the entire kill.

What is this, huh?

What is this that I'm watching?

Instead of syrup, there's just a few close-up shots of a caved in skull, blood caked over the eyes in a sickly dark concoction, looking more like grease than blood.

My pet walks dragging the body, camera pointed down at the ground.

I'm watching but I've already understood why.

The reason he did what he did. But no, I'm unwilling

to accept it; the ruin is far greater than the reason. Freeze frame on my pet with his one free hand over his face. Every shot is disgust.

Where's the rest of the kill?

This is it?

This isn't data.

I cannot label this "Data Recorded!"

I pause the tape.

I play the tape.

I pause it again.

I'm looking for something.

I'm searching for something other than why.

But the tape is more of the same.

My pet walking the dirt road alone.

My pet dragging a body until it is caked in layers of dust and dirt.

My pet leaving the body like it'll be there when he gets back.

My pet clearly aware that I'll get to the body first.

And then the camera in his hands makes for a clearer shot.

What you see: A man fending the heat, the sunlight.

What I see: My pet knew that the Candy Man shouldn't have been; he knows that it was my mistake. My mistake to have ever been involved with the Candy Man. My mistake that I let him laugh his way into my life. My mistake that I cultivated such an unmemorable legacy.

So what does my pet do?

He treats Jeff like he's just some guy in the way.

A bystander that saw what he shouldn't have seen.

And what does this tape have anything to do with his training?

With our relationship? It disgusts me. More so, it shows that he is willing to fight me on this. So egotistical after so few kills. What does this mean?

I catch her watching from the backseat.

"What did I tell you to do?!"

She's there so I take out the confusion on her.

When I regain my calm, her face is bruised.

Her nose bloody. I tell her, "You made me do this!"

I saw something in her eyes.

She thinks I made a mistake. And maybe I did. I'd be the first to admit it.

But not to her. I'm feeling inadequate so I speed up.

We're going to get some candy.

That's exactly what we're going to get.

Candy.

Yes.

6.

Data erased.

You want what you cannot have.

1.

The mystery is a man.

The mystery is a woman.

The mystery is you.

The mystery is that my pet can become anything I'd like him to become.

I know him better than anyone else. He is capable, fully capable, of anything you might like to see. More so, I'm quick to point out that he'll do just about everything to make you uncomfortable. You won't want to watch, but you won't be able to look away.

He won't be here.

He's busy. He'll always be busy.

But I'm here, so ask me. If it pleases you, go ahead and ask.

What would you like to know about him?

[Audience participation]

That's right. It's your chance to speak.

So speak up.

I'm all ears and waiting. Just don't make me wait for long.

Answer: He's smart. Smart as can be. He's good at adapting. One second he's innocent and wouldn't hurt a fly, next second he's all blades and bullets and ready to go down on me for hours. He doesn't need to come up for air.   Answer: He's capable of that too, yes. He can rig up bombs. Even if he doesn't, he can learn and I can teach him. Don't confuse the lack of explosions as a lack of intensity. We simply prefer intimacy.

Answer: He's always been a student, like me. No minimum wage shit. That's not for us. It would numb me out so much that the fight would be all I'd care for. I had an ex that I supported fully but couldn't kill. Turns out he only hated his job. He only hated people. Hating people and the act of serial killing are opposites. They don't need to be involved. In fact, I'd say that to be one of the best, a legacy worth a damn, you've got to believe that everyone's already dead. Nothing, no value to them; just bodies still moving around. It's how I've gotten to see people and it's how I'm training my pet to think. That way, there's no preoccupation, no direct hate, or disgust. Save all that for what we share: our bodies, our thoughts, his legacy.

Answer: He's got a family like you've got a family. And I've got one too. What else is there to say? They didn't do shit about my decisions and I'm sure as hell my pet's family does nothing but hope that he'll fit right in and be lost in the crowd like everybody else.

Answer: No there's no hope in that regard. I'm thinking it's kind of a wash actually. The concept of having enough to be okay is absurd. Getting comfortable is impossible. Getting comfortable sucks the fight right out of you. If you're a fighter, you won't be able to do the five-day-a-week grind. It's barely enough for me to do this academia garbage. But I'm going with it, the bare minimum, always the bare minimum; no one deserves any better except for those that keep you fighting. Moment you fucking give in is the moment you start dying.

Answer: Wouldn't say I've been abused. He's surely never been. We're just interested in what's hidden. Too much is hidden, shoved underneath the façades civility gives us. If I'm a scholar in any area, it's in getting what I want.

I always get what I want.

Answer: He's been with others like I've been with others, but it's the first time we've ever been with anyone alive. Everything else, it might as well have been necrophilia.

Answer: This is just a body. It's what he's capable of that's most attractive. He looks at me and I know what he sees; he's not just seeing my skin, my chest, my face, my curves. . .that's what you are seeing. Not him. He's seeing what's within. He's seeing beyond the pickup and beyond the seduction. He's seeing the ether of me.

Answer: I've heard of it, yes. Doubtful he's heard of it. I've lectured about it once or twice. The Macdonald triad is just another theory working to make sense of what's hidden so far underneath;

only way you can understand is by doing. Seeing means feeling. Feeling means being right there, fingers in an orifice.

To answer specifically about the triad:

No, he's not a pyromaniac.

No, he isn't sadistic. It's all about the kill—whatever factors into the kill is entirely for accentuation of reason; it's to keep you all interested. Nothing else. If he shot a person and walked away, you would forget a minute later. You've probably already forgotten how he killed that kid. Jeff. Only reason you remember is because it's on me. It's on my mind. It's still on my mind, yes. It's always on my mind.

No, he's never tortured animals. What did I say about torturing animals? You should have been paying more attention. This isn't the kind of stuff that you can watch out the corner of your eye.

No, he's not a bedwetter. He surely gets me wet. But he saves the urine for the urinal. Or the kill, if there's a need for a little something extra to get people leaning forward, edge of their seat stuff.

Answer: Stats are just that—Concrete evidence that can only resemble the past. I'm here to tell you that the momentum is too quick to ever be completely accurate. Those stats explain what happened a few years back. A few years back, to me, can sound like fiction. That's all it can be.

Answer: I don't know what you're trying to get at but let's leave it to the mystery.

The mystery can be anything and everything. And surprises outweigh expectation.

No one is spared and everyone will, at some point, be surprised.

After the pickup game, it's the game of devotion and obsession, but the switch of sex and violence is exactly the same. It's how anybody stays interested; it's how anybody gets along.

They lust for something they don't quite understand.

But want—it all starts with that wanting.

If you're like me, you'll need to find it.

You won't stop until it's all yours.

2.

I know firsthand the anatomy of betrayal.

I knew that something was wrong when I couldn't find my phone. Using a payphone to find it, I couldn't hear my ringtone. And then I couldn't find her. My phone goes missing and it doesn't just go missing. One and two equal reason.

The blonde one.

You think she'd be able to be me. I'll show her a thing or two.

No—I'm not angry. No. I'm not. I'm intrigued. To think she believed that she could replace me. Whereas, I'm sure my pet is far from interested, using her as something to fill the nothingness of our long drive. And it is a long drive.

No—I'm not angry. He's bored between each of my exes.

No—I'm not angry at all. She'd try her best. I'm sure of it.

But guess what? She's not getting away with it. I'm approximately fifteen minutes behind them, and I can only assume that she's with him in the broken down coupe.

I already know that in order for this to have been possible, she somehow took advantage of him. He's mine. You're mine.

My pet is young and full of excitement. In his excited state, he might have confused her for me. From a distance, in this dreadful heat, the bright sunlight, I'm thinking it's truly possible.

No—I'm not angry. But something is going to happen.

Got to think about what she's done to get him inside her. She probably did it all, everything she could think of, using what she observed from me. Anyone around me long enough, it usually rubs off on them, the act. The whole act and nothing but the act. The truth, it's no court case.

See it like it's some kind of recap at the beginning of

an episode. . .

Previously on. . .and then it's her but her face is blurred out. Because something's wrong. She's not me. Could never be me. But the betrayal is real. It is its own problem in need of its own punishment.

Oh, look at her. She'd look right into his eyes, never breaking eye contact, just to show that she's confident. In needing to be so obvious, she reveals to everyone watching that she's insecure. There's truly nothing like that affection for another to make them feel alive; she's doing her damnedest to make him feel good.

Look how she's blushing like any other victim.

And then she's giggling too, flirting with the threat of disaster.

I don't see him in this.

Shot for imagined shot, this is not part of the show. This is part of my imagination. And I'm only telling you what could have happened.

I'm telling you it wouldn't have been any better than this. She wouldn't have been able to replace me, much less do any better an impersonation than the one I just prefaced.

No—I'm not angry. I've repeated it enough times for it to be true.

We're getting right up to the picture, where we left off.

This unexpected juncture consists of the following:

The coupe, where it was, dirt road cast in the heat of midday.

He's as he should be. And me, where am I?

I'm where I've always been—driving.

I could crash into the coupe.

I could crash into her.

I'm thinking about it, but if I did that it would reveal that I am, in fact, angry. That would make it so that I was lying. A liar means anything said is in question of it being real or not.

I'm telling all of you this is real. Unexpected and a real surprise, the blonde so boastful of the fact that she wants him. . .when really she has no idea how to satisfy him.

You wouldn't know what to do with him even if you got him.

Look at that, then—my pet so bored that he's passed out in the driver's seat.

Where is she? She's sitting right next to him. At the last second she tries to duck behind the dashboard. Too late dearie, you're not getting away with this.

Stop the SUV in a way where the coupe wouldn't be able to steer away from me. Nothing wrong with this, babe. I'm not blaming you, my pet.

No. I'm not.

You are not his. You are mine.

All of you, mine.

I'm the driver. I'm the master.

So then when I leave the SUV, walk casually down the dirt road, open the front passenger door, remove her from the equation, this is what's supposed to happen next.

It's my right to do this.

And I'll take her, bind her with rope and duct tape, to the gas station where we should have been, where we will be, and I'll bring her in the back.

Hey, clerk, you won't mind will you? Course not. He sees three attractive girls and his pubescent self can do nothing but imagine the sexual possibilities.

Enough of him though. He's next, not now.

I'll take her back here so effortlessly.

Treat this as an outtake.

And if you're still watching it's because the camera's still rolling.

Camera's rolling and yeah, you can think of it as a little privilege. You get to see what sometimes happens when you let the study evolve on its own. Everyone gets ideas. Some ideas don't end up working for the entire production. My study, remember?

Brunette is quiet but she's still my assistant.

I'm telling her to keep up. This is not on her. Blonde's on camera now.

And then you get that one frame, the shot that changes everything:

Her betrayal is her only way out. She wants out of our endeavor.

Blonde has lost sight of the study.

I'll fix her. She wanted this anyway, right? Full attention.

So let's start.

"Tell me what happened," I'm commanding.

And her voice is shrill. Obvious that she understood the repercussions for deviating from the study, going against my wishes. Now she gets what she can only expect will be death. But I'm not killing one of my own. If she's going to be victimized, it'll be after she loses all of her worth.

She's still of some use to me.

Next we have a little back and forth session where I'm forcing her to repeat after me.

Repeat after me, same tone, same inflection, same. Everything about it the same.

Am I just another lay?

Her response: "Am I just another lay?"

Again.

Am I just another lay?

"Am I just another lay?"

Am I?

"Am I?"

Louder. Am I?!

"Am I?"

Am I really?

"Am I really?"

I'm no different than you.

She pauses.

Say it!

"I'm no different than you."

I'm Claire.

"I'm. . .Claire."

Not good enough.

I'm Claire.

"I'm Claire."

Oh that's some bullshit. I'm taking the camera from the brunette. I'm zooming it on her face so the only thing being seen is her face. Her frightened, sweaty face.

Does she think she's going to die? Of course.

But that's not why she's scared.

She's scared because she won't die. And this will continue. The study will continue.

She's scared because she's going to be quite an important part of the study.

When will I get you both to understand that we're no different?

We're all the same!

Tit for tat, that saying. We seek the mystery as much as the mystery becomes us.

They're watching us. You both like and hate that you're being watched.

I'm telling them both. You'll be me yet.

Except for one difference. Where they're searching, still searching, I've already been found. Rather, I've done all the finding and I've got plenty left to fight for. They're envious because they're the versions of me missing an important piece.

Master without pet.

That's no good. Master without pet means you're not really much of a master.

And there it is: the source of the fear.

Being me without what I need feels as much like a disaster as anything else can. It's depression and desertion all at once. They'll know and feel the loathing, the loneliness, the general disgust, the dark thoughts and many, many dreadful days I've felt when I couldn't find one that would be mine. And I mean really be mine.

You both will be me.

To the blonde I'm shouting, "You will be me!"

Accept it. I slap her across the face. Camera's still on her.

For a split second, you see only skin, you see a flash of what can only be surprise.

Accept it. Say it. Be mine.

Be me!

She doesn't want to say it.

I'll say it again, "I am Claire."

Her turn quickly results in tears.

So another slap. I'll do what needs to be done to fix you.

You'll be mine. You'll be me.

I'm Claire.

Say it.

"I'm Claire."

Again.

"I'm Claire."

Again!

"I'm Claire."

Louder and more declarative with every successive utterance, she's beginning to understand. She's beginning to accept. Again. Say it. Again.

Be mine.

She begins to anticipate the slap, so I have the brunette

use the stun gun on her, once. Twice. We'll break her down.

It won't take much.

Again.

Say it again.

Believe my words as your own.

You're mine.

You always were.

You wouldn't be anything without me.

What's your name?

What's your name?

Say it.

Again.

Say it.

What's your name?

"Claire."

Her name is Claire and she always was trying, wasn't she?

She's searching. She's envious. She'll never again think of betraying me. If she did, she'd only be betraying herself.

We don't want that do we?

Of course not.

Data recorded.

3.

To brunette from Claire: Did you see that, hmm? An assistant thought better of herself. She didn't quite understand what's going on here. The mystery can be confusing, that's for sure.

But you're not like her, are you?

Just because she has blonde hair doesn't mean she's any different.

We're Claire.

I don't have to remind you, do I?

Of course not. You're subservient. You're like I was, on the surface. I was always the good student. I was always trying to leave an impression, but only if it seemed like it would help my grade.

I was always searching for affection, but none of what people had looked anything like what I was looking for.

I was looking for it a long time.

Really was a long time. Wow. . .

But you're not like that, right?

You're not worried about how long it takes, only that you'll find what you're looking for.

There are fighters out there.

Maybe one of them will be yours.

A pet of your own. For now, watch me and be me.

You are me. I'm hoping it doesn't take as much for you to understand this. I'm hoping you've already understood the situation. This is my study, but you might get a chance to express yourself one day. Keep searching.

Find someone to be yours.

For now, you both will be me. You'll learn.

You'll identify as me.

I'm sure you've noticed, huh? Noticed that you never had much to identify with and that kind of led you in the direction of criminology. It led you to look at the bare essence of the mystery. It led you to where you're at now.

And I'll be the first to tell you:

It wasn't an accident.

It's all about finding something that completes you. That's what it's most about.

You'll learn. I keep saying that, but it's true. It'll be grueling. You'll get frustrated, but no one ever helped me the way I'm helping you. The both of you.

As my assistants, my two doppelgangers by design, being me will help you learn.

You'll learn to know what you're looking for.

More importantly, you'll understand what it looks like.

The fight is hard to find if you let yourself get desperate. I've been desperate. I've used so much, tried everything really, to fill in the gaps. I've turned to chatrooms. I've recorded myself doing everything you could possibly do to get a reaction from others online.

It doesn't fill in what's missing.

The fact that you're a master looking for a pet.

The fact that your pet needs to want to be yours.

She thought she could steal mine. She thought that by doing that, she'd find escape.

That nothing's going to happen. He's mine.

Yours is somewhere else. He's waiting for your help. Doing his best to express himself. . .and yet, he can't do it all by himself. We need someone else.

We need our other half.

A better half.

Master and pet—it all makes sense, doesn't it?

So learn from me.

Be me and soon you'll find a pet of your own.

You both are in training too. It's not just him.

You two are masters in training. I picked you for a reason. We like what we like. Just so happens that we all seem to like those that can put up a real fight.

I couldn't agree more, really. There's beauty in unraveling a mystery.

Be me and you'll understand how such simple words as "I love you" can mean a whole world, changing meaning with each declaration

Understand? I knew you would.

Oh, her?

She'll be just fine.

Be mine and one day he'll be yours.

1.

I don't want it to get out so how about we make the next few for a special audience? You know who you are: Everyone that's signed up for the forum, bought the subscription, and buy up the limited edition panties and "murder weapons." I've got a need to speak, and you all are the ones listening. Be warned. Be ready. I'm talking to you, and you know who. For a brief moment, pretend to be him, my pet.

It's how you'll enjoy this confessional piece.

Why is it so hard to understand that you're mine? First you're perfect, and then you let the blemishes show. You're everything to me and then you do something like this. I've said that I'm not angry, but who would believe it? I mean, really? Who treats me as second, if even for one brief moment? If the audience can tell that I'm lying, it's obviously true. What the audience assumes is bound to be true. On the surface, this is all for show.

My pet, you push back when all I want to do is push you towards perfection.

Your legacy—I haven't said your name and I won't say it, no, not ever, not until you begin to understand why. Why? Why I do the things I do. Why I chose you instead of another serial killer. You've killed enough to count on one hand. Normally that's nothing to brag about, and yet, have you listened? Have you heard?

The media has begun to pick up on what you're doing.

This is my work. You should understand that. And I know you do, and yet you resist. You toy with her, one of my assistants, because you're frustrated.

You go against my wishes, my commands, like you think you're the one that's right. That's confidence. It's the fight, I get it. I'm able to understand what you're doing.

My pet, my dear pet. . .

You're young. You're maybe concerned that you have no control in our relationship.

This, I also understand.

You can go ahead and say that you're a part of me. We're making the mystery possible, blurring the lines and letting the blood flow. So then why must you resist when I ask you about your reply?

Maybe it's hard to stomach. You're new, but you're a natural.

You've listened and you've loved. They want to be like me, but that doesn't mean you can.

You understand, don't you?

Then why won't you tell me why, why you didn't follow my command?

You were so perfect. . .

Why did I just say that?

This troubles me.

We're perfect for each other, and then you do something like this.

And make me say something like that.

Okay. Okay, I'll be the first to admit it:

I'm concerned. I am. I'm frustrated. The moment when the first blemish appears, when a new and idyllic love begins to age, and with age you start to see the wrinkles, it's the moment reality strikes.

Gravity—and you know what, me and my two assistants, we're beautiful.

We know what we want. They want what I want. They talk like I talk.

And they're going to hear about this, my disappointment in you.

And I also don't want to talk about it. But I also do.

And I want to just forget it all.

I want to feel something else.

I'm at once insulted and indifferent. I want to tell you, but I also don't want to tell you.

I want you to be everything you can be, yet this little blemish makes me reconsider the entire thing. Your training, this study. I couldn't care less about anyone else but myself. Then why am I so upset? So conflicted?

This is so uncharacteristic of me. . .

I'm ditching the SUV. I'm getting a different car. You won't even know. You won't know where we are, only where you need to go. I'm tired of talking about this.

We're going to get lost for a while.

The only people that'll know are those that bother to listen and watch.

But I won't be able to really be myself. I'll be preoccupied with the thought. The one thought. The one thing that keeps me from being able to forgive you.

A master disappointed with her pet is not much of a master at all.

Fuck it. I'm not going to think about this.

I think it's time for some fun.

2.

We were always listening, you know.

I heard him running back to the front counter as we left the back room of the quick stop. He had listened. Of course he listened. Look at him, he's just like my pet: so curious, so willing, so horny, and yet so oblivious to command.

Might he be a replacement?

I'm walking up to him and doing exactly what I usually do to make it clear to him that I might, and I'm willing, but only if he's my type.

What I'm saying is, are you my type?

They walk the other aisles while I'm walking right to him. In this moment, he's the only thing that matters to me. He's not you, and I let the camera capture everything in such a way that you'll know, my pet, that you can be replaced. You are being replaced.

How does that make you feel?

You're mine.

I'll say when it's over.

I'll also say that I'm not bothered about it at all. No—you'll soon feel everything I've felt.

Right ladies?

"He's going to hurt so bad," says Claire, brushing a strand of her dark brown hair over her left ear. "Mmhmm," says Claire, who has her blonde hair still in a mess, makeup smudged, from our little confrontation. That's the past and I'm thinking my pet might soon want to remedy what's already happening.

Someone else might say that this is just an argument.

People in relationships have arguments.

I'm thinking that's too general of a statement. If there's an argument, something must have happened. Guess what? Something has definitely happened. I tried to let it go, but in trying to do that, to give him the benefit of the doubt, I've lost sight of why I did that.

And now I don't understand.

I've given him everything. There was one condition and one condition only, but if you look back at the data, it went well until it all went wrong.

Maybe you're watching and thinking I'm exaggerating.

To that I'm going to ask: Have you ever really given yourself to someone, not just your affection and your body and your loyalty, but also your wisdom, your life, sharing your entire existence with someone else? Did you say yes?

Fine, then I ask: Has that person ever stolen what you gave them without a second's thought? Yes? No? If you answered yes, you understand why I'm doing this.

Why, we're going to have a little fun with the kid.

I don't want to think about him.

So the kid is easy, easy enough to render him vulnerable.

Easy enough. He thinks I find him attractive.

I'm thinking about nobody at all. I'm thinking about only wanting to have fun. I want to feel something else. Fuck the study; fuck what I'm feeling.

I just want to feel something.

I want to feel good.

So then I've got the fireworks.

They know what I'm thinking, starting with the silly string, draping the entire quick stop with different colors. In no time, the camera captures the kind of scene you probably wanted.

There are explosions. Fireworks detonated in microwaves, in cash registers, and wrapped around propane tanks will do that. But then he had to get involved, didn't he?

Walking in like nothing's happened.

My pet, deep in that fantasy of his, asking for water, asking for gas, "I want to fill this, with that, gasoline, okay?"

He acts like it's not his fault, coupe going bad and having to walk the entire way. He acts like he is the victim in all this. I'm about to jump up from behind the counter where we're hiding, but I don't. Instead, we're filming. Instead I fixate on stuffing the kid's pants with fireworks while stroking his erect penis. I'm doing this because it's hilarious. In this moment, I'm all compulsion. I fixate on now, forgetting what I'll have to think about later.

My pet's asking for a cab to be called.

My pet's lingering around like he's mocking me.

Like he's trying to punish me. Punish me.

And when he walks around and waits for the cab to arrive, I begin to wonder if he even knows I'm here. Got it all on camera.

You see it right? Does he look like he's aware or not?

Didn't think so. So then I'm starting to get excited. I really might be overreacting.

The excitement makes me stroke the kid faster, he can barely contain himself. Didn't expect the kid to be anything more than another one, someone without a single ounce of fight in him. An erection is just an erection. This is all face-value to him; kid's got no understanding of subtlety, of the undertones being cast across the entire scene.

He's got a big part in this.

Lucky for him, we're going to put him out of his misery.

When my pet finally leaves, there'll be fireworks.

We'll call it a robbery, yes.

But really, we do this because I want to.

I do this because I can.

Wasn't part of the study. There's no data to record.

But for the moment I'm happy and it has everything to do with the fact that I don't know.

We're just having a little fun, filling holes with a few explosions.

Letting fireworks fill the sky at daylight.
Nothing wrong with that, huh?
Got to let the mystery roam free a little bit.

3.

Hi Claire.

Hey Claire.

How's it going?

I've been better.

Do you want to talk about it?

What do you think?

Sure, I understand.

Do you?

Of course I do. I feel like I'm partly responsible. I mean, I did try to. . .you know.

Well, that was beside the point. It had been bubbling under the surface for the last fifty miles or so.

Are you sure you don't want to talk about it?

Talked to the audience already. Got it all in the form of a confessional.

He probably has no clue that anything's wrong.

Maybe.

He means well. I really think he does.

I'm not so sure.

Why?

What do you care?

I'm Claire.

I'm Claire.

Well I'm Claire too.

That's right. Yeah, yeah, you're Claire.

I want to apologize.

Apology accepted.

Umm. . .

What?

Do you want to go somewhere?

Huh?

It's just. . .I'm getting a weird vibe from all this.

Me too. This isn't going the way I initially expected.

Maybe he just wants to impress you.

Yeah, that's what they're all saying.

The audience is right, you know. I think he's trying to be the gimmick.

What gimmick?

See, I was going to say the same thing. I don't understand what he's supposed to be. I mean fully, as a serial killer to remember.

Well, he's not there yet. I'm not ready to tell him of his true potential.

Maybe it's because he hasn't been given enough guidance that he's acting this way. . .I mean, I'm just saying. Don't get me wrong.

I'm not getting you wrong.

But hey—that was fun now, right?

Yes, it was fun.

I can't stand to see you this way, Claire.

I'm thinking it's because you feel what I feel.

Yeah. We're both broken up inside.

I get it. Hmm. . .

Does it get any easier?

You'll give, and then right when you think they appreciate you, something like this happens.

Yeah. . .

Hey Claire?

Yeah?

Let's get out of here.

Sure.

Get Claire. We're going for a ride. . .

4.

The taste of something sweet can help wipe away what you can't help but see.

Person that could have been an eight but is instead a six because his nose is too big, his penis is too small, and/ or he has a lack of confidence that makes it hard to even talk to the guy. Look at this employee, she's straight out of some talent agency. Think: Teenage female working at yogurt store to save up for summer vacation and you'll get an image. Stick to that image.

It's better than what the camera's seeing.

We're in the middle somewhere—where are we again? Maryland?—and we want something sweet. So I'm doing my best to think of anything but what's really happening here.

To that you'll probably think: What do you mean? You're at a yogurt shop, place where you weigh the yogurt after you custom fix it with your own toppings. That kind of useless diversion that works for areas like these, where there's nothing to do and everyone's looking to get away from their thoughts, their problems, their relationships, for at least fifteen minutes.

They turn to sugar long before they turn to alcohol and other substances.

I want to taste something sweet.

But in order for this to work for me, I'm getting my assistants to create the story.

For the mystery to work, here's the backdrop. Forget all about the fact that we're nowhere and I'm doing this to try to forget about him for an hour or two.

Forget all that. This is a scene that's all about impact.

It'll be enjoyable as long as the facts are clear:

We're here to buy something sweet.

Think beyond the lines, under the belt. Lick of the finger, giggle, moan, etc.

I'm thinking we've got the entire audience on my level.

Right?

"Right, Claire."

"You're so right, Claire."

That's what I thought.

Here's what I'm imagining:

It's a frozen yogurt chain, sure, but the owner has a backdoor operation.

Every archetypal employee at these places are young females. It's not odd until you let the mystery have its way.

So I'm thinking it's a prostitution ring.

And the girls are involved too.

They are willing.

They're willing because they want to be able to pay for vacations, for Spring Break, whatever. Fickle, but immediately realized motivations.

So then, when we're doing what we're doing and my pet walks in, he's as clueless as ever and I'm enjoying every damned moment.

It's all such bullshit but it's a beautiful pile of dirt.

I'm laughing, so they're laughing too.

And when he says what he says, he's suddenly mine again.

Mine because he didn't mean to say it but somehow, I'm in his head as much as he wanted to be in mine. This is all about favor, all about control.

He says: "I'd like my snack with a blowjob on the side, please."

It's absurd and absolutely part of the mystery.

He's clueless and even ashamed. I caught him in the moment of his own fantasy.

And I'm delighted.

This proves something but I don't know what, exactly.

The scene's my counter for his arrogance. I'm wanting to break it open, the entire scene, and walk right down the middle, slap him across the face and say:

"What were you thinking?"

He's young. He's stupid. He's a genius.

I'm different but he's capable of so much more.

Really?

Would you really think it's true? Threatened by my pet? Pet threatens master?

I'm laughing, so they're laughing too.

We're laughing at the gossip.

Has nothing at all to do with that. I'm not going to lose him.

No way. He thinks I'm perfect; he thinks we're perfect. We're masters, and serial killers like him need masters if they're going to make anything of their legacy.

Fuck it—I don't have to explain it to you!

Jump cut to when the employees start screaming because, you fill in the blank:

a) They're being gutted.

b) They're being raped.

c) They're being gutted and raped. Or vice versa (one's more typical, the other is more necrophilia.)

d) You're a part of this: You've already conjured up your own conclusions.

I've got mine and to that one idea that's starting to get around. . .

No, nothing's changed.

5.

Riddles and rhymes, I've got nothing but time.
Sticks and stones may break my bones. . .
But your threats are nothing but whispers.
Cock a doodle do. . .
The camera sees you.
Roses are red and violets are blue. . .
The mystery's a murder that might just include you.
Okay fuck this too. Waste of time. None of them work.
Just shows you how stupid these things really are.

Nothing's really honest if they aren't your own words. What am I getting at?

I'm saying quit the rumors and *keep watching.*

Nothing's lost when you begin to understand that this, everything that's happening, scene for scene, is because of me. It's mine. And, you know what, because you're watching and truly invested, it's probably right to say that *you're mine* too.

So don't make those kinds of assumptions.

Don't spread those kinds of lies.

Just because you can't remember when, doesn't mean I can't.

With no effort at all, I'd prove it to every single one of you.

And then you'd be the one who's torn up, seeing what I've always seen:

I'm capable. I could have done this all on my own.
You'd realize that I'm right. You really **are** mine.
I've seen as much of you as you've seen of me.
Wave to the camera.
Now sit down and shut up.
I've had better days. Way better scenes.
Why can't a girl have a bad day?

Data erased.

You'll believe anything as long as it makes you feel better.

1.

I'm my own person. Always have been and always will. I'm able to turn off the camera and not need to turn it on again moments later. A master can be without a pet. I'm sure of it. I'm not loading in another tape and I'm not going to save the live stream. So then it's all about this moment; it's all about the candidness of a live broadcast. To watch this live, you had to pay. But I'm beginning to think you already paid for all-access, didn't you?

This is the stuff that he won't get to see.

That's how it works.

"Yeah, that's how it works."

"Mmhmm."

Thanks girls. They're there for me when I need them.

What I'm asking you is—

Are you watching?

Are you still in doubt of what I can do?

Are you still thinking there can't be anything better than this?

Have you lost sight of the show?

Did you miss a few episodes?

Where are you right now?

What does it take to have you back?

And then I'm starting to think I know, I know what everyone wants to see.

You want to see it, don't you?

Maybe I'm not so different after all.

2.

I visit him with no clear intent. I mean, the data will be erased; what's the point of these tapes when my pet won't see them? It's all me, and that's what you're going to get. So let's set the scene: The girls and I, we're at the prison early, about thirty minutes before visiting hours begin. We're already live so there's no point in waiting. It doesn't take any more than a ten-dollar bill to get us inside and then another ten to sway the guards into saying yes when they hear that I want to see him.

Derrick Muse, the one and the only. Part serial killer, part philosopher, part cultural icon. He had perhaps the most potential prior to my pet, and for that reason, he wore that label too.

You could say he was, once upon a time, my pet.

You could say that we had a lot of good times together.

You could say that I still wish what we had didn't end. But then again, he had his own idea of how to end this. He didn't agree with how I wanted his legacy to be seen. He's more into the acclaim of media. He liked the way he looked on camera. He wanted to be known not only as a serial killer but also as a musician, a philosopher, and a heartthrob. He wanted it all. And for that reason it wasn't meant to be. If he really were mine, he wouldn't have the surname "Muse."

When we were close, he had an entirely different name. Doesn't matter what he name was, it's all in the past. He had the same gimmick, though.

Either way, when I see him sitting across from me—like he hadn't been incarcerated for the past five years—we can't help but pick up where we left off.

"Claire."

He looks at the girls, one standing on either side of me,

"Aren't you going to introduce me?"

He does that thing with his mouth that gets everyone on his side. It's cute. He's so damn charming; he could have been anything he wanted. I'm aware of, at least vaguely, that he needed more than I could give him. But I was his master, after all.

"Well, you don't look any different."

He leans back in his chair, sound of ankle cuffs dragging against the concrete floor.

"I've led a very monk-like existence lately. Exercise, writing, correspondence—All I've got to keep me from going sane."

There it is again, his sense of sly humor.

Always believed in being different. He really relished in being eccentric.

Everything about the guy is practiced. What makes him one of the best killers is how he'll make you his best friend right before he'll end your life.

"Aren't you going to say anything nice about me?"

I'm watching as he inspects his fingernails, "What do you want me to say?"

"You were always a jackass, Derrick."

He laughs, "Someone's pissy today."

"You could have least said what everyone usually says."

He looks around the room, gives a sort of glare at one of the other inmates, "Oh yeah, and what do people say during these things? I wouldn't know."

I'm detecting some sarcasm.

But then he's a charmer, always has been, and what he says next makes me forget how everything went wrong.

"You're not here to see me, Claire. You don't play the game like that. I don't know what you're doing, but you never show up for a second visit."

He's right.

"You're not acting like yourself. For one thing, why is the camera on me and not you?"

He knows me.

"Tell me what's wrong." He leans forward, hands folded, his attention completely mine.

"Don't start," I'm not falling for it, no, no, "I'm not one of your fans, one of your trophies that visit you all the time, giving you whatever you need."

"All I need is you, Claire."

Ugh. When does saying something like that even work?

Then again, you're probably thinking, when does it not?

"Shut up."

"Sure thing."

We're sitting in silence but not long enough for him to seduce my girls, because that's what he's best at, after all; it won't take much, a few glances, a few words. He'll have them like, during my lonelier moments, he had me.

I'm not saying I regret it; we were perfect together. He just wanted everything I loathe.

I mean, who cares about intellectual property and making money when you're stuck in a cell with no ability to use it?

He cares—to Derrick, the legacy is a financial empire based entirely on brand.

He's starting to chuckle.

"What is it?"

"You're a wicked one, Claire."

Roll of the eyes, I'm brushing that bullshit aside, "I'm here to talk. That's why I'm here. No other reason but that."

"Sure." Ugh that grin. "Let's talk."

I catch him looking at them, "You got a problem?"

"Not at all. I just haven't seen them in so long."

I'm sighing, "Well the days of copping a feel are long gone."

"Understandably."

More silence.

This is making me look bad.

I could probably create a diversion, pretend something else is important, but I don't think he'd care to notice. It's all the same to him. And that's where I've figured him for imperfect: He's into himself and, if he were forced to live or die, he'd beg for his life. I'm sure he's staved off execution due to his level of popularity. He should have been dead by now. Can't be any simpler than that. So that's how I'll turn the camera back onto him. Let's talk about Derrick.

Derrick loves talking about Derrick.

I'm asking him, "How big's the cult now?"

"It's not a cult, Claire. How many times do I have to tell you?"

It is a cult. He has a bunch of loyal female fans and quite a few men too that do nothing but spread the word, sell merchandise with Derrick's own designs on it. They'll also print up his latest manuscript and get it into the hands of every agent in town. There's a movie in the works.

This is Derrick's idea of a legacy, and I'll admit that it's impressive, but where we disagreed so much was how much input he has in the creation of this legacy. It feels more like it's a business rather than expression. You see what I mean? Just look at him.

Everything about him is improbable.

And yeah, he's talking about his cult, explaining it all to me in clear-cut language just like this is some boardroom meeting.

I'm not listening.

The ladies don't seem to either.

They're like you, wanting to speed it up to the end, the payoff, but hey, we're live: You're getting every excruciating detail, good or bad.

I'm yawning and he notices.

I did that intentionally.

I want him to feel pressured. I want him to know that he'll never really have me. I'm here because I want to be here, not because I need to be. I'll find favor wherever I can find it. It's really good to see Derrick; he can be as predictable as anyone else.

I'm telling him I don't care.

"I don't care about all that."

I'm telling him, "I was just making small talk."

There we go. You see it? Peeling back a layer, "Then why the hell are you here?"

"I think you know," I'm saying without looking at him. Feeling tired all of a sudden, inspecting whether or not it's mental or physical exhaustion. Probably both.

"You act so tough, but I can see it."

"What do you see?"

"You're tired. You're lonely."

I shrug, "Posing for the camera gets old."

"We're in agreement there."

And then he needs to know, and this is where I have him, right where I want him, "Where is he? You're not alone. He must be somewhere."

"What makes you think it won't be me?"

He raises an eyebrow, "Oh come on." He laughs.

So I reply with, "Maybe I've learned to live with myself."

All by myself. Not a single fucking person.

How's that for believable?

He says, "That's not the Claire I know." Not very it seems.

"Oh yeah," raising my voice, "and which Claire do you know?"

The girls step forward. Good for them; they understand what I'm trying to do. In case you don't understand, I'll explain: I'm trying to confuse him with the thought of them being my clones.

"I think you're worried," he says.

Seems he's not into science fiction.

"You're worried that you're the reason for his disobedience."

What did he just say?

Looking satisfied, Derrick nods, "I was your pet once. You need to be in control."

He probably said that to provoke me. He shouldn't be provoking me. No, not here, not now. Watch as a smile outlines my face. "Let's take a look at the situation here, hmm?"

I point to his cuffs and then I point to my wrists, "Who's shackled? Who is serving life sentences in a fucking jail cell, hmm?"

He seems to understand and tries to interrupt me, but I dismiss it. He's going to listen and listen well, "It's just like you to act so calm when you've been stripped of everything. Your basic liberties, as an individual, are trashed. I did that to you the moment you got this big-brained idea to leave me. I gave you everything. . ."

Tries to say something again so I shout:

"I gave you everything!"

If this weren't live, we could cut to a quick shot of the girls going around the room with the guards, forcing all visitors and inmates to stand up and leave. If not a momentary cut, it could have been a picture-in-picture kind of affair. But instead, you'll have to keep it to a view of Derrick, the faintest of glimpses partially visible from the area around his shoulders.

Is that fear in his eyes?

Seems he may have doubted me too.

"Why do you think I can't do what you do?"

He doesn't say.

"Hey sweet talker, answer me!"

"I don't have to answer to you," he closes his eyes and does breathing exercises.

I think: monk-like, recalling it from earlier and it's enough to get right down to it.

I hum some kind of song, lyrics being, "The day Derrick Muse died."

The room cleared out, all that's left is what he's done to so many others.

I take out a mirror and shove it in his face, "Look at yourself one last time."

The ladies are laughing. It is kind of funny, isn't it?

"You'll never see it again."

Perfect last words for the guy. If you want to think about the aftermath, just think:

His empire will crumble; his worth will not double. He'll be remembered more as a businessman than a serial killer. Infamy will not be his, the element of mystery completely destroyed.

To be timeless, there needs to be an element of mystery.

You need a piece of me in your life.

3.

Warning: Zero cuts. No edits made. This is footage.

It's exactly as it happened. You'll come to use this whenever someone doubts what I'm willing to do. Consider it proof. Now see what happens. . .

I asked him right then and there, if he missed me.

Looking into the mirror, he shook his head, not even a single moment of doubt, so I put on gloves, reached behind his head, grabbing a handful of hair, and smashed his face into the mirror.

Shattering in multiple places, a few shards remain lodged into his face.

Didn't get any in the eye.

We'll have to change that.

I tell the girls, "Not a single word."

Hush.

"Derrick's got a lot to say," I pick out the shards from face, "so let this be a love letter."

Snap of a finger, signal for water, I'm pouring it all over his face, cleaning the wounds.

"A beautiful love letter to the entire cult."

She starts taking off her clothes, ties her brown hair in a knot to keep it from getting in her face, as I say, "After this, they'll understand why his empire won't survive."

Fully naked, you can see the little white string dangling from her vagina.

She takes it out and walks over to where he remains cuffed and seated.

I'm repositioning the seat so that the back of his head is pressed against the tabletop.

She touches herself, inserts two fingers inside.

It's dark, which means she's only just begun menstruating.

I give her the nod.

Straddling his face, she sits into the curve of his chin.

I've got my left hand cupping the area under his chin and my right hand pressing down on the top of his head. He can't move and he won't be able to open his mouth.

She gyrates and, for what it's worth, has a good time.

You can see red streaks all across his face.

I'm looking into the camera. I'm neither amused nor disappointed. This feels a lot like homework. Doing what needs to be done. It happens because, well, how about this reason:

Because someone, somewhere, had the idea.

It's obvious.

She keeps at it until I can hear him choking.

From there, what's done matches precisely what he used to do to all his victims.

I kick over his chair, pull down his pants, and start on him, stroking his penis while she gets ready. He never failed to satisfy his sexual urges.

When he's hard, she rides him raw.

Tears stream down his face.

I like what I'm seeing.

Waiting patiently with the knife, I watch as she lets herself have fun. I mean, why not? My assistants should have fun. I'm the only one that won't be satisfied.

He's getting close—jeez, shows how long he's really had since a good lay—so I cut right at the base. She stands up before he can really spray.

Let the blood get everywhere else.

She pulls it out, surprised to see how it has remained in shape longer than we expected.

I take it and show it him.

His eyes wide, feeling the pain, seeing what I'm capable of.

Capture this candid moment. He's going to start begging.

I'm having none of it though.

Get that tongue out of there.

I'm taking a second to look at the current status of the kill.

Hmm. I break the silence for a second, "What do you think, ladies?"

"Something's missing."

"Yeah, something's really missing."

They're really trying their damnedest to be me.

I appreciate it.

So we have one Derrick Muse. . .

Emasculated.

Humiliated.

Call it whatever you want, but for someone that has based his entire self on the opinions of the media and his fans, this is the lowest possible point.

Go ahead and start begging.

It's what's missing.

I can watch the fight drip out of him all day. He lasted a whole lot longer than I expected; he really had a lot of potential. It's true. Makes this so much better. He won't give in so quickly, not like the typical victim. I'll give him that: he's always been a fighter.

Now beg.

Life's flashing before your eyes, and what you're thinking is: Damn, I wasted it.

Could have been everything you hoped for but that's not what you think about when you're this close to the end. You're thinking about everything you lost. You think about what you didn't do, what you weren't able to accomplish.

Derrick, he's thinking about how he lost me.

If what we had was anything like loyalty, it was that I stayed loyal to him. Master gave until the pet decided to bite back.

When he finally does beg, it's really a disappointment.

You see it too—what do you think?

Really, I'm getting tired of this.

I kneel down on one knee, "It's okay Derrick. We both know you'll believe anything as long as it makes things easier. Believe that the data will be erased. Believe that your legacy will be notable. Believe that, between you and me, there may have been more. Believe what you want to believe. It's not going to prevent me from killing you."

I gesture for the saw.

I draw a line using lipstick across his bare neck.

Like I said before, keep to what they did. It works better for the media. A serial killer killed using his/her own gimmick. There's nothing more poetic than being fed the slop you sell.

I'll enjoy this, almost as much as you will.

The mystery devours all doubt.

4.

My dear pet—

It's not the same.

Being the serial killer.

I can. Apparently it was in question.

Now it's mere fact.

What's left but the actual? The realization that there's nothing mysterious about it, when there's no pet, a master is just another person, searching for missing pieces.

I'll say it, say what I didn't want to say:

I feel empty.

I feel unfound. Most of all. . .

I feel alone.

Where are you?

Where's my pet?

I looked where his tape should be, and the one before that, and the one before that one. . .I'm thinking he didn't leave one this time. Why would he? I haven't left tapes in the past three locations.

Proof that he might be doing what I'm doing. It's a good thing gone bad.

Kept so much from him. For a while, it didn't feel like he was really there. And maybe you'd get the idea that a character had been killed off, one that wasn't supposed to die, at least not unless I wanted it to happen.

I miss him. You all probably miss him too.

But where is he, really?

I thought about what I can do to reach him.

There's only one thing I can do—so I go through the trouble of having it recovered, driven the many, many mile markers to where the girls and I wait.

When I'm back behind the wheel, it feels like everything that happened after the night I found out that the Candy Man had been executed has been erased.

Data erased.

In the red convertible, I feel like I'm only a few cars behind. I can almost see his brown coupe.

By now he's fixed it. By now he must be near the south of the border.

By now. . .I shouldn't have to feel the way I feel.

Let’s get lost together.

1.

I drove through the night.

I kept filming even though I hadn't a clue what my pet had done.

I'm waiting for his apology.

I'm waiting for him to notice that master is not pleased.

It's true, what I said. That I miss him.

And it's all I can do to go on: I imagine what's happened. The way I would have liked it; the way it was originally planned.

I can imagine the entire mystery.

So much that I can lose myself for as long as I'd like.

2.

I imagine. . .

That the mystery will never end. It remains the peak of curiosity, back when we first took to the interstate. It's there that I'm exactly who I am and I don't ever feel any less than when I didn't initially get what I want. It's there that I imagine the wide-open road before anything else.

Flicker and it's back to when it was fresh. Fade in on the mystery speeding down the interstate picking up theories.

Some drive until the road ends. Some turn around and try learning a different road. Some never find a place they can call home. They commit to theories that speak of a life that only ends up coiled around mystery.

They might as well have kept driving.

Virginia welcomes you. Sign's gone as soon as it is seen.

Keep on driving. The road will soon look the same.

The mystery rides the interstate carrying the only theory that's ever mattered:

The one he learned from me.

I'm imagining the road leaning to the right as if reminding him that this is it—This is your exit. Don't want to be late. The mystery ends up at another prison, where a guard waits for his cut. Paid in full, the guard retrieves the one who would have been next. By my predictions, it's the quaint and even-tempered killer that went by the alias, "The Bystander."

The mystery poses as a social worker, would be under the basis of what I do know about Bystander: He's born-again, working to get off death row. Been saved from lethal injection once already. He's deader than dead under the illusion that conversion might bring him back to life.

The mystery drives to a nearby park.

Settle on a calm scene between two people sitting at

a picnic table in tranquil early morning sunshine. Birds chirping, gentle breeze. . .both are silhouettes long before one swiftly takes care of the other. The mystery errs towards brutality, so that means a close-up on the Bystander's body, thin blade punctured through the right eye, just enough to induce shock; the pain there but more numbing than anything else.

Eyes wide, the Bystander is beginning to see how mysterious the world can be.

The Bystander didn't expect a thing.

3.

It would have been a beautiful sight: Bystander hanging from a tree by the rope knotted at his ankles and wrapped to his toes. The sunlight bouncing off a face masked with blood. Peering into that face, I'm seeing my own reflection. As if I were there; as if I could have been there.

Rope wraps around each wrist, pulls in opposite directions.

The mystery cuts three-inch incisions wherever veins are visible.

Thin blue veins pour out more of the same, red and dripping. A pan is placed below the elevated body, collecting the blood.

The Bystander may be weak, but he still manages to fight against the rope.

I'm imagining what the mystery could have done to thoroughly enjoy the kill. . .but just as quickly, the mystery conforms to how I had planned the Bystander's gimmick.

On target with the bloodletting, the weakened victim gives into the ropc.

Rope pulls arm and leg from each socket.

Body slacking, yet the Bystander won't make a sound.

The mystery waits and watches. It's almost done.

The camera is stationary; the scene solemn and calm makes for an even more unsettling and jarring display. Heartbeat slowing as mine would beat quicker with every passing frame.

Watching it, I'd be proud. I'd say something like, "It looks so easy. He's getting better."

The mystery would leave both body and blood there, on-point with the Bystander right down to the abandoned scene. It would baffle the authorities. It would help corroborate that someone's offing incarcerated serial killers.

But the mystery would remain because of one clear detail:

No one knows that I'm part of the mystery too.

I'm the key piece of evidence—one that'll never be revealed.

Everyone watching would keep a secret too. Leave it to mystery.

If you told anyone, you'd be an accessory.

You're in this too. And so, because this is true, there's no reason why the mystery would continue to unfold with or without a new episode.

I imagine. . .

4.

Without me there, he would have no reason to film.

No reason to speak. The entire state of Virginia would pass by in complete silence.

He would continuously think of his cellphone.

But he won't call. He wouldn't film until he felt completely alone.

And then it would take everything just keep to the fantasy alive.

He'd drive faster, lured by the idea that around the next corner, I'd be there, waiting.

5.

"I need someone that'll need me, want me, covet me, consume me, captivate me, just as much as I do all those things and more to them. I'm selective in that way. But really, how can you not be?"

Just in time to keep you interested, the mystery is back with a brand new season!

A whole lot has happened since traveling down the interstate.

New love. New lust turned pure jealousy.

Fresh kills and pure potential.

Full frontal fantasy.

Betrayal. Relationship tension.

Candid "1-on-1" confessionals with the audience.

Even a few cast disappearances and one hell of a coup.

And that's not all!

Season two will now be moving to Monday and Friday!

That's two hour-long episodes a week.

Season premiere begins at 8PM Eastern/7PM Central with a special half-hour recap with the starring cast. Get firsthand commentary from the fans as we dive back in.

The mystery is about to take a sharp turn. . .

You won't want to miss a thing!

6.

I imagine the apology.

I imagine the next juncture.

I imagine how, given not a whole lot of time, it can be forgotten. One argument doesn't need to be the end.

I imagine it's all so stupid anyway.

I imagine what we'd do after he'd apologize to me.

I imagine everyone would watch.

See every part of us.

Watch as we teach you new things about sex and violence.

I imagine it would last a half-hour before we part ways yet again, conforming to our cover stories, letting the fantasy conceal reality.

I imagine me and the ladies speeding down the interstate at sunset, naked and warm, shouting and feeling empowered, a sort of celebration.

I imagine we're celebrating, my pet and I. We're celebrating what will come next. We're celebrating for the sake of celebration, once again realizing what this study will bring us.

This study, which in turn is more show than anything else, will produce results.

Any way you look at it, the mystery isn't just a road and it isn't just new love.

It's everything and, if you let it, it can be purely fiction.

A lot can be lost along the way. Can really lose oneself in the mystery.

I'm thinking this might not be as perfect as I imagined. I don't need perfect; I need my pet.

I'm thinking it's about time for that apology.

I'm thinking he's been waiting for me.

7.

No matter what the show's about, everyone ends up traveling. It's a mystery that anyone knows what the hell's going on now, after all that's happened, but I know that I've got to keep with it. I've got to be patient and observant. I can't keep getting lost in ideals, my overactive imagination. I have to keep going until I pick back up where the mystery stopped.

Keep on driving until it all makes sense.

Keep on driving until we're all caught up.

No use getting lost alone.

Sincere apologies make for an excellent aphrodisiac.

1.

She wouldn't shut up about it.

"Claire, just call him."

My reply being, "Even I'm not above the rules."

"He doesn't have a clue."

Relentless, I tell you.

"I'm driving."

Focus on the road. I don't see either of them offering to drive. They've been kicking it all casual in the backseat, giggling and having the time of their lives.

Meanwhile I hate everything and I want to crash the car into a gas truck, taking out an entire patch of the interstate in one perfect explosion.

You'd probably like that, huh? Surprise twist.

At least someone would be surprised. Yeah, so what—pretending nothing's wrong only works for like a few miles.

"Claire, you look miserable. I'm telling you, call him!"

"Look, I'm tired, okay? Shut up."

She wouldn't shut up though. Eventually I couldn't take it anymore; got the hell off the interstate and got the hell out of the convertible.

Walked into one of those newer rest stops with full-featured food court and sat in one of the back booths alone with scalding hot chai tea.

And I don't even like tea.

But that's where I am, alone.

Sipping the beverage. Not admitting that I can't see myself getting back onto the interstate in the foreseeable future. It doesn't seem like it's possible.

Can't even conjure up the image.

Maybe I'll just stay here.

These rest stops are twenty-four hours; I could live in this back booth here. I'm the back booth lady. I'd tell crazy stories to passerby's, anyone willing to listen; they wouldn't believe any of it. Like you, though, they'd listen and they would assuredly be entertained.

I'm here for what feels like only a moment, but it ends up being a couple of hours.

I see her blonde hair over the partition diving the food court long before I see her face. She's looking around for me. I'm not going to wave her over. She can figure it out herself.

Maybe she won't see—oh, too late. Spotted.

Runs over in a way that annoys me.

Everything annoys me.

She's out of breath. I tell her to calm the fuck down.

But she can't, she won't—something's happened.

It doesn't make any sense though, pure nonsense until she repeats it for the fifth time.

My assistant has disappeared.

Hits me hard. Another betrayal.

"You've got to be fucking kidding me."

It's the truth. When get back to the convertible she's not there.

"How the fuck could this have happened?"

Here's how she explains it:

Apparently the coupe pulled into a parking space. Neither paid much attention to it until, sure enough, it was my pet that got out of the driver's seat. One assistant remained voyeur while the other ran for the coupe, got into the coupe, and before she could be stopped, my pet walked back with a coffee in hand, playing up his side of the fantasy, completely immersed in his self-conscious self. Probably didn't notice her in there until much later.

She's told me everything she knows. My assistant sighs and says, "So now what?"

I'm speechless.

It took her disappearance to make me do something

about it. I don't know, it's just that sometimes I don't feel like myself. Everything's going my way, yet I feel like it's all washed out, numb. I don't feel much of anything. I could hear him apologize and I'd probably feel nothing at all. Maybe I'm tired—that's my go-to excuse. Maybe I'm miserable because I've lost sight of what this is, and the mystery's bound to get old sooner rather than later. Maybe I'm just jealous. But I dismiss that almost immediately.

I give them everything and this is what ends up happening.

It's so much easier for others to let go, but not me. I hold a grudge.

My phone rings.

We both look down at it, safe and stowed away in a cup holder. We listen to it ring over a dozen times before I can get my body to move.

Pick up, can't bring myself to say much of anything this is so fucked up. . .

Her voice comes through loud and clear. Of course.

"Claire. Claire?"

What the hell. . .

"Claire??"

"You know who this is."

"It's me."

No shit. When I get my hands on you, they'll add this to the highlight reel. . .

"Look, you're angry. I get it. I know, but hear me out."

Why?

"Are you listening?"

Let's just say. . .my jaw is clenched so tightly I can feel my teeth starting to ache.

"Hear me out: It's all in your head, Claire."

Digging your own grave.

"You make things out to be so much more than they

really are."

Yup—you can forget about everything I told you. Your part ends here.

"He likes you. He's always liked you. More importantly, he's afraid of what you might do."

"What are you saying?"

"He didn't know."

I'm cupping the phone, telling my other assistant to start up the car and drive.

"He assumed you were testing him. He only wanted what's best. He wanted to impress you."

"Where are you?"

She tells me where they are. We're about a half hour behind.

She's also saying that he didn't pick her up, "I snuck into the back of the coupe. I knew you wouldn't just talk to him. I tried and tried and tried to get you to realize what's real versus what's just some idealization of what didn't end up going your way."

I'm sighing and she must have heard it because she's apologizing.

"He's headed for him. We're on our way to Scott. But we left a tape."

I hear a voice that's not hers.

I'm not sure what he said until she says it for him, "He's sorry."

Then he's saying it. My pet is apologizing, "I'm sorry, Claire. I'd do anything for you. I want you to know that nothing's changed."

I know where the tape should be.

I'm telling my assistant to drive faster.

Before she hangs up, I hear him say, "What does she want me to do?"

It's enough to get me excited.

2.

How it feels to be depressed, I imagine, is something like being completely disappointed. Coupled with the anxiety of things not going as planned, I'm thinking depression is finding out that your car won't go as fast as you want.

Go, go, go—my excitement leads my assistant to tears.

I'm too excited to tell her that it's not her fault.

Too excited to tell her it's okay.

Too excited to tell her to slow down when we get there.

Too excited to feel the pain when I fall face-first while getting out of the moving car.

Too excited to look and see whether or not anyone's watching as I walk into the men's restroom, into one of the stalls, lift the lid and reach in to remove the plastic sealed bag containing the tape. Too excited to wait and watch it back in the car. I sit down in the stall, shut off the camera, and load his tape.

As it starts, I see nothing but grass. Camera is held down low, haphazardly, as if he's mocking me. I can't tell if he forgot that he turned it on or that he wouldn't have been able to turn it on later, after everything started. I don't have a lot of time to think about it since it cuts to a long continuous shot of my pet speaking to a guard.

The guard isn't interested in bribes.

It's not the same when my pet tries to do it all on his own.

He tries and he fails. Though it's never said, he shows me that I am not only missing but also missed. He really misses my guidance, my aid.

The shot continues despite a lack of light when it gets interesting.

I don't care. I don't care that I don't know what's going on. I don't care because it's not what's on camera that matters; it's what isn't captured on camera. It's what he can't quite do.

It's what he ends up having to do in order to still keep with my plan.

Not his plan, my plan. He has to follow orders. He must follow master's command.

Where he ends up, the camera cannot follow, but as the shot abruptly ends, I'm treated with a sudden glimpse of someone I could never, ever forgot. Her name was Macy, but people referred to her as the Damsel. She and I met when Damsel was only beginning to explore what she might be able to do with herself, trying out new things, setting boundaries.

We were close, real close.

We tried everything together. Back then I didn't really have a type. I didn't have it in mind to look for the fight. But I knew what to look for. She had it and really, she tasted so good.

And it's nice to see that she accepts him. It's nice to know that my first accepts my last.

They talk about me. Macy looking a whole lot older and I'm kind of, you know, shocked to see that she still bothers to be well manicured.

It's really what makes this possible—the promise of a conjugal visit.

There are places where they can go. I'm watching as he straps her down and doesn't wait. Inserts himself into her and fucks her for a few minutes. She wasn't ready, I can tell. He was horny; my pet so lonely. No lube meant it was tough to begin with but soon even she felt pretty good.

Then he stops, takes the camera, and points it down to her naked body.

She says, "Hello Claire."

He zooms so that I can see her face.

Then she says, "I'm so happy for you."

We always understood each other, Macy and I.

When we parted ways, I didn't lie to her. She would know better anyway. She'd see right through my lies. I told her what I'd do. She told me, "Do what you need to do." It was my first breakup and, even though it was mutual, it still hurt so much. It hurt so much that I made it happen. With the evidence, the authorities quickly connected the dots. Made it look like they found it on their own. All I had to do was put it near the crime scene.

And then it was data fit for her jaunt to death row.

It's good to see that she's still alive.

I'm glad that she approves of him.

The tears dripping down my eye aren't out of sadness. I'm watching my pet fuck her hard, then gently, and then hard again, imagining it were me.

When I want him to hurt her, he does.

When I want him to kiss her, he kisses her nice and long.

He beats her to a bloody pulp because it's the only way she can come.

He stops to say, "What do I do now?"

Damsel, she takes the lead. Teaches him a thing or two. Lets him taste a little bit before his tongue licks the small of her back. There, and here, right there: Perfectly they indulge and, in the cramped stall, smelling of bleach, hearing men pissing in urinals without washing their hands, I get lost in the fantasy. Two fingers are all it takes. Gentle motions are all I need. The tips of both fingers brush against the inner wall, close enough, the feeling close enough to exhale.

But I don't. Held back. Waiting for him.

I want to come when he comes.

They keep going, thrust after thrust, as he slaps her and she slaps him. Blood drips down his mouth. Familiar fluids trickle out of his penis as he pulls out quickly.

But not yet. He writes with black marker on her forehead, "I'm sorry."

Turns her over, changing positions, and sticks it back in.

Muffled speech. Faster and faster: Each thrust is matched by a careful strike.

She punches him hard in the chest.

He elbows her in the thigh. She comes twice.

He waits until the third time to pull out, pausing a moment to look into the camera, to tell me it's time. She lies there, watching, breathlessly and beaten, as him and I make up.

In the stall, men can hear me moaning.

None dare to have a look.

As he comes, he says it one last time, "I'm sorry."

I'm pleased, so pleased to accept his apology.

So pleased to be able to say:

Data recorded.

3.

Truth is, she wouldn't have made it past his visit. Macy, the Damsel, begged for him to make it right, "If you are, let me show you how. Don't fuck it up." It involves work as much as it is an act of wanting, the things we do to know someone else, to know someone fully, is absurd.

I'm surprised that anyone can be anything but alone.

But anyway, I accept his apology. I'm taking off my panties and wrapping it around a new tape. I'll leave it where he knows to look. When he's ready, he'll be the one that'll slip it back on me.

I'm walking back to the convertible and we're back on the road, speeding to catch up.

My assistant calls, asks if I got the tape.

I'm asking to talk to him.

Yeah, she warns me that it breaks the rules but really, by now, the rules have been broken enough to be stripped clean.

"Shut up and drive," I'm telling her.

With him on the phone, we don't need to say much.

And we really can't because it might be that someone's listening.

Instead, we listen to each other's breaths.

Listen calmly as we pick up speed, switching lanes and pushing the limit.

Listen as it all starts to form into something bigger.

What we still need to accomplish.

What the authorities are beginning to find.

How his work, his gimmick, will be no clearer until we finish, until the number left is zero. When done is done. My pet is quiet and patient.

He accepts that the most important information will remain unrevealed until the end.

Like any great narrative, I'd tell him, the mystery can't

be solved until the end.

His name, his reason, the nature of his legacy, all that won't work if I just tell him now. He'll get comfortable; he'll lose the fight. He'll get tired of driving. He might pull over and put up roots.

Got to keep moving. Our need to express is outweighed only by our need to explore.

Explore every single extent of our tastes.

Memories, so many memories, yet every time I see my exes again, it's like we've never been apart. I'd like to tell them that they could be so much more; I'd like to tell them that I can help them, but then, really, I'm here to show off my new pet.

I'm here to tell them it's over.

It's all over.

The data being recorded is for our own purposes.

The world won't end, but ours, it'll finally involve more than our own egotistical selves.

Master lectures.

Pet listens.

Master will provide instructions.

Pet will learn.

He's done so well. I'm thinking it's time we get caught up in ourselves.

A legacy is a structure built around bodies.

Bit by bit, it becomes something recognizable.

It becomes the story you can't help tell to your friends and family.

My dear pet, you'll be remembered.

And I'll be there to help you remember.

4.

Somewhere, on some website, leaked footage exists to be viewed by those deeply invested in the mystery.

They deal in lies and, at a cursory glance, it's fake and has no real connection. But if given the full analysis, the handful of the audience would realize that it's not just something similar. It's not coincidental.

He looks like him but doesn't act like him.

He drives the same coupe, but seems to do different things during moments when he would have been filming, would have been feeding the mystery.

However, looking scene-for-scene will get you nowhere. There are too many gaps, too many missing spots to tell the difference. Instead, you have to take a step back.

You have to look at the footage for what it is:

Something made to deter.

Something made to be dismissed.

It's a story, sure, but a very peculiar kind of story.

For the fans, the handful of you that would keep watching something over and over again, no matter how gruesome, no matter how boring, to capture more of the world created using video, you'll see what I've created for him.

You'll understand.

The basics become the most difficult pieces to fit into the mystery.

A college student with student loan debt. A criminology major with no interest in solving or understanding crime. A brown Japanese coupe that has maybe a thousand miles left before it says goodbye. A student that doesn't seem nearly as lucky to be my pet. A student that has a decade of loneliness to suffer through. The days to follow no longer feel the same as they did when he was younger, as recent as senior year at Archbishop High. Perhaps he had something to look forward to, back when the days, the col-

lective "tomorrow," were palpable. It was danger, and danger had always been captivating.

There are black clouds on the horizon and they're looking for revenge.

If you made out with the fantasy, you might be able to look through the cover story.

The road starts to mess with your eyes. Excuses, excuses. Things that used to be fantasy become factual.

If you accept it, you'd see through the bits and pieces built to steer you away from solving this mystery.

For it to work, my pet and I need to remain barely anything at all. . .a story in some book on some shelf that's maybe read or maybe left dog-eared and forgotten.

It's the fantasy that hides our true form. Footage is never "just footage." Every frame reveals so much more than it takes away. The film adds more even when you swear it contradicts itself.

This footage is perfect. The filmmakers are professionals. They are perfect, really. They meet every requirement Stephen has for film and a starring cast. Perhaps they're only a glimpse, but they really are beautiful.

The one driving is blonde. The one sitting up front is a redhead. The third, a brunette, straddles the handbrake. Their footage matches his. He doesn't find it unusual.

And he knows who's who. It has nothing to do with hair color.

The girls seem to do exactly what it takes to make you more interested in the footage. What does it take to get you more excited, more intimidated? It takes the brunette and the blonde touching each other and making out. It takes the redhead speeding down the interstate chasing after a scared driver, a fleeing car. It takes the redhead shooting out one of the car's tires. It requires narrow escapes, the car speeding away slinging sparks. It takes a cliffhanger ending, omitting any and all reason and possibility for this footage to make any sense.

What am I saying?

Nothing. Nothing at all.

Just talk between scenes.

If you're willing to look, and I mean really look, you'll see so much more.

Things are bolder when you imagine what's been purposefully left out, withheld.

Yeah, I'm not saying anything.

This is our fantasy.

This is our reality.

Just talking, that's all

This is our mystery.

Thanks for watching. I don't think I've said that yet.

Thanks. I'm as beautiful as you think I am.

5.

Rules are designed to be broken. It's the reason someone like me can even be possible. I mean really—the rules I make are built using the cadavers of previous canons.

Anatomy of a true love; or, a lesson in successful manslaughter.

1.

It was like it never lost any meaning, like saying the words wasn't cliché—I love you.

We started saying it early in the morning and by the time we had cut him to pieces, my pet and I had turned it into an echo, a refrain for every deep cut of the knife, the snapping of bone, every pull of the trigger, the tortured cries of each victim.

I love you.

It was all we needed to say.

Our actions meant far more, filling in the blanks.

The rest, we leave it for you to clean up.

2.

Scott the Slaughter. Guess who came up with the name?

Yup. He didn't have a name in mind. For such a creative fellow, Scott kept his cards close like he didn't really trust me. After a dozen, a fleshed out gimmick, and he still failed to trust me. So I'm not that angry for what my pet and I do. I'm good like that: Easy to bargain with dollar signs, with batting of an eyelash. We're hanging in Scott's jail cell in no time.

And then it's happening so quickly, him and I.

Scott led from the cell back to the convertible. Held down by the ladies.

My pet returning to his coupe, looking sad, but I tell him, "Cover story."

He gets it. I'm probably who's most hurt by the forced separation; if he's going to make it onto the front page of magazines, front page of websites across the globe, yeah:

We have to keep the study alive.

Fine by me—though we break the rules to be closer, we're no different than anyone else wanting to remain free.

Down the road, to the right, and make two lefts so that we won't miss our exit.

Cut to the house I rented for the hell of it. Used a lot of the money we got from the gas station. Sure it was a nice financial boost, but I'm not even worrying about the cost—not worrying about anything but how the next few scenes will look like on camera. I'm first out of the convertible.

I unlock the front door, run inside to open the garage door for both cars.

We're home for the time being.

I'm going to teach him a thing or two about taste.

It's got to be tasteful.

Getting a closer look at Scott, he's in poor shape. I'm asking him, "When's your date?"

Only he knows what I'm talking about, and only he tells me its three days from now.

"Then you shouldn't care that it's been pushed up to today."

Scott shakes his head and coughs.

"Harsh cough," I'm saying while directing the assistants into the right room. The whole house carpeted, I had plastic laid out in what's probably supposed to be where the TV goes. This is the room where all of you are likely watching this happen. If that's irony, use it in a situation where irony isn't annoying. I'll let the audience have it.

Scott doesn't say anything.

"I'm thinking it's been a decade since your last physical."

I'd be right. Stripped down, he's thin, malnourished-looking.

"Haven't been eating the food they give you?"

He coughs and spits, "Stomach can't take it."

"You'd think you'd acclimate. Build up immunity. Something."

The ladies get the camera ready, stationary so that we can all have a turn.

"This'll be fun," I'm winking at my pet.

Scott shivers, "I'm not going to do anything with my last three days."

My pet is the last to enter the room. He seems shy.

I'm not going to ask him why.

We'll start soon—don't be frustrated.

"Stand there," I'm telling Scott.

He does what I tell him, same tone of voice that I use on all my pets. I like that he still remembers me well enough not to test me.

This will go smoothly.

Scott standing in the center of the room, my pet at the door, one foot in, one foot out (probably some kind of metaphor there, right? Committed, but only to what's approved), and my two assistants laying out the black tarp, the tools, tending to the camera so that there aren't too many jump shots and lost footage.

"Ready?" I'm asking everyone.

I give my pet a nod.

He walks in.

Won't look at anyone but me.

I lick my lips, "Okay let's do this."

3.

Scott coughs up a wad of phlegm. He won't stop coughing and it becomes tiresome. Every time I lean down to inspect his body, he coughs in my direction, our direction. It's disgusting, but he's saying that he can't control it. He says that there's something stuck in his throat, lodged there for years. I duct tape his mouth shut, clearly having enough of his bullshit, and feel his forehead.

"He does feel a little warm," I'm saying.

They can't resist feeling his forehead after me, repeating what I had said.

"Warm, definitely."

"Definitely warm."

"It's okay," I'm telling him. We're here to take the pain away.

The interesting thing about the mystery is how, depending on context, my pet and I can assume the role of healers at the same time we do what we like to do.

That's about as blunt as I can get, you know.

We like that we're doing this. On Scott's benefit, he won't have to be sick for much longer.

So what's wrong? It's not just a cold. You're wheezing, have a fever, clammy skin, a constant sweat, discoloration of the tongue. You're finding it difficult to focus, right? You're losing sight of what's happening here. Start talking only to forget what you were talking about a couple words in. Where are we? What are we doing? My name's Claire and you used to be mine.

Now you'll make for a great little experiment.

I'm going to show my pet how to make the act of killing poetic.

Oh, that's right—you two haven't met.

Say hello.

Scott, meet my pet.

Pet, meet victim.

He's great, isn't he?

I slap Scott once across the face. I don't always need a reason.

It felt good. I'm feeling good. Things are in place and everything I care about is in this room. I can feel the pressure from before settling, easing off. Tapes are ours to keep; the camera captures what you want to see. Everything's in motion.

Now for a little anatomy 101.

I'm starting to get worked up. Showing him what's what, this versus that. . .this happens and then that happens. What happens next? Use your imagination. We cut here. Remove that. If you want to keep him conscious, don't go for it first. Amble around major arteries and organs. Cut skin. Break bone. Let cartilage make that satisfying crunch. Just don't be so hasty. I know it's sometimes more efficient and better for the scene to be brutal and have gore splatter across the walls. It really does look good, I know, but if you're going to settle into the gimmick, you've got to do what he did.

"What did you do, Scott?"

He's all mumbles and garbled noises due to the duct tape.

So I'll go ahead and continue my lecture then.

You see, Scott earned the "Slaughter" part via the way he dismantled his victim's bodies with surgical precision. He'd cut each and remove them like a surgeon. He was training to be one, after all, and it became his gimmick (and later his obsession) exploring how much can be removed before crossing the line and seeing the victim die.

It was more for effect until, well yeah, he started doing it less for the game, the thrill, and more for some far off idea that I couldn't understand.

But who had to clean up the bodies?

Who had to make it so that we were invisible?

Who explained how crime works, how anything criminal can be more popular and memorable than anything civil?

He wanted to be invisible.

Too bad he didn't think clearly enough to understand what that meant.

Invisible.

If you're invisible, you are alone.

You can't be invisible without expecting to leave me, and I'm kind of wondering if he ever figured out why what we had ended. It wasn't because he lost interest in me, became less loyal; it was because I became a source, something to rely on, and nothing more. He did what I wanted him to do, but he no longer wanted to do it. When I commanded him, he was obedient but dead.

The fight had faltered.

Shit, it's getting hot in here.

"Turn up the air conditioning," I'm telling one of the assistants.

Knives up.

I tell him to make the first incision.

"Cut where you think it'll make me happy."

4.

This here, I'm lecturing, holding the scalpel over Scott's forehead, cutting thin lines, just enough to draw blood. You cut here and he won't be able to blink anymore.

My pet went for the stomach, and that's fine, but I warned him: It's a sweet spot.

The whole midsection of the human body is where you have to be extra careful.

We want Scott to feel this.

This is his physical.

His last hurrah: As a victim he must be completely and wholly victimized according to the manner in which he dispatched his own. During his time.

We must do him some justice, you know?

Sure as hell can't stand the guy, not anymore. His smell is enough to annoy but you see, you're here with me, my pet, and so what we do is what we have to do to make it better for you.

Your legacy.

So cutting here, good. Cut evenly. Good.

You've got a steady hand. That's good.

Cutting there and also here, I'm pointing at the upper eyelid; will make it impossible for him to see for any longer than it takes for his eyeballs to dry out.

It'll be pain and discomfort before things get worse enough to have him focus his attention on something else. Cut right there to make it seem worse than it actually is.

Good.

There was never any doubt, huh girls?

"Not at all," says one.

"No Claire, no doubt about it," says the other.

Sometimes you really got to use the girls to make a point.

Control the blood flow. Make sure to have it splatter across the sides, not on the body or else it'll be a pain in the ass as we start cutting deeper.

There we go.

Now over there, yeah, you see it? Right there.

Lift the skin. Careful now.

Okay. . .umm.

Here, let me do it. Just watch.

See how the skin doesn't quite separate from the muscle? When you do this, you'll have to pull everything up from the skull.

You get used to hearing them scream.

I'm sure you haven't gotten to that point yet, huh?

Didn't think so. I can tell. You wince when they get loud and you react when they beg. That should all be white noise while you enjoy the act.

The act is what matters most.

With that removed—here you can go ahead and place it on the table over there—you'll notice that his eyes are unfocused. Don't be deterred, we're not done with the face yet.

I'll let you cut where I've drawn the lines.

I'm going to work on another area of the body.

No, that's correct, cut that line. Don't worry about how deep you go. You'll know when you've gone too far. You'll hit bone. You'll probably see him wince.

Yeah, just have at it.

Fun, huh?

That's my pet.

5.

Oh, it looks like he's starting to pass out. Inject this into the muscle of his arm, any muscle will do, bicep is best, to keep him awake. We want him awake for this. Got it all cut?

Great—go ahead and remove it.

You can see his jawbone.

Now we're going to start removing extremities.

Scott used to break an arm or leg before removal.

Do you want to break or cut?

You want to do both?

You know just the right thing to say, don't you?

Mmm, fine. "Ladies, the sledgehammers."

"Scotty, this is going to hurt a bit, okay?"

I'll target the right leg; you go for the left.

We'll do this on three, okay?

One.

Two. . .

Three—ouch, close but we need a bit more.

"Poor Scotty. Just think of your number. How many did you dispose of, wasn't it—oh I don't know—thirty? So yours won't be nearly as big of a deal. Everything we're doing, we're doing in your image. So Scotty, why not enjoy it, hmm? Enjoy the pain. Not everybody gets to be immortalized in someone's legacy."

Again, on three.

One.

Two. . .

Three—there we go. Now looks like they're both broken. Shattered, actually. So what happens next needs to be precise. We can't make any mistakes.

"Someone get me the bone saw."

You can watch.

Don't look away now, my pet.

If it isn't a rule, it should be:

Never censor the best part of the kill.

Keep the camera right on the action. They always cut or fade when it comes time for the payoff. But not this time. We'll watch. You're already watching.

I've always hated the sound of the bone saw.

Such a shrill obnoxious kind of thing, buzzing in a way that you can't ever imagine. It's what still gives me goose bumps. But this thing really does a great job. See, I'm not going to cut where the fracture is; I'm cutting right above the fracture.

Right where the bone is broken, but still attached.

This will take a moment. . .

There.

He isn't making a sound.

"Hey girls, check to see if Scott's conscious."

Watch as they both scramble to check his pulse.

"Well?"

He's alive. Barely.

"Good enough," I'm saying as I hold up the bone saw. "Want to try?"

Of course my pet says yes.

That's a good cut.

I'm holding up the bone saw, "Someone take this," and I'm moving on to show him how we'll cut into his chest.

Now most of the organs, if removed, will quickly result in failure.

Scott will die.

My question to you then is, which shall be removed?

This? That? Scott removed the brain. That was his. He didn't listen to me.

If you ask me, I'd remove what he'd miss the most.

These are the kinds of things I'm interested in teaching you. It's the small things—not the broad strokes—that need to be taught. Subtlety not sanctity. You've got the basics down. You're a natural. You never needed to be taught the basics. You've got a good stomach; no nausea or vertigo when it comes time to deliver the act. I'm impressed. I really am. There's a whole city to explore, and we'll explore it together. My jealousy was out of my affection and loyalty for you. Master needs her pet, after all. I'm not going to be able to continue the way I'd like if I didn't have you with me. What we have borders any body; what we do will be remembered as a whole.

We look into each other's eyes.

I hand him the scalpel. "Ladies, give him some room."

We leave the room, tending to other aspects of the kill. What I've left him you'll see. What he'll do, is between you and him. I've let him mark it as his own.

I ask him, which will you choose?

The camera will spread the word.

My pet, I'll give you the option.

Go ahead and choose.

6.

I can ask you, I can ask him, but I won't. I already know what he chose.

There's only one way to truly express ourselves and it's by marking what we, up until now, haven't been able to find. So he removes what I had lived without until I found him, my perfect pet. He removes the heart, because I'm not quite sure I had one. I'm not quite sure I cared about much, save for the fight. For the fight to be more desirable, I needed to understand what it's like to lose it all—to feel absolutely nothing—in order to appreciate a fighter.

We get what we want, but we're also the ones that keep us from getting there.

It could be so easy. I could have found him right from the start.

Truth is, he was just a teacher's assistant.

He was there, in my classes, and was there, as one of my own, but I hadn't let it settle. I noticed but never bothered, favoring the established killer, the killer with a flavor, the ones that had begun to tap into the fight in order to be fully featured. I looked there instead of looking directly in front of me. And when I did, I had made so many mistakes.

This is what we're doing.

We're fixing what I did.

My pet, there can only be one of you. No one can ever know what I gave them.

My failures, my exes, cease to exist.

I kept myself from being found.

It took me this long to figure that out.

We'll wrap up the body parts and freeze them. We'll tend to the mess that was once the feared serial killer, Scott the Slaughter.

But one thing I will take with me is the heart.

The authorities will not find the heart.

7.

You probably want to know, right?

What it takes to kill?

What it feels like to pull the trigger and see the body fall to the ground?

Understandable, and honestly, for a long time, I couldn't think of anything else. I imagined what it might feel like. I made love to the idea, made it more than it could ever be. There might be something in this, reason why it took so many to get to him, and why I need him so much more than I need myself.

But, you know, it's a mess.

We could have avoided the mess; we would have killed him with little to no trouble. There is an art to manslaughter, and it's often about quickness and efficiency.

For instance, you can simply inject a poison. The stronger the better. It's a silent killer. No one will suspect the seizure or other reactions to the poison to be yours. Sodium thiopental is the most effective, not that just anyone can get a hold of the chemical. But you get the idea.

Another would be to enact a situation where the target explodes, typically not by way of just exploding, but rather in relation to something else around the body exploding and, as a result, the body is broken apart and rendered obsolete at the same time. This is expensive but utterly satisfying. Not very practical, sure, but it'll be tough to find the body.

I'm thinking the easiest is also the most "natural," if murder is something you'd admit as a natural act. It's been around since life began. Life's sole counterpoint is death. Perhaps murder is the opposite of mystery. It's obvious. It is final.

A gun will deal the best results. It's not as impactful and not as gruesome. You're probably thinking that it's a predictable answer, but fact of the matter is that it's true.

Killing a person swiftly means aiming for the head and pulling the trigger.

More effective than shooting them in the head is hitting them in the heart. Hit them with a shot right where it matters most, the one organ that makes any of this possible, and they're dead before their body can hit the ground.

Even more effective is not listing out effective ways to kill. Manslaughter is an act with reason, a motivation underneath. I'm sure as hell that few would bother to go through with it if they didn't have something imbedded, something that enforces reason or defies it. There needs to be a pulse, a prospect, behind the act.

And that's why I'm a believer in the slaughter.

It's nothing without creativity.

The creativity is what renders a crime scene worth taking extensive footage of for all to see. Not just those assigned to the case; not just the eleven-o-clock news.

The scene that defies all other scenes. . .now that's beautiful. What we have is beautiful.

And I'm thinking I still want more.

We always want more. You probably want me to say something else. . .

This is another confessional. Hmm.

Well, I'm probably going to step down. Let all you have a chance to watch and react. It's going to be a great season. Lots will happen in a short amount of time.

It's an important season.

It's the one that'll provide a real ending.

I'm sure they'll get someone else to speak for the mystery.

I'm going back to living it.

Thanks again for continuing to watch.

"Say it. Speak up."

I want you to hear his voice.

I want the camera to finally catch it, mark it as a moment.

This is the moment he finally says, "Yes master."

And that, my, my—it's enough for me to climax right here.

Data recorded.

We were close once.

1.

I drove through the night.

I drove through an entire day.

We couldn't stop. Not even for the tapes we were supposed to leave for each other. We hold onto ours in hopes of getting to watch them later.

It was because of the house. I had rented it on a whim, forgetting that it would lead the authorities on our tracks. And now, they are four or five cars back, the threat of being spotted so very real. It didn't stop us then—I drove faster—and it won't stop us now—I'm driving fast enough to create distance. We'll get to him in time. My pet and I will need to keep track of our turns, but other than that, what's one chase, one wrong move when we're moving so quickly?

My pet, my perfect little pet, don't you worry.

The road might be lengthy and tiring, but we're almost there.

Into the phone that becomes our only link, I'm hearing myself say, "We're almost there."

Soon we won't have anywhere else to go.

2.

This is the part where she takes the fall.

She had blonde hair and I wanted her to keep it the same. No need to change the color. No need to change anything that wasn't her. All I asked was that she be as close to me as possible.

Understandably, she tried to replace me, thinking it would be her only escape. I forgave her, and this is why she will do what needs to be done to keep this convertible running.

I have my pet on the phone, the tapes running thin; the line clear and there for good. Don't hang up. Don't pick up any other calls. "We'll be okay," is all I have to say to him and he'll do what needs to be done. And we'll be okay. There's never been any doubt.

He's not the one being followed.

This convertible has been marked.

When the number of squad cars littering the interstate became one too many, I started to get nervous. Both of them, they of course know. They can sense that something's about to go wrong.

I'll keep driving. That's what I'll do.

I turn up the music—let it drown out any and all potential deceit.

I won't have them thinking lesser of me.

My pet's not in question here. He's safe and sound and that's about as important as anything else. I'm not going to be lost, downed on the side of the fucking road.

I refuse.

So listen to this music.

Nothing's wrong at all.

Nope. I'm getting them to sing along.

"Sing," why don't you sing?

That's not enough. I'm telling them to dance, "Do it!"

We need to look like we're just any other car, the wrong convertible. Oh, hey officer, guess you got the wrong red convertible. Us? We're headed for tropical waters. We're all about getting tanned.

Maybe I'll show some skin.

Pale, porcelain skin. Show him and say something like—don't you think I need a tan?

Then have the girls echo my thoughts, what I'm implying, and the officer would forget all about pulling us over. He'll treat us nice, like he's at fault, and we'll continue down the interstate.

And if not that, I've got the cover story.

Always had the cover story.

It'll work, yes—we're criminologists. The camera? It's part of the study. Got to gather data somehow. Be more elegant about it. Elegant, seductive—something like that.

Ugh, I hate this song.

With the radio off, it's kind of obvious. It's left out there, for the three of us to comprehend.

I guess I'm concerned because I don't want to have to do what I know needs to be done.

"You know," she starts, "we managed to have our clothes match the entire time."

I'm nodding. My other assistant replies, "Wardrobe without any malfunctions."

Them I'm saying, "I'm not taking the credit on that one. Sometimes the scene falls into place perfectly, and all we have to do is take off the clothes. Never have to put them on."

But by the time we reach the next sign, it's clear, and I'm not telling her because she's already agreed. I'm saying, "Are you sure?"

Again, she agrees.

"Someone's got to stay interested," she says as she begins

to remove her clothes. My other assistant films the undressing, capturing the urgency alongside the quick look at her curves. Is the audience interested? That shouldn't be in question.

Not to worry: The camera will never cease to be a part of this.

Leave the worry to me.

She puts on something else, a dress, something that I hadn't planned on wearing.

I speed up in order to pass the car to my right.

Once I'm in the right lane, I'm looking at her. She seems so calm.

I'll give her a moment, or two. But eventually it'll have to happen. She'll take the wheel. She'll drop us off at the next rest stop. My one remaining assistant and I will go inside, seeking food despite having no appetite. I'll walk back outside the moment she pulls out of the parking space, the convertible visible as it rejoins the momentum of the interstate.

I'll see the car, the one that followed me, taking the bait.

This will happen so smoothly, it'll seem like it was scripted.

My assistant will ask the one question on the audience's mind:

"Aren't you worried she'll say something?"

To that I'll say with ease, "She's not going to get far."

She has less than a fourth left in the tank and she'll drive approximately a mile and a half down the interstate before finding the right sacrificial vehicle.

Doesn't take a whole lot to flip the convertible at that speed. Danger drives easy and well at 95MPH. She'll angle in on the turn just enough. She'll lead them to a dead end, and what they'll end up with is another mess to clean up. You would have seen it if you'd been there.

She did it for me. She did it for us.

Down and out, we're aiming for the aftermath. I can almost see it.

This'll end how I want it to end. You'll see.

Maybe she'll talk about it later.

3.

This is the part where my pet takes to the back roads so that he can visit the Villain. Phone with him at all times. Even though I can't be there, I'm listening.

I'm listening as we pick up speed, renting a car that'll never be returned. I'm listening as we buy another camera, one that uses the same tapes. I'm listening as we plot out an alternate path to where we need to be a few hours from now.

I'm listening the entire time.

Without a camera, the scene takes on a different sort of atmosphere. Instead of visual cues, I have his voice. Everything he tells me is his choice. He sculpts the scene with my pleasures in mind. So when he's finally with the Villain of the Carolinas, I pictured it as a scene I had designed on my own. He told me what I needed to know and, much like the mystery, everything left out is mine to explore. Let my imagination run wild.

The Villain deserves a little pity.

I had known him as a childhood friend, of sorts. A man that was meek but loyal, he'd do pretty much anything if it meant upholding a friend's dignity. He was my pet long before I knew what I was looking for. Early, sure, but he was kind of always there. I did my best to relate to his problems, his interests. Sometimes I'd get the feeling that he directed attention away from himself because he lacked the most basic of needs, the self-image, to function with true cause. He'd do anything yet he wouldn't know why. It's why he did everything I said. And I really do mean that: He did everything.

But he never lost the confusion.

The Villain operated under the concept of cages. I came up with the idea because I wasn't really very creative back then, probably saw the idea in some horror flick, and I was all about seeing what he would do. The Villain caged people for weeks. He fed them like they were rats. He treated the living like they didn't deserve to live. . .but didn't deserve to die either.

It was the one kid that changed it. For six kills, he had done well, real well. I tried to make sense of it; I'd explain why he was feeling the way he was feeling (or wasn't) but I was young. I hadn't figured it out either. But when he started liking kids, I lost interest.

I'm not about the nubile. I'm not at all interested in the exploitation of the naïve. The naïve provide no sort of affection; they are merely childish and lost, right to the final gasp.

The Villain wasn't my name. He earned it all on his own.

Yeah, that's him, pitiful and pathetic.

I'm listening when my pet wants some guidance.

Wants to know how best to deal with the Villain.

I'm not saying anything. Instead, I direct him to vacancy, the act of letting the Villain kill himself. Because he truly can, it might be the best means of pulling out from this world.

I'm not saying anything when my pet humiliates him, muffled sounds and sobbing can be heard clearly above everything else.

I'm not saying anything even though I'm curious about where they are, where my pet decided to do the deed.

I'm not saying anything as I hear a more familiar sound and then nothing.

Previous sounds followed by clear and plain coughing, lungs grasping for air.

I'm not saying anything when I hear him talking, saying the words I couldn't have fed him, louder and louder until I imagine the Villain licking up his own tears with his tongue, a mouthful of dust and dirt licked from the floorboards. One nail pierces through the Villain's tongue.

A little torture goes a long way.

I'm not saying anything when my pet delivers the command once, twice, a third time.

For a brief moment I feel pity for the Villain, how oblivious and fearful must be facing him, alone in whatever place they're in, faced with death, the only person to share these dying moments being the one being he cannot fully comprehend.

My pet is confusion.

My pet is the reason there's no longer a place for him.

I'd say something, say something like goodbye, but it doesn't feel like the right time and place for it. What's a childhood friend when you haven't seen each other in over a decade?

We were young then I'm thinking as I listen to my pet explaining how to properly take the bullet. We were young and curious I'm realizing as I hear my pet telling him how quick it'll be, how painless, no more painful than the nail through his tongue.

I'm listening to the Villain gag on his own blood.

I'm listening to the gun being loaded.

I'm listening to the gun being given.

I'm listening to the gun being placed in his mouth.

I'm listening to the solemn shivers of a confused, mentally underdeveloped man, someone I used to know, someone that I might have kept around but, well, fuck it, I didn't and this is how things happen. Things fall in line or fall away from the limelight. We do what we need to do to stay in the light. I'm fine either way. So the sound of the gun isn't all that spectacular. I've heard it before and I'll hear it again. It's the silence afterwards, the gentle and oh, so satisfying ringing that I enjoy.

I'm on the line the entire time, listening.

I drive the interstate inconspicuously. Headed for the one and the only, the man that might have made me, but instead I made it so that every waking moment is bled-through wonder about why, why I did what I did to him. Why did I do that to any of them? My exes didn't deserve it, did they? Create a dialogue. See if others agree.

I'm not so sure they'd choose differently if they had a second chance.

I'm pretty sure they'd still choose to be my pet.

Who could resist this beautiful voice?

Hear me sing, my pet.

Hear me sing.

4.

This is where she'll turn herself in. It's her idea, not entirely mine. I had her set to end her part of the study shortly before the Florida state line, but she told me she had enough.

"I've had enough."

See? That's proof that she said it.

She cowered under the idea of what they'll try to do, and because I said that, you're probably wondering about the authorities. The authorities are an entirely different brand of fetishism.

If you let them, their nightsticks and firearms would take on a manifold of seductions.

Give them an inch and they'll try to stick it all the way in.

Just because they wear a uniform, it doesn't mean they aren't curious. They'll bite; they'll bite right through if you let them. I'd never make an officer my pet; there wouldn't be any fun in it. They'd do anything to make me happy. Making me happy would make them ecstatic. They'd be turned on by the approval. They'd desire my full approval. I'd grow tired of them and leave them tied up in some basement somewhere.

But she'll be okay.

I know it.

She'll confess.

She'll tell them everything which will only make it easier for them to let her go.

Doesn't sound real. Sounds like something imagined.

Something stupid and unbelievable.

They said the same thing about every single killer before they found enough evidence to turn the tale into something personal and very real.

But this is where she wants to be let off. Her part of

the study ends.

Leaves only you and me. My pet and I. And the camera.

You'll be here to the end, won't you?

You'll watch as long as there's a show to watch.

You'll never leave.

5.

This is the part where I'd say something like, Long time no see. Not that I'd say something like that; who says that while being serious? I mean really?

Busy room. Inmates get a taste of the world outside these walls. I sit down and wait for him to arrive. I place the camera to my side, lens adjusted so that it'll capture him, and only him. You'll only need to hear my voice. He walks in like he's a different person. It wouldn't take a whole lot to convince me. That look, what I see his face turn into when he sees me, it's clear that I'm the same.

I am who I am and I just want to say hello.

He sits down.

I lean forward.

Take it all in.

He's staring back at me.

If he were a true gentleman, he'd initiate the conversation. You get where we're at, I say the line, the one that started this all, and that would have sent him over the edge if there was anything left. There isn't so we'll just talk. Talk like this is exactly what it seems: a visit.

"When's your date?"

He tells me, "Next April."

"What's the holdup?"

He doesn't say.

He doesn't ask, "What are you doing here?"

"We had some good times."

Doesn't say anything.

"No use mentioning why."

"Yeah," he nods, once.

"I had never been with someone like you. . ."

"And never will," he finishes my sentence.

I'd have to agree. There's no one else.

"Who is he?" he asks me.

"He's sweet, charming, from the same department. He wants to be a criminologist."

"Just like you." I can almost tell that he's happy for me.

That's just for show, you see. I'm saying that it seems amicable, our discussion, but really he's tired. He's tired and nervous. Most of all he's waiting; everyone knows what's next.

"You don't think you'll get tired of him?"

I shake my head.

"You get tired of everybody."

"Not true," I make a pouty face "It's not that I get tired; it's that the people I'm with never ended up being who I thought they were. Every single time, something was discovered as missing."

He shuts his eyes, "What was I missing?"

"What do you mean?"

"What was I missing?"

I think about this. Need a minute. And then I decide that he wasn't missing anything in particular; it's that he didn't keep up. Couldn't keep up. A lack of trust.

"A lack of trust," I tell him.

A moment passes until he says, "You should be in here."

I shrug, "What did I do wrong?"

He could have said something, but he chose to remain silent.

He looks at what I'm wearing.

I explain, "Independent study."

"I see. And when's my turn?"

"Soon." I click my tongue, "Sooner than April."

We sit facing each other, two people, two pieces of a very particular past, not sizing each other up, nowhere near any sort of collision. We're two pieces that didn't quite fit, but could have, and because we didn't, it's at least my duty to make sure that he fits in somewhere else.

My gentleman killer and I, we were close once.

We spend this time like we spent so much time watching each other on camera. We look past the flesh into what we see underneath. I imagine he's not worried about me. Things have worked out. Things will continue to work out. He hasn't done well. I see nothing past the façade he maintains. I see a man that has already taken stock of his life. He's ready to get lost. Won't even look, not ever; there's nothing left after this. He has no interest, no need, to find anyone else. There'll be no one there as he is erased. It's then that I know it was right to speak to him. I could have let my pet handle it. I wasn't sure whether or not it would be worth the risk, given the lingering interest, the threat of authority, but then again, I'm okay. We'll all be okay. And this gentleman, the Gentleman Killer from a different phase of my life, it's here that I understand that it was an important phase. It's a phase worth remembering. The mystery took shape then, and quickly became the reason to keep on going, keep searching, finding the pet perfect for my needs.

Consider it done. I've decided it'll be the least I can do.

I give him one last kiss before leaving. My pet will be there, and I will be watching and listening. He won't have to die alone. Before being nobody, he'll know that he meant a whole lot more to me than most others. My pet and I, we'll take his life, but in turn we'll also take his legacy.

A true gentleman would have preferred to remain anonymous. Invisible.

With a fleeting kiss, I bid you goodbye.

Data erased.

6.

Greetings, and thank you for letting us speak today. It isn't customary for national airtime to be set aside so that we can completely break the fourth wall, potentially ruining the mystery, but we were given the opportunity by the network and, well, we felt it was necessary to speak today.

Indeed, we're here today to speak about the issue, not the substance; the theory of the mystery rather than the material at play. We're wearing these masks for an explicit reason. Not to confuse. Not to abstract our identities. Rather, it's because we want to remain objective.

You know who we are. We were close to her, and as such too close to say anything about her, or him, or anything at all about the cover story, the so-called study.

That'll resolve itself without any hinting on our part.

Yes—we want to talk about the root issue, what both of us noted throughout every episode.

To put it simply, we want to talk about sex.

And violence.

We want to talk about sex and violence. The concern for what the camera captures is rendered as less concerning than the fact that through the continual participation of a large audience throughout the entirety of the mystery, it was their preference to omit the abstract.

The viewing public actively preferred the explicit portrayal of physical and often dire acts over the scenes that may or may not involve characterization and context.

As her assistants, we both quickly understood and abided by using anomalous yet vivid depictions of sex combined with violence.

Yes—we both noticed this.

We're both invested in the act so normally there's no difference—no separation—between context and portrayal. We are who we are and that's all there is.

We are not implying that the mystery conformed completely

to the audience's demands.

Not at all.

Rather, we are here today to make note of the pattern.

A very important pattern.

For you see, nine times out of ten, when the scene exhibited received critical acclaim, it involved the merging of both seemly acts.

Sex and violence.

When a scene had one, it wasn't nearly as highly received.

When sex and violence merged—became two essential underlying nuances of the delivered scene—the rating skyrocketed. The data studied, or rather the theoretical data as per the "study" of the show, exhibits a fascinating similarity.

The average audience member fails to discern a difference between sex and violence. With both extremes imbedded, the extremity takes on strangely seductive properties no matter how violent, no matter how sexual the scene.

Sex at its most extreme is violence. Violence at its most extreme becomes sex.

The average audience member is compelled, but they don't know why.

Use of both extremes fuels any mystery that's unsolved.

Use of a mystery fuels the need to continue watching.

It produces a reaction not unlike commitment in another individual.

When an audience member is committed, it's not unlike developing an intimate relationship with the material.

We find it both compelling and alarming.

What we want to leave you with today is the information we've gathered.

We want to leave you with the notice, the understanding that it's seldom as simple as dividing the viewing material by fact and fiction. What you see is not always what you get. In fact, you should assume that what you're watching has additional properties. Always seek out what doesn't seem to be there.

We did and found a pattern.

If you choose to look, you just might find a mystery all your own.

7.

In dreams that I'll never need to have, I am with him riding the same interstate, dead end of night, but the situation's reversed. I've been hunted. He's been hurt. He bleeds more blood than I'd ever think a person could have; I drive the entire way. The headlights are relentlessly there, blinding me whenever I try to look into my rearview mirror.

Their sirens are loud enough to ruin any show.

I'm not quite sure how long we drive, but we are chased.

We take part in a chase that's scripted to end with our incarceration.

But in dreams we can hide from anything. I'm able to keep the convertible running long after the tank runs dry. I'm able to keep him awake until they shoot out our tires and the sun blinds me and it's clear that this is the part where we're written out of the script.

It's our turn to die.

He leaves me before I design the way it passes.

Spin out the car, hitting others, flipping twice, my body launches into the air, his is crushed under the weight of a nearby semi.

Airborne, I witness the entirety of what it feels like to have been found.

I'll die with their cameras on me. They'll be filming my fall.

Right before I can hit the ground, I wake up.

If traveling south of any border, make sure to be well manicured.

1.

I had data. More data than originally expected.

I had enough data to finish a study and corroborate three more.

I had him at my side, the two of us posing as people without purpose, loitering and wandering around a nearby lake.

No one was here.

We were alone.

I wasn't master. He wasn't pet.

We were simple people.

We had gifts for each other.

He had every single tape I had missed, and in turn I had an equal share.

And so we traded.

After that we walked. We talked. We were just some couple.

We felt no urge to assail, no urge to assign extraneous meaning.

I heard sirens in the distance. They got close, but quickly faded.

We were alone here. We were simple people.

They wouldn't see who we really are.

It was a lake in the early afternoon.

And he was mine.

No camera would exaggerate the scene.

The scene was as simple as stock footage.

2.

This part isn't captured on film.

But it's worth mentioning that something happened here.

Time elapsed, and if we are both still alive, know that we're both still trying. A lot happened here, a lot that is shaved off clean, well-manicured, wondrously smooth.

And explored. Explore the final stretch of the mystery.

The best part. The best part you'll never see.

It's left for us, master and pet.

3.

I asked him to tell me a little bit about his part of the fantasy. He laughed it off, "Nothing in particular. Shitty roadside attractions, a lonely clerk or two, a lot of road. A lot of driving."

He asked about mine. I told him, "It's all on the tapes."

He nodded, "Mine too."

Then he said, "It's never the same as how we remember it."

I replied, "Nope."

And then added, "But that's why we have the data. No one's going to see those tapes."

He agreed.

Data recorded.

4.

I had something else for him.

My pet deserved a gimmick.

My pet deserved a name.

I handed him another tape wrapped in one of my panties.

Told him that it was his, the label read, "For Stephen."

He took the tape. I told him not to watch it until it was safe.

Save it for the bedroom, I whispered.

Until we were there, our one and only destination.

And then he put my panties back on.

He drove while I slept in the backseat.

Time would pick back up.

Time would erase all potential suspects.

Time would erase all probable leads.

Time would bring us home.

Home sweet home.

5.

The mystery is that we get along at all.

Home is where my heart is hidden.

1.

Close up shot of asphalt, moving at high speed, camera aimed low enough to see the blemishes, the stains, the cracks, faded blotches of asphalt.

The shot holds, resembling the passing of time as we hear the following voiceover inserted—lines from the prequel, the film before the show, the scene before there could have been any clear sense of a person's wanting.

She wanted so very much to find and be found. But now we're moving, quickly moving to the conclusion. It's enough to let the lines ring out.

"But you see, I was different. I knew what he had planned. What I offered him no one else has ever offered. I offered him more than my body. More than my love. I offered him my home. My kindness, my secret, my safety. He would be mine and I would keep him to his craft."

Get the sense that we're going somewhere.

"I support you financially. I give you a place to hide. I make sure you are never under suspicion of being what you really are, a cold-blooded psychotic killer (so hot), and, in return, you clue me into your process. You become mine.

"You do what I say.

"When I say it.

"Master and pet. This isn't unreasonable."

Getting closer.

"I need someone that'll need me, want me, covet me, consume me, captivate me, just as much as I do all those things and more to them.

"I'm selective in that way.

"But really, how can you not be?

"That girl, that guy, doesn't need you.

"They'll get what they want. If they are being picked up, it's because they're not the aggressors, the players; they aren't capable

of putting up a fight. They know they don't have any fight in them so they wait it out, hoping to be found by the other fighters, the ones capable of getting anything they want, be it one hour or the rest of your life.

Closer. Any minute now.

We will arrive.

"He didn't know what he was getting into when he first agreed.

"Have any of your exes?

"I'd like to think my breakups are always mutual."

Though the road never seems to end, it will, and soon. Much sooner than you think.

"You might as well begin and end all comparisons on the violence of our everyday actions and reactions because that's where the victim's chance to break free ends. And when that weapon is made murder weapon, and the location is made crime-scene, the last thing that's important is whether or not the victim was a good human being or not.

"So no matter what, the media's going to make the victim as innocent as can be. No matter what the victim might have done, there'll be this disconnection from reality and fiction when it comes to serial murder, so it doesn't really mean that much to answer why, and I'm really trying not to answer the question why because no matter how hard I try, I'm not going to be saying what you want because I don't really know what you want and I don't know the answer."

A jump cut to final scene.

The scene where mystery becomes more method for every kill that'll ever occur.

"The mystery will consume everyone, and I'm the only one that'll have known every inch. I'll have seen everything before it turned into common knowledge. I'll have been there, telling him what to erase and what to keep. And I'll be saying to him every line that no one else will hear.

"Every line of that mystery.

"Every line of you and me."
Now let this fade. Let go.
And watch the final episode.
The lines, they ring true.
"A pickup isn't over until they ask you where you want to go."
Where do you want to go?

2.

It's only him and I, master and pet. It's only him that can do it, but I'll teach him. I'll tell him every step of the way what needs to happen. What he'll do, no matter how heinous, this is the last scene, you see. This is the last scene of the mystery.

"You need to make them happy," I'm saying.

There needs to be interest.

"You need to keep me interested."

My pet and I sit in his coupe, the cool night air seeping in through the vents.

I look around, the neighborhood hushed, snuffed until dawn. Houses of little to no variation line the street. Cars parked on driveways, garbage cans on the curb waiting to be collected. I'm reminded of where I used to live, and where I'd like to live again, someday. The serenity of a neighborhood like this affords a lot of privacy. Seems like Florida is packed in with tons of these neighborhoods. Makes sense—there's little to be done that can't be done indoors. So go away. It's like an owner's saying, we're consenting adults; we'll do whatever it takes to please us. You can't watch with the curtains down.

My parents before me had a home that might as well have been in the middle of nowhere. As long as we abided by the homeowner's association code, we could host any number of spectacles indoors. I'm looking at the clock. 4:35AM.

Yawning, I recline back in the seat.

All we can do now is wait. You can't rush this.

With my eyes closed, I coach him on what's going to happen next.

He's silent, though, which concerns me.

I'm forced to ask, "You understand, right?"

He should have said yes. With no hesitation, yes.

I recline the seat back up. Turn to him and look deep into his eyes, "Say it."

He doesn't say it.

"Look at me and say it."

He looks at me but doesn't say it.

"This is how you'll prove to me that you're mine."

He sighs. And it's a sigh that answers more than anything he could have said.

I take his face into my hands and, an inch from his lips, I whisper the command. I tell him that it's necessary. The tapes recorded as cover, part of his fantasy, will inevitably be found by his father, or his mother, or worse. Much worse.

He has to do this if he wants to ensure his legacy. Our legacy.

"It's them or me." I'm saying a little louder now, "You have to choose. What's it going to be?" And then you have to understand what it means to set fire to a home. You have to understand what he's going through. But then, with his reply, I'm quickly regretting why I ever doubted him.

He massages his forehead, "No contest—I'm just a little exhausted. Wondering if I'll have time to nap for a half-hour."

This is the first time I kiss him.

I bite his lower lip, just enough for him to wince, and he bites back.

We share this moment and it's secure. All we do now is wait.

I decide to rest in the backseat, that way his father won't see me. He nods off with his arms wrapped around the steering wheel.

It is 4:49AM. His father doesn't knock on the car window until around 6:30AM. approximately. His father doesn't see me, and I don't see him. But I hear everything.

Father says, "Finally made it back."

My pet nods, providing an appropriate excuse, "I didn't want to wake anybody up."

Next words being his, "What time is it?"

I glance through the rear windshield as my pet and his father walk into the house.

I look at the time. 6:45AM.

I'm not going around back, slipping into the house via the basement door, until around 7:30AM. By then, his mother is collecting dishes, cleaning up after breakfast. My pet's in his room, waiting. His father's reading the newspaper at the kitchen table.

There's no convertible. There's no conceit. It's just me. Him and I, we no longer need any fantasy. I'm tiptoeing up to the second floor. Inside his room, he sees me and stands up from his bed. I look at the TV. He watched the tape. We share another kiss. We know that it's time.

For the first but not the last, I address him in name, "Stephen, only you can do this."

He nods. But that's not enough. I want to hear it.

"You understand why. If you're going to own up to that name, the gimmick I've designed for you, there can be no leads, no links. It has to be like you never were. Nothing but an apparition, a ghost. A killer of killers: and in that way a media saint."

I hand him gloves and a knife, "Now I'll hold them down, but you have to cut."

We put on gloves. Hear footsteps at his door.

Lindsey walks in, says something like, "Who's this?"

He tells her to walk over and shake my hand.

"Why are you wearing gloves?"

I'm saying, "It's cold in here."

I give my pet one last moment to say goodbye.

She asks me, "Are you my brother's girlfriend?"

I hug her, saying, "Thank you for saying that."

With my arms wrapped around hers, he cuts her from the back of her neck, and stabs her a few times in crucial points on her back.

Good—I command him to make sure by cutting the stomach too.

No matter the smell. We'll get used to it.

No matter the blood; it's just another bodily fluid.

I grip on tightly making it hard for her to breathe.

I'm saying, "This is yours to design, do whatever you like as long as you do it."

Do it with confidence. There shall be no killing with kindness.

Some of those closest to us only end up holding us back. My pet and I will never be happy, never be impossible to track, if there are people that expected him home, knew of his cover story, knew of something suspicious. His father could sense that something was wrong. His son had changed, grown into his potential.

Lindsey's a bleeder. I get it all over my shirt, so I take it off.

He gives me one look. I pose for him, back arched, shoulders back, letting it show.

Lindsey tries to scream. "Hush now," I'm telling her, "can't do that if I won't let you breathe." She quickly bleeds out, four-foot frame rendered slack in my arms.

I lift her up and wrap her in his bedsheets.

He's got a choice but he can't have that gun. I'm shaking my head. Snap of my fingers, he hands me the gun. I offer him the wire or the chemical.

He takes both.

"Good pet," I say.

He descends the stairs on the balls of his feet.

I wait until I hear a mother's screams. That's my cue to supervise.

Downstairs, he has his father hog-tied and stripped down to only his shirt.

His mother's screaming, face red, eyes shut and swollen.

How creative, he used the chemical on her, not him. I stand back, arms crossed and watching. You watching this? How's it faring, so far?

The father tries to move, wiggling towards the front door, but falls over in a way that makes it impossible to move at all. My pet tends to his mother, whose screams quickly become irritating.

If you don't shut her up anytime soon, few will be able to stand it.

We'll have to hit mute.

I command him to get her to eat the chemical. It's not possible until we make it possible. It's a powder that burns and ruptures skin with little effort. Ingesting it would quickly cause hemorrhaging. Of course, I base this on nothing. I've never tried it before.

But I want him to try it.

He can't hold onto the powder chemical for long. Even with the gloves, it burns.

I hand him a scooper found in the cupboard. It was used to scoop out flour for baking.

Bake this—my pet pries his mother's mouth open.

I'm shoving a funnel into her mouth.

He's pouring the chemical in.

I've got the duct tape.

He tapes her mouth shut.

We stand back for a moment, watching.

I command him to tend to his father while I watch and wait for the big payoff. Mother's going to have a reaction, but what will it be?

My pet's dragging his father in a way that shows that neither cared for each other very much. The one that may have hurt the most is already over. Lindsey didn't feel much. Well, actually she did. But it's over now. My pet will be able to move on. He's got me.

I command him to hang him by some hook, but while I'm finding a hook that can hold the weight of an adult male he proves, yet again, why I can't resist. Why he's my perfect pet.

Why he's everything—he hangs his father by the tallest banister in a way that uses the entire structure to hold up the hog-tied man.

I tell him, "Go for it."

So he does.

The wire is sharp enough to cut anything.

I look down at the mother, no noticeable change, "She's seizing a little."

He cuts the father's left ear off and shows it to him.

Father's crying. Keep with it. Cut the left ear.

This time he tosses it aside, no bother.

My pet takes a step back, observing his creation.

He's taking suggestions. What would you like to see?

The wire could cut his genitals off, but that's to be expected and not very entertaining.

The wire could cut a few fingers off. That's more like it.

The wire could shave skin like a knife cutting butter. Pleasant image?

The wire could cut straight through his father's neck, but that's the kill. That's the final act. Shouldn't there be something else here? Something to enjoy?

He removes the father's ball gag.

Father spouts pained gibberish, more a sobbing with poorly enunciated speech.

Cut the lips. Oh, never seen that before.

I command him to play dentist. People like to cringe. They like to see teeth removed even though it causes them to look away in horror.

Plyers?

"Don't mind if I do," he says.

One front tooth and two molars later and I think his father loses consciousness.

Thrilled, we stand there and watch blood drip from his mouth.

"Oh shit," I remember.

We run back to his mother's body, but it's too late.

"Shit," he says, covering his nose.

We poured enough chemical into his mother's mouth to burn through her stomach lining, burn through her skin. It's uncanny, the resemblance:

It looks a lot like how celluloid looks like when you set it on fire.

I have to get a close up shot of it. All for you. No need to thank me.

With only the father left, we take our time.

Cut this, cut that—he's not going to regain consciousness.

Eventually there's not much left of him to cut without disemboweling him or essentially cutting the cord—ending his life. We sense the conclusion of the scene fast approaching.

He looks at me. I nod.

He wraps the wire around his father's neck twice and pulls.

Afterwards, there's a lot to clean up but without black light, we don't have to worry about anyone noticing. My pet and I make it look like nothing's ever happened. Anything worth hiding, we file them away in the basement.

The basements of America are full of secrets and dead bodies. Lies will only get you so far; you need a place to stow away the loneliness, a place to be alone when you need to be invisible. You can't be invisible without first losing the right to have another.

Dead bodies will soon become skeletons. With the skeletons file away the missing links and missing pieces, the doubt and the depression that may one day resurface. Keep the door locked. It's like it'll never again be a problem. I don't look forward to spring-cleaning. But the tapes, we keep them on our shelves. Never know when we'll crave another viewing.

Filed away, not for long: It feels like maybe it never happened.

But there, in the dark, dank forgotten corners of the basement, my heart will rest. I no longer need it. My pet and I only need the one. Together we beat to the same brutality; we hunger for the same chances, whatever that means.

Might as well imagine an epic soundtrack set to the entire thing, followed by a calming closer track, something that is more piano and foreboding than anything else.

My pet and I, we can take care of this without so much as a single sound outside. None will be any wiser. Outside it's early morning, the only thing that can be heard are the sounds of screeching tires, rumbling engines, and churning gears, the garbage men making their rounds.

Data recorded.

3.

What we have is unbelievable, absurd. Absurdity is an excuse.

What I find to be interesting is what so many others deem impossible, ridiculous, downright obscene. I must say, we all have our perfect type. And in order to have a type, there must be more than one. The audience needs to be large enough to fund the operation.

And you see, I'm well-funded.

I don't see why this is a problem.

Everyone's got a Feature Presentation. Some just require more commitment, suspension of disbelief, in order to fully comprehend the mysteries of its reality.

It's not that absurd when you think about it.

True love is worth whatever it takes to find it.

And when you find it, I'm going to say it just this once:

Don't ever believe that you'll be alone forever.

Don't you ever let go. You heard it from me. You'll never know how far you'll go to find it until you're already too far gone. The search will be the beginning and the end.

4.

So say it with me.

For there to be a worthwhile mystery, it ought to be truth. It ought to be so true it's impossible to accept. You want it to be fabricated, turned upside down, inside out.

When, really, this is what we have, these are the facts that remain:

The mystery was a man.

The mystery was a woman.

The mystery included you.

The mystery revolved around me.

We told no stories. We spoke in measured lies.

The element of mystery made sure that we were never telling a story. We revealed shades of reality, shades of ourselves. And now, more than ever, it's clear:

The mystery consumed us all.

Let's skip right to the honeymoon.

1.

One night in many, they were a couple, two sharing the same bed, huddled underneath a thick blanket, their warm bodies sharing the warmth. Perhaps there's only the one light, a little lamp setting the mood. It might be apt to pan out to show the house as a whole. The same house that had been his parents has now become his. The aftermath of senseless peril glazed over yet another cover story. Stephen as victim, he appeared as awestruck and emotionally broken by the news. His family brutally murdered, the killer(s) have yet to be neither named nor apprehended. Under such a cover story, one Stephen Chonrei is turned into yet another one of the countless faces affected by senseless tragedy. With his girlfriend, Claire, they are merely two people grieving, two people attempting to pick up after what the media branded as a life ruined.

They hold each other close, like they can't bear to be apart.

"When are you going to go back to your natural hair color?"

She nestles her chin into the curve of his arm, "I thought you liked it red."

"I do," he runs one long strand through his fingers, "I just figured you'd get tired of it."

"I'm fine if you're fine."

She turns to face him. He leans in for a kiss. She bites his lower lip, drawing blood.

He grins as she lets go, a single droplet hitting the white of the bed sheets.

They enjoy what they share; it keeps them one step ahead. It keeps their relationship fresh. Every moment of their lives shared, much like the information that'll never be made viewable to the public. He wipes the blood on the back of his hand and looks out the window.

After a while, she reopens her eyes and looks up at him, "What's wrong?"

"Nothing. Just thinking."

She sits up, her bare chest visible, "Tell me."

The forcefulness of the command rouses him to speak.

"What do you think our children will be like?"

With little debate she says, "If it's a boy, he'll be just like his father."

He looks into her eyes, "And if it's a girl?"

Her face forms a grin, "She'll be just like her mother."

In the next few moments, we're left with what's been implied just now. But then, without too much observation, it would be right to assume that they could be anybody.

The illusion of safety would offer enough.

Nothing like that could ever happen, right? The mystery is a thing of the past. Life moves on. With time it's something people learn to accept.

Eventually it'll be our turn. We will put our hearts on the line.

2.

Things are the same. Not much is different, really.

This is exactly what you'd like to hear.

With every kill we grow older.

I'm not above the thought of sagging skin and dimming sight. Much to my delight, we'll grow old, but the legacy, and every attraction we've had, will continue as new and fresh as the day the first victim was slayed.

As professor, a master role in and of itself, I share some of the responsibility; I study and explain his legacy. I provided the data that derived his name. I produced the study to end all studies about the state of deviant behavior in this age and the next.

I sit on the other side of the table at department meetings.

I am one of the cushy and the comfortable with tenure, sipping her latte, wasting time like there's plenty. But you see, beyond all that, nothing's really changed.

I'm the same person. I'm Claire and I was there from the beginning. After awhile, the middle portion fades in favor of the first and the last, what is and will always be.

I will attend the class.

I will lecture and, if anyone's willing to learn, I will teach.

My pet,
my perfect pet.

0.

The Judge (also known as The Patron; or, The Patron Saint of Poetic Justice) is a serial killer said to have operated on the east coast during the summer of 20[redacted]. The killer's identity remains unknown despite the efforts of the Federal Bureau of Investigation (FBI) as well as the activities of a devoted community consisting of both professional and amateur members. The Judge reportedly murdered incarcerated serial killers in Maryland, Virginia, North and South Carolina, among others. A lack of evidence has resulted in a lot of hearsay and conjecture, stories and myths. In recent months, though, the authorities have confirmed that the murders belong to the same killer. Due to the nature of the killer's victims, as well as the killer's method, the associated press quickly coined the name, "The Patron." Not long after, the namesake evolved to "Patron Saint" and "The Patron & Judge." In recent weeks, the FBI listed the killer as "The Judge" in all federal files; as of this writing, it is considered the accepted namesake (citation needed). The killer's method has produced its own share of media attention. Victims were reported to have been highly brutalized and disfigured, extensive torture and trauma in nearly all reported victims. Investigation revealed a pattern in the killer's preferred method. The killer adhered to the victim's own methods to torture.

A lack of suspects and conclusive evidence has resulted in the FBI marking the case "inactive" while keeping the file open for further investigation. The status of the case as unsolved has drawn attention from academia, with prominent social scientists studying the proposed killer.

A film produced, by [redacted], will be inspired by the Judge.

Confirmed victims (needs citation):

Malcolm Ames ("The Demon")

Giles Keller ("Giles the Great")

Derrick Matthew McPherson ("Derrick Muse")

Henry Borski ("The Bystander")

Macy Calmshores ("The Sweet Damsel")
Scott McCarthy ("Scott the Slaughter")
Edgar James Andrews ("The Villain")
Victor Hent ("The Gentleman Killer")

The killer has generated interest in Hollywood and a film inspired by the killer has been announced. Filming is scheduled to begin in the spring of 20[redacted]*. Rights have been secured and sold for a television series under the same franchise to begin airing shortly after the film's release.*

A community of conspiracy theorists called into question the lack of conclusive evidence, suggesting the serial killer as a government cover-up attempt to "personify media attention the wrong direction while entities worked to clean death row."

The Maryland Police Department reportedly tried to corroborate the murder of a young male in conjunction with the killer. A lack of evidence and its contrariness to FBI profile led to the dismissal a connection.

In a recent university lecture, popular philosopher Stanford Bilbek spoke about the "metaphorical nature" of the Judge's method and his explanation helped give rise to another name for the killer, "The Patron Saint of Poetic Justice." The following is from the lecture:

"The killer killing killers, it's worth the baffling effect it has produced in our culture. We are not ashamed to be so captivated. Its metaphorical nature pleases me. I see in the Judge the exact replica of our cultural habits. We consume. We are consumed. We are consuming—we see only suggestion and we create myth due to our bafflement. We are inadvertently suicidal in our need to be satiated. It is to no fault of the serial killer, as symbol, to set him or herself out there. Because they are out there, it is quickly obvious that someone else may be interested. The interest may be us, and one of us may be interested in taking the killer's life. This not far removed from the ruthless modern dating environment. We set ourselves out there. What becomes of us? We are consumed. We

are consuming. We are the ones consuming others. There is poetic justice in this. We are killers, though we do not pick up a weapon; killers, though we do not take lives. We take emotions; we break hearts. We consume as much as we can though we haven't a clue why we like what we consume. We don't know why; we merely do. Perhaps there is a killer that knows what s/he wants. If so, s/he is the killer that shall exceed consumption and be that oft-used but wholly impossible emotional state: Happy. The majority of us are being served through a mystery we'll surely be unable to solve. We consume that and in turn justice is served."

ABOUT THE AUTHOR

Michael J Seidlinger is an Asian American author of a number of books including *Dreams of Being*, *Standard Loneliness Package*, and *The Fun We've Had*. He serves as Library and Academic Marketing Manager at *Melville House*, Editor-at-Large for *Electric Literature*, and is a member of *The Accomplices*. He lives in Brooklyn, New York, where he never sleeps and is forever searching for the next best cup of coffee. You can find him online on Facebook, Twitter (@mjseidlinger), and Instagram (@michaelseidlinger).

FANGORIA

FANGORIA.COM

@FANGORIA

DALLAS, TX

CPSIA information can be obtained
at www.ICGtesting.com
Printed in the USA
LVHW112015281018
595012LV00004BA/4/P

9 781946 487025